FLOWERS OF DESIRE

For Dorothy)
who once thought
in silence —
Fred
1-5-1990

A Novel By
Frederick Manfred

Flowers of Desire

DANCING BADGER PRESS
SALT LAKE CITY
1989

Copyright © 1989 by Frederick Feikema Manfred
Printed in the United States of America.
All rights reserved under International and Pan-American
Copyright Conventions.
First edition.

Published by Dancing Badger Press:
1260 East Stratford Avenue
Salt Lake City, Utah 84106-2727
(801) 484-8273

Cover Art: Arnold John Dyson
Typesetting: Jeoffrey R. McAllister
Camera and Imposition: Natalie R. Howard
Printing: Publishers Press
Binding: Mountain States Bindery

The paper in this book meets the standards for permanence and durability established by the Committee on Production Guidelines for Book Longevity of the Council on Library Resources.

LIBRARY OF CONGRESS CATALOGUING-IN-PUBLICATION DATA

Manfred, Frederick Feikema, 1912–
   Flowers of desire.

   I.Title.
PS3525.A52233F58   1989   813'.54   89-23569
ISBN 0-9624298-0-5 hardcover   (alk. paper)
ISBN 0-9624298-1-3 paperback   (alk. paper)

DEDICATED TO
RALPH EARLE DICKMAN
NOW GONE

BOOKS BY FREDERICK MANFRED

*From 1944 through 1951
Frederick Manfred
published under the name
Feike Feikema.*

The Golden Bowl. 1944.

Boy Almighty. 1945.

This Is the Year. 1947.

The Chokecherry Tree. 1948.

The Primitive. 1949.

The Brother. 1950.

The Giant. 1951.

Lord Grizzly. 1954.

Morning Red. 1956.

Riders of Judgment. 1957.

Conquering Horse. 1959.

Arrow of Love. Short stories.
1961.

Wanderlust. A one-volume
trilogy incorporating revised
versions of *The Primitive, The
Brother,* and *The Giant*. 1962.

Scarlet Plume. 1964.

*The Man Who Looked Like the
Prince of Wales*. 1965. Reprinted
in paperback as *The Secret
Place*. 1965.

Winter Count. Poems. 1966.

King of Spades. 1966.

Apples of Paradise. Short
stories. 1968.

Eden Prairie. 1968.

Conversations. Moderated by
John R. Milton. 1974.

Milk of Wolves. 1976.

The Manly-Hearted Woman.
1976.

Green Earth. 1977.

The Wind Blows Free. Reminis-
cence. 1979.

Sons of Adam. 1980.

Winter Count II. Poems. 1987.

Prime Fathers. Essays. 1988.

*The Selected Letters of Frederick
Manfred, 1932-1954*. Edited
by Arthur R. Huseboe and
Nancy Owen Nelson. 1989.

I. THE FLOWER

CHAPTER ONE

CARLA

It was the last week of May, 1941, and the sun shone golden on a green world and the fox squirrels skirred happily in the oak trees and all the streams twinkled with sweet running water and life sap dripped out of the ends of twigs. Bones ached with spring's love.

Carla Simmons had just finished her final exam as a junior in high school and, in happy relief, decided to go to the last baseball game of the season with her confidant, Tracy Cadwell. The Whitebone Indians had a pretty good team that year.

Carla and Tracy decided to walk across town to the baseball diamond in the bottoms along the Big Rock River. Tracy wanted to talk about something private before they climbed into the stands.

Carla was a virgin. She was sixteen, a slim girl with fleshy legs, a firm waist, a good bosom, strong slender neck, and a shapely head of milkweed-pod hair. She had a fine nose and tender smiling lips. Her blue eyes could burn silver when she thought about the way Tracy's boyfriend, Brent Goede, treated Tracy, and would become soft as milk when she considered Tracy's sinful ways. Carla wore a green dress. Her muscled calves were bare, and she wore a pair of short white sox with black loafers. Carla walked along in an easy willowy manner.

Tracy was short. She worried about putting on weight, especially around her seat. She was an orange blond with a round face and peach-slice lips. An impish look worked at the corners of her dark blue eyes. She was known as a honeypot in school; boys buzzed around her like bees. Tracy wore a light-blue blouse, dark blue skirt, and also wore bobby sox. Tracy walked a little like she talked, in spurts and a little breathless.

Tracy worked evenings at the Palace Theatre selling tickets and was usually finished around ten o'clock. She drove an old blue Ford to school and to work.

Tracy said, "Brent followed me home after work last night."

"I hope you told him off."

Tears showed in Tracy's eyes. "He caught up with me under Norton's hill and waved me over."

"I might have known."

"I tried not to. But driving two abreast like that on the highway I was afraid we'd meet someone and then there'd be a collision. So I pulled over." Tracy lived with her mother two miles from town. Her father Bill Cadwell was a salesman who had a passion for women and was always getting them into trouble. He bragged that he never took precautions, just as he hadn't with Tracy's mother the night Tracy was conceived.

Carla gave Tracy's arm a shake. "You always give in to those oil salesmen. You've got to say no, hard, to begin with."

Tracy chewed gum with her mouth open. "I said no when he got into the car with me."

"Oh, Tracy, I don't know what we're going to do with you."

"This time I asked him what he's going to do in case I get a baby."

"What did he say?"

"He said, 'Well, Babe, tough titty for you, then.' I said, 'You're not going to stand up in church with me when the baby's baptized?' He said, 'How will I know if it's my baby the way you run around with all those other guys? When you lose a finger in a buzzsaw, who knows what tooth cut it off?'"

"He said that! Dear Lord, I'd never see him again, ever, if he said that to me."

They passed under a tall maple tree. Sunlight filtering through the branches cast moving mottles of light on them. Some tossing deep-purple lilacs grew along the walk. A soft perfume floated off them.

Tracy said, "But then he touched the inside of my leg . . ."

"For goodness' sakes, how did he get that far?"

"Oh, Carla, you don't understand. Once you've done it, and you like it, you just can't say no anymore. It's like that slide down at the playground. The more you use it the slicker it gets and the faster you slide down."

"But it's a sin not to wait until you're married."

"You just melt, and then pretty soon you just swoon away. And it's so sweet to swoon. Even though I know it's a sin."

"Well, at least it's only with Brent your intended." It was too bad that Tracy had such a wastrel for a father. Carla's father would never have let Tracy grow up loose and wild. Tracy with her little blue car could run around town, while Carla was forbidden even to drive the family car.

They turned the corner past the First National Bank and headed east down Main Street. Three boys in an old Ford jalopy drove by. They honked the horn and whistled at the two girls.

Tracy said, "Brent isn't the only one."

Carla stopped on the sidewalk, aghast. "What!"

Tracy blushed. "Well, I was trying to forget Brent by dating somebody else."

"Who?"

"Brent's buddy."

"Not Reuel Darland?"

"Yes. Brent must have told Reuel about us. Because Reuel moved in on me like he knew I would do it."

"And my father thinks Reuel's banker father is a thief and a looter."

"Reuel's even bought me flowers."

"How can you be doing it with both at the same time?"

"I know. That's why I wanted to talk to you." Tracy squeezed Carla's arm. "You're so good for me. You help me stick to the straight and narrow."

"Trouble is, you started too early."

Tracy let go with a laugh. "Isn't it awful?"

At the east end of Main Street they headed for the ball park tucked in between the Big Rock River and the Milwaukee Railroad embankment. Some twenty cars were already parked behind the green wooden stands. A dozen players in blue uniforms were gathered around the visitors' bench, some pulling on spiked shoes, some going through stretching exercises. The home team in gray uniforms were already out on the field going through their pre-game warmup, with a stocky coach whacking out hard vicious grounders to the infielders and an older fellow clouting fungo flies to the outfielders.

Carla said, "It's too bad you don't go to my church. Reverend Holly is wonderful with young people." Carla loved her Presbyterian minister. He often said the young were more apt to inherit the kingdom of heaven than the old because the young were still idealists, still hadn't become cynical hypocrites.

"Your minister is too strict for me. He likes to point the finger."

Some two dozen fans were already in the stands behind the wire-mesh backstop. Most of them were high school students. Tracy threaded her way up through them, Carla following her. The two girls settled near the center of the second row from the top.

The river winked where it curved away from centerfield. Tall elms bordered it on both sides, and on the far side of the river spread a park. Several families were having picnics at log tables under the cottonwood trees.

Carla asked, "What are you doing tonight?"

"I promised Reuel I'd see him after the movie."

"You're hopeless." Carla shook her head. "I don't understand what's gotten into you kids."

An older woman, mother of one of the Whitebone players, turned on the bench below and said over her shoulder, "And I don't either."

Both Carla and Tracy fell silent, abashed.

A fellow sitting beside the woman smiled to himself. He was Oren Prince, reporter for the local Whitebone *Press*. He had glossy black hair combed straight back and brown artful eyes. He said, "I fear that's an old complaint."

"What do you mean?" the older woman snapped. She was quite hefty, and when she wiggled the bench undulated. She had rough features, almost mannish, and her blue eyes were like frost holes.

"I just meant that every generation has that thrown at them." Oren had a clipped way of talking out of the corner of his mouth. "All the way back to the time of Noah and his sons."

"Hmff!" the woman snorted.

Carla knew Oren Prince. He was the son of the local Methodist preacher, the Reverend Clifford Prince. Oren had been five grades ahead of her in school and that put him in with the grown-ups. After graduating from high school, Oren had gone on to a junior college in Blue Wing, and after that had taken a job with the *Press* as a reporter. Part of his duties was to cover all the high school games: baseball, basketball, and football. Oren was dressed in dapper clothes: powder-blue suit, white shirt with red tie, two-tone tan oxfords, blue socks with a flashy white arrow. His skin was swarthy and already he had a heavy beard. He was of average height, five ten to Carla's five eight.

The home team finished their pre-game warmup and ran off the field; and the visiting Blue Wing Falcons ran onto the field to have their turn at it.

Oren smiled at Carla. "Here to cheer on the boyfriend?"

"I have no boyfriend."

"What a waste."

"What's the rush?"

"You got a point there."

Carla had made up her mind long ago, from the example of her mother, that she was going to save herself for her husband. Christ would want her to be a virgin on her wedding day. One fellow in high school, Dink Sunstrand, first baseman for the Whitebone Indians, had once made a pass at her in the hallway, and it made her so angry she'd written a poem about it:

> You're wasting your time
> at my door, bud.
> Find some other girl to paw.
> Your hands are rough,
> your tongue is rough,
> I have no time for roughnecks.
> You look at me with the eyes of a calf.
> I know what you want.
> Well, not here, bud.

The poem was published in the school paper, and that made Dink so mad the next time he saw her he called after her, "You ballbreaker!" At first Carla hadn't known what he meant. She thought it had something to do with baseball. But when she mentioned it to Tracy, Tracy burst out laughing. When Tracy told her what it meant, Carla cooled off even more about boys.

Tracy touched Carla on the elbow. "Don't look now."

Carla had already seen why. Brent Goede had driven up in his jazzed-up Chevy. It was painted a garish purple, with flowing white stripes along the sides, and had been outfitted with a set of balloon tires. It was the thing just then for young sports to put on thick balloon tires that hardly fit under the fenders. Brent's father, a rich farmer, had kicked Brent out of the house because he was such a spendthrift. Brent, eighteen, had promptly quit school and had taken a job with a local painter. Brent next rented an apartment over a drugstore and lived it up even more.

"Don't move or he'll spot us."

"For goodness' sakes, I can move if I want to. I'm not having any trouble telling him off."

Brent looked over the crowd in the stands. He was impatient and revved up the motor in little spurting roars. At last, unable to spot Tracy, he snapped open the car door, got out, and headed slowly toward the stands, sullen blue eyes moving from face to face. He had on a blue shirt, blue tie, and a pair of blue trousers.

Tracy said, "I didn't know he was off work today."

Carla said, "All you have to do is mean it when you say no. It's so simple, really."

Then Brent spotted Tracy. He climbed the plank seats to where the two girls sat. "Coming?"

Tracy said, "Brent, I can't see you today."

Brent jerked Tracy to her feet. "C'mon!"

"Ow! Brent. No!"

Carla glared icicles at Brent.

Oren had been listening too, head turned away, but when Brent touched Tracy, he spoke up. "Leave the girl alone."

Brent snarled at Oren. "Who asked you to stick your nose into this?"

Oren slowly stood up. "Why you punk you. Spoiled rotten."

"Look who's talking."

Everybody in the stands turned to look.

Brent changed his tune. "Tracy, please."

Tracy, aware of all the attention they'd drawn, lowered her head. Brent gave her another tug, this time winning, and she gave in. Meekly she followed him down the plank seats.

Carla was disgusted.

More cars drove up and the grandstand filled. Some fans elected to watch the game from their cars. Others sat on the grass just outside a cable strung from post to post on either side of the infield. The May sun turned warm, and heat rose from the sandy diamond and touched the faces of everybody. After a long cold winter, it was wonderful to be able to relax in summer warmth.

Some half-dozen fathers and mothers of the enemy Blue Wing players began to push into Oren's row.

Oren decided to make room for them by moving up one row beside Carla. "Mind?"

"Not at all." Carla wondered if Oren had a girlfriend.

Two umpires clad in deep blue gathered at home plate with the rival coaches.

Oren stood up. "Would you hold my seat? I think I'll go down to the pop stand and quick get myself a snack before the game starts." He placed his clipboard where he'd been sitting.

"Sure." Carla set her purse on top of his clipboard.

A few minutes later Oren came threading his way up through the crowd carrying two bottles and two hotdogs. He had gotten her a snack too.

She picked up her purse. "You didn't have to do that."

"I've got a grape and a cream soda. Which do you prefer?"

"Oh, the grape, I guess." Carla took the bottle as well as the hotdog wrapped in a slip of wax paper. "Thenk you."

"Not at all." Oren settled beside her, moving his clipboard over. He waited until she'd taken her first bite and then he too helped himself. "I hope you like the mustard on it."

"I love it." Carla did like the breaking snap of wiener skin in her mouth, followed by the sweet release of meat juices. She also took a sip of the grape soda and relished the way it prickled against the roof of her mouth. The pop reminded her of the wine she took at Lord's Supper.

"Got a question to ask you. Are you the one who did all those backdrops for the class play last month?"

Carla felt herself blush. "Yes."

"Well! you can draw. Are you interested in art?"

"I intend to major in it when I go to college."

"Good for you. I thought they were swell. From where I sat, that grass looked real enough for a fellow to want to take off his shoes and go walking in it."

"Well, thenk you."

"No, really, I mean that."

Carla felt herself softening toward Oren Prince. She watched his fingers as he checked the visitors' line-up. They were the fingers of a city boy, thin and quick. Carla never liked the blunt-ended fingers of Dink Sunstrand. Her father was a mason but he still managed to have good-looking hands. Her father wore gloves at work and at night just before going to bed always rubbed his hands with a glycerine preparation.

"You're good friends with Tracy, aren't you?"

"Yes. And I feel for her."

"She maybe feels for you."

She studied Oren's smooth-shaven face, fine chin and cheekbones. With his dark hair slicked back he was very handsome.

A sly look opened around Oren's brown eyes. "You and Tracy complement each other. You live the good life for her, and she lives the loose life for you."

"I'm not sure I like that."

Oren finished his hotdog and pop. "Through?"

"Yes."

Oren eyed some barefooted boys playing tag under the stands. "I think I'll take these bottles down to that waste barrel. If they should happen to fall and hit that cement below there, there'll be glass all over." He set his clipboard on the seat. "Hold my place." He picked up the two bottles and pushed his way down through the crowd.

Carla was touched by his concern.

Before Oren could come back, Meddy Queen showed up. Meddy had come late to the game and spotting the open place beside Carla had climbed toward her. Meddy saw the clipboard, pushed it to one side, and sat down.

"That seat's taken," Carla said.

"I don't see anybody," Meddy said airily. Meddy was a gold blond. She was Carla's stiffest competitor for class valedictorian. They both had the same marks for two years, a straight-A average, but Meddy had the advantage because of her extra-curricular activities. Meddy sang in the school choir, played in the band, debated, had the lead in the class play, and was editor of the high school *Trivia*. Carla sang in the choir and did the artwork for the *Trivia*, but that was all. Meddy had coy blue eyes, not much of a bosom, and could run with most of the boys in school.

Meddy said, "I'm surprised Tracy isn't here with you."

"Brent came and got her."

"I don't see how you can stand her."

"Well, she needs somebody for a friend."

Oren came back. "I see I've lost my seat," he said with a smile at Carla. He picked up his clipboard.

Meddy bounced to her feet. "Oh, I'm sorry."

"It's all right," Oren said. "I can sit down there on the grass." He looked at Carla. "See you around."

Carla nodded. She was sorry to see him go.

Meddy sat down again. "I didn't know you knew Oren."

"He just happened to land next to me."

"I'm sorry if I spoiled something."

"You didn't." Carla watched Oren step down through the crowd, politely touching people on their shoulders to let them know he wanted to get through.

A loud voice, the umpire's behind home plate, called out, "Play ball!"

For the next two hours the athletes in gray and the athletes in blue ran and leaped and swung and dodged and fell on the greensward. There were shouts of joy and cries of frustration. The crowd in the stand cheered and groaned by turns. It was all a play in youth's faery world, here one moment, a brilliant iridescent bubble, and gone the next, invisible atoms. It was at once forever here and forever gone; scintillating dew one second, cold dust the next.

The lead seesawed back and forth. Then in the bottom of the seventh Dink Sunstrand hit a homerun with two men on and the Whitebone Indians won 9 to 7. Just before he did it, as he stepped into the batter's box, Dink blew his nose farm style, first a finger against his left nostril, then a finger against his right nostril.

In the push of the crowd leaving the baseball grounds, Carla couldn't find Oren. Perhaps it was just as well.

Carla took the path up toward Main Street, then took Spring Street north. Children played tag around her.

Whitebone was a city of beautiful trees, elms and maples, with huge spreading umbrella branches. One could walk all the way across town in the shadow of the trees. It was also a town full of birdsong: fat robins, darting bluebirds, dippling martins. Every patch of hollyhocks had its hovering hummingbirds.

Carla walked along very straight in an easy rocking manner, thinking about Tracy and her weakness for that awful Brent. Carla tried to imagine what they were doing right that minute up in Brent's apartment. She got as far as seeing Brent unbutton Tracy's lightblue blouse, then could go no further. Carla looked down at her own green dress, with its buttons in front, and blushed to herself.

Carla also thought about Meddy. How very funny that Meddy should always be trying to make up to her. Meddy, who'd lost her father and mother in an automobile accident, lived with her rich grandmother, Rilla Queen. Stylish Rilla Queen had inherited some forty farms that were once a part of a huge English-owned estate. Meddy was really to the manor born.

Meddy envied Carla her parents. "Your father and mother always look so happy together when you see them in church."

Meddy didn't know. Dad and Mother might look happy in church, but at home it was different. It wasn't that they fought. It was just that they were both mostly silent around each other. When they did talk, they had a way of acting as if the other one wasn't in the room. "Carla, you might tell your father that the fireplace smokes again." Or, "Carla, you might tell your mother that she should put a little more grub in my lunch bucket."

It was lovely going down the last block. Deep purple shadows hung under the tall trees. Rising fumes shimmered off the lilacs in the yards.

Carla saw her young sister Ivoria shooting baskets with some neighbor boys at a hoop attached to a garage. Ivoria was fourteen, a freshman in high school. She had brown hair with a touch of gold in it, deep blue eyes, and high round cheeks.

Ivoria spotted her coming. "Mom's looking for you."

"I suppose."

"She just got home from Mission Society and is afraid she'll be late with supper. And I've got my chores done."

"Well lucky you."

Carla moved up the cement walk. Dad had studded the walk with flat stones, some pink, some brown, some gray—stones like those he'd put into the fireplace. The stones made the walk attractive, though it was hard on high heels. Carla liked their home. Dad had made over a simple structure into a good-looking cottage, blue siding with windows trimmed in white, shakes for a roof, and low-growing junipers under the picture window.

Carla opened the screen door and walked in. "Hi," she called out.

Mother emerged out of the cellar, blond head first, carrying some potatoes in a pan. "Well, there you are at last. Hurry, put on an apron and peel these for me, will you? I'm late."

"I can't help it that your meeting lasted so long."

"Where were you?"

"To the ball game."

"With that Tracy Cadwell I suppose."

Carla decided the less said the better. She took the pan of potatoes from her mother and led the way into the kitchen. She found herself an apron to cover her green dress and, sitting down, placed the pan of potatoes in her lap. Her mother handed her the potato peeler and poured a little water in the pan and set out another pan with fresh water nearby. Carla had nimble fingers and she peeled the potatoes deftly, taking off only the thinnest of the skin, twirling out the deepset eyes with a twist of the wrist. She dropped the peeled potato in the clean water.

Carla looked up. "Mother, when you and Dad first met, did you right away fall in love?"

"Huh? No. I was never gonna get married. Last thing in the world I wanted." Mother still had the smooth face of a young girl. Only her neck showed age where wrinkles had begun to form.

"Why was that?"

"After I saw what happened to my older sister Ada with that big fat windbag of a Barry Simons, and my sister Allie with that sex-crazy Willie

Alfredson, I knew better. That men were heartless when it came to falling in love."

When Aunt Ada caught Uncle Barry lying on top of the hired girl by the calf pen at the time when she herself was heavy with child, she had finally had enough. Shotgun at the ready, Aunt Ada'd chased him off the yard. It was even said they got divorced. Ten years later, repentant, Uncle Barry had come back. And about Aunt Allie, who'd been a beautiful gold blond, there'd been rumors back then that on Sunday mornings, when everybody was supposed to be in church, Allie used to do something with Willie Alfredson up in the haymow.

Mother went on. "You want to remember Jake was Barry's younger brother. Heh! it was like asking for double trouble." Mother buttered the biscuit pan first before dropping in little mounds of fresh bread dough. "Everybody in Bonnie knew Jake had been a wild one before he went off to war. Raising Cain with the boys."

"What changed your mind about Jake? I mean, about Dad?"

"I liked his hands." Mother sighed. "I figured anyone with hands like that just couldn't be mean." Mother pushed the biscuit pan into the oven of the blue gas stove and closed the door. She set the heat at the required temperature. "But a month after I was married, I found out he was just like other men. A pest in bed."

"But at least Dad doesn't carouse around."

"I know that. And that man works hard. Lifting stones and blocks of cement all day long, it's a wonder his back hasn't gone out before this. He's been a good provider, all right."

"Why did you two move away from Bonnie?"

"We wanted to make a fresh start in a new town. Get away from all that mean gossip."

"Goodness, I might have gone to the Bonnie High School instead."

"Thanks be to God not."

The white-walled kitchen was alive with light. Mother had a modern kitchen all because Dad was so handy around the house. He'd made the blue counter and the natural wood cabinets and had put in a blue tile floor. Mother had done the rest with pretty knickknacks in the corners and the startlingly white curtains in the windows.

Mother said, "I think I'll call Ivoria. She's getting to be too much of a tomboy for me."

"She says she's already done her chores."

"Ha. What she calls done. A flick here and a lick there. What she calls dusting is only moving dust from one place to another. When what I want is to have the dust removed."

Carla laughed. "But isn't that what re-moved means?"

"Don't get smart on me now."

Carla picked up the fattest potato. It had at least a dozen eyes. A regular grandmother of a potato. If one were to cut it up for planting, there'd be some dozen potato plants. It was almost a shame to cut it into halves for boiling.

"Are you about done?"

"Just a couple more."

"If we can get them to boiling in the next couple of minutes, we'll have dinner ready when Dad comes home."

Carla loved her father. He could be firm with his two girls, but he was always fair. He always first listened carefully before he issued an order. He never flew off the handle. Though he did with Mother. My, how Dad and Mother could bristle at each other sometimes. With bitter lips Dad would sometimes call her, "Sister!" and equally harsh Mother would call him, "Brother!" It was obvious they weren't lovers anymore.

Carla finished peeling the potatoes. She poured the peelings into the slop pail under the sink. Then she put the finished potatoes on the stove.

Carla next set the table in the dining area just east off the kitchen. The furnishings in both the dining area and the living room were Carla's doing. She'd once asked if she could arrange the furniture and pick the wall paper. Mother had been a bit exasperated by the request. "So it ain't good enough for you?" And Carla had said, "It's not that, Mother. It's fine the way you have it. But can I try it once?" When Dad had finally said, "Why not let the kid try it once?" Mother had given in. When Carla finished, having picked a gold-and-blue flower design for both the wallpaper and the chair seat covers, as well as a light blue carpet, Ma was so astounded she sat down suddenly. "Well, holy cats, now I know you're ready to be a housewife."

A motor roared up outside, then fell silent. Dad was home. Dad believed you should always goose the motor just as you shut it off to make sure the carburetor would be full of gas the next time you wanted to start the car.

Dad came in through the kitchen door. He'd shed his cap and jacket and his outer overalls in the garage. Except for his lime-edged hands, he hardly looked like a mason. Dad had the high forehead of an aristocrat, with light-brown hair graying over the temples, an aquiline nose, fleshy lips, and fair skin. He was a good six foot tall, slim, muscular, with a quick snappy step. His eyes were blue and had the piercing aspect of a falcon always on the watch. He had gone through the horrors of the First World War, but, except for bad ears, it didn't show. He didn't suffer from war nerves, didn't drink, didn't smoke.

Dad saw that the table was set. "Well, I see everybody's alive and kicking here." He barely touched Mother with a look and smiled at Carla. "Who won?"

"We did. Nine to seven." Carla spoke directly at Dad.

"I hear your boyfriend Dink hit a homer."

"Yes, and he blew his nose too like a dumb clodhopper."

Dad laughed. He sat down at the head of the table and took off his shoes. He wiggled his toes a moment, then thrust them into a pair of slippers. "Where's Ivoria?"

"I'll go find her."

While Dad washed up and combed his hair and slipped on a light blue blazer, Carla went out the back door and cut across the alley to the neighbors'. Coming around the side of the Norcross house she saw Ivoria was still playing roughhouse basketball with the boys. It made Carla smile to see how Ivoria gave as good as she got. Later on, when Ivoria's breasts became sensitive at certain times, she'd play a bit more gingerly.

Finally Carla had to break up the game. "Dad's home."

Ivoria was about to protest, basketball in hand. But on second thought, reflecting it was really Dad calling her, she threw the basketball high in the air and joined Carla. "So long, you guys. Lucky for you I had to quit."

At last all four were seated around the table, one on each side, potatoes steaming in a huge bowl, porkchops neatly arrayed on a meat platter, fresh biscuits in a basket, and a side dish of peas next to each plate.

Carla said the blessing. It was the thought of both Dad and Mother that they were never to eat without first asking the Lord to bless a bountiful table. "Amen."

They were well into their potatoes when Mother said, "I found some mouse dirt in the kitchen again."

Dad paused in his eating, holding knife and fork crossed over his heaping plate. "Again, eh?" He thought to himself a moment. "Well, I'll set four traps facing each other, so that no matter which way they turn those little rascals won't have a fightin' chance. Regardless."

Eyes rolling upward, Ivoria pretended to vomit. "Ulk. Please don't talk about mice when I'm eating."

Mother went on. "And that washtub faucet still drips."

Carla didn't like it that Mother brought up her troubles at the table. "Dad, how did work go today?"

Dad was laying brick for a new creamery a block north of the First National Bank. "Boss had bad news."

Mother was instantly on the alert. "How so?"

"Said he had to cut us a nickel an hour. Or he'd lose money on the job."

"Well, but that's his lookout, ain't it?"

Dad held his head sideways, as if trying to handle two strong winds coming from opposite directions. "If he goes broke, where do I go then?"

"But shouldn't wages be going up, with us helping England fight Hitler?"

Dad finished his plate. "Yeh. Here I am, in a trade that is probably one of the most important in the country, and yet I don't get my just dues. If it weren't for us masons there'd be no skyscrapers, no arches of triumph. Without us masons, we'd all still be Indians. Regardless."

Mother next said, "Carla still hangs around with Tracy."

"Now Mother," Carla said, "Jesus had time for Magdalene."

Mother said, "That was in Bible times."

Dad said, "One thing you've got to say for Tracy. She's got spunk. She works in the theater nights. Money she turns over to her mother."

Mother's face turned purplish. "Ya, I've noticed it already. Whenever Tracy visits here you can't get your eyes off her."

Dad picked up his dish of peaches and began dipping the slices up with his favorite silver spoon. "She's full of fun, too."

"Hmf. Well, I think Tracy is way too young to have dates."

Carla could feel herself reddening. "Mother, Tracy often talks about how good I am for her."

"Does she ever talk about how bad she might be for you?"

Dad said, "I've had sufficient. Please pass the toothpicks."

CHAPTER TWO

JAKE

Jake could smell his daughter Carla. There was always about her the sweet smell of a yeasty maiden in spring.

Jacob Simmons had a keen smeller. As his deafness worsened, his sense of smell sharpened. His nose had once saved his life at work. It had smelled out that the dirt walls of a trench he was working in were going to collapse, and he'd leaped out just as the walls began whooshing down around him.

As he picked his teeth Jake remembered Mimi, who'd given herself to him between two haycocks in France. She couldn't have been more than fifteen. In America she would have been jailbait.

. . . . The camp kitchens had not yet arrived, so the word went out for the men to scarf around for whatever they could find. "Help yourselves first, and if you have anything left, bring it back here."

Jake was chasing a white chicken near a barn, out of sight of a peasant's house, when he came upon Mimi with her white-gold hair and shining brown eyes, wearing a lightblue smock and leather sandals. She was sitting on a haycock with a mischievous look on her lips. Right away Jake had ideas. She wasn't unwilling, and it wasn't long before he was diving into sweet oblivion, forgetting the chicken.

On his next furlough, he went straight to Mimi's farm and had himself introduced to her parents. They didn't know English and he only knew a few words of French, but they got along. The young mother seemed to like him, seemed to favor his seeing Mimi, but the old father, though generous with the family wine cellar, always remained distant.

His furlough lasted a week and he spent all of it with Mimi. They made love in the nearby woods. But the best was at night, when her folks were asleep, and Mimi would come stealthily to his room over the kitchen. They made love so often that his fingers began to shake when he picked up a cup of tea. Mimi was insatiable.

Before he got another furlough, Jake's battalion was sent to the front near Argonne, the farthest point of an advance made by the previous battalion. The order had come down to hold it to the last man. Regardless.

The shelling started in the afternoon, and everybody dug in deeper. When the shells began to zero in on them, they dug side trenches. Some of the men tried to make caves. But the shells came and came; first a whoosh, then, on impact, an incredible explosion and a terrifying shaking of earth. The shelling continued all night long, pounding, numbing; and detonating and blasting and crushing everything in the area. Jake sat as still as a mouse while the great cat of destruction pounced all round him trying to find him.

But Jake knew he was going to survive. He was eighteen and he believed it.

Toward dawn the bombardment suddenly dropped off.

Jake waited. Dust trickled down on his steel helmet.

To his surprise the first thing he heard was a bird singing. Slowly Jake raised himself erect, and when he still couldn't see the bird, he hoisted himself up a couple of feet by stepping on a loose board. He spotted the bird sitting on a strand of tangled barbwire. It had a gray back and a white belly and a black head.

He called out, "Hey, where is everybody?"

The bird flew off.

He dared to look toward the German lines. To his still further surprise he saw lines of dirty-helmeted Germans running away from the front. It was as though they knew something terrible was coming and they wanted no part of it. Jake looked around, sharp-eyed. And saw it. Gas. Somebody, the Germans, had laid down a gas attack. He could see where it was rising out of a dip in the pitted land. He understood why the Germans were running. The wind had shifted and it was blowing the gas toward the German lines. He could just make out the gray stuff in the slowly pinkening dawn.

Jake jumped out of his hole. "Where's everybody?"

No answer. The trench they'd been in, except for the little spot where he'd been sitting, had been obliterated. Gone. In its place were huge holes and blowouts. Yellow clay and black dirt lay splashed in all directions. He took a couple of steps toward his command post. He stumbled over a human leg, blown off at the hip. Then he stepped on an open hand, ripped off at the wrist. Abrupt piles of earth were soiled with blackening blood.

"Hey!"

His voice sounded muted to him. With finger and thumb he jerked the lobe of each ear. Still that odd silenced sensation. He pried a forefinger in each ear, wondering if maybe the shelling had pushed the wax in too deep. His forefinger came up dry.

"Hey!"

Finally a vague shout sounded behind him. Then there was another shout to the right of him.

"Over here!"

Soon figures emerged in the pink light. Soldiers. American khaki. They appeared to come out of shrunken horizons.

An officer from the next battalion to the west was first to arrive. He stared at the devastation. "My God! Wiped out." He turned to stare at the floating fog of gas slowly vanishing toward the German lines. "The Boche bastards!"

Jake saluted.

The officer returned the salute. "You the only survivor?"

"We was told to hold it to the last man. Regardless."

"Well, you sure as hell did. Come with me, soldier."

Jake was sent to a hospital for examination. There wasn't a scratch on him. When he complained about his hearing, they couldn't find anything wrong. They told him it was nerves; his hearing would eventually come back.

They kept him in the Army hospital for two weeks for observation. No improvement. Finally they told him he should take a furlough for a month and then come back.

Jake did. He went directly to Mimi's farm.

It was gone. Blasted out of existence. The haycocks had burned down; so had the barn and the house. All he could find was a soft silver spoon. He remembered it was Mimi's. He stood staring. Up until then he had stared in innocent farm boy bewilderment at all the death and the destruction after the bombardment, and had managed to stay glued together. But this? Mimi gone?

He began to shriek. He shrieked a series of high yells, peels of them, one after the other.

No one was around to hear him. He barely heard it himself.

After a while his voice turned hoarse, and then finally it quit on him. All that came out of his mouth was a series of gushes of air.

He stayed there panting until dark.

The Army finally discharged him and sent him home. He arrived a hero in Bonnie. Everybody had a slap on the back for him and the good word. Girls had a wide smile and a little wave of the fingers for him.

He noticed after a while that people looked at him kind of funny sometimes. His older brother Barry advised him to get hearing aids.

Jake hated to admit his hearing was almost gone. Instead, as his sense of smell sharpened, Jake worked at reading lips. His smeller told him where somebody was and then he'd look at the lips. One piercing look and he'd catch what they were saying. He began to read facial expressions like a detective. He also developed uncanny peripheral vision. His brother Barry said Jake had eyes in the back of his head.

Thinking back, Jake had trouble remembering exactly what Mimi's face looked like. He could remember what her mount of love was like but not her eyes.

Soon he ran into Sadie Engleking at a Young People's Meeting in the Little Church. Hotblooded, a warrior and a lover, he went after Sadie as though it was a war he had to win. Sadie was still innocent and read his intentions as pure true love. She managed to hold him off until they were married. To her disgust, she'd discovered he wanted to make love all the time rather than live in religious true love with each other.

By the time Jake realized he'd rushed Sadie too fast, it was too late. Sadie continued to like him but her love for him was lost. And now that they had two children, both in their teens, she felt she no longer had to submit to him. It was a sin, she said, if they didn't intend to have more children.

Sadie urged him to get a pair of glasses with hearing aids attached. No one would see it, she said. He almost exploded at that. Glasses was the one thing he didn't need. His eyes were perfect. He could spot a fly on a dog across the lawn.

Jake remembered those first times dating Sadie as though they were songs. She had gold hair trailing down her back and her blue eyes were full of trust and her waist was as thin as a bundle of wheat. He used to take her for a spin in his copper-nosed Ford after church on Sunday, sometimes out to the Big Sioux River, sometimes to the Fourth of July celebration in Rock Falls. With the top down and the wind flowing over them, he thought the shiny copper and her gold hair all of a piece of paradise . . . .

Carla had left the table, and when she came back she announced that the toilet off the kitchen was flooding over the floor again.

Jake woke up out of his memories. "Say, that's right. There's something I've been meaning to talk to you girls about." He got up. "I'll be right back."

Sure enough. The stool was running over. Something had clogged it down below. He knew what it was too. He reached behind the seat for the plunger and thrust it down into the neck of the toilet. Working the red suction cup up and down a few times, using the water to make tight suction, he managed to unclog the line below.

He next opened the little cabinet door and reached in for a spare roll of toilet paper and took it back with him to the table.

All three of his women looked at him startled.

"Look," he said, sitting down. "Somebody in this house is using too much toilet paper."

"Now, Jake," Sadie warned, "not right after we've eaten."

"I don't care," Jake said, "I'm going to speak my mind on this. Uk! Uk!" he quick said to Ivoria, who had begun to slide away from the table. "You too. You may be the guilty one." He held up the roll of paper. "I'm sure it's not when you do number one. It's got to be when—"

"Dad!" Carla said.

"You don't need more than seven squares of this. Four for the first"—he tore off four squares and neatly folded them together—"and three for the second"—he tore off three more squares. "Four for the heavy duty work and three to polish."

Ivoria began to shriek.

"Seven is all you need. But it seems someone here is pulling off enough paper to choke a Case threshing machine. That's why that toilet gets plugged. Have you ladies got that now?"

"Oh, Dad," both girls cried, eyes rolling.

"Really. And it's also expensive to use so much paper."

"But maybe it's Ma!"

"She knows better." With a wrinkled smile, Jake added, "Your Ma goes back to the days when it was first a red cob and then a white one."

Sadie glared at him. "I never used them, I'll have you know."

Carla laughed so hard she slid down in her chair. "Oh, Dad, you sure are a case."

Sadie said, "Let's have no more of this disgraceful talk."

Jake gave Carla a loving look. He liked it that she could laugh about the way he went at things. And he especially liked the way she sometimes talked as though she still was a little girl with a lisp. He made up his mind that if Carla still wanted to go to an art school when she graduated, he'd help her. He'd do it even if Sadie disapproved.

CHAPTER THREE

OREN

On his first Saturday afternoon off in July, Oren slipped into a white shirt and a pair of white ducks and heavy tan walking shoes and took a hike out to the Blue Mounds. Arriving at their base, he climbed over a steel gate and strolled up a winding red path. The path rose up through a patch of plums. He pushed through a fringe of chokecherries and entered the front of a red quarry. The quarry had been cut a city block square into the side of the huge cliff of Sioux Quartzite.

For the fun of it he called into the quarry. "Hel-lo-there."

"El-lo-ere," it called back.

The acoustics were perfect. Many a choir in the area came to the quarry to iron out the flaws in its singing. A person right away knew when he was off.

His cry and its echo awakened some pigeons high on the far wall and they flew out in alarm. They clappered around for a minute, flying balls of white and purple and brown, and then slowly resettled on their pink ledge.

He let his eye wander over the quarry walls, noting the various deep cracks, the immensity of that bit of skin of the earth. Revealed were eons of layered history, pink and purple and red and gold, of a time when sand slowly became sandstone became quartzite. What a place to hold a pageant. The gold-and-blue sky above, the dazzling red striations on three sides, the crushed-rock pink floor, the deep green elms standing sentinel in the entrance on the east side made for a perfect outdoor amphitheater.

Oren followed a winding red path north out of the quarry. The path curved around fallen old boulders hoary with lichen, skirted a fallen bur oak, dipped through a passageway between the wall on the left and a row of fallen rock on the right, at last opened onto an animal pass.

Oren moved stealthily. Sometimes one could surprise an eagle sitting at the top of the animal pass. Oren had once been startled to see a piece of rock fall off the cliff above and turn into a pair of great wings and swoop past him and pounce on a rabbit. He peered up past a boulder. No eagle that he could see.

He mounted the worn wriggling path, a hand to each knee. By the time he reached the tableland above he was puffing. Wiping sweat from his forehead, he settled on a smooth red boulder and rested a while.

A soft north wind rustled through the top of a gnarled old oak and cooled the back of his neck.

Rested, he got to his feet and took a cowpath south along the edge of the cliff. He checked to see if any cattle were around. Sometimes a tough bull ran with the cows. But there were no animals around. He was alone on the undulating plateau.

Sweet William waved pink at his feet. Occasional birdfoot violets blued shy in the shadow sides of stones.

As he approached the north precipice of the quarry, he ran into some western cactus. In the midst of a dozen prickly lobes, each the size of a hog's ear, bloomed two lovely rich yellow flowers. He knelt down on a knee. A bumblebee was working one of the flowers, dropping its menacing tail into the yellow blossom's vulva pink center. The bumblebee moved as if it were humming to itself. It buzzed over to another blossom and inspected it thoroughly. Then, quivering, moving clumsily, it lifted off and zoomed up past Oren's nose and was gone.

He stepped to the edge of the precipice and looked down into the deep quarry. The sun beat shimmering down into its red floor. The shadow off the far wall deepened its red colors into layers of frozen wines.

He skirted the quarry, going west. Above the west edge men had piled up the overburden. Grass had completely grown over it.

He was following a cow path heading south again when he heard voices. Soft voices. He looked up.

Two girls. Naked. The soles of their feet toward him. They were sunbathing on a patch of skin-smooth rock.

He'd forgotten that young people, both boys and girls, sometimes climbed the Blue Mounds and sunned themselves here, sure that they couldn't be spotted by anyone in town. Through a mist in his eyes he became aware that the silver blond, the long-legged one, had flaxen pubic hair, that the orange blond, the thick-hipped one, had light-brown pubic hair. As he stared his vision cleared and he saw their faces. Carla Simmons and Tracy Cadwell.

The girls were so busy talking they hadn't heard him.

Tracy said, "But I did say no to Brent finally."

"Good," Carla said.

Oren thought: "Tracy's got the one that's been tapped."

Tracy gave her bottom a little bounce on the smooth pink rock. "What I don't understand is, that the Lord could give us these nice bodies and the fun we can have with them, and then he tells us we can't have that fun. It really isn't fair."

"You can have that fun after you're married."

Oren thought of retreating, was afraid they'd hear his heavy shoes crinch on the crushed rock.

Carla seemed to pick it out of the air that somebody was present. She lifted her head and held a hand over her eyes against the sun.

Oren hung balancing between steps.

Carla made out who it was. She quick smiled and gave Oren a little wave of the fingers. "Hi."

Tracy lifted her head too. She also smiled, a wad of chewing gum showing pink between her white teeth. "Hi."

Oren said softly, "Sorry. I . . . I came to have a look at the cactus."

Tracy said, "We came to sun ourselves."

"I see that. Well . . . see you around." Oren turned and left.

It had come about so sudden the girls didn't have time to turn shy.

He didn't know which smile was the loveliest.

Oren followed the cow path. He brushed through a thick patch of wolfberries. He hopped over a long row of stones.

He came to a thick patch of cactus. They were everywhere in the grass. The sward near a huge cracked rock was yellow with them. Some had blossoms a good three inches across.

"Absolute miracles. The longer the stickers the thicker the flower. Hard to believe."

He climbed a ledge and found himself a large stone to sit on. At his feet bloomed another kind of cactus, tiny, resembling small dark green pickles covered with fuzzy stickers, and in their midst, stunningly, a tiny couched bronzy flower the size of a gold coin.

He looked up at the sky. Utterly blue.

He couldn't get the naked girls out of his mind. The healthy glow of their gold-pink bodies was of a piece with the beauty of the flowering cactus. How lovely. Especially Carla.

CHAPTER FOUR

CARLA

What a gentleman Oren Prince was. He hadn't looked at her in a nasty way.

During the next few days the picture of Oren standing in front of her silhouetted by a bright sun came to her often. She wondered what might have happened had he been the one to be sun-napping on those smooth pink rocks and she the one to find him there.

He was handsome. He had a good job as a newsman. He was a minister's son. His brother was a comer in the banking business. His father and mother were important people.

One evening, after she and Ivoria had finished washing dishes, she went to her room to rest. It was August warm out. She undressed down to her panties and lay down on the smooth creamy coverlet of her bed. A little breeze came through the open window and it teased the fuzz on her belly. Carla luxuriated in the tender touches of the breeze, stretching her body out several times to its full length, arching her feet and wriggling her toes. She fondled her breasts.

It wasn't long before she began to daydream about Oren. Yes, it was true he was a good five years older than she was, but wouldn't it be fun to go to a concert with him in Sioux Falls. At intermission he'd take her arm and guide her out into the lobby and he'd ask her what she thought of it and she'd . . .

"Carla? The phone. It's for you." It was Mother calling.

Carla got up. "Just a sec." She reached into her clothes closet and grabbed her flowered housecoat.

The phone was in the kitchen, up on the wall. She drew up a stool. "Hello."

"Carla?"

Carla began to smile. "Yes?"

"This is Oren Prince. I didn't interrupt something?"

"No."

"Good. I thought maybe you might like to go see a movie with me at the Palace. It's cool in there, you know."

Carla's smile widened.

"We can still make the nine o'clock show."

Carla looked at her gold wristwatch. "Yes, I suppose we could."

"We're going to have to walk it. My old Ford is on the blink. Will that be all right?"

Heavens. Walk it? Everybody in Whitebone would know about it by morning. "Let me ask a minute."

Carla stepped into the living room where Dad was reading the Sioux Falls *Argus Leader* and Ma was mending an apron. "It's all right if I go to a movie, isn't it?"

Ma said, "Who with?"

"Oren Prince."

"The minister's son. I guess so."

Dad spoke up. "What's the movie?"

"I don't know. He didn't say."

Dad spoke sharply. "You better find out. I'm not having you go to a dirty movie."

Carla went back to the phone. "What's the movie?"

"*Carefree* with Fred Astaire and Ginger Rogers."

Carla told her father.

"Well, all right. But be home early. Mind now."

"I will." Carla turned to the phone. "Okay."

"I'll be right over."

Oren was, too. Ma gave Carla a frown when they left the house just to let Carla know she had to be careful around men.

By the time they arrived at the Palace Theatre there was a queue a block long. But once it got moving Oren was soon buying their tickets.

Tracy was in the ticket booth and had a big smile for them. "Well, Carla, so he took the bait."

Carla blushed. Oren pinkened.

Tracy had on a low-cut pink dress and when she leaned over a person could almost see her rosy nipples. "Have a good time, you two. And don't do anything I wouldn't do."

Oren said, "That doesn't leave us much choice."

Inside Oren handed the tickets over to tall gruff Old Jessup, who tore them in half with a quick twisting motion and gave one set of halves back to Oren. Oren then took Carla by the elbow and steered her up the brown carpeted stairway to the balcony. Lights shone dimly. Oren managed to find them two front seats. "These okay?"

"Couldn't be better. All this nice leg room."

In a few minutes the house was full. Talk began to rise. Everywhere hands began tossing popcorn into open mouths. The smell of fresh butter on hot cornstarch became heavy on the air.

Then the dim lights went out, everybody quieted down, and the screen came on, silver, dancing, with flying flecks like spots before the eyes.

First the newsreel. Hitler was shown stomping triumphantly into yet another country. There were scenes of soldiers being blasted to bits, of mothers crying piteously over mangled children.

Oren muttered in Carla's ear, "We gotta do something about that wild man pretty soon."

A half hour into the main feature, Oren gently picked up Carla's hand and held it, warmly, squeezing it.

Carla withdrew her hand.

The romance in the movie wasn't much. Every time things seemed to warm up between Ginger and Fred, when a person could expect them to begin kissing, they'd instead somehow figure out a way to glide into a dance.

Some boys in back, bored by all the polite palaver on the silver screen, began to horse around, throwing balled up empty popcorn bags at each other. In a moment old Mr. Jessup appeared in the stairwell and growled, "All right, you hoodlums, you're going home. Now." He went straight for the culprits, grabbed two of them by the shirt collars, and hauled them out of their seats, down the aisle, and then down the stairs and outdoors. A watchful silence settled in the theater.

Toward the end of the movie Oren once more reached for Carla's hand and gave it a soft squeeze.

Again Carla withdrew her hand.

Carla thought the last dance in the movie miraculous. Generally she didn't approve of dancing, but she could see that the way Fred Astaire threw his slim body around, the way his feet flashed and flitted, had to be beautiful.

Movie over, the two of them pushed out with the crowd. Talk about the movie remained subdued until everybody was well past where Mr. Jessup stood glowering. Then, out in the lobby, everybody became animated. The young made skipping motions as though they too were on a dance floor with a Fred or a Ginger.

Carla and Oren walked up Main Street, past a lighted jewelry store window, a dimly lit general store, a smoky noisy restaurant. They turned the corner at the Northwestern Bank and headed north.

Oren asked, "You ever go dancing?"

"My folks are against it."

"Mine too." Oren took her arm. "That's the pity of being a minister's son."

Carla saw they were going to pass under a row of maples heavy with foliage, where it was dark. Sure that he was going to kiss her, she said quickly, tongue turning fluttery and making the words blur into each other, "What I liked best about the movie was all the beautiful sets." She hated it that her voice sometimes made her sound as though she still were a little girl with a lisp.

Oren slipped his arm about her hips.

She had to admit it. It was thrilling to have a man's arm around her waist. She could feel a shiver at the base of her spine. She tried to hurry them through the dark passage. Gently she removed his arm from her waist. "Oren, please. I like you, but not so fast. After all, I'm still only sixteen and know nothing about dating and such. While you're a grown man and probably have had a lot of girls."

"Not really."

"'Really' usually means you have." They were almost home. Ahead Carla could see that Dad had put on the porch light.

"Tracy is hardly in your class, you know."

"Oren Prince, that's a mean thing to say."

"But it's true. You like art. And she doesn't have a mouse's notion of what art is all about."

They turned up the walk. Carla took the step up onto the cement landing in front of the door. She turned to face him. "Tracy may surprise us someday."

"You hope."

Carla reached for the doorknob. She decided not to invite him in. "Thenk you for a good time."

Oren stepped beside her and again slipped his arm around her. "Kiss?"

"No."

He leaned in to kiss her anyway.

She pushed him away, smiling. "What you don't know is that I've made up my mind not to have a steady until much later."

"May I call you again though? Sometime?"

"Not right away."

"All right, Carla."

CHAPTER FIVE

OREN

The grandfather clock at the far end of the living room struck two o'clock just as they sat down to Sunday dinner.

Father sat at the head of the table, Bon the older son sat on his right, Oren the younger on his left, and Mother across from him. Father asked the blessing and then, with four stacked plates in front of him, took up the gleaming carving set and began slicing the roast beef. He cut several neat slices for each plate and sent the plates on. He next helped himself to mashed potatoes and gravy, to steaming snap beans, and passed them on. Mother at her end filled four salad bowls and passed them around. Mother tried to pretend everything was all right.

The shades were drawn halfway down, softening the faces in the family portraits on the upright piano. Light tan walls, rose carpet, walnut chairs filled the room with a mellow translucence.

Father had removed his black frock coat for a maroon smoking jacket. Bon, always formal, still wore his Sunday black suit. Mother still had on her blue church dress. While Oren, who hated restraint, had removed his blue suit jacket and red tie. The blue suit was a hand-me-down from Bon.

Bon had coal-black hair like his mother. When he used Vaseline to make it stay in place, straight back, his hair took on the glossy purple look of a grackle. Bon had a heavy jaw, thin-lipped mouth, small ears. When he spoke his mouth took on a square look. He had solid wide shoulders. He took the *Wall Street Journal* and read it religiously every morning right after breakfast. He also kept a close eye on the tax deficit listings in the weekly newspaper. Investing his savings in land he picked up for a song, he was, at twenty-six, a wealthy man. Yet for all his wealth he preferred to live in his father's house, in a room he'd always had.

Bon's manners were meticulous. His gestures were deft and sure. He cut his meat in precise squares. Lately he'd taken on the English manner of loading the back of his fork with potatoes plus beans and then of lifting it all with an even smooth motion into his mouth.

Oren had once loved his brother. But as Bon became more and more lost in his monied world, and joined the Chamber of Commerce and the

Rotary Club, Oren gradually began to detest him. What especially galled Oren was that Mother approved of what Bon had become.

Father remarked that the collection was poor that morning.

Mother smoothed that over by saying the collection would get better when the farmers started harvesting their crops.

Bon spoke up, looking straight at Oren. "I heard you took a high school kid to the movie the other night."

Oren misswallowed and had to quick help himself to some water. "What of it?"

"She hangs around with that wild Cadwell skirt."

Oren put down his fork and knife. "Want to make something of it?"

"People talk."

"How come you're not dating women?"

Mother broke in. "Boys, it's the Lord's day."

Oren kept picking at it. "Maybe you're not the marrying kind, Bon."

"I'll get married when I'm ready."

"And when will that be?"

"Dating is a good way to get trapped before you're ready."

"What are you doing for it in the meantime?"

Bon paused in his eating, fork lifted halfway to his mouth. His eyes slowly took on the color of hailstones. "It's a mistake to get married before you're well-fixed financially."

"I suppose you can turn it on like a faucet."

Bon continued to stare hard iron at Oren. "I've set a date when I'll start looking. Until then, nothing."

Mother smiled. "What's the rush? Many a mother never sees her sons again after high school. Except maybe at Thanksgiving."

Father said, "Oren, what's troubling you?"

Oren said, "I don't like the way Bon talked about Carla Simmons. Carla is worth a dozen Bons."

Again Bon drilled Oren with a shiny iron look. "I heard you the other night."

Oren flamed red.

"You left your door open."

Mother whitened around her lips. "You're pointing the finger again, Bon."

Bald head held sideways, smiling at life rivering past him, Father said, "'He that is without sin among you, let him be the first to cast a stone at her'."

Bon said, "It's all in your head anyway. A person can control himself if he wants to. I can."

Oren said, "You with your stock market graphs, you're just like a machine. Pure machine. No heart. Eight hours' sleep every night as regular as a clock—"

"—except when you make all those bouncing noises in your room."

Oren exploded to his feet. "Goddammit, that's enough. Either you apologize or I'm leaving."

Bon sat up stiffer. "I'm not apologizing. Not to a gossip-mongering reporter!" Bon almost spat out the words. "Not an issue goes by but what there aren't some gross errors in your rag."

"Listen, you. My boss is known everywhere for getting things accurate. That's why we win so many prizes."

"You and Ian McEachern keep making mountains out of molehills."

"But your *Wall Street Journal* doesn't?"

"Only good newspapermen work for the *Wall Street Journal*."

"You see?" Oren cried to Father and Mother. "There's never any arguing with him. He's always dead right."

Mother said, "Oren, won't you please sit down? I'll serve the dessert."

Oren threw down his napkin. "No. No dessert for me. I'm leaving. I can't stay under the same roof with that hard-hearted robot." Turning, Oren stomped upstairs to his room.

He found a small upstairs apartment, furnished, on Cedar Avenue across the street from the pink stone city hall. Entrance was on an alley, which he liked; it would allow him to enter his rooms without being seen from the street.

He sat in a stuffy brown easy chair hating Bon. He thought of ways to get even with him. He wanted to be especially devilish about it.

Finally it came to him. He snapped his fingers. "I'll turn him in to the Director of Internal Revenue. Bon probably hasn't cheated on his income tax, but he'll sweat for a couple of days while they go over his tax statement. I'll get my revenge without his knowing it. Nothing could be sweeter. I'll just sit back and smile."

It got dark in his apartment. The darkness fit his mood. Searching, he found an old table model radio in a closet. He set it under a window and turned it on. Soon classical music from WOI in Ames, Iowa, poured into his rooms.

He caught himself sitting with his legs crossed, big toe hooked an extra turn under the calf. He wondered why his legs on their own always seemed to want to cross themselves that way. It was as though they sought each other's comfort, as though they were cold and needed to be cozy with each other.

He crossed his legs the other way. Silhouetted against the window his raised knees reminded him of a human head. How interesting. How strange.

Then it hit him whose head it resembled. The Minneapolis *Chronicle*, in its rotogravure section, had published a remarkable picture of the body of a woman around twenty. She'd been found in a Danish marsh.

Her body had remained well-preserved in the marsh brine. Even her clothes, a rough-weave smock with a leather belt, were intact. She had been garroted, and the rope, its strands clearly visible, was still tight around her neck. There was a martyr's smile on her lips as though she'd gone happy into the darkness. What was remarkable about the smile was the way her eyeteeth were clearly outlined beneath her upper lip. It gave her the look of a wolf woman. Autopsy showed her stomach to be full of choice wheat grains. Apparently she'd been sacrificed to the harvest gods. The chosen one. Anthropologists estimated she had lain in those Danish marshes some four thousand years. Over all those years her skin and her hair had slowly turned brown.

Oren couldn't imagine anyone dying willingly with a smile on her lips. When he'd examined the picture in detail, he'd noted that she actually was smiling only on one side, where the lip caught her wolf tooth. The other side had the look of a scared person trying to look horror in the eye.

The ancient Danish woman haunted Oren in his dreams. In one nightmare, just as the enbalmer was about to pick her up, the figure moved, her head slowly turning toward Oren. She winked. Oren gasped. Then to his great surprise, Carla suddenly showed up at Oren's side, crying, tugging at his arm. Carla told Oren he was making a mistake about that "face in the mud." Then Oren woke up.

In another nightmare the face-in-the-mud woman was still back in the village. It was a gloomy spring day out. The faces of the people were all sad. They were worried. It appeared the gods were not going to give them a good harvest. Something had to be done to appease the gods. So lots were cast, and as it turned out she was chosen. Men came and grabbed her by the arms and after forcing their best food down her throat they led her toward the fatal marsh. She was young and beautiful, still golden. Suddenly she tried to wrestle free. She cried out, "I want love! Let me go!" Then Oren, struggling in his sheets, cried out, "Wait! Let her go!" And woke up.

Well, he couldn't do anything about Mudface. She was long gone. While Carla was still alive and lovely. And most lovely of all, Carla, when excited, had a fetching way of lisping, of slurring her words.

CHAPTER SIX
CARLA

Mother baked an angel food cake for Carla's seventeenth birthday, September nineteenth. It was a three-decker with lemon filling and rosebud frosting. Tracy and Meddy came after school for tea and a piece of the cake. Later that day, after Oren had taken Carla to a musical at the Palace Theatre, more of the cake was cut. It was scrumptious.

For the date to the musical Oren had given Carla a rose corsage. It was her first one and when she went to bed that night she placed it in a saucer of water on her bedstand. She could smell the roses in the dark.

She was pleased that Oren hadn't tried to kiss her. Once she was eighteen then things could be different.

Then on December 7 the Japanese attacked Pearl Harbor, and the United States declared war on both Japan and Germany.

A week later Oren met Carla on Main Street. He told her he'd been given a high draft number, 1 B, and that he probably would soon be called up.

Carla blanched. For the first time she became aware of the real world outside Whitebone. The sun seemed suddenly to cloud over. "Oren, I'm sorry."

"Luck of the draw."

At night Carla began to dream about Oren. She heard him calling her from a foxhole: "Carla! Carla! Where are you?" He lamented that now they'd never get a chance to really show their love. "Now I'll never have you."

The day before Christmas, Carla found an unusually large package at their door. It was addressed to her. She put the heavy box under the tree.

Christmas morning, after breakfast, the family retired to the gold-and-blue living room to open the presents. Most presents really weren't presents; they were clothes and school supplies, practical things.

Carla opened the big package last as Dad and Mother and Ivoria watched her. The present turned out to be a handsome wooden painter's box, along with an easel, a selection of paint tubes and water colors, and a dozen different brushes. Inside was a card from Oren Prince. A noble gift. Maybe Oren really would be the kind of man who would let her paint after they got married. So many talented women who'd had dreams of glory before they got married had them shattered when they learned that what their husbands really wanted from them was sex and good cooking and their shirts ironed on time. If they were farmer husbands they wanted sons, and more sons, so they could buy more farm land.

"Well," Dad said, "that fellow sure spent a lot of money on you." As Dad became more and more deaf, his voice became harsher.

Ivoria showed big round eyes. "Gee, someday when I get a boyfriend, I hope he'll give me something great like that."

Carla said firmly, "But I don't have a boyfriend. Yet."

Mother said, "Then you better return it."

Carla said, "No, I think what I'll do is write him a nice thank-you note. In such a way he won't get any ideas."

A month later, Oren called her on the phone.

"Carla, thank you for your sweet note. And for the little sketch you enclosed."

"Oh, it was nothing really."

"What are you doing tomorrow night?"

Carla took a deep breath. "What's going on then?"

"Your basketball team is shooting great guns this year and I thought maybe you'd like to see the game up at Marshall since it'll decide the championship."

"I'm not really all that wild about basketball."

"Not? All those flying bodies, those different forms and figures out on the floor, why, that should be perfect grist for the mill for you."

Dink Sunstrand was the star center and she didn't exactly care to see his big form flying through the air. "It's so far to Marshall."

"I'll have you home by at least eleven-thirty."

"With that old clunk of yours?"

He laughed. "Father is letting me use his Plymouth."

"I don't know if I should, Oren."

"Tell you what. Why don't we leave right after your last class? Then up at Marshall I'll take you out to dinner before the game." His voice became grave. "I have a special reason for wanting to see you alone."

Again she took a deep breath. Had he been called up?

"Please?" Oren had a winning voice over the phone.

"Okay."

She dressed in her long blue flowered dress, which she knew became her light hair and deepened the hue of her eyes. Her mother made her put on her rubber buckle boots just in case it snowed, as well as her long black-and-red mackinaw.

The first few miles up Highway 75, neither had much to say. Oren kept fussing with the heater in the blue Plymouth and worrying if Carla was warm enough.

Just as they passed through Pipestone, the sun disappeared behind an oncoming roll of gray clouds.

"Gosh," Oren said, "that's the one thing we don't need. We've already had about thirty inches of snow this winter."

"Dad's been complaining about it too."

They next took Highway 23 angling off to the northeast. Near Ruthton the clouds began to spit. Fine snow pelleted the windshield.

Oren kept looking up at the darkening sky. "This kind of snow usually means a bad storm is on the way."

Oren found the Copperplate Cafe on Main Street in Marshall and parked nearby. They settled in a booth in back and a pretty brunette waitress came to take their order. Carla loved fish and so did Oren and they both ordered lake trout.

The fish, pink and succulent and running with lemon-flavored butter, was very good.

The pretty waitress came back. "Dessert?"

Carla shook her head.

Oren considered a moment. "Yeh. A butterscotch sundae."

Carla smiled. "You have a sweet tooth."

"Yeh. Bon says it's the baby in me."

"You sound like you don't get along with your brother."

"Not always." The waitress brought the butterscotch sundae and Oren began to dip into it. "Everything is so mechanical with him. He gets up at exactly six-thirty. He shaves and dresses by seven. Sits on the can at exactly seven-thirty."

"Oren."

"Yeh, he's got it all figured out. By the age of thirty, he's going to be a millionaire twice over. And then on the first day of May he's going to pick out a woman and marry her on the first day of June. He'll lay down the law to her. Neat house. Meals on time. Make love on Saturday at two o'clock after a nap. No coupling during the week as that will interfere with clear thinking at the bank."

"Oren!"

"I'm sorry. I'm in a bad mood today."

Carla waited.

"I got a letter from Uncle Sam yesterday. I've been drafted. I have to report April tenth at Fort Snelling." Oren fixed her with a burning look. "Yeh, when what I had in mind instead was to ask you to marry me next year. After you were eighteen." Oren pushed his icecream to one side. "I love you, Carla. You know that, don't you?"

Carla felt her mouth go dry.

"But God only knows what's going to happen to me now." For a moment it looked as though Oren was going to cry. "Oh, well, I guess the fates never meant for me to be a happy man."

"Don't talk like that."

The waitress brought the bill and Oren paid up with a generous tip.

When they stepped outside they found the snow had become heavy and fluffy, like wet eiderdown spilling. A good two inches of snow lay on the sidewalk.

Oren helped Carla into the car and then got out a brush and cleaned off the windshield and the back and side windows. Then he got in behind the wheel. "Wow. If this keeps up, we're going to have trouble getting back tonight."

The thought flashed through Carla's mind they might be marooned. "I don't have any relatives in town either."

Oren's chin set out. "Well, don't worry. I said I'd get you home by eleven-thirty and I will."

At the Marshall high school gymnasium Oren found a seat for them in the row behind the official scorer's table where the Whitebone fans sat. With clipboard and pencil in hand he was ready.

The gym filled rapidly.

The rival B squads played first. The crowd laughed indulgently at some of the clumsiness; cheered lustily when some fledgling got off a deft pass or a slick basket. The Marshall B squad won handily, 27 to 19.

While the A squads went through their routine warm-ups, cross-passing, driving lay-ups, jump shots, free throws, the Marshall band came out and played pep numbers. When the band as a matter of courtesy played the Whitebone song, the visitor fans cheered. When the band played the Marshall song, the local fans roared.

When the band played *The Star-Spangled Banner*, Carla and Oren rose to sing with the crowd. Carla was surprised at Oren's voice, a rich clear baritone, overriding most of the voices around.

Then the game was on.

Slowly Carla felt herself becoming more and more excited by the bright lights, the shiny varnished floor, the flying forms of players and cheerleaders, the noisy earnest band all dressed in red. She jumped up with the Whitebone fans to cheer and clapped her hands in rhythm. Everybody on their side of the gym was family.

Marshall had a hot first half: Marshall 26; Whitebone 17.

Oren and Carla trailed the crowd out into the hallway during intermission. Oren bought them each a bottle of grape soda.

"You remembered," Carla said.

They stood close together. Occasionally they were pushed breast to chest by the shoving crowd. Little boys chased each other in a game of tag through the standing clusters of talking adults.

Then they were back in their seats for the last half.

In the fourth quarter, Dink Sunstrand suddenly got hot. He'd spotted Carla up in the crowd and began playing over his head. He rebounded, passed off, shot brilliantly. His playing brought the Whitebone crowd to their feet again and again.

Dink made the last basket of the game and Whitebone won, 37 to 35. At the final whistle the Whitebone high school kids surged down off the stands onto the playing floor. They hugged each other in sweet victory. The Marshall fans shrugged glumly into their overcoats and went home.

Oren smiled at Carla. "Your boyfriend has gone and done it again. What a honker."

"Can we go?"

"Sure." Oren helped her into her black-and-red mackinaw and then slipped into his own black overcoat. They followed the happy Whitebone fans out through the main doors.

It was snowing more heavily. The Whitebone drivers hurried the students aboard the yellow buses. Red lights blinked. People slipped in the slush, almost falling.

Oren helped her into his car. Once more he cleaned off the windshield and the windows, then jumped inside. "Good thing we got those buses ahead of us. They'll make a good track for us."

"If they get stuck then we'll all be marooned."

"They won't. We'll make it."

Slowly the big bulky yellow buses, resembling windowed jack-o'-lanterns, turned off the parking lot and lumbered ahead. Oren started the car. Skidding, sliding to one side, then the other, the tires slowly took hold. A dozen Whitebone cars were up ahead between Oren's car and the last bus. Headlights shot wavering shafts of light through the falling clots of white.

Carla felt a chill in the cold car. She slid over to sit near Oren.

"Maybe you better not sit too close. You might get an elbow somewhere if I have to whip the wheel around."

Wheeling and steering, slowing down at each corner, looking both ways twice, mostly in second gear, making sure there was a safe distance between his car and the car ahead, Oren managed to make good headway.

Snow began to collect on the windshield, and as the heater began to throw warmth up against it the clicking wiper thickened with ice and moved sluggishly.

"I'll bet there's eight inches of snow out there," Oren said.

"Just so we get home okay." The vague blue illumination gleaming out of the dashboard instruments made Carla feel safe and snug for the moment.

The buses and cars all stopped in Ruthton and the drivers got out and cleaned off the iced-over wipers.

There was some tire-spinning and skidding when the snaking line started up again. Headlights wiggled at cross angles. Gradually the line straightened out and made progress.

As they headed south out of Pipestone, still last in line, they ran into a hard west wind blowing across the road. It made the going treacherous. Sometimes the gusts pushed at the cars, making them slew around.

Oren said, "I'm not sure I like it we got nobody following us."

"How so?"

"Suppose we slip into the ditch. Nobody will know."

They had just passed the Edgerton turn-off and were heading for the slow curve toward Hardwick, when the lights of an oncoming car appeared ahead. Both the buses and the cars slowed down to make sure they were on the right side of the road.

Abruptly the oncoming car jumped out of its track and almost hit the car ahead of them. The driver over-corrected and then it appeared he was going to hit Oren's car head-on.

"Look out!" Carla cried.

Oren wrenched his wheel over. The front wheels, caught in the track made by the cars ahead, didn't respond. Again Oren rolled his wheel over, and then the front wheels caught. The blue Plymouth skidded along sideways, the rear wheels still in the old track. Somehow the oncoming driver got his front wheels back in the proper tracks and whirled past, vanishing behind them, horn howling.

The blue Plymouth hurtled forward slantwise. Oren whipped the wheel over the other way, trying desperately to get the front wheels back in the track. The snow in the track was packed down higher than on the rest of the road.

Suddenly the rear wheels zigged left and the next thing they knew they landed in the ditch, almost rolling over, first one way, then the other.

"Just as I thought!" Oren cried. He gave the engine the gas, tromping the footfeed down to the floorboard, hoping to bounce out of the ditch again. But the car mounted a snowbank and the rear wheels spun free. The motor roared uselessly.

"We're hung up!" Carla cried. "Stuck."

Oren let up on the gas. He sat in thought a moment. "Maybe I better go have a looksee." He reached around and picked up a blue stocking cap from the back seat and pulled it well down over his ears. "Be back in a jiff." He jumped out, closed the door, and vanished in the driving snow.

Carla could see him in the headlights leaning over the hood of the car checking the front tires, then saw him go check the back tires. There was a moment of silence. Then she heard him open the trunk.

A few seconds later he opened the door on his side and pushed in two sleeping bags. Then he got in himself. He was puffing. "We're done all right." He puffed some more. "Well, we better not let carbon monoxide get us." He turned off the ignition, then flicked off the headlights. Darkness lapped around them. "Good thing Father always puts sleeping bags in the car come fall." Oren couldn't quite look her in the eye. "This might turn out to be one of them old-fashioned blizzards."

"Then we might be here days before they find us."

"Could be."

"What will we eat?" she asked.

"Worse yet, how do we go to the bathroom?"

"Yes, that too."

Oren sat troubled. "Well, Carla, we'll just have to bear with one another." He slipped an arm around her. "Carla, I didn't mean for our date to end this way."

Carla was surprised to find herself smiling.

"Maybe God sent this storm to test us," he said. "And if we have to do odd things here, like relieve ourselves, well . . ."

"Does that really bother you? When you gotta go, you gotta go. All girls know that." A part of her was quite daring.

"We better each get into a sleeping bag and then huddle together. Here, I'll help you."

"Maybe I should go to the bathroom first," she said.

Oren's eyes flashed.

"I'll just open the door a little. If you'll look the other way."

"Of course."

Somehow Carla managed it. When she'd finished, she was shivering. She shut the door with a hard slam.

"Shucks. With you having to go now I have to go."

"Like when somebody runs water."

"Yeh." Oren opened the door on his side. When he finished he too was shivering. He cracked the door shut.

"Now help me into that sleeping bag. I'm cold."

Oren unzipped one of the bags in the dark and started to help her into it. After some struggling, mostly to get her booted feet inside, Oren finally got her zipped up. "There."

"Thanks a million. I feel warmer already."

Oren nuzzled his head between her head and shoulder. "You smell so nice. You know," he said, and she could feel him smile against her cheek, "with your hands tucked in like that, you can't defend yourself much if I decide to kiss you."

"I've been wondering when you'd think of that."

Oren turned her face with his chin and nose. She could just make out the white corners of his dark eyes. Shyly he lifted her chin in his hands. Then he kissed her. "I want to marry you."

"Don't you think you better slip into your sleeping bag?"

After some more wrestling, Oren managed to get into his bag. Just before closing himself in, he gave her a final hug and then drew her along the seat against himself.

The wind increased. It wasn't long before the snow began to pile up against the window on Carla's side.

Carla could feel Oren inside his bag trying to get closer to her. He was like an affectionate dog that couldn't get enough of licking her face. It hurt to think that perhaps in a year he'd be lying dead somewhere on a battlefield.

"Carla, there's about six weeks left. Could you possibly think of marrying me before I go?"

"Mother and Dad would never let me."

"If I don't come back from the war, then I'll never have had you."

"I know."

Oren whispered, "I'd like to just once before I go."

Carla began to feel very strange in her thighs. "No, Oren."

Oren sighed. "You're right, of course." He sighed again. "But oh, how terrible I'm going to feel when—"

"Shh!" she whispered.

The wind began to blow at them from the northwest. A tiny drift showed up along the right edge of their windshield. It slowly began to blot out their vision up front.

"Oren? I've always wanted to see what you do at the paper. Before you go, could I come down sometime and watch you get it out? And go along with you when you deliver the bundles?"

"Sure. But I warn you. The day we put it out you have to take a whip and a chair to get into the place. It's that wild."

"I want to remember you at work."

"If we get out of this alive we'll do it."

The blizzard roared and soughed around them. Carla soon became sleepy. She could feel Oren relax next to her. She wondered if it wouldn't be wise for one of them to stay awake. It was so easy to fall asleep when one became numb with cold. People had often been found frozen to death in snowstorms.

CHAPTER SEVEN

OREN

Cold slowly worked in through his sleeping bag. Carla lay heavily on his right thigh and soon it turned numb. She slept in slow even falls of breath. Her near breast pushed against his arm like a soft balloon.

He thought again about that afternoon up on the Blue Mounds. He couldn't get the vision of her naked body out of his mind. The high sun glancing off the bare pink rock had been at just the right angle to highlight the golden flesh of her firm legs and slim belly and full breasts. That fleece of hers, covering her mount of love, that lovely pillared door, he'd never enter that.

Mating was so problematic. It was asking a lot of fate that it should provide a man with the perfect wife, with the right color hair, the right bosom, the right fleece, the right voice. It would be a piece of absolute luck if a man ever found them all in one woman.

He thought of shifting his position to relieve the numbness in his thigh but was afraid he'd awaken her.

He nuzzled his head inside his sleeping bag. He could just make out the point of her nose silhouetted against the white snow outside the car window. Every time she took a breath her nose emerged a little.

He let himself slip into fantasy. He saw himself taking a lonely walk over the Blue Mounds again. Only this time he found Carla alone. He just had to look at her long nude limbs. Next he stared at her face. There was a look on it suggesting that, had she been born a Roman Catholic, she'd have made a wonderful nun. Well, he wasn't going to let that happen. He was going to make a lusty loving woman out of her. He was going to be the perfect lover. His heel caught on a small rock. There was a slight noise and she turned her head and saw him. She smiled lazily. After a moment she placed a finger on her lips and beckoned him to come lie down beside her. The sun shone very bright on the pink rock and on the nearby clumps of yellow-flowered cactus. He lay down beside her. Then, dreamily . . .

"Oren?"

He started. "Yes?"

"We mussent both fall asleep. That's dangerous."

"I know." The blizzard raged above the roof of the car. "Are you warm?"

"Mostly. Are you?"

"Not really. There's a leak in the door behind my back." His right leg had gone to sleep. From his hip down he didn't know if he had a leg there.

"My feet are cold." By the way her legs tensed back and forth he knew she was wiggling her toes.

"Maybe we'd be better off making one sleeping bag out of these two. That way it'll be much warmer."

She thought it over. Finally she said, "All right, if you think that'll work."

They helped each other, he with her zipper and she with his. It was very awkward getting the sleeping bags out from under themselves and aligning the zippers so they fit into each other.

"Here. Let me get this side under me"—groaning he managed to get half of the doubled bags under him—"and then this side over the top of us. And this time let's sit a little differently. This way."

She reached under herself and brushed her coat and dress down. She laughed. "All this wiggling around, it's warming me up."

After a while his right leg woke up and began to sting all the way from the nail of his big toe up to the jut of his hipbone. There was even a spear of pain running into the base of his skull. "Godd."

It took several minutes for the stinging to quit and for his leg to return to him.

The strong wind shifted again, coming out of the north, pushing at the rear of the car, hollowing out the snow around the trunk and dumping it up front, soon covering the entire windshield.

He could feel them both warming up in the doubled sleeping bags.

Carla asked, "What's that bump there?"

He'd become aroused. The stinging sensation that had been in his leg seemed to have jumped into his fellow. It was a strange wild sensation. "It's because of how much I love you." With his arms now free in the roomy double-bag, he took off his right glove and slid it inside her mackinaw and, daring, cupped her breast. "Oh, Carla, it would be awful if you and I couldn't be good to each other at least once before I go."

"Oren."

He thought: "Everybody's gonna think we did it anyway, being as we were out together all night in a blizzard." He reached in under her dress; and waited for her to protest. When she said nothing, he slipped his hand down into her pants; and waited again. He could feel her thinking to herself, weighing, wondering. She didn't resist his touch nor did she melt under it. He breathed into her neck.

He rounded his hand over her mount of love. She was very full. He wanted to say "fulsome" but remembered how his boss had once jumped him about that word. "Fulsome," Ian had said, "means 'offensive, repulsive, disgusting'." Oren later looked up the word in Webster's Second and discovered it had other meanings: "Plump, fat, copious, abundant, lustful, wanton," all listed as obsolescent. Too bad. Fulsome could have been a lovely American word.

"You're so rich," he whispered.

She reached down and pushed his hand away. "Don't."

Again he rounded his hand over her sweet fleece. He had to have her. "Carla, after having touched you like this, if I went to war now knowing I'd never have you, I think I'd kill myself."

"That'd be one sure way of helping Hitler win the war."

He was too full of wanting her to laugh.

She wasn't lying quite right, and as she made an undulating movement to straighten out her leg she pressed herself up into his hand.

He almost fainted. She was swelling under him. "If we freeze to death here tonight I won't have to worry much about going to Fort Snelling on the tenth of April."

"They better not find us dead like this."

He decided not to push any further. Just rest easy. Wait. Have patience. The cut-rhubarb-root aroma of her mingled with an old smell of mothballs in the sleeping bags.

Suddenly with both her hands she took his hand away and threw it aside. She zipped down her side of the bag and slipped out of it and, turning, got on her knees on the front seat beside him. She began to beat the back of the front seat with her fists. "No! No! No! I mussent! I mussent!"

Oren was astounded.

She began to bounce up and down on the seat, long hair flying up and down as though someone were vigorously shaking out a dustmop. "No! No! No! Please God, forgive me for even going this far. After all the lectures I've given Tracy, this is awful! I don't want to start a baby until I'm at least married. And I don't want to get married until I'm through college and well-started as an artist. I'd be so disappointed in myself if I didn't wait."

"Carla, not so wild. Of course we won't do anything if that's what you want. Carla."

Carla continued to bounce up and down on the seat.

Oren didn't know what to do.

"No! No! No!"

Finally Oren thought of something. Best was to cut through it all with what he hoped was a humorous remark. "Well, Carla, bouncing up and down like that is one way of making sure you won't freeze to death."

She turned and grabbed him by both ears. "All right, Oren Prince, you minister's son. I've just now won the battle over lust and licentiousness. I've got my emotions under control. Now you get yours in control. There's no excuse for the way we behaved tonight. And you know that."

She'd beaten the back of the seat so hard Oren thought he could smell the air of the factory in which the car had been made.

"Did you hear me, Oren Prince?" She gave his whole head a hard shake.

"Yes, Carla." Oren's ears cracked and rang as though she'd broken bells in them.

He loved the sound of her voice, especially when she became excited. Her words slurring together would be with him forever. Already it seemed he'd heard her voice all his life.

CHAPTER EIGHT

CARLA

There was an ice-crunching noise above them.

Carla sat up with a start. A gray sliver of light showed in the left corner of the windshield. That's right. The night before they'd slid off the road in a blizzard. Dad and Mother. They'll have been up all night worrying their heads off.

Again there was a crunching sound on a cold morning.

"Oren!"

"Mm-yup?"

"Wake up. There's somebody on top of us."

Oren jerked erect beside her. "There is?"

"We've slept the whole night through in here."

Oren rubbed his eyes with his knuckles.

Once again there was a snow-crunching noise.

Oren cocked an ear. "Sounds like a snowplow."

"Really? I hope they see us in here."

"Part of our top must be sticking out."

Abruptly there was a voice nearby. Very clear. "I told you there was a car in the ditch here."

"Yeh," another voice said, "one sweep of our wingblade along here and we'd have buried it."

"We better have a look-see."

"I'll get a couple of shovels."

Carla's eyes opened very wide. "Oren! We can't be caught in here with our sleeping bags zipped together like this." After her outburst the night before Carla had quietly crawled back in with Oren. "Quick. Let's get out of this. Separate the bags."

Numbly, somewhat stiffly, they rustled around and finally did manage to separate the bags and then crawl into their own bags once more.

Carla said, "I know this is kind of dishonest, pretending we slept separate, but I'm not going to have the whole town talking about us."

The voices came back. Rubber buckle boots skrinched on the snowbank on top of them. A shovel stabbed into the snow and a chunk popped up. Another stab and then the point of the shovel hit the roof of the car.

One of the voices called down. "Anybody in there?"

Oren called up. "Hey!"

"By God, there really is somebody alive in there."

Shovels began to whack into the snow and break out big stiff chunks of it. Twice shovels ticked the roof. Then a shovel pinged on the window near Oren's head. Instantly bright sunlight flooded into the car. Both Carla and Oren had to hold up a hand against the brilliant flare off the sharp-white snow. In a few moments one of the snowplowers had dug out a deep hole.

"By golly," the digger said, "two of 'em."

Oren opened the door. He slipped out of his sleeping bag and ducked into the dazzling blue-white cavity in the snowbank. He turned to Carla. "Here, let me help you."

Carla wriggled out of her bag, then got out of the car. Two hands above her helped her to the top of the snowbank. "Am I happy to see you guys," she cried. Then she helped Oren up.

Both men were about forty. They were dressed in six-buckle red boots and heavy sheepskin coats and sheepskin hats and lamb-lined leather mittens. Big white smiles gleamed out of their red faces. The taller one asked, "What happened?"

Oren said, "Met an oncoming car who zigged toward us, and in getting out of his way we slipped into the ditch."

"You're lucky you didn't freeze to death. It's ten below."

Carla began to shiver.

The shorter fellow said, "Pete, go get me that long chain, and we'll hook their car onto our snowplow and haul it out."

It didn't take long. A little more scooping around the Plymouth, some grunting as Pete scrambled under the car to hook the chain on its frame, and then, with some blasting from the huge yellow snowplow engine, their car was back on the road. The blue Plymouth was so plakked with snow it had the look of having been painted with coarse whitewash.

Oren got in and gave the motor a try. The engine fired on the first revolution.

"Lucky you," the shorter man said.

Pete said, "I'd keep that motor running now for at least an hour."

"Why?"

"With all that snow blown in around the engine, the only way to get it all out of there is to melt it out. Or you'll have shorts all over the place."

Shivering, Carla thanked the two men and then got into the Plymouth on her side. She covered her knees and legs with a sleeping bag.

Oren leaned out to thank the men and then with a wave of the hand put the car in gear and they were off.

Carla watched the landscape go by. They were in another world. Snowdrifts changed the earth's contours. Ditches were hard to make out. Fields had bumps where before they had been flat planes, muted blue edges in a sweeping white waste.

The engine had just begun to push warm air at their feet when they came over the top of the last rise, the Blue Mounds. Whitebone lay below. Sunlight gave the town's red buildings and bare-limbed trees set in the white snow a Christmas rock candy look.

They pulled up in the Simmons drive. Someone had been out to scoop it free of snow. A little path to the front door was scooped out too. They got out.

Just as Carla reached for the knob, the front door opened, and there, inside, standing as though they were a reviewing board, were Dad, Mother, and Ivoria.

Dad said, "Well, I see you finally made it."

Carla found a little laugh. "Yes, and all in one piece. We landed in a snowbank and this morning two men in a snowplow came along and pulled us out."

Mother looked as though she were trying to read what might have happened under Carla's dress. "Where did you sleep then?"

"In the car."

"Just the two of you?"

"Yes."

Dad said, "Well, step in. Let's leave the weather outside."

Oren said, "I'm awfully sorry about this. You don't know how bad I feel. I promised to bring your daughter—"

Dad cut in. "Well, maybe not on time, but at least safe and sound."

Mother said, "We hope."

Oren didn't like that. "Mrs. Simmons, you don't—"

Dad cut in again. "Uk! Uk! Everything's going to be all right. The main thing is, you're here." Dad turned on Mother. "I *told* you he'd be responsible."

Mother said, "How did you keep from freezing to death?"

Again Carla had a little laugh. "Oren's father always keeps sleeping bags in his car."

Oren said, "Well, time for me to go." His eyes didn't slide off to one side. "You're all right, Carla?"

"Everything's fine. It was a real adventure."

When the door closed behind Oren, everybody moved to the breakfast nook where the coffee was perking.

As they seated themselves, Mother said, "Carla, how many times haven't I told you, when you sit down, to please brush your dress down first. It keeps your dress from wrinkling."

"I'll try to remember, Mother." Carla stood up and ran her hand down over her seat, then resettled herself.

Ivoria leaned forward to sip at a glass of milk. "Then there really were two sleeping bags in Reverend Prince's car?"

"Yes. Two people can hardly get into one bag, silly. Unless they're beanpoles."

"Nah," Dad said, "that's enough now on that subject."

CHAPTER NINE
CARLA

After some watching, Mother decided nothing had happened the night of the blizzard after all. Mother even began to have a smile for Oren when he called on Carla. Mother's friends thought it rather cute that her daughter should be dating the son of a respected reverend in town, making it forgivable that a high school girl should be dating an older man.

Gradually Carla became aware that she and Oren were playing games. She didn't like it. True love shouldn't involve stratagems. When a person loved someone, a person should love with all their heart. Scheming was low and common. When the proper time came, sex should come about naturally, a lovely dream in the night.

It was obvious Oren was troubled too. But unlike her, because he was full of hot ardor, he was always on the alert for a softening on her part. Just when it would be time for him to go home, that look would appear in his brown eyes, which meant he wanted to get inside her pants again.

People teased her a lot about Oren. Even their egg man got in his nickel's worth. It was Carla's job on Saturday morning to walk out to Henry Crouch's to get their weekly supply of eggs. Henry Crouch was a widowed farmer living a mile north of town.

She usually knocked on his door around ten in the morning.

"Don't be bashful. Come in."

"How are you today, Mr. Crouch?"

Eighty-year-old Henry Crouch had a spry way of moving about. He had a slightly bent stance and it gave him the look of a fast-skittering spider. "Pretty good, considerin' they still hain't tucked me away in a grave."

Carla set her empty pail on the counter near the sink. "Four dozen again?"

Henry Crouch handed her a full pail. Bits of straw, even mustard-colored chicken dung, clung to some of the eggs. The clean eggs gleamed pink as though each had a little light on the inside. With a little wiggle of his gray head, meant to be humorous, he said, "I guess I can let you have four dozen of those that didn't hatch out."

Carla laughed.

"Now if some chickens hop out of those eggs, those are mine."

"Mr. Crouch, you're such a funny man."

"I put the biggest eggs on top so you'd think you're getting a bargain."

Carla glanced around in the dingy bachelor kitchen. The smell of eggs fried in rancid bacon fat lingered in the room. "I see you've already been washing dishes this morning."

"Yeh, now and then I agitate 'em a little in water."

"Mr. Crouch, there are a lot of old maids in town who'd be more than glad to come over and wash them. Let alone widows."

"Well, I tell you, the truth is I've got my eye on you."

"Oh, Mr. Crouch."

"What's that minister's son got I haven't got. Except maybe good looks."

Carla noticed Mr. Crouch had a shotgun standing ready near the screen window overlooking the garden. "Afraid of burglars?"

"No. Just that there's been a rabbit working over my lettuce patch. It's worse than having a louse in your hair." Henry Crouch fastened his shiny grey eyes on her. "How is your love life?"

Carla blushed. "How much?"

"The usual. Thirty cents a dozen."

"A dollar twenty cents then." Carla laid the money on the yellow checkered tablecloth. "Thank you so much."

"Don't mention it. So you'd rather be his girl then, huh?"

"Oh, Mr. Crouch."

Henry Crouch abruptly turned his back on her and skipped over to the sink and began putting dishes away.

Carla strolled home slowly in the morning light. She walked along with the gracious step of a dove. The hardened snow on the ground had melted some, turning glossy, and light bounced off it making the whole valley appear to be a frozen pond.

English teacher Miss Kildare assigned the seniors a final paper for the year on a subject of their own choosing. That gave Carla an idea.

On a Tuesday after class she went up to Miss Kildare's desk. Miss Kildare, a spinster some forty years old, was a tough teacher. She had nothing but scorn for laggards and was sometimes in trouble with the school board for being too sarcastic in class. She was a tall woman, dark-haired, fleshy, with thick features. The boys hated her. They said her trouble was she wasn't getting her regular sex.

"Miss Kildare, can I talk to you about my paper?"

"Of course." The teacher liked Carla, one of the few so privileged. It was mostly because Carla had decided that the only way she was going to be able to stand Miss Kildare was to regard everything she said as humorous. Miss Kildare in turn misinterpreted Carla's smile as one of friendship.

"I'd like to write a paper about a day at the newspaper."

"Wouldn't that be more of a project for Journalism?"

"I've been thinking of making a story out of my visit. And then I'd like to illustrate it too."

"Oh." Miss Kildare's thick lips came out in a large square pucker. "Well, far be it from me to throw cold water on enthusiasm. Go ahead. Let's see what you come up with."

"Then can I get off tomorrow, the whole day?"

"Yes. I'll write out a pass for you. And say hello to Oren for me."

Carla turned fluttery. "Why him?"

"Oren was one of my best students. He could write."

As she stepped through the front door of the *Press* the next morning, Carla was startled to hear Ian McEachern, publisher and editor, going at it with Oren. McEachern was furious about something. They were standing near the door to the composing room. Oren, head bowed, listened sullenly. McEachern's blond Scottish face was plum red, and the few strands of blond hair over his bald head stuck out. Oren and McEachern were the only people in the front office; all the rest, the clerks, had skedaddled.

"I tell you, Oren," McEachern was saying, "I've watched her grow up into a Christian beauty."

"And I'm not a Christian?"

"Look, you're too old for her. Why, imagine you getting your slimy hands on her . . . uchh!" McEachern waggled a finger in Oren's face. "I have half a notion to fire you. And I would too if you weren't about to leave for the war."

"Thanks!"

"Let's hope the war makes a man out of you." Froth began to edge along McEachern's lips. "You modern kids, with your loose morals and your wild ideas, maybe this war will straighten you out."

"Mr. McEachern—"

"This generation is going to the dogs!" McEachern had a considerable potbelly. As he ranted and raved, the belly bounced around like a volleyball loose in a gunnysack. "Why, just this last year, my old friend Hod Cornish, sheriff down in Woodbury County, showed me something I'll never forget. She was a student at Morningside College. There she lay, a beautiful gal perfectly naked on a cold slab in the morgue. Long blond hair. Slim well-proportioned body. Hips"—McEachern shuddered in memory, pale blue eyes closing—"beautiful. A lovely flower of a woman. Hod said he was sure she'd been a virgin before the rape, by the way she'd bled. But now she was dead. And all because some foul viper of a man got his slithery slimy claws on her and indulged his satanic passions on her body . . . uchhh!" McEachern waved his gartered arms around so hard a pencil flew out of his flapping gray vest, a pencil which he caught in midair with a darting snap of his hand. "This generation! Suppose there is a terrible bloodletting? So what? Sometimes a blood-letting is very good for the purity of our fair republic."

Carla had heard enough. Discreetly she backed out the front door and softly let the door close by itself. She turned up the street. She decided to walk around the block. That would give Mr. McEachern time to cool down. Some of the things Mr. McEachern said made her a little sick to the stomach. Yet at the same time she had to smile at the funny way his belly bounced around.

The streets were busy with men going to work, some driving, some walking. A few of them stopped at Gert's Cafe for a quick cup of coffee.

Soon she went back to the *Press* and was glad to see Oren busy at his typewriter and McEachern sitting at his huge rolltop desk talking on the phone. Two clerks, middled-aged ladies, were busy at their desks too. "Hi," Carla called out.

Oren glanced up, face still sullen. "You made it."

McEachern dropped the phone into its black cradle and whirled around in his swivel chair. His face opened into a smile. He bounced to his feet. "Glad to have you on board today." McEachern opened a little gate in the wooden partition for Carla.

"Thenk you."

Oren pulled up a chair for her next to his desk. He let her read his story about a farmer who'd invented a cowbarn gutter with an auger which automatically shoved manure outdoors the moment any kind of weight fell on it. Oren next took her with him when he carried the copy out to the linotypist in back. There was a sweet acrid smell in the composing room. The oily floor was speckled with silverish strips of spilled hot lead.

Carla took notes on her clipboard. Carefully she stepped around the greasy presses. Several times she had to fold her gray coat tight up around her knees to keep from getting it soiled.

When all the type had been set, Oren helped the pressmen lock up the forms on the stone and then helped them put the forms onto the press. Soon the great heavy machine began pounding out the pages, folding them in their proper sequence and ejecting them as a finished newspaper.

McEachern came out back. With a warm smile he said, "Oren, don't you think it's about time you took the young lady to lunch? You've got time now before we begin delivering papers."

"Good idea." Oren took Carla by the arm and began steering her through the jumble of machines.

Out on the street Oren said, "How about a quick bowl of soup up in my apartment?"

Carla was willing. She'd been wanting to see his rooms.

They turned off Cedar into an alley, entered a side door into a brick building, mounted some narrow stairs, and then emerged into a long tight apartment. The place had flat-white walls, tall thin windows, a shining kitchen, and a white immaculate bathroom.

"This is cute," Carla said.

Oren hung up her coat and his jacket on wire hangers. He next got out an aluminum pan, filled it with water and a package of ready-mix chicken soup. "You sit there." He pointed to the far chair at a little table. He poured them each a glass of milk and set out a plate of fig cookies. "It won't take but a jiff."

Carla liked the way he kept the place spick-and-span. Many wives had slobs for husbands, men who never picked up after themselves.

Finished with her lunch, Carla got up to look around in the little apartment. It was when she went to look at his bedroom and pushed down on the single narrow bed to see how hard it was, she realized she'd made a mistake.

"You like hard beds?" Oren asked, coming in behind her.

Carla tried to slip past him. "We better get back to the plant."

"Oh, we got a few minutes yet." He put his arm around her waist and pushed his nose inside her long hair.

She could feel herself begin to melt. "He'll fire you."

"Not before I leave for Fort Snelling." Oren moved his hand up over her breast. "Come, a real kiss now."

They began to wrestle a little and soon fell across the bed, Oren on top of her.

Carla said, "This is something we haven't done before."

Oren held her close and began to kiss her. "Carla, when can we make sweet love?"

"Wow. You sure get to the point, don't you?"

"I want to reach deep into you."

"That's just what I don't want you to do."

"Oh, darling, I'm going wild."

"But I'll have a baby."

"You never get a baby the first time you do it."

While Carla was busy keeping one of his hands out of her pants, his other hand tried to sneak into her blouse. When she was busy pushing his other hand away from her breasts, his first hand snuggled still farther inside the rubber band of her pants. "You pest you!" At the same time for the life of her she couldn't understand why Mr. McEachern could refer to a man's hands as either slippery or slimy. Oren's fingertips thrilled her.

Oren began to groan love.

She tried to make light of it. "Got it bad, haven't you?"

"Just let me a little ways. So I can at least take that memory with me."

"Hoo," she said. "I know you. Give you an inch and you'll take a mile." She could feel her nipples becoming erect. "We better get back. Or really, Mr. McEachern will fire you."

"The heck with him." Oren's half-closed eyes flashed silverish.

"Remember what he said about some foul viper of a man getting his slithery slimy claws on a young Christian girl."

"What? You overheard him say that?"

"Yes. I quick backed out and walked around the block."

Oren let go of her and lay back in the pillow. "Damn him anyway. He's crazy."

Carla quickly got to her feet. She brushed down her blue woolen dress to make sure she hadn't picked up any wrinkles. Next she got her comb from her purse. She leaned far over, head almost to her knees, and began combing her long blond hair down, with it almost reaching the floor, to get the tangles out and get it all flowing one way. Finished, she raised up and threw her hair back over her shoulders.

Oren began to pound his pillow. "You once said, 'No! No! No!' Well, I say, 'Yes! Yes! Yes!'"

She could feel how thick he was with it, almost in agony, and she couldn't stand to see anyone hurt, denied. But she got her coat and put it on. Then she took his jacket and held it out to him. "We've got to get back."

"That damned McEachern. Now I've got another reason to be mad at him." He got to his feet and slipped into his coat.

They went single-file down the narrow stairway. Once out on the street, she noticed how stiffly he walked and wondered about men and their needs and how it was with them. Spring seemed to come earlier for boys. She smiled at his dark flushed face and gave his arm a pinch. "You better get that look off your face."

"I'll be all right." Then, after a bit, he said, "I'm sorry I'm that kind of fellow."

"It's okay. That's boys, isn't it?"

They turned the corner by the bank and headed for the plant. There were only a half-dozen cars in town, parked at an angle like blue hogs at a trough. Wednesday was sometimes a shopping day for out-of-towners.

When they entered the *Press* front door, they found McEachern standing beside his rolltop desk. "Oren! Where were you? The boys are already making up bundles for delivery."

"They got the old clunk backed up to the delivery door?"

"No. That you can do. And get on it." Then McEachern said to Carla, "Sorry to be so testy. But I like to stick to a schedule. If we don't, we miss the last mail at the post office, miss connecting trains, miss getting the papers distributed in the restaurants around town before dinner. People depend on getting the paper on time. Especially the merchants and the shoppers. They pay our bills."

"I understand," Carla said softly. "Can I go along with Oren? It's all going to be part of my paper."

"Go ahead." McEachern gave her a pinched smile. "Mind that you keep him hustling along now."

"I will."

Oren hurried her out through the back door to a battered red Chevy pickup. "She ain't much, but she always runs, come snow or rain. The only time she's unhappy is when the sun shines. Then she floods."

Oren started the pickup and backed it to the delivery door. He got out and, with the motor slowly smoothing over, helped the pressmen hurl various sized bound bundles of the *Press* into the pickup. They filled it to a heaping mound. Again Oren got in and they were off.

First stop was the delivery door of the post office, then the restaurants and various drugstores and grocery stores, and finally the two depots. Carla helped with the smaller bundles. When they were finished, Oren brought the red pickup back to its spot in the alley behind the plant.

"That was fun," Carla said.

"Yeh, I kind of liked it myself. With you along."

"Working at the *Press* you really get to know this old burg down to its last clothesline."

Oren gave her a look. "I'm done for the day. How about coming up to my rooms . . ."

"You sure don't give up, do you?"

"At least let me walk you home part way."

"No. I want to walk home alone and collect my thoughts. I'm going to write my paper yet tonight."

"Suit yourself."

She leaned across the seat and pushed a dry little kiss against his cheek and then stepped out. She waved at him once and, clutching her clipboard under an arm, headed out of the alley and into the street.

CHAPTER TEN
CARLA

Oren's train was due at midnight. He was to take the sleeper coming in from Sioux Falls, and an hour later in Blue Wing the sleeper would be hooked onto the night train coming up from Omaha, and from there he'd ride straight into St. Paul. The next day, the tenth, he'd be inducted into the Army.

Carla helped Oren pack his little bag and went with him to his parents' house. Reverend Prince had a kindly smile for Carla, while Mrs. Prince fell into occasional reveries. Brother Bon was at a bankers' convention and that eased things in the Prince home.

At eleven-thirty the four of them walked over to the depot five blocks away. There was a fine glowing lemon of a moon out. April had opened fair and the few showers that had come along had greened over the lawns and started the buds in the lilac bushes. The perfume of a new season was in the air.

They were early. Lights were on in the yellow-brown brick depot. Their footsteps crackled sharply on the dark square bricks in the floor. After Oren bought his ticket they sat down on a long hard wooden bench facing the railroad tracks. Sturdy armrests for each seated person divided the bench. Nickel radiators cracked with hissing steam.

The station master, Olaus Northey, whose mother built the first cabin just east of the Blue Mounds a decade before the Civil War, was bent over the telegraph sending key, tapping out a message.

Carla let her hand rest on Oren's shoulder. She noticed a spiderweb hanging in a nook of the rounded-off corner of the ceiling. Another spiderweb hung from the top of the shoulder-high brown wainscoting.

Mrs. Prince asked, "You sure you packed everything, Oren? That little pocket Bible we gave you?"

"We're not supposed to take much along, Mother."

"You packed extra underwear?"

"Mother, they furnish all that. Government issue."

"What'll happen to the clothes you have on?"

"I'll have to send them home."

Reverend Prince had a godly smile for Oren. "I wonder if it wouldn't be fitting to offer up a special farewell prayer."

Oren squirmed. "Here?"

Reverend Prince said, "God's ears are everywhere, son."

"Oh, all right. I suppose if you must, Father."

Reverend Prince folded his hands under the gray hat in his lap and closed his eyes. "Our heavenly Father, we come to Thee in the late hour of this day, in this humble public place, to ask a special farewell blessing."

Olaus Northey kept working his sending key. Click. Clack. Click click. The sound of it had a way of emphasizing Reverend Prince's phrasing.

"Our son has been selected to serve his country in a holy war. The enemy is indeed of the Devil and means to destroy the Christian way of life, love for one's fellow man."

The nickel radiator gave off a low pounding sound.

"If our son's life must be offered up on the battlefield, Thy will be done. But we pray, O Lord, if it be at all possible, that his life be spared. We are mindful, dear Father, that you in your infinite wisdom once offered your son for all our salvation. It was the supreme sacrifice. Thus for us to ask for a special exception is perhaps an arrogant thing. Forgive us. We are mere human beings with tiny frets." Reverend Prince had a fine baritone voice, and in the brick-walled depot it took on dignity. He was utterly sure of being heard. "Bless our son wherever he goes, give him strength in his hour of hurt and despair, fill his heart with a real love for Jesus. Bless also his friend Carla Simmons, who has become as a daughter to us and whom we love dearly."

The telegraph transmitter abruptly fell silent. Olaus Northey had finally noticed that he had a family praying in his waiting room.

"Father, give strength to our President and to all our generals and our armed forces. Give them wisdom so that, whatever we do in this war against darkness, it will redound to Thy honor and glory. We ask it in Jesus' name. Amen."

The door opened at that moment and to Carla's surprise her father and mother walked in. Carla jumped to her feet. "How wonderful." She skipped over and hugged her father.

Dad smiled at everyone. "Wal," he said, voice as usual sounding like clashing gears, "we thought we better plant a few shade trees for ourselves. Just in case."

Reverend Prince got to his feet. "Shade trees?"

"You know, pretty soon these kids of ours may set up housekeeping, and then, who knows, someday we may have to go to them for help. So we better stay on the good side of them. Regardless."

Reverend Prince laughed. "I see what you mean. Well, we're honored that you've come." He bowed to Carla's mother. "How very nice to see you here."

Mother said, "We thought it the right thing to do."

Oren got up and took Carla's mother by the elbow and helped her to a seat next to his mother.

Mrs. Prince said, "Too bad you weren't here a few minutes earlier. You could have joined us in prayer for Oren's safety." She spoke in a soft voice.

Dad smiled a laugh off to one side as he settled next to Mother. It was obvious he hadn't caught what Mrs. Prince had said. Dad kept surprising Carla with his many different stratagems to cover up that he was hard of hearing. Dad said, "Were you in the last war, Reverend?"

"I was a chaplain. But I didn't go across."

Carla got to her feet to have a look out of the west window. After a moment her eye caught something and she looked more carefully. Where the two tracks curved southwest a light seemed to catch their slick surfaces. The curving reflection moved slowly toward the depot. That had to be the train from Sioux Falls, headlight still out of sight behind the houses.

In a moment Oren would be gone. Possibly forever. She should have given herself to him as a last present. Full of soft giving, she stepped back to Oren. Then, unaccountably, directly in front of him, she squatted down on her heels, knees opening in invitation. She gave him a wide opening smile. Still smiling, she rose and settled close to him and kissed him.

There was a long whistle, moaning, haunting.

"There she is," Olaus Northey announced. He looked at the big railroad clock up on the wall and then looked at his pocket watch. "The Chicago, Minneapolis, St. Paul & Omaha is always right on time." It was a moment of much satisfaction for him.

Everybody looked at each other, then slowly stood up.

Oren picked up his little suitcase. He put his arm around Carla and leaned his head against her head.

They straggled outdoors onto the brick platform. The train's brakes took hold with the sound of anguished iron. The enlarging big eye of the diesel engine owled up in a slowing rush. The engine and the cars swayed from side to side. The single big light rose above the waiting party; then with a huge whosh moved past them. The big driver wheels skated on the iron tracks, setting off sparks. With a final vast pinching sound the train stiffened to a complete stop.

A conductor in a dark blue uniform swung down from the last set of steps. He waved his flashlight toward them to indicate that that was where the sleeper was, the last car, a dull-green affair different from the rest of the cars.

Oren and Carla led the way.

Carla reached up a warm wet kiss. "Oh, Oren."

"It's all right. We'll have a good time on my first furlough then, huh?"

"Yes, yes. Oh, I'm so sorry." Knees weak, Carla sagged.

The conductor said, "This way, sir. We're not stopping long."

"Yes sir." Oren let go of Carla. Turning, with a forced smile, he shook hands with Mother and Dad, then his mother, and last his father.

Oren gave Carla a quick dry kiss and then, whirling about, took the steps up into the sleeper and was gone.

The conductor waggled his flashlight and stepped aboard. There was a toot from the engine ahead and the train began to slide forward.

Carla walked along with the train, hand to her mouth, hoping to catch a last glimpse of Oren through the sleeper windows. But the shades were drawn. Carla slowed to a stop.

The engine ahead tooted again, and in a few moments the rear red lights of the sleeper began to fade down the track.

II. THE POLLEN

CHAPTER ELEVEN

OREN

It was ten o'clock in the morning and the sun shone slantwise through the high narrow windows of the processing hall at Fort Snelling. There was a musty smell of dried fungus in the building. Cigarette smoke drifted about under the long low ceiling.

Most of the men in the long line waiting to be inducted were young. They'd been called up from the farms and the little villages and the big cities in the Upper Midlands. They came in all shapes and sizes: tall and self-conscious, short and cocky; long rooster necks, short fat necks; long flat feet, short broad feet; dark-featured, stunning light-gold hair; large wide mouths with narrow-set eyes, tight pinched mouths with round startled eyes.

Oren had never seen such a menagerie of human beings. By narrowing his eyes until sight blurred off a little, Oren saw every man there metamorphosed into an animal: the sensitive alert deer, the stubborn heavy dog, the gawky year-old colt, the smooth-muscled elegant hound, the waddling goose, the elongated giraffe, the sneaky weasel, the dangerous cat, the staring antelope, the playful otter.

A few of the men, who'd served in the Army before, stood in a group and talked by themselves.

One humpneck with lively mocking brown eyes had the most to say. He had the air of one who knew he was going to be rejected. "I hear this time they're going to be more careful about letting in queers."

"How would they do that?"

"If the examining doc doesn't like your looks, he sends you over to an army psychiatrist for further examination."

"Hey, that would be a good way to get out, wouldn't it? Put on a la-de-da act and home you'd go."

The humpneck said, "I think they'd spot that pretty quick."

Oren hated standing in line. His little suitcase began to feel heavy and he shifted it to his other hand.

"We had one in basic camp. A lieutenant. He was overly polite around the ladies. One kid complained he'd made a pass at him in the shower room. Looking for a chance to bugger him while he was bent over picking up his soap."

A slow-smiling fellow spoke up. He had old lips and sunken grey eyes. "Yeh, a friend of mine ran into one of those officers once. He said the cupcake caught him with his rod all soaped up in the shower."

"What happened?"

"He let the officer bawl him out for a few minutes. But finally, when he'd heard enough, he stepped up to the fellow and said, 'Sir, this is my soap and this is my pride, and if I want to soap it up real good, that's my business'."

The waiting men laughed.

"Yeh," the humpneck said, "officers are lazy bastards. They're generally dirty. Really dirty. We always had to clean up after them high nuts. Course, we would have been gigged for it anyway. So it was all part of camp life."

Oren said, "You make it all sound pretty awful."

"It's tough titty in basic. You gotta crawl on your belly while they're firing live ammo just sixteen inches above the ground. Raise your butt an inch too high and you've got a second canyon."

More laughter.

"But, then, you got your furloughs to make up for it." The humpneck let his brown eyes close in memory. "Man, when I was based in Hawaii, I used to visit this tiny little thing. Black hair. She was my favorite. Once, when I came back to camp, I could hardly walk. Thought maybe there was something wrong with me. But the medic said it was only strain."

The line shuffled up a few feet.

"Talking about them pansy loots, the way you spot them is, they like to hold a lot of short-arm inspections."

"Maybe the cook is short of cheese," one said.

"Yeh. Likely." The humpneck spotted an unusually tall fellow in the line ahead. "Now there's one guy who's sure to get bumped home. Anything over six-six is too much. The Army has to buy special clothes and special shoes for him. It takes him twice as long to dig himself a foxhole. He just oddballs up the whole outfit."

"Yeh, when the general comes by to inspect the troops, he sends those long gears to the rear. Nothing but your five-foot-ten boys up front."

Through the window Oren could make out the long narrow bridge he'd crossed that morning while riding a streetcar. Below the bridge rippled the Mississippi, the biggest river he'd ever seen. The Mississippi curved through a yellow canyon. It was a wild and romantic sight. He had trouble believing it could be part of the same world in which a deadly war was being fought.

The line of men shuffled up. Those carrying heavy suitcases reset them near their feet.

Oren imagined himself being sent off to Africa. He saw his sprawled body, eyes closed, drying up on hot sand even before maggots could get to work on it. Like dried jerky. He imagined himself being blown to a thousand bits by a bomb, one moment rifle in hand, the next moment nothing, not even toenails left.

Oren became aware everybody around him had fallen silent. Turning, he saw two officers talking in a doorway across the hall. Something was up. Every now and then they cast a look at the line of men.

The humpneck said, "One of them looks like the C.O."

The company commander finally nodded. The other officer picked up a bullhorn and began blasting. "We've run into an emergency here at the fort. One of our clerks was called home because his father died. Only male left in the family, so he has to go home to run the farm. We need the produce to help fight the war. So. Anyone here know how to operate a typewriter? Write up reports?"

The humpneck muttered, "You never volunteer in the Army."

"You won't have to go to basic training right away," the second officer went on to say. "You'll be put to work right here and now."

Oren awoke from his gloom. Hey. If he volunteered maybe he wouldn't have to go to the front after all. He'd certainly be more apt to get furloughs to go home working here at the Fort than he would at the front. Maybe he could even talk Carla into coming up on the train to see him weekends. Again he saw Carla on impulse sitting down on her heels in front of him, knees open.

"Nobody?"

Oren raised a hand.

"You there. Step forward."

The humpneck sneered. "Look who's bucking for a clerk's job."

Oren walked over and presented himself. "Yes, sir."

"Can you type?"

"Used a typewriter at work."

"What did you do?"

"I'm a newspaper man."

The company officer looked Oren up and down. He appeared to like what he saw. Slowly a smile broke across his smooth Nordic face, revealing an even row of white teeth. He was as tall as Oren, but much heavier in the shoulders, with narrow hips and strong thick legs. His blond hair was cut short. His small ears were set close and tight to his skull. "So you'd rather sit than fight?"

Oren didn't like the question. "Sir, writing reports, isn't that a form of fighting the war too?"

"It is." The commanding officer smiled slantwise some more. "I'm Colonel Simpson. When you've passed your physical, report to my office on the grounds. They'll show you where it is." He saluted.

Oren saluted in turn. "Yes, sir."

As Oren walked back through the line he got the razz: "You always run into one guy like that, an ass-kisser." "Ding-donger." "What's the C.O. want, have you hold his pecker while he takes a leak?" Oren could feel his face turn red.

Oren passed his physical. He was outfitted with an olive wool uniform, blouse and trousers, and shoes and cap. He was then shown his cot in the barracks, the first one on the left near the door. Beyond ran two rows of cots, all neatly made up, khaki blankets as tight as a drum.

At three o'clock an orderly came to show him his desk at the headquarters. They walked briskly down a long sidewalk. On their left loomed a row of old stately buildings, yellow brick with black slate roofs. Farther on stood some red brick buildings, the officers' quarters. On the right across a paved road spread a very long and wide green sward, white goal posts at the ends.

"They play polo here?" Oren wanted to know.

"Yep. Before the war they had a great team here. Beat England, Virginia, Australia. Now it's the parade grounds."

They walked across the top of an anvil of earth. North of the anvil ran the Mississippi and south of it ran the Minnesota River. The tips of massive cottonwoods growing out of the bottoms resembled little trees.

They turned left up a cement walk. The orderly skipped up a flight of steps and held the door open for Oren. They passed through a short entry, wheeled right through a hallway, and entered a large room with a half-dozen desks and high wide windows. The room was flooded with afternoon sunlight. Maps had been tacked up between the windows, the European sector, the northern half of the African continent, the vast Pacific Ocean. White pins showed where the Allied battle lines were and black pins the enemy. Oren spotted a desk with some drooping red roses. There was also a smell of dry paper and old ink around.

The orderly pointed. "That's your desk there in the corner. These other desks are for your secretaries."

Oren pointed to the desk near his with the collapsed roses. "Whose is that?"

"Teresita Wendt's."

"A girl? Here in the Army?"

"The Fort's always employed women secretaries. From General Services."

"For godsakes." All the desks, except for some files, looked neat. "Where's everybody?"

"Coffee break. Downstairs we have a snack bar. Ah, shall I take you up to see Colonel Simpson now?"

"No. I'll find my way."

After the orderly left, Oren sat down in the swivel chair and whirled himself around in it. And smiled. What luck. He checked the drawers in the honey-blond oak desk. The wide top drawer had the usual pencils, letter opener, paper clips. The top side drawers had envelopes and stationery, and the lower drawers, deep ones, had files. There were three trays on the desk marked Out, In, and Hold.

A black Remington typewriter stood on a rolling typing stand on his left. That gave him an idea. Quickly he slipped a sheet of Army stationery into the typewriter and began writing Carla a letter. He told her about his great luck that day. For both of them. "I want to marry you as soon as possible now that this has happened. Ask your father and mother to waive the age requirement for you and then go to the clerk of court there in Whitebone and take out a marriage license for us. We can get married on my first forty-hour pass. I heard in the doctor's office that married service men here get separate quarters. Please do this for us. I need you so." He thought once more of those opened knees. "A big hug and a kiss for you, my darling sweet. Tons of love. Yours, always, Oren."

He had just addressed the envelope, licked and sealed it, and tossed it into the Outgoing tray, when there was light laughter of women out in the hallway, along with klokking heels, and then in a moment four women filed into the room. The first one was short, dark-haired, about twenty, demure and silky in her walk. She was wearing a white linen dress and red shoes. She had a red feather caught in a pink comb in her black hair.

Oren gulped. He hardly noticed the other three women because the first one was a deadringer for that Danish woman who'd been found garroted in the peat bog. He stared. She even had wolf-like eyeteeth. It wasn't possible! He blinked; and then looked again. He almost expected to see a rope around her neck.

Oren got to his feet. "Hi."

"Hi," they all said.

"I'm Oren Prince, your new head clerk."

The dark young woman said, "And I'm Teresita Wendt. And this is Chris Anders, and this is Mabel Seilman, and this is Josephine Handley."

He nodded. "Well, as you were." He waved at their desks, then sat down himself.

Teresita settled at the nearby desk with the faded roses. She sat with her back arched, black hair cascading down the back of her white linen dress. She studied some papers to one side of her typewriter a moment and then slipped two fresh sheets with a blue carbon between them into her typewriter. Just as her fingers touched down on the keys, she threw Oren a smiling look, part of the smile catching on an eyetooth. She had wide-set eyes, slightly slanted, very black, with glowing blue pupils.

That smile was exactly like the one Mudface had given him in his dreams. His heart began to pound in his chest.

Knitting his brows, he forced himself to read a sheaf of papers on his desk. He finally managed to make out they had to do with various requests from divisions abroad for radio operators, communication engineers, experts in explosives, mechanics to repair Sherman tanks. He turned to Teresita. "I'm afraid I'm going to need help with these."

Like a sinuous kitten Teresita rose from her chair and leaned near him. "These go to Colonel Simpson upstairs. You mark them as received with your initials in the upper right-hand corner and then he goes over them." There was a soft lilt to Teresita's voice, animal husky.

"I see," he said.

"Initial them and I'll bring them up to him now."

"I'll do it. I still have to report to him."

"As you wish."

Oren initialed the pack of papers, slipped them into a folder, and hurried out of the room.

Out in the hallway he felt his hair to make sure it was in place and then climbed the stairs, hand trailing along the blond oak balustrade.

He found Colonel Simpson's office on the far right. He knocked.

"C'min."

Oren entered and saluted. "Oren Prince reporting, sir. And here's some papers for you."

Colonel Simpson reached for them. "Oh, yes, I've been expecting these. I've had two telegrams from that wild man George Patton. His aide-de-camp has been shooting off requests to every induction center in America for tank mechanics. You'd think Patton was going to win the war alone." Sunlight bounced off Colonel Simpson's polished honey-blond desk. He asked, "How's it going down there?"

"Fine. Say, that Teresita Wendt now, she's . . ."

"Ha! You noticed, eh? Well, she's not only pretty but she's got her head screwed on right. Nobody, but nobody, is going to get his hands in her pants. So far as I know she don't even date anybody. Her father's of German descent, a dentist, and strict. And her mother was a Filipino, from the upper classes there. So you see, our little Teresita isn't going to be throwing herself away on just anybody."

Oren could feel the power of the colonel radiating toward him. The deeper self of the man was letting him know it liked him.

"Yeh, she comes from a close tight-knit family. They'd rather spend their evenings together than go gallivanting around." Colonel Simpson swung to his feet in an easy graceful motion. He got out a pack of cigarettes and offered one to Oren. When Oren refused, he nodded, and then helped himself. He lit his cigarette with a lighter, then strolled over to the tall windows. "She runs a good office. Neat." Colonel Simpson pointed with his glowing cigarette. "She sure is a helluva lot neater than our yard detail. Look at the crud out there on the parade grounds." Colonel Simpson's voice sharpened. "Prince, I want you to get in touch with Sergeant Honkers and tell him to police up the joint. Right now. Tell him it's on the double." Colonel Simpson flicked imaginary lint off his impeccable brown blouse. "Goddam, I hate clutter."

"Yes, sir." And saluting, Oren turned and left.

Back at his desk, Oren turned to Teresita. "Sorry, but how do I get in touch with Sergeant Honkers?"

"Oh, him." She handed Oren a stiff cardboard covered with transparent plastic. "His number is on here."

Oren dialed the number.

A voice coarse with saliva answered. "Honkers here."

"This is Oren Prince, new clerk here at headquarters. Colonel Simpson just told me he wants you men to police up the parade grounds. On the double."

"We just did."

"You didn't do a very good job then. I just heard the colonel cussing a blue streak about the crud out there."

"Shi-ite."

Sergeant Honkers showed up with a detail of six men. Oren went outside to show them where the crud was. Honkers was a hulking six-foot-two, wide shoulders and heavy legs. He seemed to have grown into his name. He had a wide loose-lipped mouth with big white horse teeth. Oren wondered how Honkers could eat without biting into those lips. The other six men were average.

Honkers said, "I don't see it. Just a couple of cigarette butts." Honkers stooped and picked up several butts.

A balled-up envelope lay nestled in the mown grass ahead. Oren went over and picked it up. "This is what he means."

"Yeh, but a fellow can't see that unless'n he's standing right on top of it." Honkers sneered elaborately.

"I saw it from where you're standing."

"All this fuss over a couple bitty pieces of paper." Honkers stared at Oren's left sleeve to show he didn't think much of taking orders from an E-1 private desk clerk.

"The colonel said to get on it."

Honkers nodded to his men. "Well, I suppose we better go through the motions." He bent over and picked up another cigarette butt. His men began searching the grass at random.

Oren heard a low crackling sound in the grass behind him.

It was the colonel. For a second he resembled a grinning chimpanzee. "A bit of rebellion here?"

Honkers pouted. "We just scoured the place this morning."

Colonel Simpson drew in his belly. He was the perfect model of a commanding officer, brown uniform just pressed without a wrinkle, brown military shoes shining as though they'd been shellacked. "Honkers, tomorrow some big brass is coming in from Washington and I want this place as neat as the inside of a milk pitcher." He paused to take breath, lifting his chest even higher. "Now, goddammit, get on it! Cigarette butts. Cellophane. Pencil stubs. Cigar butts. Buttons. Kotex."

Honkers thought that pretty funny. "Hoh. We're likely to find lady napkins on the grounds all right."

"Get going!" Colonel Simpson stepped up and aimed a swift kick at Honkers' high butt; and missed. It left the colonel a little red-faced. "Police up, damn you. Down on your hands and knees. Down! I mean that. All I want to see moving is asses and elbows."

Slowly, elaborately, as though they were tired down to their very bones, Honkers and his men got down on their hands and knees and began looking through the grass.

Colonel Simpson watched them a moment. "That's better." And with that, he saluted sharply at Oren, and whirled on a toe and marched back up to the office.

As Oren turned to go too, he allowed himself a smile. He could just see seven agitated asses and fourteen elbows moving across the old polo grounds like hurrying grasshoppers.

Settling down at his desk again, Oren noticed something. "Teresita, what happened to that letter I had in Outgoing?"

"The mail clerk just picked it up. You wanted it mailed, didn't you?"

"Well, I guess I did."

The sound of Teresita's voice, soft, catchy, sent a quiver up his spine. Certain phrases of music had the same power to make him shiver from neck to toe. For every man there was one note on the clavichord which, when struck, woke up his private tone. Each man had his own private prevailing tone of being.

It was as though he had in his head a certain set of cells, a certain configuration of them, that had been handed down to him intact by way of hundreds of generations, great-grandparents ad infinitum; cells that had once, five thousand years ago, responded to and loved a certain shape of face; and then over the centuries had lain dormant, unresponsive; until now in him they had awakened, had responded, first to a picture he'd seen in a rotogravure section, then to a real-life face he'd met at Fort Snelling.

He dared a glance at Teresita. She was sorting papers, jouncing them on their edges, first lengthwise, then sidewise, to make neat piles of them. She had that same Mudface smile all right.

A voice in him spoke up. "But you love Carla."

"Yes," he said aloud, "yes, I love Carla."

"What?" Teresita said beside him.

Promptly at five o'clock he went to his cot in the barracks and lay down with the worst headache he'd had in years.

He ate dinner with Honkers and the boys in the mess hall.

Honkers told about how once he went with a Greek girl. He'd wanted to marry her, he said, but they had a problem. Her family had strict rules about their daughter remaining a virgin. She was to send to her father, still in Greece, a sheet stained with blood on the night of her marriage. "Impossible," Honkers said, "because we'd been screwing already for a year. She wanted me to nick my chin with my razor for the blood. I told her to go jump in a lake."

Oren hated the way Honkers licked his coarse lips.

The shortest man in Honkers' squad, Elton Saxneat, spoke up. "Never let a woman tell you what she wants. You tell her what you want. I went out with a babe here a couple weeks ago who had all kinds of rules."

"Was that the tall titsy one?" Honkers wanted to know.

"Yeh, that one. Said she wasn't gonna do it until she at least had a sparkler on her finger." Saxneat sneered. "Well, I told her off. 'Come to it, or you can walk home.' Most generally they come to it. She liked it well enough at the time."

Honkers laughed. "Yeh, I know about her. I took her home once too and fixed her."

"You fixed her too?"

"Sure. I just plowed right in."

For a moment Saxneat looked as though he might hit Honkers.

Hubie Roach, the fat one, had a laughing way of talking. He was occasionally approached by men because of his soft pink skin. "I had a woman almost rape me once. Man, was that fun. Her husband was one of the first to go off to war and she wanted a man to take care of her while her husband was gone."

"Rape you?" Honkers cried. "How could she do that?"

"She opened my pants. When it wouldn't come up right away, she started to flick it with a fingernail."

"Oh, come on now, that's pretty strong."

Hubie laughed. "Fact. Pretty soon I couldn't get enough of it. She told some of her girlfriends whose husbands had also gone off to war. The next thing I know I'm servicing three Army wives on the home front."

"Ain't it nice when you like yourself so well."

"Oh, I hain't always had it so easy. I had a sergeant in basic who almost killed me. He hated my fat. One day he took me aside. 'Look, Fatso, there once was such a thing as a six-month soldier training period. Then there was a three-month training period. Well, my boy, there is now a special seven-day training period. Just for you. It'll be hell, heaven, or hobo by Christmas. But by God, we'll make a soldier out of you yet'."

Honkers looked at Hubie's belly. "You know, really though, for your own good you ought to get rid of that tub."

"Oh, no," Hubie cried in pretended shock. "I just got it."

Honkers' lower lip finally got in the way as he chewed on a tough piece of beef. He bit into it; and jerked erect.

Oren said, "Honkers, pass the salt and pepper."

Honkers' lip hurt. "What's the matter, mister clerk, those creamed foreskins not quite to your taste?"

Oren noticed how sharp his sense of smell had become. He could not only smell the chipped beef and potatoes and cutbeans and butterscotch pudding on the tray before him, but also the gassy odor of the wax on the floor and the acrid scent of old paint on the nearby wood. "Just pass them, will you?"

Honkers handed the tin shakers to Saxneat who in turn passed them on to Oren.

Saxneat said, "Trouble is, if the girl don't invite you in, where are you gonna jazz 'em?"

Honkers snorted. "Do a wall job on 'em."

Saxneat went on. "You can't do that here at the Fort."

A long discussion followed about the ideal place for coupling: hard bed, couch, floor.

Saxneat finally said, "Well me, all I ask is enough flesh to keep it off the ground."

It took a while for that to soak into Honkers' head, but when it did he laughed like a horse.

Bald Harry Dent, oldest man in the squad, smiled to himself. "Have your fun while you may, boys. What I used to do all night now takes me all night to do."

Saxneat couldn't resist getting in one last jab at Honkers. "Oren, did you hear what happened at short-arm inspection the other day? You didn't? Well, we had a new castor oil artist here doing the inspectin', and when he came to Honkers here, he took one look and said, 'Holy smokes, you mean to tell me that all belongs to one man?'"

Honkers glared. "Right now your wife is in bed with some man she just met. And there's nothing you can do about it either, private."

The next morning Oren was at his desk a full hour before anybody arrived. He quick wrote another letter to Carla. "Please get your father and mother to okay our getting married on my first 40-hour pass. I know you'd like to wait until you're eighteen, but, sweetheart, a terrible war is on and precious days are rushing past. I'd so like to hold you in my arms each night to help me forget this awful place. I'm sick of the men I have to live with. No future to look forward to here. Everything seems so hopeless. Especially when I remember the wonderful pushing kisses you gave me at the depot."

He finished the letter, signed it, affixed several X's, addressed the envelope, sealed it, and tossed it into the Outgoing tray. He loved Carla.

He had started to work on a folder file marked Roster At Fort Snelling when his four secretaries walked in.

"Good morning, Mister Prince."

"Morning, ladies."

The three older women settled down at their desks like old meadowlarks resettling in their nests in the grass. Teresita sat in her chair with her back arched, hair hanging free past her shoulders. She was wearing a red dress with a white belt.

They'd all worked about an hour when Teresita got up to place some fresh mail in the Outgoing tray. She spotted Oren's letter to Carla. "Ah, homesick already, I see. That your girl?"

"Yes."

"She must be beautiful."

"She is."

Teresita returned to her chair. She sat more arched than before, thinking to herself, once more resembled the Danish Mudface.

That afternoon, around coffee-break time, Oren was surprised to have Teresita ask him, "Could we interest you in some icecream?"

Oren said, "Of course. But where do you get it?"

"We office girls have a custom of making icecream every Friday afternoon."

"You have a freezer?"

"A little one in the basement. You'd like some then?"

"You bet. Icecream is my middle name."

Soon everybody was chattering away as they lipped their icecream. It was the confidence hour of the week. To Oren's surprise, the three older women talked about sex much like men did.

Chris Anders told about a friend of hers who'd got in a family way with a worker at the Ford plant up the river. "It's her own fault too. She always had open drawers for him. Though she claimed he always tore the buttons off her drawers when he did it with her." Chris, once a slim blond, had become plump and liked to lick her spoon twice to make sure she got all the icecream.

Mabel Seilman had remained skinny. She had deep lines around her sad grey eyes. "Men. Well, what I tell 'em is, they can damn well leave my skirts alone."

Josephine Handley, a brown-haired divorcee, was the smallest and the most fleshy. She had to wear a girdle to keep from looking fat. "I know what you mean. But sometimes, when they moon around so, and carry on as though they are about to die, you finally just say, 'Oh, what the hell, it isn't going to hurt me all that much'."

Chris said, "I know one sure-fire way to cool 'em off."

"What's that?"

"A cozy fart at the wrong time can surely ruin a relationship. That's the perfect way to give a man the air."

Oren almost choked on his brownie. Teresita beside him didn't laugh. She watched to see how he would take feminine frankness. In the midst of it all his interior commentator spotted something. The way Mabel had pronounced one word, "re-lay-shun-ship," there was an ambivalence in it. To lay a woman was one thing, to shun her another.

Icecream finished, Teresita gathered up the paper plates and threw them in a wastebasket and took the spoons downstairs.

While Teresita was gone, Mabel had to tell Oren something. "You want to be careful around her. She's beautiful, and she's a good girl, but she's a schemer. I've seen the colonel upstairs try to outfox her but he loses every time."

"Thanks."

The next afternoon, Saturday, with nothing to do until Monday morning, restless, Oren decided to get a pass and go for a walk. Most of the men were lying on their bunks, mending clothes, reading mail, napping. A few were sitting on the waxed cement floor playing cards.

Neatly dressed, shoes polished a rosy tan, he walked across the bridge over the Mississippi. A streetcar came trundling along behind him, then rushed past. It made the old bridge tremble. Iron braces far below cranged.

Off the bridge he turned left and followed a footpath. The path wound around rocks and oak trees, descended into a little gully, climbed a small mound, then leveled out once more. Below, on his left, the Mississippi sparkled in the falling sunlight where the water ran the swiftest. There was one boat out on it, two boys with fishing poles.

He stopped on a sandstone ledge overlooking the river and sat down. Sunshine warmed his right cheek. A huge oak, just budded, cast a shadow like a hairnet over him. He picked up a stone and threw it far out over the river, and waited until he heard it go p-lunk.

He wondered what Carla thought of his two letters.

All that talk about sex by the men at the Fort, as well as by the women . . . it was funny, but when a human being found himself forced to do a job he hated, his thoughts naturally turned to sex. To ignore it or forbid it was about as futile as trying to freeze a flame.

The hard sandstone began to hurt his butt, and he got to his feet, brushed himself off, and went on strolling down the narrow path.

He'd just turned a corner, when there she was. Teresita. She was wearing a man's sweat pants and sweat shirt and was running toward him. It startled him.

She too was startled; and, slowing, stopped in front of him. She puffed a little. "Hello, Mister Prince."

"Hello yourself. I didn't know you liked to run."

"That's how I keep in shape." Her eyes barely came to the chest pockets of his brown tunic.

"How'd you ever get started running?"

"My father and mother both run. I guess you might say we're exercise nuts."

He admired the dark rosy flush in her cheeks. She glowed as though a bright lamp had been lighted inside her. He said, "Maybe that's what I ought to do. Get rid of the blues."

"Why don't you go out with the boys and paint the town red?"

"I'd much rather have a date with a woman."

"I'm afraid I can't help you there."

He looked at his watch. It was going on five. On an impulse he asked, "How about dinner with me tonight?"

She looked up at him with great dark eyes. "Oh, but I don't date anybody from work."

"I'll have you home whenever you say."

She looked abashed at her hands. "Well, really, I don't date much."

"Are your parents that strict?"

"Oh, no. In fact, they're afraid I'm going to turn out to be an old maid." She laughed, full lips thinning at the corners.

Oren stared at her features, at the rich play of expressions over them. Her face had the exact likeness of his Mudface haunt all right. Whoever Teresita was, a real flesh-and-blood woman or a visitation from another time, she was slowly sucking him into a whirlpool. "Maybe you're ashamed to be seen with me."

"Oh, no no. That's not it. It's just that I haven't gotten around to thinking much about boys."

"Then it's about time. Come. I won't hurt you. I just want a sociable evening with a lady. You." Even as he spoke, there flashed before his mind's eye the vision of Carla suddenly sitting down on her heels, knees apart, in the depot back home. "I heard Colonel Simpson say that Gambino's Dine & Dancing is a good place to eat. Just off the bridge back there."

"But that's where the officers usually go."

"So?"

She pinkened over like Carla sometimes did. "Well, all right, just this once then. Promise to have me home early?"

"I promise."

She turned. "Come. Then we'll have to go back the way I came. I'm not going to dinner in these clothes."

Teresita lived in a brick house overlooking the Mississippi. It stood back from the River Road up a sloping lawn. Four white columns flanked a white porch and a white front door.

Stepping inside, Teresita called out, "Dad? Mother?"

Within moments a slim blond man appeared. Behind him came his short dark wife. He had lanky arms and legs and moved with the elaborate correctness of a German officer. She had spike heels and tripped along with an easy bearing.

Teresita introduced Oren and then went upstairs to dress.

"Have a chair, Mr. Prince." Mr. Wendt waved Oren to a brown plush armchair, while he settled on a brown davenport. Mrs. Wendt settled beside her husband. The room had tall windows and fronted on the river. There were German paintings on the walls and Filipino family pictures on the grand piano. There was an odd air of the correct exotic about the place.

Mr. Wendt asked Oren about his home. Mrs. Wendt listened with stabbing black eyes. Twice she stroked her yellow dress down over her knees. Mr. Wendt had long fingers and every now and then out of habit bent them back at the knuckles.

Soon Teresita came down dressed in a long yellow dress. It made her look taller.

Mr. Wendt looked Teresita up and down in approval. "May we know where you two are going?"

Teresita said, "Gambino's."

"All right."

Teresita got her topcoat, a light tan thing, and Oren helped her into it.

Mrs. Wendt finally spoke. "Have a nice time."

"We will," Teresita said, taking Oren's arm.

As they went down the front steps, Oren thought: "Man, now there's one fellow I wouldn't want to tangle with. And Mrs. Wendt, she's got stilettos for eyes."

They were early and chose a booth in a darkened corner. The booth had sumptuous shiny red leather seats and the table between them had a hard black linoleum surface.

A girl waiter came along and lighted a little candle inside a glass chimney on the table. The yellow candle gave off a soft light, bathing both their faces in gold. The waitress took their order, lake trout with baked potato, and then disappeared into the kitchen.

Teresita said, "You don't smoke, I see."

"No. I once heard smoking makes your lungs look like a couple of folded tobacco leaves."

"Dad doesn't either."

"He's pretty strict, isn't he?"

"Not really. That's just a front."

"I'll bet your mother is though."

"She's not much for touching." Teresita rolled her firm narrow shoulders. "Have you heard from your lady friend yet?"

"No, I haven't."

"She'll write you. You're too nice a man to let go. What's she like?"

"Tall. Blond. Like you, athletic. She's going to be an artist. She can draw like a dream."

"She sounds wonderful." Again Teresita had the look of a woman from another time, of woman as comforter and listener.

"She is. And there's one thing in which she's like you."

"What's that?"

"She's still pure."

Teresita's black eyes looked at him in a level direct manner. "Good for her. Once a girl has lost that she's up for grabs."

Oren laughed outloud. "That's a funny way to put it."

"Well, she is." Teresita's eyes began to sparkle with an inner fury. "Once you men know that we aren't, you treat us like chippies. We're expected to hand it out like sandwiches at a party."

Again Oren laughed.

The lake trout was pink and soft and broke apart in long flakes. Between bites of buttered potato, both Oren and Teresita relished the fish. Oren remembered the last time he'd had lake trout, with Carla in Marshall when he'd asked her to marry him. He pushed the memory aside.

Oren asked Teresita if she'd like some wine to go with the fish. She declined.

He told her about his family, that his father was a preacher and a kind man, that they were Methodists. "I suppose you're Catholic?"

"Yes." She said it in a way to suggest mystery.

He told her about his hard-headed brother Bon. Curiously, Teresita showed interest in Bon.

Oren left a generous tip when he paid the bill. Then he helped Teresita into her coat and they were off for home.

It was chilly out and she shivered the first couple of blocks. They walked briskly. By the time they entered the path on the cliffside of the River Road both had warmed up. They had little to say. Some low clouds had pushed in from the north, and the river gorge was dark with shadow.

They were almost home when she stumbled over a root in the path. He caught her and held her up. Then he held her close for a moment. She didn't resist him; nor did she encourage him. As she got her balance she slowly straightened up in his arms. Again, on impulse, knowing it was wrong, but doing it anyway, he placed both hands around her face, making a creamy cameo of it in the dark, and then gently kissed her.

She stood a moment uncertainly, as if she weren't sure how she should take it. Finally she said, softly, so softly he almost didn't hear it, "Thanks."

Thanks?

An odd little ache set off in his head. An inherited cluster of brain cells, asleep for centuries, had awakened. It awakened exactly like a leg might awaken from having been sat on too long. It stung.

The odd ache would eventually take him over, he somehow knew, and neither he and all his good intentions about Carla, nor Carla and her love for him, would be a match for the Mudface spell. He could hear the hoarse hollow sound of an old wind blowing down a long corridor. And in the middle of that hollow wind there was that voice of Teresita's, one he now knew for sure he'd heard all his life, heard it as a baby, heard it while in his mother's womb, heard it even while in his grandmother's belly. He had kissed an ancient ghost.

He shook his head. "Come, I promised to have you home early."

They had no more to say all the way to her front door.

"Would you like to come in for some hot chocolate?" she said. "My father and mother always like some just before going to bed. It helps put you to sleep."

"I shouldn't. But I will."

Both Mr. and Mrs. Wendt were pleased to see them back so early and went out of their way to make Oren feel at home.

Oren had a second cup of hot chocolate. "Your daughter tells me you both like to exercise a lot. Run."

Mr. Wendt nodded. "My doctor once gave up on me. But I didn't. I made up my mind I was going to live. So I started to run. I got to like it and kept it up."

"What did you have?"

"Some kind of fungus or other, eating away my lungs."

"You look fine."

Teresita said with a smile, "And mother took it up because the American foods were making her fat."

Mrs. Wendt smiled too. "A short person doesn't have much room to put on fat."

Oren finished his chocolate and set his cup on the coffee table. He smiled at Teresita sitting beside him on the brown davenport. "Well, all that running shows in Teresita. She walks more from her hips than she does from her knees. Like a man does."

Mr. Wendt nodded. "That's true." He ran a lean freckled hand through his bristle blond hair, then cracked his knuckles. His light-blue eyes twinkled. "Did you know that if you throw a knitting needle at a woman's lap, she opens her legs? While a man closes his?"

"Oh, Father," Teresita said.

"Try it sometime. When they don't expect it."

Oren was thinking that in the case of a man it was probably for a good reason. Throw a knitting needle at a man's lap and he'd close up to protect his genitals.

Mrs. Wendt said, "Did you ever watch a man try and thread a needle? No? He holds the needle steady and then moves the thread into the needle. Women do it the other way. They move the needle towards the thread."

It was time to go home. Teresita accompanied him to the door. He wanted to kiss her again but decided against it.

"'Night."

"'Night."

He followed the path back along the river. Ahead through the thick buds on the trees he could make out, across the river, the lights of Fort Snelling.

CHAPTER TWELVE

CARLA

Back from the depot, Carla and Dad and Mother gravitated toward the maple breakfast nook in the kitchen. Ma put on a pot of coffee and Carla set out cups.

Dad got out his silver spoon saved from the war. "He's a nice boy. May he have my luck."

"God forbid," Mother said.

"What?" Dad said, cupping a hand to his ear.

"Those awful nightmares of yours, I don't wish that on my daughter. The way you used to yell and hit at me in your sleep . . . ugh!"

Carla said, "And here I was wishing I'd married Oren before he left."

"Holy cats," Mother said. "You better get down on your knees and thank God you didn't. Forget him. Besides, you won't be eighteen until September nineteenth."

"But you and Dad can sign a paper and let me get married early."

"Never. Ha, Dad?"

"Pardon? Oh. No, I've read the paper already."

Mother said, "You better go talk to our minister. He'll talk some sense into you." The coffee began to perk and Mother poured them each a cup.

Carla smiled to herself. Carla Prince, famous artist.

Mother sipped her hot coffee. "Dear God, I hope you don't follow in the footsteps of your cousin Frances. Having to get married so early, standing up in church for all the world to know you broke the Seventh Commandment. Or have you already?"

"Mother! Don't talk that way about Frances. She's sweet to her babies."

"And well she better be, to make up for what she did." Mother shook her head. "That whole dummed Simmons bunch is bad news. Yes, you come from blood with a wild hair, girlie, don't you ever forget that."

Dad heard that of course. "Yeh, Carla, it's a miracle you turned out as good as you did, with your mother's Engleking gang just as bad. There's rascals on both sides of your family."

Carla got up and rinsed out her cup in the sink. She said over her shoulder, "I'm still going to ask you both to give me permission to get married early."

"Oh, go to bed," Mother snapped.

Four days later she got Oren's two letters. The second one had caught up with the first one. She was overjoyed to learn that Oren had a job as a clerk at Fort Snelling. And she leaped for joy when he asked if they couldn't get married right away. He was right. Precious days were rushing by.

But on a 40-hour pass? That would hardly give them enough time if they were to get married in Whitebone. He wouldn't be able to make the right train connections in time. She decided that instead she'd go up to the Twin Cities and marry him there.

She talked it over with Mother some more.

"Over my dead body," Mother said. "Graduate from high school first, you silly snip of a girl. Have you talked to our minister yet?"

"No. But I intend to."

"You be sure to do that now."

Carla found Reverend Wayne Holly in the basement of the Presbyterian Church. He was alone in his dark mahogany study. Light from the two north windows gave the room a somber cast. There was a smell of good leather about.

Reverend Holly had a big warm smile for her. His manner was one of youthful vigor. He was about thirty-five, slim, with curly brown hair and vivid blue eyes. When not preaching he liked to wear casual loafing clothes, blue jeans and a blue shirt open at the throat, affecting to be just like any other layman in his parish. His face was oddly speckled with blackheads, a few of them as large as peppercorns around his eyes.

Reverend Holly tipped back in a red leather swivel chair. "Have a seat, Carla."

Carla sat down.

"No no, sit over here. Let's not have a desk between us."

Carla, smiling, moved to a red leather chair close up.

"How are your folks?"

"Fine." Carla wondered why he didn't pinch out those blackheads around his eyes. Or get a face massage to have them removed. Were she his wife she'd pinch them out for him. Apart from the blackheads Reverend Holly was a handsome man. Women in church swooned over him when he gave one of his impassioned sermons. Carla remembered one sermon in particular. He'd preached it a year ago when he got after the fat cats in his congregation for being so commercial-minded every December. He ended his sermon with a ringing cry, slowly lifting a finger to the heavens, "Oh, how that Chamber of Commerce loves the

Christ Child when Christmas shopping season comes around again."
There'd been a lot of red faces in the front rows that Sunday.

"What can I do for you, Carla?"

"You know of course I've been going with Oren Prince."

"Yes."

"I want to marry him right away."

His thick brown brows swept up and his eyes became wary. "Surely
you're going to wait until you're through high school."

"No. I'm ready now."

"Really, you ought to wait."

"Reverend, I love him. And I feel sorry for him that he had to go off
to war. It's the least I can do for him."

"You're so young. So young. Later on you'll regret it."

The smell of old psalters and peppermints hung in the air. Religion
was an aged perfume. "I'm ready for him now, Reverend."

Reverend Holly leaned toward her. "What you need to do is keep
busy. Have other things to do besides just your school work. Help you
pass the time until he has safely returned from the wars."

"No."

"I've noticed you have a good voice. We could use another good
soprano in our choir. We're weak there this year."

"Oh, I can't sing that good."

"I've heard your voice. When you sit up front in church."

"Well . . ."

"And we're also short a Sunday-school teacher, after Howard Hoiland
left for the wars. You're good with children, I hear."

"I do like babies."

"There you are. We'll expect you in both the choir and Sunday
school." Looking at his watch Reverend Holly wound it up a few turns.

"Reverend, have you got anything against Oren Prince because he's
a Methodist?"

"Not at all. His father and I are good friends. We serve together on
the local pastors' council."

Carla left dissatisfied.

But she had it in her to be the dutiful Christian, so she taught Sunday
school. She liked the eight-year-olds in her care; they were so full of
questions, often wonderfully embarrassing. They were calves that still
hadn't run into any stinging barbwire fences.

She also went to choir practice. She knew most of the hymns by heart.
When she sang them polyphonically with altos and tenors and basses,
she discovered a new joy. The other three voices seemed to fill out her
chest and gave her the sensation she was riding on wings.

The third Sunday in the choir loft, facing the congregation, she had
a great thrill. They were singing "Bringing in the Sheaves," when, a few

bars into it, her voice took on an extra dimension, an overquaver. She'd heard an overquaver several times before, listening to opera singers over the radio, but this was the first time she experienced it herself. She let her whole soul pour into it, until she could feel her nipples harden in her brassiere.

After the sermon, Reverend Holly tugged at her sleeve. "See? Didn't I tell you? You really have that extra quality."

She smiled. "Someday I'm going to find that extra thing when I'm painting. Because that's what I really want to do."

She wrote Oren daily.

As the days passed his letters took on a frantic note. Reading them, it came to her that he was beginning to beg. She much preferred him when he was in his confident smoochy moods.

One night, turning off the light and nuzzling her head deep in her pillow, thinking about one thing after another, the thought struck her like a flying drop of rain: "I wonder, he's beginning to sound like there might be another girl."

She sent him an invitation to her graduation, along with a graduation picture. She also sent him a clipping from the Whitebone *Press* announcing that there had been a tie for valedictorian that year: "Meddy Queen and Carla Simmons share top scholastic honors for the class of 1942."

He thanked her for the picture, saying he was going to take it out of its folder and put it in his wallet. He also thought her idea that they get married at Fort Snelling a good one. Fort Snelling had a lovely chapel.

Oren next sent her a battered copy of a sex book by Margaret Sanger.

The Sanger book Carla handled as if it had been bound in poison ivy. She kept it in the house only one day, hidden under her mattress, and then sent it back. She wanted to learn how to make love with a man God's way, natural, as a doe and a buck might out in nature.

It was shortly after he had sent her the Sanger book that Carla began to have the uneasy feeling that someone was nosing through Oren's letters. She kept the letters tied in a packet with a silver ribbon. The bow she sometimes found in the ribbon was not the same bow she tied. Carla liked to flatten out the wings of the bow, neatly, after she'd tied it.

Carla decided to set a trap. She stuck a small piece of toothpick in the bow she made. Sure enough, the next time she looked at the packet, the little splinter of toothpick was gone.

Mother had to be the guilty culprit.

Carla thought of challenging her mother, but after more thought decided not to bother. It would only alert Mother all the more. Carla hid the letters in the basement. She put them in an old carpenter's toolbox that Dad no longer used in a far back corner of the basement. Mother would never think of looking there.

CHAPTER THIRTEEN
OREN

The door to the barracks whanged open and the raucous voice of Sergeant Honkers ripped the morning air. "All right, you men, drop them cocks and grab them socks!"

Groans rose from every cot. Slowly vague forms stirred under the khaki Army blankets.

"Get up!" Honkers roared. "In the summer when it's hot and sultry it's too damned hot to commit adul'try."

Honkers went on, whacking the metal end of each bed with an iron rod, down the line along the right and then back on the left. "Another Mister Big Balls is flying in from Washington. We've got to police up the joint again. So hurry it up."

"It's always hurry up, hurry up," Saxneat muttered.

Honkers paused at Oren's bed, the last one. "Well, well, I see the colonel's pet sleeps with his hands crossed over his crotch."

Oren sat up suddenly, throwing his blanket to one side, thrusting his face up at Honkers. "Butt out, buster!"

Honkers continued to stare down at Oren with a lip-raised sneer; then, humping up his shoulders, turned on his heel and left.

Oren had to admit Honkers had taught him one good thing though: how to make a bed that would pass inspection. And Honkers had done it in an interesting manner. After Oren had done what he thought a good job, sheets and blankets tucked in tight and smooth, Honkers looked at the bed, and then, digging into his pockets, came up with a nickel. He tossed the nickel on the bed. When it didn't bounce, he knelt down beside the bed and retightened the sheets and blankets until the sides of the bed came up a little to form what looked like a wide shallow drum. Then Honkers tried tossing the nickel again. This time it bounced up a good four inches. "See? Your dream sack needed just a hair more tightening."

"How come you know so much?"

"Simple," Honkers said. "When I'm around a smart man I never say a word. I shut up and listen to everything he has to say. So then I know what he knows plus what I know. While he doesn't know what I know and only knows what he knows." Then Honkers tapped Oren on the shoulder. "And look, bud. Don't always be so offish with me. The time may come when you need a friend."

One morning at headquarters, after the girls came back from coffee break, talk got around to how lonesome they were. The three older women remarked that lately dates for them had been few and far between. Officers their age at the Fort no longer asked them to dinner and a night on the town.

"Really," chubby Chris Anders said, "if it weren't that we're suppose to help our country in its greatest hour of need, why . . ."

Josephine Handley, the plumpest one, was inclined to ride with the times. "You wanna remember that a lot of eligibles are off to the war somewhere. We'll just have to wait until they get back."

Mabel Seilman pushed up what little breasts she had. "The Army has a big base down in Omaha, doesn't it?"

"Yes."

Mabel wetted a fingertip and then traced out her blond eyebrows. "I know what. Let's go down to Omaha and start over again as virgins."

Mabel's remark broke Oren up.

Teresita didn't laugh much.

Generally, though, the three women's chitchat rubbed Oren the wrong way. They were always talking doom and destruction and divorce and did it with a show of toothy glee.

Late one Friday afternoon, when the three had indulged themselves in a particularly vicious bit of gossip about the President's wife, Oren abruptly whirled in his chair, stood up, and shouted, "Shut up, for godsakes, you goddam magpies! I can't hear myself think with all your stupid small talk. Roll up your flaps."

There was a breath-sucking silence.

Teresita kept on typing steadily as though nothing had happened.

Then another kind of silence spread in the office.

Looking around, Oren was stunned to see Colonel Simpson standing in the doorway, blue steely eyes glinting.

"Well, well," the colonel said, "I see you can lose your temper too. Good. I wondered if you ever would."

"I'm sorry."

"Don't apologize." The colonel gave the three women a reassuring wink. "Oren, it's Friday and the end of another week. You've worked hard since you joined us. Why don't I give you an eighteen-hour pass and you go have yourself a ball on the town? All right?"

Oren saluted. "Yessir. And thanks, sir."

The colonel saluted back, and turning on a heel, went back upstairs.

Promptly at five the three older women covered their typewriters and left the office.

Finishing a report, and stapling it, Oren covered up his typewriter too and got up to go. He tossed the report in Outgoing. Then he glanced down at Teresita. "I suppose you have a date this weekend."

She erased a word.

"What I don't understand is that you aren't just besieged with men trying to date you," he added.

"Maybe I'm being picky."

He looked at her dark head, at the neat parting down the center of her hair, then down to where her hair flowed into two long heavy black braids, revealing the lovely nape of her neck. He whispered, "What a waste, what a waste."

She looked up, modestly. "What is?"

"Your not having a date. And me not having a date."

"Maybe we should do something about that."

"Like what?"

"How would you like to come along with me? I'm going to Wisconsin to open up my parents' summer place. Usually the three of us drive out to open it up for the summer. But this weekend they're going to a wedding."

"Where will you get the car?"

"They're riding with some friends. So I can use Dad's."

Oren could feel his heart begin to pound in his collar. "Where is this place?"

"Across the St. Croix River. We call it Skyhawk." She looked at him with a shy smile. "I'm leaving in a half hour."

"When would we get back?"

"It takes about an hour to drive up there. That'll still give us two hours of sunlight to get things in order. We can easy be back by eleven."

He thought of Carla and her sweet open smile. Too bad Carla didn't resemble the garroted woman found in the Danish marsh.

"Unless you're afraid of my driving."

"Oh, what the hell. I'm going wild here trying to live the life of a saint. Where do I meet you?"

She straightened up, braids riding free of her shoulders. "I probably better not pick you up at the barracks. Why don't I meet you in front of Gambino's diner, say, at six sharp?"

"Done." She had such a lovely small puckered mouth. Impulsively he leaned down and kissed her.

She blushed, and said, "Thanks."

He went back to the barracks. He changed his tan shirt for a fresh one, put on his tan tie again, polished his shoes and brushed off his jacket.

He strolled out to the bridge. At the north point of the old fort walls some uniformed men were having drinks on the porch of the commanding officer's house. As Oren crossed the bridge he looked down at the dippling Mississippi. Sunlight glanced off the little waves like a flight of golden arrows.

When he approached Joe Gambino's Dine & Dancing, he saw a soldier with a leg missing sitting to one side on the front steps. "There but for the grace of God go I. And some luck." The fellow held up a small cup for handouts. Just then two women alighted from a chauffeur-driven car. They spotted the cripple, whispered together a moment, their faces taking on teary sympathy, and then both dug into their purses. They each gave the fellow a ten-spot. The cripple smiled in thanks, eyes also teary, ashamed of the role he had to play.

Then Oren saw a surprising thing. The moment the two ladies disappeared into the diner, the pathetic expression on the cripple's face vanished. What had been a young boy, blond-haired, blue eyed, ashamed at having to beg, suddenly changed into an older fellow, someone in his thirties, hard, smiling in twisted contempt that he'd hoodwinked a couple more suckers.

"Why, the son of a bitch," Oren whispered to himself.

The cripple spotted Oren's scowl, and immediately put on the young boy's suffering look again.

The conniving bastard.

When the cripple saw his boy-smile wasn't working, he studied to himself a moment; then, reaching for a pair of crutches standing to one side, hoisted himself up and came swinging over in a pendulum motion. "You didn't like what you just saw, hah?"

"No, I didn't."

"What's the harm in me panhandling the rich?" The fellow touched his nose with the edge of his thumb like he might be paging a book. "I ain't puttin' the touch on soldiers, you unnerstan'."

"What's your unit?"

"Hey, I'm Henry Kempner. Sometimes also known as Skip."

At that moment a shiny black Packard pulled up in front of Gambino's. A horn sounded. It was Teresita, Mudface, waving at him. Relieved, Oren skipped down the steps toward the car.

"Hey, whadda y'u mean, running off like that?"

"Sorry, but my gal is in a hurry."

Skip Kempner made a violent motion with his thumb. "Up yours."

Oren opened the door of the Packard, only to find Teresita had already slid over onto the passenger side. She was wearing a casual blue cotton dress. "What's this, Teresita?"

"You drive."

"If that's your wish." Oren stepped around the black car and got in on the driver's side. "Wow. You have to be rich to own one of these."

She laughed softly. "Not really. Dad's a saver and he either gets the best or goes without."

"Like my brother Bon with his bonds."

Oren could feel the soft purr of the motor through the brown wooden steering wheel. He shifted into low and they were off. The Packard rolled easily with a slowly gathering rush. It was a dream to drive. The steering wheel felt as big as a bicycle wheel. The dashboard was made of finished walnut and the nickel instruments gleamed silver.

They took Highway 12 out of St. Paul. Small truck garden farms lay in the flats, and little groves of elms and maples grew in the draws, and dazzling green pastures curved over the lifting slopes. Highway 12 soon tipped down toward the St. Croix River, crossed a long trestle bridge, and entered Wisconsin. At Hudson they turned north and followed a gravel road skirting the east bluffs of the river. More open country came along, mostly dairy farms. In the low falling sunlight the purple shafts of shadows deepened the emerald greens of the pastures and the darker citrons of the oak groves.

After some twenty miles, Teresita pointed ahead to a sign tacked onto a tree on the edge of a thick grove of maples. "That's our place. Slow down."

Oren turned in. They followed a narrow rutted lane, grass growing in the center of it. Soon brush on either side thickened and deepened. They seemed to be driving down a green tunnel. Elms and maples lapped together overhead.

"We're almost there."

In a moment a little clearing appeared. "That it?"

"Yes. From here we walk in."

Oren pulled up, then deftly maneuvered the long black Packard around until he had it facing out.

They got out. To Oren's surprise, when Teresita opened the back door and reached in, she came up with a hamper full of food. "I brought along a little supper for us. After we've finished opening up the house."

Oren smiled. "A picnic. I was wondering when we'd eat. Good. Here, let me carry it."

Teresita led the way down a path into a thick stand of gnarled white oaks. Above them the slanting sun shone bright on the treetops while below he and Teresita walked in shadow.

"You people always have to carry your stuff in?"

"On our backs. Even when they built the house, everything had to be carried in."

The trail ended abruptly on the edge of a cliff. Below, through the trees, Oren saw a hump protruding out of the cliff. Steps cut into the rock wound down to the hump.

Teresita started down ahead of him, blue cotton dress floating off her knees on each step, dark braids swinging free behind her back. They brushed through black raspberry bushes and wild honeysuckle down a lush steep drop of rock.

The steps ended on a little shelf of land to one side of the hump. They crossed a narrow plot of thick grass, and turned the corner around the edge of the hump, and there in front of them were ranked rows of boarded-up windows and a tall oak door. Below and on their left lay the St. Croix River, twinkling through the leaves of the white oaks.

"For godsakes," Oren exclaimed, "a kind of a cave with windows. What a great idea."

Teresita laughed. "Yes, Dad found the cave one day when he was out hiking with Mother. The cave was a tiny thing then, but he built it out by adding some cement walls and a cement ceiling. The best part is that in the back of the cave there's always some water running. And it never freezes."

"God, a man could hole up here in a war and never have to worry. Except maybe trap some rabbits coming by."

"Dad says a general would take this over in a war." Teresita fingered through her pocketbook and came up with a key attached to a leather fob. She opened the tall oak door and stepped inside and snapped on a light.

"My God, where do you get the electricity?"

"Dad laid it underground along the gravel road back there."

"Got a good smell too. Like fresh walnuts."

There was a fireplace of gray rock in the west wall. A log coffee table and several lounging chairs were arranged in a semi-circle facing the fireplace. A long dining table with four chairs and a food cabinet took up the center. A high wooden-legged bed was set against the east wall. The floor was cement with fur rugs thrown here and there.

Teresita set the hamper on the table. "Now to get to work. First, we open up those boarded-up windows."

It took them an hour to open up the house. Oren had to remove his tunic and his shirt.

Teresita laughed to see him in his pale-tan skivvy undershirt, muscles showing. "You don't mind working, do you?"

"I may be a minister's son, but I wasn't pampered."

"Too bad we don't have time to light a fire. It would be so romantic."

Oren slipped on his shirt and tie and jacket again. "Where do I sit?"

"Here. It's where Dad sits. So he can admire the fire."

They heard a rattling clap of thunder. With a look of surprise, both got up and stepped outside. Standing on the narrow ledge of grass they looked up through the leaves of the oaks. Sure enough, a wall of black clouds was rolling toward the river, coming in from the northwest.

"A line storm," Oren said. "They sometimes come up in a hurry back home. It can be perfectly clear when you go in for supper and then before you can get to say, 'Lord, thank you for,' there's the storm."

The river at that point was as wide as a small lake. Even as Oren looked, the first winds touched down on the green water, and spread hurrying fans and tossing rings across its surface. Then the black storm boiled down over the steep cliff on the far side of the river and dropped like it might be an avalanche of tar. In a flash the river turned into a wild lake.

Teresita tugged at Oren's elbow. "We better get inside."

"Wow. There's a lot of wind in that one. All lathered up."

"Please, Oren, let's get inside."

Oren retreated reluctantly. He loved storms.

Teresita closed the big oak door and then shot the bolt.

They stood at the tall windows and watched. In a moment the dark boiling wall of cloud hit the cliff on their side of the river and lapped itself around the mound cave. The first brush of air hit so hard the great oaks outside tossed about as though they were being given electric shocks in their roots. Several hailstones hit the glass. When the second blast of wind hit, the plate glass panes bent inward a good two inches.

Oren jumped back several steps, sure the windows were going to shatter. "Get back! Flying glass can be a killer."

Teresita dodged behind Oren, peering from under his elbow at the boiling gray outside the windows.

Heavy rain next splashed against the tall panes of glass. There was a roar as of a great electric dynamo running wild . . . and then, abruptly, like a kite fluttering down to earth, the storm passed over them.

They stepped outside. After-drops fell on them from the branches above. Dead twigs lay scattered over the narrow strip of grass. Teresita began gathering them up, saying they'd make good kindling. The rain smell was marvelously sweet.

Oren helped her gather up the loose dead twigs, held the door open for her, and like her carefully piled the wet kindling on the firebrick to one side of the fireplace.

"Well now," Teresita said briskly, slapping bark dust from her hands, "time for our picnic lunch." She washed her hands, dried them, and set out the sandwiches and the thermos bottle of tea.

Oren settled in her father's chair, and soon they were munching dried-beef sandwiches lined with lettuce, and sipping tea, and smiling at each other.

Teresita chattered away like a joyful phoebe. She spoke of her love for wild flowers.

"What I'll never understand," Oren wondered, "is how come someone hasn't come along and glommed onto you for his wife."

A soft glow appeared in her eyes. "Thanks."

"I mean it. You're easy to be around."

She stood up. "I think it's time we started home."

They cleaned up the table together.

Oren picked up the hamper and headed for the door. Just as he stepped outside, the sun ovaled out from under the flying clouds.

Raindrops hanging under the silver sides of the oak leaves gleamed like yellow diamonds. The river shone a luminous blue.

They climbed up the notched trail in the rock wall, Teresita leading the way, and then, reaching the ground level above, headed for the car. As they wound their way along the narrow path through the oaks, they came upon many down branches. On that high flat of earth, the storm, compressed from having to brush up over the cliff side, had hit the oaks hard.

They entered the clearing; and saw disaster. A great old maple had crashed across the opening to the road, just barely missing the black Packard. Beyond it lay yet another huge tree, a cottonwood, and it too blocked the lane.

"Holy mud!" Oren cried. "Now how do we get home?"

Teresita didn't seem to mind the devastation. "We can get Ole Tryg-vold to help us with his tractor. He sold us our plot and this lane here. Only trouble is, he moonlights. Both he and his wife work in a bullet factory from four until midnight."

"You mean, we're going to have to wait until morning?"

"I'm afraid so."

Teresita got out her car key and opened a door and set the hamper inside. "Too bad we ate all the picnic goodies. We could have had some for breakfast." She sighed and locked up the car again. "But there's coffee in Skyhawk. And sugar. And I think I saw some salt crackers."

A holy blue darkness slowly fell around them. Lightning crackled and spangled in the far east. Above them stars pricked out from north to south.

Oren said, "Don't you think we should try to call your home from somewhere to let them know you're all right?"

"The nearest phone is at least two miles from here. That was another reason Dad liked this place. The isolation of it." Teresita pursed her lips in thought. "Maybe we better take the flashlight with us. Dad always keeps one under the front seat." She unlocked the car again and reached in and found the flashlight. She flicked it on. In the dim light, as she looked up at Oren, more than ever her face resembled the face of the garroted Cro-Magnon woman. Even her eyeteeth were more pronounced. She was a beautiful wolf woman.

"Come," she said, and she started down the path, spraying the ground ahead of her with the beam of the flashlight.

With their toes they felt their way carefully down the steps in the rock wall. The trees were still raining drops and the going was slippery.

Opening the door again, they discovered, when Teresita snapped on the light switch, there was no electricity. "Aha," Teresita said, "there must be more down trees east of here somewhere. Well, that gives us a good excuse to light the fire."

Oren helped her. They found dry kindling in a box in back, found three dry logs stacked against the far wall, and soon had a brisk fire going. The red flames flittered up the throat of the fireplace and cast a warm pink glow throughout the cave house.

They each sat in an easy chair, watching the fire. She took off her shoes and so did he. When it became warmer he took off his blouse and tie. The oak fire in the darkened cave made for a cozy corner against the world.

She got up once to push the logs closer together. "Would you like some wine? Dad doesn't drink but he has some wine here for special occasions. Like birthdays and so on."

"That would be a dream."

Using the flashlight she rustled around until she found a bottle. "It's some port," she said. "Do you mind if it's sweet?"

"Port will be fine."

She poured two glasses and soon they were sipping wine together and watching the titting fire.

He said, "Then you've never been in love?"

"Never."

It became late and she stirred restless in her chair. "I think we better go to bed. We'll have to get up early to get that road cleared."

"I suppose we better. I'll sleep on the floor."

"Nonsense. You're my guest and you take the bed. I can easy make a comfy bed by pulling up these two chairs."

"But it's important that the host stays happy. Company will just have to shift for itself."

"Nonsense. You're going to take the bed. I'll go hunt up some sheets and blankets." She rummaged through some drawers built into the side wall. She found the bedclothes and smelled into them. "A little musty but they'll do." She made the big bed in the corner, moving it around efficiently, snapping the sheets square at the corners and then tucking them in all around. "All right, sir, your bed is ready."

He got to his feet. "Really, Teresita . . . "

A mischievous smile pulled at her small lips. "You better watch your step. Dad taught me jujitsu." She approached him as if she meant to throw him in the bed right then and there. "Now, if you will just step aside, I'll make up my bed."

"Teresita, I have a suggestion to make." His belly tightened. "That bed is so big two can sleep on it without touching each other. If you will agree to stay on your half of the bed, I'll agree to stay on my half."

She looked up at him with somber eyes. She took him seriously, and slowly changed her mind. Then she held out her hand. "All right, as you men say, let's shake on that. Because"—she allowed herself a little laugh—"sleeping on those two chairs wasn't going to be all that hot.

They have a way of separating during the night and then you fall to the floor."

"It'd take me all night to cross over to your side."

They undressed in the light of the dying fire, he on his side and she on hers, their backs to each other. He undressed down to skivvies and she down to her slip.

He remembered that when he was a boy and his parents went visiting somewhere, he always felt better sleeping in a strange bed if he first kneeled beside the bed and prayed. He recalled the little prayer his father taught him:

Now I kneel and fold my hands,
My eyes I close and bow to thee.
Dear Lord, I pray my breath to keep
While I visit Thee in eternity.

Bless all the little birds that fly,
Bless all who creep upon the ground.
Bless mother, father, brother,
Bless all those heaven-bound. Amen.

He'd often wondered, back then, about those who might be hell-bent. They probably needed prayer more than those heaven-bound.

He slid in on his side of the big bed.

Teresita didn't go to bed right away. He heard her go back to her chair to watch the fire a while. Her bare toes made soft callus noises on the cement part of the floor.

He thought of Carla. He remembered Carla breaking free of his arms as they sat in his father's car in that awful blizzard and, on her knees, begin pounding the back of the front seat, crying, "No! No! No! I mussent! I mussent!"

Presently he heard Teresita coming on soft feet and slowly opening up the quilts on her side and then slipping into bed. He could just make out the whispering of the sheets.

The crackling fire slowly died away. Flame shadows played over the log beams in the ceiling.

She whispered, "I'm glad you're such a gentleman."

"'You never know when a good penny will show up'."

She laughed. "Dad likes to say, 'A spoonful of kerosene will ruin a jar of honey.' I wonder how you'd change that?"

"'A spoonful of honey will improve a can of kerosene'?"

"I like being around you. A woman feels she can trust you."

A ruckling rose in his throat. "Well, and I trust you."

"We'll always be friends."

"Yes."

"What we have is solid now."

"Yes, Teresita."

"Good-night, Oren."

"'Night."

They slept.

Around midnight, both woke up a little and turned over at the same time. Teresita sat up as if she wasn't sure for a moment where she was. Oren could sense her looking at his side of the bed. Then she lay down again.

He whispered. "We forgot to give each other a goodnight kiss."

"Maybe it was best we didn't."

"If I promise to just kiss you," he went on, "and then get back on my side, may I?"

Silence on her side of the bed. Finally she stirred, letting one limb slide over the other. "All right."

He didn't move right away. He didn't want her to think he'd been lying there tense all that time waiting for a signal of some kind so he could jump her like a bull might a heifer. He nuzzled his head once in his pillow, and then with his left hand he reached for her under the quilt. He found her shoulder, slid over, and with his nose found her nose, and with his lips found her lips, and kissed her, dry and chaste, and then slid back to his side.

"Thanks."

A deep sigh escaped him. "I wish you wouldn't say 'thanks' always. Thanks for what? Because then I should say 'thanks' in turn." He realized as he spoke that she hadn't really kissed him back. Nor had she the other two times when she'd thanked him afterwards. There was just a dry shaping of her small piquant lips and that was all.

She lay silent beside him. She was every bit as mysterious to him alive as the Danish Mudface was to him dead.

The fire died away into ashes. It became very dark in the cave retreat.

Then he said something he'd heard himself say before. "When can we make sweet love? I want to reach deep into you."

"I can't."

"Then you really never have before?"

"No."

"Did you ever dream of wanting to?"

"Yes."

He recalled a limerick he used to recite when tempted:

> What should I do . . .
> masturbate
> or wait.
> Cockle doodle do.

Warmth flowed from her.

"Oh, Teresita, dear Zita, we don't have to do it, but let me hold you in my arms a little. It has been so long . . . can we?"

She slid over an inch toward him.

With a groan he slid the rest of the way and slowly slipped his arms around her and hugged her, hard then soft, first kissed her along her cheek and then her neck, and taking her head in his hands kissed her on the lips, and kissed her and kissed her until she kissed him back, until he could feel her eyeteeth cutting him a little. "Zita. Zita. Darling."

Soon her hands were busy with him, short slim fingers sliding up and down his arm. Once her hand touched his belly.

He found himself wonderfully aroused. He wanted to slide his hand between her thighs. Yet somehow he managed to remember that she should probably touch him first. Gently he took her hand and placed it on himself.

She hesitated, at last let it rest. "You said, 'We don't have to do it'."

"Please."

Again, as always, after what probably was some soul-searching, she stirred and began to fondle him.

"How lovely." Slowly he slid his hand over her taut belly, and onto her mount of love. He was surprised to discover her pubic hair was stiffish, not silken. He played, and then was further surprised to discover how far under she was. Carla's was higher up. He could feel Teresita stiffen under his hand, tighten her legs together. She ceased fondling him. He retreated an inch; and played. He waited until she resumed her fondling and then explored some more. Lord, she truly was far under.

She had become swollen. Two short tubers had come swelling up. And she was wet.

"Zita, my darling woman, I'm so in love." Fumbling, urgent, he didn't know how to touch her little bump.

She took his hand. "Lightly, lightly," she whispered. "Real lightly."

"This way?"

Of a sudden she pushed up her hips, her whole body rising in an arch, from her shoulders to her heels, holding herself up like a wonderful bridge, and then abruptly she shuddered, and she left off fondling him and clutched at his hand and pressed it hard onto her little wet bean.

He could feel her pulsing under his hand.

Gradually she let down her bridge.

"It happened," he whispered.

"Yes."

"How lovely."

She sighed, still breathing fast. "What about you?"

"It's all right. I'm only happy for you."

"Oh, no," she said, and began fondling him again. Urgently.

"It's all right. It's better if I don't. Then I can believe, truly, that we didn't do it."

She withdrew her hand. She lay a while in silence. She seemed to subside like the dying fire in the fireplace. She straightened out her limbs in a long easy stretching motion. And slowly went to sleep.

He lay thick and trembling.

The last hot cinder in the fireplace made a crinkling noise.

How could this woman lying in his arms have so affected him that for a little while he forgot Carla? This woman had a hold on him he didn't understand. It had to be, yes, that he'd inherited a certain set of cells in his brain that had in it a specific instruction that, should he someday run into a certain face, he was to respond to it. And it would have such a powerful hold on him that it would override all other loves he might have.

At last he too fell asleep.

He dreamed he'd been chosen by lot to be sacrificed to make sure there'd be a good crop the coming year. The leaders slipped a noose around his neck and led him toward a big swamp northwest of Whitebone. It was expected of him to smile, and he did smile, though the smile hurt him like the time when his dentist had a finger pried into each corner of his mouth the better to get at his teeth. They hadn't bound him and he thought of suddenly breaking into a run, bursting out of the circle of singing villagers. Then a weird creature came floating on its side toward him some six feet above the ground. It smiled at him. It was a she-creature with two heads, one at either end, one of them blond and the other very dark, and it was hard to tell which head went with which feet. The creature had two sets of breasts and two bellies, but only one mount of love, and it was positioned exactly between the two navels. Every now and then all four hands covered the creature's pudendum, one on top of the other, like two batsmen going up a bat to see who'd bat first. Then in a moment he and the crowding villagers were at the edge of the slough and his bare feet slid into the slucky stuff. Then the two-headed woman-creature floated up close and took hold of the noose and proceeded to strangle him.

A voice called him. "Oren! Oren!"

"What?"

"You've had a nightmare, Oren."

He lay stiff, with every muscle near spasm. He also found himself erect.

She hugged him. In hugging him she found him and then she hugged him all the harder. "Oren, if you want me."

They made love sweetly and fondly, whispering to each other; then just before he rose to a wonderful point, she rose under him, just as before, making an arching bridge out of her body so that he could reach her all the better so far under, lifting him up as though he were a boat on a wave. They cried out together.

Presently she let the bridge down and they descended to earth.

He found himself strangely wrung out from both the nightmare and the loving.

Again they slept, this time intertwined.

Oren's dream continued. But there was a difference. The floating woman parted and became two women, one blond and one dark. They held up their hands and stopped the press of villagers. They conferred, with nodding heads, with odd looks at him. Then the two approached him again, and they took hold of the noose once more . . .

Again a voice called him. "Oren! Oren!"

"What?"

"You had another nightmare."

"Yeh. And it was all mixed up."

They were still twisted through each other, legs and arms. She began to rub his belly. After a moment she made a discovery. "Why," she said, chuckling, "all you've got to show now is a little puddle of puppies."

"Keep that up and they'll turn out to be a pack of wolves."

"I never knew it was like this with a man."

He was surprised at the change in her. The swoon had mellowed her.

Women were surely not the same as men. A woman could never have the same feeling a man had when he swooned, feeling his seed jetting into a woman. Squirting juice, as naughty boys said. A woman might swoon, yes, but she could never have the sensation that she was thrusting seed into another body. "And he strengthened her," as the Bible said. On the other hand a man could never do what a woman could, make a bridge of her body all the better to receive him. Perhaps the receiving of another person into one's self was a great thing.

"What are you thinking?"

"A man acts out his sperm, probes like a searching arrow, a woman acts out her egg, waiting like a target."

She flung the puppies away. "You men! I get mad when I see a rooster jump on a hen, the way he pecks ahold of the feathers on top of her head, and forces her down so that her tail lifts up, and then clamps down on her."

"Where did you ever see that, you a city girl?"

"At Ole Trygvold's place. I sometimes go there in the summer and visit with the Missus."

His hip began to hurt him because of the odd position he was in. Gently he moved to straighten out his leg.

"Am I hurting you?"

"No, Zita." He reached for her and couldn't right away find what he wanted. "Where's your little hen?"

"Little hen?"

"Well, if you can talk about a cock, then I can talk about a hen."

"I said 'rooster'."

"'Rooster' is an old-maid word. Chaucer called it a 'cok'."

"Chaucer's dirty."

"Says who?"

"Our priest."

"A priest would."

After a time she whispered, "You're some sort of magician."

"How so?"

"One of the puppies has suddenly changed into a big rooster."

A smile moved in his belly. "Is the little hen ready to tip up her tail again?"

"She is."

When he awoke in the morning, he heard water making laughing sounds nearby. He sat up. Ah. The electricity had come back on and Teresita had put on a light in back. He could see her taking a shower against the rock wall on the other side of the table. He smiled. He watched the water streaming down her body, off her long black hair and down her breasts and belly. It made him shiver to see the delicate look of water streaming down her fuzzy legs.

He got up and found a long towel and fastened it around his middle. Then, thinking how silly that was after the love night they'd had, he threw the towel to one side and joined her in the shower.

She let out a little squeal when his hip touched hers. Then she laughed merrily. Truly, Teresita had changed.

She toweled herself off first and then he followed. She wrung out her hair as best she could and then folded it up in a turban made with a towel.

It was eight o'clock when they locked up the cave and started up the cliff. Everything was still wet from the storm.

When they came to the clearing, the morning sun, striking across the grass, caught hundreds of little circular spider webs just right, making glittering diamonds out of all the dewdrops.

Oren pointed at the dew-spangled webs underfoot. "Look at those natural diadems."

CHAPTER FOURTEEN
CARLA

There was a job open at the Great Plains Manufacturing Company on the south edge of town. Several tool and die men had been drafted and the company boss had decided he'd hire women with a mechanical bent to run the machines. The pay was good and Carla thought it a good way to earn some money. Soon she and Oren would need to buy furniture.

The Army had let out a subcontract with Great Plains Manufacturing to make struts for a moveable lightweight bridge. The Army assault units were going to use it to cross rivers and swamps. The company president had invented a way of making a blind hole that was roomier at the bottom than at the opening to make sure the bolts in the struts wouldn't pull out. Hot rivets were then driven into the tapered holes.

Carla, in overalls, caught on quickly how to adjust the milling machine. By working the wheel slowly she made excellent blind holes after only a few tries. The expanding tool or boring head slowly widened the hole as it fed down into the steel. She had to make sure that oil drops fell onto the cutting edge at all times. When an occasional drop of oil was slow to fall, the machine began to squeak like a stepped-on mouse. Little tails of steel curlicued off the cutting edge and fell underfoot. There was a good hearty smell of oil in the shop. Overhead belts slapped and popped. Dust rode in the air under the high ceiling.

One day the company president, Thomas Lovinger, came into the shop. He stopped by Carla and her machine and watched a while. He seemed to like what he saw, and during a break, when she had to change the boring head, he complimented her.

"Thenks."

Mr. Lovinger had wide shoulders and powerful arms, with short underpinning bowlegs. He rocked from side to side as he talked. He had brilliant dark eyes. "Like your job?"

"It's okay."

They talked a while, and then he asked, "Carla, how come you never look me in the eye?"

Carla lifted her head. "Oh, it's that if I look a strange man in the eye I might encourage him—"

"To be fresh with you?"

"That's right."

"Good girl."

"And by looking at a man's mouth I can tell sooner what he's up to than by looking him in the eye."

Mr. Lovinger twisted his head around and up to consider her remark.

In two weeks Carla came home with her first paycheck. She showed it to her father and mother and then banked it. She wrote Oren about her job. She told him how proud she was to help him fight the war against the enemy.

On another day, when Mr. Lovinger stopped by her milling machine, Carla had a suggestion to make. "Must these holes be put exactly where they're marked on these beams?"

"Yeh. Why?"

Carla shook her head. "The way you've got them now, stippled here and there, it doesn't look nice. I could make a much better design if you'd let me."

"Show me." He handed her his clipboard and the pencil from behind his ear.

Carla swiftly sketched what she thought looked like a handsome design.

"Hm," he grunted. Then, without a word, he walked away.

Carla thought maybe she'd made him angry.

But an hour later he came by again with his clipboard. "Just talked to the engineers and, by God, they say your design will make that strut even stronger. So go ahead, do it your way."

"Art always knows," she said.

"I ain't usually got much time for wild hair art guys, but I guess this time it works."

A few days later she found two checks in her pay envelope. The extra check was a bonus for her original idea.

Then Dink Sunstrand came to work at the milling machine next to hers. She'd read in the local paper that he'd been rejected by the draft board because of a bad knee. She'd also heard the rumor that he and a buddy had gone the rounds of a whorehouse in the Black Hills. It was said that he'd been thrown out of a crib for roughhousing. It made Carla sick to her stomach to see him.

The first couple of days Dink didn't say much; just cast her sidelong glances. But when he saw how the other men in the place teased her, he joined in. "Yeh, working at that machine should help you core out an apple better when you start making apple pies for your old man."

She ignored him.

She was almost finished with another hole and was working the wheel carefully, wanting to finish it before changing the bit, when she sensed he'd stopped work to watch her. The bit was screaming it was so dull.

He called over, "Gently does it."

She gave him a fleeting look.

"Yeh, and the longer the harder," he added.

She stopped her machine. "Will you keep your nose to your own grindstone, please?"

"So, you can't take a joke, eh?"

"Not yours."

Some of the other men picked up Dink's remark and with a leer bandied it about the shop. "The longer the harder, boys."

With Oren gone, Dink seemed to think he now had a chance with her. He was always underfoot, at their machines, at the long zinc tub where they washed up after work.

She decided to damper his interest in her. Whenever she spotted him starting to turn his head toward her, she'd say, "See, there you go again, about to get that look."

"Don't tell me you're still carrying the torch for that Oren Prick fellow."

"His name is Mister Oren Prince to you."

Once she was having a little trouble with her crescent wrench while changing a drill. The edges of the wrench's mouth were so rounded off from use she could no longer get a good purchase on a nut.

Dink stepped over. "Carla, you're fightin' it too hard."

"What I need is a new wrench."

"What I mean is, you're working too hard at pushing me off. Take a good look at me. I ain't all that bad."

"I don't care a straw for you."

"What you need to do is to think about that 'the longer the harder' part."

"Just because you defiled yourself in a Deadwood whorehouse doesn't make you an expert in what I need."

"Don't working at that machine give you any ideas?"

His remark hit home. She had begun to have dreams about the way the machine worked. "I think I'm going to tell Mr. Lovinger you're molesting me."

Dink went back to work.

Then she got a letter from Oren in which she instantly spotted that something had happened. He sounded as though he was about to have a nervous breakdown.

About ten o'clock the next morning, after having drilled her tenth tapered hole, she shut off her machine and headed for the front office.

She knocked on Mr. Lovinger's door.

"Come in."

She pushed in and closed the door behind her.

Mr. Lovinger looked up from some blueprints. "Well?"

"Can I sit down?"

"Please do. Excuse me. What's wrong?"

"How about me working in the drafting department?"

His face crinkled up in irritation. "What's wrong with the job you got?"

"If I have to drill one more hole that gets bigger as it goes in . . ." She blushed.

"Oh." Just in time he covered up a male smile. "I see."

"Otherwise I'm gonna quit." She hated it that she'd blushed. "Maybe I should anyway. Oren wants me to marry him right now and maybe I should do that."

"Can't wait, eh?"

That made her blush all the more. She stood up. "All right, if you don't have room for me in the drafting department, I quit."

"But I've already got too many shiny heads in there."

"Thank you. Just send me what money I've got coming." And turning, she went out the door and left the plant.

On the way home she saw some children playing skip the rope near the grade school. They recited a line of verse with each circling flip of the rope:

> If you wanna go to war
> Go to war and shoot.
> Shoot the Kaiser, shoot the Hitler,
> Shoot shoot shoot.
> If you wanna go to war.

When they noticed Carla looking at them, they sang:

> Carla and Oren, sitting on a fence,
> Trying to make a dollar out of 99 cents,
> The grass was so tall it tickled their chin,
> Carla opened her mouth and a kiss popped in.
>
> Carla had a baby, named it Tiny Tim,
> Put it in a bathtub to teach it how to swim,
> Drank all the water, ate all the soap,
> Died the next day with bubbles down its throat.

Mother saw her coming and opened the door. "What's the matter, you sick?"

"I quit. I've decided to marry Oren right now."

"No."

"No?" Carla was incensed. She started to jump up and down, hitting the floor so hard with her heels that the dishes rattled in the glassfront china cabinet in the dining room. Her voice became shrill. "I want to get married rightaway! Oren needs me now! I love him and he loves me."

"Temper temper."

Carla continued to stamp up and down. "Don't you stand in my way. Or I'll run away and elope with Oren."

Mother was wearing a blue apron and she slowly wrapped her hands and arms in it, folding it over her belly. "Well, before I say yes, I want you to go see Reverend Holly first."

"He'll just give me some more of that pious crap."

"Carla! He's our minister. God's chosen."

"I don't care. My mind's made up."

Ma plumped herself down in an easy chair. "Well, and I've made up my mind too, you headstrong snip you. You're not going anywhere until you've talked with him again."

The upshot of it was that Carla finally did agree to go see Reverend Holly one more time.

Just as before, Reverend Holly sat in his swivel chair and she in a red leather armchair.

There was one change in him. His big blackheads were gone. Apparently his wife had at last persuaded him to have a facial massage. He looked unusually clean shaven and very young. "What is it this time, Carla?"

"I want to be with my man."

"Can't you wait until you're eighteen in September?"

"No."

"I take it that your parents still don't want you to get married?"

Carla felt another tantrum coming on.

Reverend Holly's sensitive vivid blue eyes read the turmoil in her face. "You've taken this up in prayer?"

She thought: "All they can think of is how they feel about it, not how I feel about it. When it's me that's getting married, not them."

"Would you like it if we got down on our knees before God in this matter?"

She stared at him. "There he sits now, safe in the middle of all his worked-out arguments," she thought. "He'll never change his mind. Just as Mother won't change hers."

He looked at her in pastoral love. "Carla, are you being a good Christian in this matter?"

Carla sagged down in her red armchair. She was hurt to have that question thrown at her. She felt very close to Jesus, and often in the night, awakening from a dream, really had prayed to Him for guidance. "Reverend, how else but through his guidance could I have remained a virgin?"

"Carla, dear girl . . . and you are a dear beautiful woman . . . then you already know that purity in life depends on purity of the mind. Because a mind left to revel in voluptuousness will sooner or later lead the possessor to overt acts of sin."

Carla threw him a scratching glance. He was looking at her the way Dink Sunstrand sometimes looked at her. Her minister?

He went on, looking at his fingers, which he kept building up into a church with a steeple and then collapsing them. "I'm glad to learn that you have not indulged in premarital sex. The loss of modesty these days, especially during this war, is one that may, in the long run, cause incalculable damage to the integrity of our nation. A bashful girl is much more difficult to find nowadays than it was a quarter of a century ago."

Her chest began to hurt.

"Those nasty dances and all those other late-at-night gatherings have brought out the bold and the flippant in the natures of our young women. A mind once sullied with vice is marred forever. Once the seed of sex is planted in the mind, it is very easy for a young woman to fall victim to sin with vile young men." Reverend Holly dropped his finger church and leaned across the desk. "Carla, I'm going to ask a blunt question. That night you and Oren Prince got caught in a blizzard and you had to stay in his father's car all night, did you do it with him?"

"No! I just told you I was a virgin."

His vivid blue eyes stared into her eyes a long moment, and then he slowly nodded. "Good. You're the better for it."

Maybe she was. But not Oren.

"Persist in what you are doing now and everything will turn out to the good. Oren can wait. After all, he is a minister's son." Reverend Holly looked at his wrist watch and got to his feet. "Oh dear, I'm late. Carla, I have a parishioner who is at death's door in the hospital, and I promised her I'd be there to pray for her one last time."

Carla got to her feet too. "I'm sorry I took so much time."

"You'll be all right?"

"Yes."

"Sure now?" Reverend Holly put his arm around her and gave her a hug. It lasted a bit too long.

"Reverend Holly."

His sleekened face took on color. Then he waved to her and hurried out of his office.

Carla walked home slowly.

When Mother opened the door, where she'd been waiting, she immediately asked, "Well, what did he say?"

"I don't think he's going to object if you let me take that marriage license with me when I go to Fort Snelling."

"What!" Mother brushed back her gold hair. Some white had begun to show along her temples.

"Call him and find out for yourself."

Mother closed the door. "I'm disappointed in my minister."

Carla settled in an easy chair. "Do you suppose we can talk Dad into taking an hour off and going to the courthouse with us?"

"Before we talk to your dad, I first want you to read something." Mother went over to her mending pile near the Singer sewing machine and, lifting the top layer of socks yet to be darned, drew out a handsome red-and-gold volume and handed it to Carla. It was a book by a family doctor, *The Ladies' Handbook*.

"Mother! You always had this around?"

"Yes. I had it hid under my underwear in my commode." Mother settled into her favorite easy chair near the fireplace. "There's things in there I didn't want to discuss with your dad."

"Why not?"

"I didn't want him to get any ideas."

"Like what?"

"Carla, please, for goodness' sakes, as I've so often told you, brush down your dress in back when you sit down. I noticed when you came back from the minister's it was all wrinkled up in back. And I just ironed it this morning."

Carla got up a second and brushed down her green dress in back and resettled in her seat. She looked down at the thick book in her lap. "I wonder what book Adam and Eve read."

"Don't be the smart one now, you snip."

"They did all right though, didn't they? We're all here now."

Mother's blue eyes slowly turned a hard grey. "Maybe I did wrong to let you have a room of your own."

Carla sat up straighter. "What do you mean?"

"Maybe you're one of those daughters who practices the wicked vice in secret."

Carla stared at her mother.

"Oh, I know about you girls. I have friends who complain to me about their daughters. If they get a lot of sideaches, then you know."

"I've never had a sideache in my life."

"Then you've never tried self-abuse?"

"No."

"You don't know anything about it?"

"Oh, I know about it. Tracy talks about it."

"That's why I hated it she was your friend. She's a little stinker."

Carla opened the red-and-gold book in the middle. A paragraph caught her eye. "Listen to this, Mother. 'The exposures and excesses of a wedding journey have cost more than one young bride her life and in hundreds of cases have laid the foundation of a disease which has for years baffled the skill of the most experienced and sagacious physicians'."

"What's wrong with that? It's true."

"You mean, because of your wedding night, you had some kind of disease?"

"I was sore for months."

"Then you and Dad didn't have any fun?"

"None whatsoever."

"Even when you made me?"

Mother turned a mottled red. "That's none of your business."

Carla read aloud another paragraph. "'Women's sexual organs, when brought into legitimate use, are delicate and liable to inflammation if subjected to excesses. The most heroic battle which many a man can fight is to protect his wife from his own lustful passions.' Mother, this is a bad book. To think black like that about something that should be wonderful."

"How can you read that stuff without blushing?"

A thought came to Carla. "Mother, did you date someone before you met Father?"

Mother gathered herself up into a tight ball. "Yes, I did."

"Did you love that someone?"

"Yes."

"What happened?"

"He got killed in a motorcycle accident." Mother started to cry. "He met another fellow on a cycle on top of a hill. Both were going down the middle of the road." Mother's whole tight face changed, loosened by an old sorrow. "Poor Billy, he never had a chance."

Maybe that was why Mother never enjoyed it with Dad.

Mother wiped her eyes with her apron. "And now I'm sorry I never let him kiss me."

Carla stared at her mother. Then she got up and placed the red-and-gold book on the coffee table in front of her mother and retired to her room.

That evening Carla and Mother and Dad sat outdoors on the lawn behind the house to enjoy the air. It was an easy kind of evening, cool, a slow north wind whispering around the house and bushes, now and then brushing over their hair.

Dad was tired but he listened patiently to Carla's account of what had happened that day. Finally, at the end, after noting Mother's troubled resistance, he said, "Tell you what, Carla. I want you to think it over for two more weeks. If after that you still want to get married, okay, I agree, you get married. I want my daughter happy."

CHAPTER FIFTEEN
OREN

One weekend Teresita's parents went visiting some relatives and Oren and Teresita decided to make love up in her bedroom. As he draped his uniform over a chair beside her bed, he could still smell the disinfectant stink of the barracks in it, a vague kerosene-like smell. That stink followed him everywhere. As he took Teresita in his arms, he sought out her flesh odor to be rid of it for a time.

Teresita was as lovely and as wonderfully furious as ever.

After he'd slept an hour and had awakened to her importuning fingers, he discovered he was unable. No matter how she tried to arouse him, it wasn't there.

He thought he knew what was the matter. He was afraid of her father and mother; also he felt guilty about having betrayed Carla. "I'm sorry," he said.

"Let's just rest a while."

His hand lay on her belly. When she talked it was as though he was listening to her through his hand.

She said, "By morning everything will be all right."

"I'm sure it will be."

She undulated against him, from her neck down to her knees. "I just love your smooth skin."

"Mmm."

Presently she turned over, her back to him. She fit her bottom into his lap and nuzzled herself into her pillow, and then gradually began to breathe in slow even falls.

A half-moon was out and it lighted up her room dimly through white curtains. He could make out the mirror over her dresser. The big oval mirror looked like an opening to a deep cave. Every now and then a pair of eyes glowed in the oval opening, yellow becoming a gas blue and fading to yellow again. He couldn't make out what it was. Distant cars? He was too tired to sit up and find out.

The voice in the back of his head said, flat: "This gal lying here beside you, there's more going on in that head of hers than you might know."

Suddenly one of Teresita's legs stiffened straight out, bending back his leg. Her leg quivered several times, then slowly quieted. Gradually too it went back to being bent at the knee.

"She's having a dream," he thought.

Her long flowing black hair lay drifted across his face. He could smell shampoo in it.

The interior voice said, "She has it in her to be a worse boss than her father or mother. As any only child born to such parents, she's bound to be wilful."

An occasional car whoshed by on the boulevard below.

The interior commentator said: "Though she's also one of those who if she is for you will gnaw her way through steel for you."

He drifted off to sleep. Dreamless.

Once again he was awakened by urgent fingers.

Teresita, turning over, awakening, had found him up. She whispered in admiration, "See? I told you. Hmm. Mmm."

He took her hungrily in his arms.

Again he lay with his hand on her belly as they talked. He fancied he could feel her think there.

"Wonder what time it is," she whispered.

"Isn't the clock there on your side?"

"Yes." She twisted around some. "Four."

"This has been one of the longest nights."

They drifted off to sleep again.

It seemed but a moment later when a light snapped on in the room. Oren was lying facing Teresita's curved back, and the overhead light caused her tousled black hair to glow with a low auburn iridescence.

A woman's voice, so high it was almost falsetto, cried out, "Teresita? Who is that in bed with you?"

Teresita froze into stiffened flesh.

A man's voice, also risen, crackling with anger, growled, "All right, the jig is up, you two. Get out of bed. Right now."

Oren couldn't move. He felt as helpless as a bit of metal caught in a magnetic field.

Mr. Wendt said, "Teresita, after all we've put into you, you pull this stunt on us?"

Mrs. Wendt said, "What will our friends say? We managed to get them to accept our own marriage, but now this?"

Mr. Wendt said, "Giving you the best of everything, clothes, education, church."

Mrs. Wendt said, "Teresita, how could you do this cheap thing to us? It's dreadful, dreadful."

Mr. Wendt stomped his foot. "Get out of bed, you little—"

"Husband!" Mrs. Wendt interjected. "Let's not use a word we'll regret afterwards. She is after all our daughter. Teresita, here, slip this housecoat on under the quilts. We now must talk to you."

Mr. Wendt went on. "In our house, in your own room which your mother helped furnish with the nicest things we could find for you . . . you wind up becoming a—"

"Husband! Don't say it. We don't need that."

"Wife! I am the head of this house, and it's—"

Oren flipped back the sheet and quilt and stark naked stood up in front of Mr. and Mrs. Wendt. He could feel heat spreading across his shoulders. "Shut up! All I've heard from you two so far is how much you've been hurt. Me me me."

Mr. Wendt staggered back a couple of steps. His face changed from outrage to surprise. Mrs. Wendt threw one look at Oren's naked body and then turned her face away and leaned against her husband. She came only to his elbow.

Oren took a step toward the two. "You should be worrying about Teresita, too. Trying to understand why she invited me up here." Oren snatched the multi-colored housecoat from Mrs. Wendt and reached it back to Teresita. "Here, honey, take this thing and put it on. The sight of your beautiful body might be too much for their poor miserable sensibilities." He waited until he felt Teresita tug the housecoat from his hand. "After all, she is of age and she is old enough to be in love with someone."

Mr. Wendt held his wife close.

Oren could feel himself turn dark with rage. "Back up a step so I can reach my clothes."

Both Mr. and Mrs. Wendt almost jumped back to get out of the way.

Oren stepped into his underwear and proceeded to put on the rest of his uniform. "If it wouldn't be for your wonderful daughter here, I'd never—"

"Stop!" Teresita cried behind him. "Oren? Don't say anything now that you too may regret."

"Regret, nothing. I don't ever have to see these people again."

Teresita folded the many-colored housecoat around her body and came flying around the end of the bed and took hold of Oren's arm. "Shh, but maybe you do."

"After I leave this house, I'm never—"

"Oren, there's something I've been meaning to tell you."

"What?"

"I'm going to have a baby."

There was suddenly a wide silence in Teresita's bedroom.

"What!"

"Yes. It's been four weeks now since my last period."

There was a tiny eeek of a sound from Mrs. Wendt. Then she cried, "Teresita! Oh, Teresita." And she darted past Oren and embraced her daughter.

Oren could feel his face turn white. There went Carla. Carla was lost to him forever. "Why didn't you tell me before?"

"Well," Teresita said coolly, "I thought maybe if we'd make love a lot one night, hard, we could knock it loose."

"Where did you ever hear about that?"

"Mabel Seilman in the office said she'd knocked hers loose that way."

Mr. Wendt collected himself. "Maybe," he said, pushing out his lips, "maybe we should all go down to the kitchen and have ourselves a cup of coffee and talk this over."

"Yes," Mrs. Wendt agreed, "yes, let's do that."

On the way down the stairs, Mr. Wendt said, "Oren, two things. I have to admire the way you stood up to me. That took a lot of guts. And, I'm pleased with the way you took our daughter's part. It told me that you really love her."

Over coffee they planned an immediate wedding. All four managed to do some smiling. Mr. Wendt kept picking up Mrs. Wendt's dainty hand and brushing his dry lips over the back of it. Teresita had soft shiny eyes for Oren. Oren held himself slightly aloof.

CHAPTER SIXTEEN

CARLA

Dad looked up from finishing his apple pie. In a rasping voice meant to be jocular he said, "Well, young lady, the two weeks is up. What have you decided?"

Carla's heart began to flutter. She cut off the point of her slice of pie. The evening sun, striking across her face, lit up her hair falling past her eye and made it seem she was looking at Dad through an ambience of gold.

Ivoria finished her pie and pushed her plate aside. "Excuse me," she said, and started to get up from the table. "I think I'll go out and help the kids round up more tin cans." Ivoria and her neighborhood friends had lately taken to collecting tin. The Army and Navy needed more and ever more metal for their guns and tanks.

Mother snapped, "Not so fast there, you. It's your turn to do the dishes. And Carla's to sweep up."

Ivoria settled back in her chair. "Shucks. Well, it'll be your fault then if we lose the war."

"Nevermind now with your snotnose opinions. We all know that our old enemy has always been a war somewhere." Mother helped herself to a piece of apple pie too. It always made Carla smile whenever they had pie. For a spatula Mother had appropriated one of Dad's smaller cement trowels. It fit the slice of pie exactly.

"Well?" Dad demanded.

Carla could feel her heart beat hard.

Mother said, "Oren hasn't been writing you much lately, has he, Carla?"

It was true. Oren had written only one letter the past week, a funny pinched letter. It almost sounded like he was trying to weasel out of it. Or else feeling very down.

"Well?"

"I've decided I want to get married right away."

"Goodie, goodie," Ivoria cried. "Can I be your flower girl?"

Carla laughed. "You'll make a wonderful flower girl. The trouble is, I'm getting married in St. Paul."

"Shucks."

Mother's face slowly darkened over. She bit on her lower lip. "I don't like it."

Dad smiled at Carla. "Don't worry. I'll sign the release."

After everybody got up, Ivoria to do the dishes and Carla to sweep the floor, Mother continued to sit at her end of the table. The mantel clock struck the half hour. Ivoria took Mother's plate and her fork and knife and washed them, and still Mother sat deep in thought.

Carla longed to talk to her mother about the wedding, what should she plan to take with her to the Twin Cities, where should they get the wedding gown and could it be folded up in a box without wrinkling, and what would be the best date of the month. It made Carla sad that she and Mother weren't closer.

Finally Mother got up from the table. "Where's your engagement ring? And your wedding ring?"

"We've talked about that in our letters and we've decided we'll buy both later on."

Mother shivered. "I just know in my bones that something bad will come of this."

Carla went to her room.

The next day at one o'clock, Dad took off from work and drove Carla to the courthouse and signed the release so she could get married.

Carla got yet another strange letter from Oren. He'd apparently written parts of it in different places because the handwriting was uneven:

> Dear Carla,
>
> You are a wonderful gal and I shall worship you always. But you are so young and perhaps it is wrong of me to ask you to commit yourself so early in life. Maybe your mother is right that you should wait. Maybe at that you should go to college first so that you can develop your talent for art. Maybe we shouldn't let the hysteria of war suck us into its whirlpool. We have to think about you, and what's good for you.
>
> And really, you are too good for me. When I think of the bad thoughts I sometimes have and then think of how good you are, then I know that I don't deserve you.
>
> You are a sweet pure chaste girl. I'll always respect you for that. So, search your heart, and if you find the least doubt, the least hesitation in yourself, call the whole thing off. I won't complain. In fact, it might be best if you didn't come, all around.

The reason I'm putting it to you this way, is that I want *you* to say no, not *me*. It is better that I get hurt with you saying no, than that you should get hurt with me saying no.

You are a golden darling. I shall never forget you.

So if you say *no* . . . all right, I accept. Good-bye and good luck and much love, yours,

Oren

P.S. Absence doesn't always make the heart grow fonder. Propinquity is everything when it comes to love. Fact is, constant touching is the secret of love. Thus maybe it would save us both great pain if you decide that you should go your way and I should go mine.

Oren

Carla was blind to the darker parts of the letter and fastened her mind on the happier phrases: "Constant touching is the secret of love." "You are a wonderful gal and I shall worship you always." "You are a golden darling." "Much love, yours, Oren."

To relieve Oren's mind, she wrote to say that she still loved him, that she was not writing *no* but writing *yes*, that she would arrive by train the next Friday morning, that he should arrange for a thirty-six-hour pass for that noon, that he should get those married soldier quarters for them.

When Tracy and Meddy heard Carla was going ahead with the wedding, they immediately planned a bridal shower for her. Meddy begged that it be held in her elegant home on the hill where she lived with her rich grandmother, Rilla Queen. "There'll be a big crowd," Meddy said, "and we've got the room."

The shower was held on Tuesday. Carla received many gifts: a complete set of gold-edged dinnerware, silverware, a fancy can opener, linen, mixing bowls, electric mixmaster, cookbooks. Oren's mother gave her a sealed envelope which she was to open when she was alone. It turned out to be a gift of two hundred dollars, which Carla promptly put in her account. Even Oren's brother Bon at the bank had something to give; he arranged to have a war bond certificate made out to Carla.

There was some talk about who should accompany Carla to St. Paul. The problem was transportation. The government had set up gas rationing during the war and a person couldn't drive anywhere without gas ration coupons. Dad used all of his coupons for his job. Besides, Dad said, his boss wouldn't let him take off. Oren's father was in somewhat the same predicament. He had to use all his coupons for calling on his parishioners, the sick, the elderly. Mother for her reasons also said she couldn't leave home. Tracy and Meddy couldn't go either; both had taken summer jobs to earn money for starting college in the fall.

Carla said she was perfectly happy to go alone. Once she got to the big city she'd have Oren to help her. As for a bridesmaid to stand up for her, Oren had mentioned there were several nice ladies working under him in his office who could help out.

Going over her shower gifts, Carla decided to take along only her silver. With that she could dress up their dinner table should the Army silverware be plain government issue. There was something about a good-looking fork or knife that made a dinner a success. She packed them in a corner of her suitcase.

Mother tapped into her private savings account and bought Carla a sequined gown to go with Oren's light brown uniform. Ivoria also dug into her savings to buy Carla a white veil. Both were carefully packed in an easily carried box.

Meanwhile Dad bought Carla the railroad ticket and, when Mother wasn't looking, tucked two fifty-dollar bills in Carla's blue purse.

Next Ian McEachern called to say he wanted to put an item about the wedding in the Whitebone *Press*. Could he have the details?

Carla was pleased with the story when the paper came out on Thursday morning, the day she was to leave:

> Mr. and Mrs. Jacob Simmons announce the engage-
> ment of their daughter Carla to Oren Prince, son of
> Reverend and Mrs. Clifford Prince. They are to be
> married this coming weekend in the chapel at Fort
> Snelling.
>
> Oren Prince was formerly a reporter at the *Press* and
> is serving in the Army as a clerk at Fort Snelling.
>
> The bride, Miss Simmons, was co-valedictorian the
> past spring at the local Whitebone high school, is a
> member of the Presbyterian church where she sings
> in the choir, and is well-known for her art work. A
> bridal shower held for Miss Simmons at the Queen
> residence was one of the social highlights of the cur-
> rent summer.
>
> The *Press* and all her friends wish her well.

Carla bought two copies of the paper, one to put in her album and one to show Oren.

On the way home from downtown Carla got her marriage license at the courthouse.

Carla next stopped off at her family doctor's office to pick up the results of her Wasserman test. Her doctor, Sherman Manning, had a

smile for her. "You're in perfect shape, young lady, and I wish you well."
Then he asked, "Do you and Oren plan to have children right away?"

"No."

"Have you given some thought then to birth control?"

Carla turned red. "Oren once mentioned condoms."

Dr. Manning was a lean spare man with a balding head of light fuzzy
gold hair. "Safeties are not very safe. A rubber diaphragm is much
better."

"How does that work?"

Dr. Manning handed her an illustrated folder.

Carla turned an even deeper red. She blinked at the picture of a
woman's vagina and uterus. "Does that mean a doctor has to put it in?"

"The first time only. As a demonstration. After that, if she is at all
competent, she can do it."

"I better ask Oren what he thinks about it."

"All right. But don't say I didn't warn you. A woman can get pregnant
the first time as easily as any other time."

Outside on the street again, Carla ran into Dink Sunstrand. He was
all dressed up in a zoot suit, the current rage in young men's fashions—
exaggerated wide shoulders, extra-long jacket, pants tight at the knees
and loose and wide at the bottoms. He looked exactly like a strong-arm
man for a gangster. The zoot suit on Dink's hulking farm-boy frame
made him look ridiculous. It was as though the designer in making the
drawings for the suit had let his pencil slip at the corners both at the top
and the bottom.

Standing on his good leg, Dink tried to act nonchalant. "I hear you're
going to the Cities to get married."

She tried to walk past him.

Dink moved to block her path. "If that business in the Cities turns
sour on you, you can always come back here to me."

"Will you please get out of my way?"

Dink's raw blond face turned serious. "I mean that."

"After what you did in Deadwood, you haven't got a leg to stand on.
With me." She looked directly at the game leg that had kept him out of
the war.

That hurt and Dink showed it. A sobering look softened his blunt face.

"Will you let me by, please?"

Dink stepped to one side and watched her go, looking longingly
after her.

Thursday night she went to the depot to take the midnight train, the
same one Oren had taken. Except for Oren, they were all there: Dad
and Mother, Reverend and Mrs. Prince, and telegrapher Olaus Northey.

No one had much to say. Mother sat all bunched up. Dad sat with a private smile. Reverend Prince kept working his tongue into his teeth as though a piece of food had got caught in them. Mrs. Prince sat like a plump ewe.

Carla finally couldn't stand it. "What a send-off this is! It's more like a funeral than a happy wedding party."

That woke them up.

Mother said, "You want to be careful with that suitcase now. Where you put it, with that expensive silver in it."

"Yes, Mother."

Dad said, "Remember that in a big city a pickpocket can come running past and easy rip your purse out of your hand."

"Yes, Dad."

Reverend Prince said, "Be sure to tell Oren how sorry we are that we're not able to attend his wedding. Marriage is one of the most important things in a man's life." He nodded to himself. "This war has certainly ruined a lot of plans."

"Yes, Father." It was the first time she'd called him that.

Mrs. Prince opened her big black leather purse and took out a small brown package. "Here is something for your wedding."

"Oh, thank you, Mother. What is it?"

"Nothing much. But maybe you should wait until the ceremony."

"Oh, but I want to know now!" Carla tried to infect everybody with excitement. She smiled until it hurt under her ears. "Can I please open it?"

"If you wish."

With a prying finger Carla opened it carefully. Inside were four things: a silver thimble, a little nickel scissors, a strong darning needle, and a blue pincushion.

Mrs. Prince's cheeks pinkened over. She brushed back her black pompadour hair. "You know the old saying about a bride. At her wedding she should wear 'something old, something new, something borrowed, something blue.' The silver thimble is my mother's. Since I have no daughters of my own, I thought it would be nice to give it to my new daughter. The little scissors is new. The darning needle I borrowed from Ian McEachern's wife. And the little pincushion as you can see is blue."

Carla's eyes moistened over. She went over and hugged Mrs. Prince.

The depot doors were open and a slow breeze from the north breathed through the place, bringing in the smell of someone's freshly cut grass. The breeze was as sweet as a fresh pear. August might be hot during the day, but at night it always cooled off.

There was a long piercing whistle west of town, and in a moment the big single eye of a puffing steam engine appeared around the curve, lighting up the paired tracks, making them glow like filaments in an electric bulb.

Everybody stood up. Dad picked up Carla's suitcase and the specially wrapped package and led the way out to the platform.

Ma pointed at the package. "Be careful with that now. It's going to be wrinkled as it is."

Carla looked up at the sky. The Milky Way arched over them, going from southwest to northeast, glowing like a vast throw of silver veils. Carla said, "Oh, I'm so happy, Dad." She made a little jump on the brick platform.

The big looming engine with screeching brakes and pulsing steam slowed to a stop in front of them. Four cars down, a conductor leaned out from some steps, one hand hanging onto a bar, and then, when the last brake fell silent, stepped down. "All aboard. This way, please."

Dad said, "I'll carry these inside the train for you."

"Good, Dad."

Carla kissed Reverend Prince good-bye on his dry drawn cheek, Mrs. Prince on her powder-scented cheek, and Mother on the neck. Then, turning, hiding a tear, smiling, she mounted the steps into the green sleeping car.

Mother cried after her, "Remember now. Brush your dress down in back."

Carla laughed. "I won't forget." She gave a final wave, and then turned up the aisle.

"Board!" the conductor cried and the train began to move.

Dad set the suitcase in the aisle and turned to hurry off the train. He caught Carla in his arms, very unusual for him, gave her a warm wet kiss full on the lips. "Be good to yourself now, girl." And was gone.

Carla steadied herself against the train's rising speed.

The conductor appeared. "This way, Miss." He pointed out a lower berth at the far end. He reached in and pulled on a light. The berth was nicely made up, covers opened on the near side, white pillow set up against the head.

"Thanks."

"I'll take care of your bags. Sweet dreams, Miss."

Carla looked up and down the aisle, and when she saw no one was looking, quickly peeled off her blue dress, kicked off her blue slippers, and crawled in. She found a hanger overhead and draped her dress over it and tossed her slippers in the corner of the berth. The train began to move faster. The set of wheels on her end of the green sleeper click-clicked comfortingly over the steel rails.

There were odd smells in her berth: freshly washed old sheets, a residual alien musk odor.

Her dreams were crazy. In one of them Oren was talking to his typewriter, saying one thing, and his typewriter was rattling on by itself, saying something else. She awoke sweating.

She thought: "Now I'm glad I waited. Not like Tracy. Tracy sort of ruined herself. She can never kneel pure into her honeymoon bed. Poor girl. Yes, it pays to wait. It's the right thing to do."

She awoke in the morning when the train began to rumble across a long bridge. Pulling back the curtains she saw they were crossing an immense river. On either side were high bluffs covered with trees. She heard someone getting up above her. It was time to get going. In a little while she'd be married to Oren and they would begin living in his married quarters at Fort Snelling. Somehow she slipped on her dress in the berth, found her slippers and put them on.

When the train stiffened to a stop in St. Paul, she discovered the conductor had set out her suitcase and special package near the iron platform.

"How does one get from here to Fort Snelling?" she asked.

"Best is to take a taxi."

Carla nodded.

The taxi took her through downtown St. Paul. She kept staring up at the tall buildings. Oren had been living near this ever since he left home? It was bound to have changed him.

Soon they were cruising down Seventh Street. That she liked. There were good-looking homes on either side with now and then a neighborhood grocery. They passed a very high hill covered with oak trees. Next they rolled onto a long spanning bridge. Below flowed the wide river again.

"Where to at the Fort, Miss?" the taxi driver asked over his shoulder.

"Headquarters."

The taxi driver took a right and drove up to a checkpoint. Two young guards looked at Carla in the back of the taxi and then waved them on.

Carla watched the strange buildings go by. She was struck by how neat everything was, flower plots at the corners, trimmed trees.

The taxi pulled up in front of the largest yellow brick building on the left. "Here we are, Miss."

Carla paid him and got out.

The driver lifted out her suitcase and the special package. "Shall I carry them inside?"

"No, just leave them on the walk here. I can carry them in." With a smile she said, "I want to collect my wits a minute first."

The driver set her things down and then with a nod got back into his taxi and drove off.

A detail of soldiers came stomping by on the grass beyond the road. A sergeant stalked haughtily alongside them, chanting, "Lef ri lef ri, lef ri lef ri. Faster mister big butt on the end there faster! Lef ri lef ri." The sergeant had big loose lips.

Carla thought: "So this is Oren's life."

The sergeant didn't like what he was seeing. "Halt. At ease. Now. Henbeck! Can't you move that butt of yours a little faster?"

"Yes, sir." Henbeck had a small chest with a considerable stomach and butt.

"What? I can't hear you."

"Yes, sir!"

"Are you a queer, Henbeck?"

"No, sir."

"I can't hear you!"

"No, sir!"

"That's better." The sergeant's thick lips thinned out. "We'll try again. Harch. Lef ri lef ri. Move it, Henbeck. Dammit, move it. Move it. Move that big fat buttocks. Lef ri lef ri." And marching, arms flashing, legs flickering, the detail rapidly moved away across the wide green sward.

It was time to find Oren. Carla looked up at the three-story yellow brick headquarters, wondering where Oren's office might be.

She picked up her suitcase and her package and slowly climbed the steps into the building. Inside the building smelled like a rusty tin can.

A pretty dark-haired young woman emerged from behind a stairwell and headed toward the door on the right. She saw Carla looking at the sign over the door. "Can I help you?"

"I'm looking for Oren Prince."

The dark-haired woman had a foreign look about her. She glanced at Carla's suitcase and package. "Your business with him?"

"Oren and I are going to get married today."

The dark woman's black eyes widened until white showed all around them. "I'm afraid you're mistaken about that."

"Why? He knows I'm coming."

"May I know your name?"

"I'm Carla Simmons."

The dark woman looked like she was going to faint.

"What's wrong?"

The dark woman stepped into the office. "Oren, there's somebody here to see you."

"I'll be with you in a sec," Oren said from inside.

Carla set down her luggage and followed the dark woman into the room. She saw Oren busy fingering through a file folder, lower lip doubled up in thought. "Oren?"

At the sound of Carla's voice, Oren jerked erect. The folder slipped from his fingers and fell to the floor. "Carla?" he squeaked.

"Oren?"

Oren flicked a guilty look at the dark woman, then threw an agonized look at Carla.

There were three other women in the room. They stared at Oren and the dark woman and Carla.

"Oren? What's going on here?"

Oren stood up and, shaking, came around his desk toward her. "Carla, uhh . . . let's go outside and talk about it there."

Carla pointed at the dark woman. "Who's she?"

Oren took Carla by the arm and tried to push her through the door. "Come, we'll talk about it outside."

"You tell me who this woman is first."

"Well . . ."

The dark woman said, "Oren, so this is the girl you were writing to so much when you first came here."

Squinching his eyes, trembling, Oren nodded.

The dark woman's eyes closed over for a second.

Carla clutched her silk purse tight to her bosom. "Oren?"

Oren's brown eyes turned milky-sick. "Please. We can't talk here."

"Are you ashamed of me, Oren?"

"Oh no, Carla. No no. It's just that I, uhh . . ."

The dark woman pulled herself together. "Why don't you just tell her that you and I got married this past week?"

"What!" Carla cried out.

Oren was a dog caught in a corner. He turned on the dark woman, showing teeth. "Shut up! I'll handle this, Teresita. My way."

Teresita showed teeth too. She took Oren's arm and smiled at Carla. "Yes, my husband and I just got married. And we're already expecting. Isn't that wonderful?"

The other three women sat like waiting owls.

The bottom fell out of Carla's belly. Oren married? He was already going to be the father of a baby? She saw the room slowly start to revolve around her. She staggered back several steps, grabbing the side of the doorway. "Oh, Oren, what have you done?" Then she started to fall.

With a wrench Oren broke free of Teresita's grasp and jumped to catch Carla.

The moment Carla felt his arm around her she jerked upright. "Don't you touch me!"

"But I want to—"

"Leave me alone!" Carla threw his arm to one side. "I don't need your sympathy. You two-timer!"

"Carla, I can explain—"

"Don't talk to me." Carla turned to leave. In her mind's eye she saw again all the women who'd attended her bridal shower.

"But what will you do?"

"I can take care of myself." Blood up, Carla stalked into the hallway and onto the steps outside.

Oren followed her. "Your bags, Carla."

"You can have them! There's some new silver in the suitcase that I got at my bridal shower. Take them for your wedding present. And you can sell the bridal gown to pay for your baby."

As Carla stepped off the walk onto the paved street, her heel caught on the edge of the curb and again she almost fell. Throwing out her hands to catch herself, she lost her grip on the blue purse. The purse hit the black tar with a thud and burst open, spilling its contents.

She began to cry as she kneeled to gather up her things. "Sure, now everything can fly apart." She picked up the little package given to her by Mrs. Prince, her wedding license, her little pocketbook, pencils, a little notebook, hairpins, several bobby pins, comb, mirror, compact, a small-print New Testament, a roll of mints, several crayons, charcoal pencil, tissue paper, and the clipping from the *Press* about her trip to the Twin Cities, and stuck them all anywhichway back into her purse.

A cold numbness spread in her belly.

It came to her that the other woman looked rather nice. Oren's type all right, dark like he was. Carla wondered if the other woman had chased Oren, or if Oren had chased her.

How had it been for them in bed. My God.

Things all picked up, she closed her purse and started down the paved road toward the bridge. She didn't look back. She thought if she could just get across that wide river then at last she'd be out of Oren's sight.

"Now what am I going to do? It's going to be awful to go home."

CHAPTER SEVENTEEN

CARLA

The moment Carla crossed the Fort Snelling bridge she turned left down a rock-studded footpath. She followed the path until she came to a spot immediately above a steep drop-off. Below lay a wide twinkling river. She guessed it was the Mississippi.

She stared down at the deep green waters. It would be so simple to just let herself lean over and slip off and go down and down. Stumbling on, she came upon a smooth boulder. She brushed off the boulder, then brushed her dress down in back, and sat down.

"Oh, Oren, what you've done."

It was a clear day out, with the sun bright and warm.

"What am I going to do? How can I go home with this news?"

Blue purse in her lap she leaned forward, elbows on her knees.

So the other woman had the privilege of lying in Oren's arms in their married quarters and learning what that swoon was that Tracy Cadwell couldn't say no to.

"How I hate being duped. Ochh!"

Absent-mindedly, she looked in her purse. Ah, there was the wedding license, neatly folded, covered with lovely calligraphic flourishes; and slipped into one of its folds was the release signed by her father allowing her to get married before she was eighteen. She looked at it a moment, then angrily tore it up and threw it down at the Mississippi below.

Her eye next lit on the little leather-bound New Testament. She was a Christian and perhaps should take counsel from the Lord's word. She opened it at random and the first thing she saw was 1 Timothy 2: "Let the woman learn in silence with all subjection. But I suffer not a woman to teach, nor to usurp authority over the man, but to be in silence. For Adam was first formed, then Eve. And Adam was not deceived, but the woman being deceived was in the transgression."

She snapped the book shut.

"Men! It's always in their favor. Come to think of it, there isn't a single book in the Bible written by a woman."

She shoved the little book into her purse again.

She remembered the night of the blizzard when she and Oren had been marooned and she'd beat the back of the front seat and cried "No! No! No!" The memory of it ate like an acid into the middle of her brain.

"Though Dad's a good guy."

She cried. The shame of it! She couldn't even tell her friend Tracy about what Oren had done.

Carla shook her head. What a mess.

"Suppose Oren had just betrayed Tracy?"

Well, Tracy would probably just shake her pretty blond head, try to laugh it off, and say there was more than one bullhead in the brook. It'd never taken Tracy long to find a new boyfriend. Ha! Find two boyfriends. Tracy had already become wised-up enough about life, callous enough, to sneer an Oren right out of her mind. She'd say, "So maybe I did warm him up for the next woman. Well, diamond cut diamond. And toot toot to you, tootsie."

A strangled laugh escaped Carla.

Maybe Tracy had been right all along. To have fun when fun was offered. It was probably the healthier way to go even when very young.

Carla got up and walked around the shiny granite boulder.

"Well, Oren, maybe you warmed me up for the next man, did you ever think of that? Tit for tat."

She sat down again.

"I know that what you just did to me wouldn't stop Tracy from enjoying life if you'd done it to her."

She watched the green river slide by below.

"Maybe I ought to play being Tracy for a while. Because otherwise what have I got to look forward to now?"

Later, Carla dozed off on the big boulder. She dreamed the boulder was her Rock of Ages and that no matter how she clawed to hang on she kept sliding off.

When she awakened, she found parts of her body had fallen asleep: her back, her legs, the back of her head.

"Part of me has turned numb. While another part of me feels wide awake."

The sun sank. Shadows darkened over the flowing Mississippi.

Hungry at last, she started back up the path toward Seventh Street.

She could feel her heart hardening. She had all that money Dad had given her and could live it up for a while. It's what Tracy would do. Nothing to lose, really. Oren had already violated her.

As for Dad and Mother, and Ivoria, and what they would think about what Oren had done to her, well, she'd deal with that later. Right now she was in no mood to go home. Impossible.

"Ohh! The shame of it all. That skunk."

Just as she reached the street again where the rush-hour traffic poured off the Fort Snelling bridge into St. Paul, she ran into two soldiers, a short one and a fat one.

The soldiers' eyes lighted up. "Hey there, you chick."

Carla turned and looked them over. She shook her head to herself. They weren't the right kind. They were too common. She set her face away from them and hurried on.

The short soldier caught up with her and slipped an arm around her. "Not so fast. Let's get acquainted."

"No. Sorry."

The short soldier slipped a hand over her breast. "Enough here to keep it off the ground."

Carla shifted her purse from her right hand to her left hand and slapped him lightly across the cheek. "You lay off me or I'll call the sheriff."

"Wow, Hubie," the short soldier said, "we got us a wildcat here. A real titsy."

Fat Hubie came puffing up. He had a good look at Carla and his round cherubic face turned serious. "Saxneat, I don't think I'd monkey around with her much if I was you."

"They all like to say no at first. That makes it all the sweeter later on."

Hubie said, "She's not that kind, Saxneat."

"They all like it once you put it to them."

It was kind of nice to have a man's hand cup her. But she broke free again. "I don't know who raised you, mister, but whoever it was didn't have any manners." She pricked her eyes into him. She could see the striations in his pale blue eyes. The striations opened away from the black centers like the petals of a blue gentian.

Saxneat backed a step.

Carla turned and headed up Seventh Street.

She spotted Joe Gambino's Dine & Dancing ahead. Ah, a place to eat. As she approached its ornate front, a taxi pulled up. Two well-dressed couples in silks and blacks stepped out, all talking animatedly as they headed for the front door. Just as they were about to step inside, a soldier on crutches appeared from one side and held out a cup. The soldier had lost a leg. The formally dressed men were of a mind to brush past the crippled soldier, but the women slowed them down. When one of the women opened her purse to look for some loose change, the other woman did the same. They gave generously. The cripple thanked them with a sad pale face, bowed slightly, and then stepped back. One of the women brushed a tear out of her eye as she went on into the eating place.

Carla felt sorry for the crippled soldier too. At least he'd fought in the war. Instead of staying home working at the Fort Snelling headquarters and getting a woman in trouble. Opening her blue purse, Carla fingered through her little pocketbook and found a five-dollar bill.

The cripple had just finished emptying the contents of his cup into his pocket when he saw Carla coming toward him. Instantly he put on a sad smile, eyes turning moist, lower lip trembling in shame that he had to beg. He had boyish blue eyes and his hair was freshly cut and his soldier suit was neatly cleaned and pressed. He held out his cup.

Carla folded the fiver over and dropped it into the cup. "Don't you have a home? A mother somewhere?"

"No, ma'am."

"You an orphan then?"

"Thank you very much for your gift, ma'am."

"Oh, that's all right. I feel kind of down myself."

He looked at her, light-blue eyes narrowing. "A beautiful gal like you? Sorry to hear that."

"God's will, I guess."

"You went through a roughty then, huh?" His eyes swept over her body as though he were mentally undressing her.

She found she didn't mind the look. "Yes, I came to town expecting to marry my soldier boyfriend . . . only to find he'd married somebody else in the meantime."

"The son of a bitch. Well, there's always more pebbles on the beach."

"That's what my best friend would say." She winked back a tear. "Well, I better go now. I haven't eaten all day and I'm getting awfully hungry."

"Say," he said, rocking between his crutches, "how about me springing for your dinner?"

"No, thank you. It's very nice of you, but . . ." She turned and started up the steps.

Carla found a small booth in back on the other side of the dancing area. Tobacco smoke swirled against the ceiling. There were soldiers in the crowd. Several officers stood sipping at the bar. The two couples she'd seen entering the diner sat near her in a large booth. Someone had filled a jukebox with nickels and one record after another dropped onto the turntable. She recognized one of the songs, "When It's June in January."

A waitress dressed in tan with a pretty green apron came along and gave Carla a menu and a glass of water.

The glass was already beaded over with sweat. Carla moved it around, making a series of wet ovals on the black tabletop.

Another waitress came along and lighted the candle in the little glass chimney. It cast a warm glow on the black surface and softened the deep red of the leather cushion seats. "Care for a drink?"

"No, thank you. But I'd like to order some food."

"I'm from the bar. The other waitress will take your order."

Carla studied the menu in the light of the candle. Her glance lighted on the lake trout entry. She thought of ordering it, she liked fish so, but then remembered what she and Oren'd had in Marshall the night of the blizzard. She made a face. Brushing back her blond hair, she went down the list on the menu. Steak she could get better at home, living as she did in farm country. Maybe she should try mutton.

The first waitress came back. "Ready to order?"

"Yes. I'll have the mutton. French fries. And some tea."

The waitress nodded and vanished into the back.

Another record dropped on the turntable, "Smoke Gets in Your Eyes." There was a ripple of a cheer near her and the two couples in the next booth got up and threaded their way through the crowded tables onto the dance floor. With easy grace the women lifted their arms to their consorts, and in a moment they were swirling with their handsome partners across the shining floor. A purple spotlight followed first one couple then the other to cheers from the onlookers. The two couples were good dancers.

The waitress from the bar appeared with her little tray and a drink on it. She set the drink on a napkin in front of Carla.

"I didn't order that," Carla said. "What is it?"

"Whiskey sour."

Carla's nose came up. "Take it away." Carla noticed the waitress had a heavily made up face and plucked brows and wide empty black eyes.

"Compliments of the officer at the far end of the bar. He said to say, 'To the most beautiful lady in the place'."

"Puh!"

"I'd feel complimented if it was me."

"After what I went through today you wouldn't."

The waitress shrugged, and left.

Carla pushed the drink to the edge of the table.

Another record dropped on the jukebox turntable, "The Shadow Waltz." Immediately the whole floor filled with paired bodies dipping and swinging and turning. Again the purple light coned down first on one couple and then another. The noise in the place thickened. Smoke curled in little clouds against the dark ceiling.

The bar waitress appeared with yet another drink.

"Take that away! Or I'll pour it on the floor."

"Hey, hey," a voice called to Carla. It was the crippled soldier swinging toward her like a hurrying spider. "Don't get excited now. That's just orange juice. I saw you push the other one away. So I knew better than to order you hard liquor."

"What!"

"Mind if I sit with you? Unless someone else is coming."

"I've got nobody."

"Good." Setting his crutches in ahead of him, the crippled soldier slid into the booth. He smiled at Carla, very boyish. "Really. That is orange juice."

Carla sipped a little of it.

He nubbed his nose with a crooked finger. He smiled down at the drink the officer at the bar had ordered for her. He picked it up and sniffed it. "Can't let a good drink go to waste, now can we?" He was about to take a sip when there was an awful roar at their table.

"Pri-vate! Don't you drink my drink, you warped little twerp you! I ordered that for the lady, not you." It was the officer at the bar. He made a swipe at the drink to take it, but the crippled soldier was too quick for him, jerking it out of his reach.

The officer was muscular and broad-shouldered, had good skin and well-groomed hair. But, scowling, his face broke down, giving him the loose-lipped look of a sissy.

The crippled soldier's eyes slowly turned a hard blue. Then he exploded out of his seat and grabbed the handsome officer by his shirt and tie. "Back to the bar, you himmer, you half-and-half." The crippled soldier's eyes took on a luminous grey-white look. "You may be a lieutenant over at the Fort, but off limits we're equals. Get it? Calling me a private and trying to steal my woman. Get, or I'll spill your guts." The crippled soldier made a motion as though he were going for a knife.

The lieutenant wrenched himself free; fell back a step. Everybody around them fell silent. The lieutenant, conscious of all the attention they were getting, finger-combed his hair and readjusted his tie. "You'll hear from me again, pri-vate." He turned and left.

The crippled soldier settled back in his seat.

Carla sat with a hand over her mouth.

The crippled soldier made his face young again; and smiled at her. "You know, I haven't introduced myself. I'm Henry Kempner. Sometimes they call me Heinie. But don't you ever call me that. I hate that name. I prefer Skippy. And you?"

She spoke before she could think. "I'm Carla Simmons."

"Sorry to make a scene. But I don't care much for officers."

"So I've noticed."

"D'bastard had it coming to him, know whad I mean? Damned queer. Bisexual."

"Is that what you meant by 'himmer'?"

"Yeh. Him-her. Plays it both ways."

"For goodness' sakes."

"Yes, Miss Simmons, it takes all kinds, you know."

The waitress came with Carla's order of mutton. She set it all out neatly, then turned to Skippy. "Do you wish to order?"

"Yeh." He looked at Carla's steaming plate. "That looks good. I'll have the same."

"Coming up."

Skippy smiled young at Carla. "I'm honored that you let me sit with you." He looked at what he could see of her above the table. "I like my women tall. When you have a big tall handsome woman at your side, it's like having a continent support you."

"You mean, one that'll give you all the more room to walk over on."

Skippy cocked his blond head at her. "Where you from?"

"Whitebone. And you?"

"Chicawgo." He looked at her plate. "Don't wait for me. Pitch in, babe, and enjoy it while it's warm."

"If you don't mind." Carla began to cut her meat.

"So it's 'God's will,' eh?" Skippy shook some salt from the salt shaker into the palm of his hand and wetting a fingertip of his other hand began dipping up a few grains at a time. "I've got a mother and a sister back home who've gone Christ-crazy. They want me to take the sawdust trail."

Carla tasted the mutton. It was juicy and good. "Well, I've found Christ, but I don't push it on other people."

"Good." Skippy touched the side of his nose with the edge of his thumb as though he were paging a book. "They've got my father so completely under their thumb, he don't dare cough outloud anymore."

"How did you lose your leg?"

He sipped at the officer's drink.

"I'm sorry. You don't have to tell me."

"It's okay. Know whad I mean?" Tears appeared in the corners of his eyes. "I lost it in Hawaii." He shook his head in memory. "I can still see those Zeros coming in over the mountains and begin dropping those bombs on the ships in the harbor. We were ordered out on the double. Just as we were climbing aboard our Jeeps, a couple of Zeros came like hornets straight for us, spraying us with bullets. We tried to duck under the Jeeps, but I was the last under and I got it in the leg."

Here now was a true hero.

"Oh, well, a card laid is a card played."

"Doesn't the Army give you something for that loss of limb?"

"Oh, they will in time. But they're so slow. Paperwork, you know. Bureaucracy."

"Can't your folks take care of you in the meantime?"

"Me stay with those fanatics? Never. No, in the meantime I can get by."

"But begging? Panhandling?"

"Well, what else can I do?"

"But the shame of it."

Skippy didn't like the word 'shame' and showed it. He leaned across the table, blue eyes lighting up with that mad white look again. "I've got a lot comin' to me and I mean to get it! They owe it to me. See whad I mean?"

Carla nodded numbly.

He turned shy and boyish again. "Forgive me for blowing my stack. You're such a nice girl, such a fine looking fresh-cheeked country girl, I'm a bad boy for ruining your dinner."

"That's all right." Carla went back to her mutton.

His mutton came and he deftly went to work on it. His table manners were like Dad's, faultless.

She wondered what Dad was doing right that minute. When she got home what was she going to tell Dad?

Skippy caught something. "Every now and then I see such a sad look cross your face."

"It's nothing."

"You can tell me. In one ear and out the other."

"Oh, it isn't what you think."

"You didn't lose your cherry then?" He tried to make it sound as if it were a little joke between old friends.

She turned red.

"Hey, you're pretty when you blush. You won't ever have any trouble landing a man."

"Thenk you. But that's just the trouble." Like always when she got excited her words ran together. "I lost the man I wanted." Slowly, as she finished her mutton and the side dishes, and while sipping her tea, she told him what Oren had done.

"D'bastard. Doing that to such a nice woman. A beautiful woman."

"Thenk you."

A well-dressed woman with gray hair and a blue hat stood suddenly at their table. "Pardon me, soldier boy, but I can't resist telling you that I saw you outside with your hand out when I came in. And I know you must have suffered, really suffered, losing your leg on the battlefield. But . . ." She shook her head gravely in disapproval. "You're not helping the nation's morale any sitting in the street wearing a soldier's uniform at the same time that you're out begging."

Skippy erupted out of his seat. "Whad do you mean, the 'nation's morale'? It's me what's lost his leg, not you, you bitch! And it's me what's gotta worry about his next meal, not you." He shook his fist at her nose. "Get ouda here!"

The woman jumped back a step; then, once again shaking her head in disapproval, retreated to her table.

Carla was shocked. She was sitting with a wild man.

He saw her look and was instantly subdued. "Sorry about that. But d'bitch had it comin' to her. Know whad I mean?"

"Such rough language."

"Well, Miss Carla, when you've gone through what I've gone through, your dauber comes up quick. I'm sorry." He reached across and gripped her wrist gently. His touch was warm, melting. "Really, I'm sorry if I've offended you."

Carla pushed her plate to one side and picked up her purse. "Excuse me, but I've got to go to the ladies' room."

"Oh, sure." He popped up on his leg, using his strong arms to hold himself erect.

Carla threaded her way through the noisy dining room, past the dancing area, then down a hallway toward two doors marked *Goose* and *Gander*.

There was a woman in the ladies' room washing her hands in the white bowl and smiling to herself. Every time her left hand turned through her right hand in a washing motion a diamond ring and a wedding ring sparkled in the dim light. Drying her hands, the woman left.

Carla remembered how back home in Whitebone the young married women proudly wore the two rings, at church, at parties, at work, everywhere.

"God had better forgive Oren for ruining my life, because I'm not gonna."

She grimaced when she remembered Oren calling after her and asking what he should do about her luggage. Besides using her silverware, his new wife could also sleep in her nightgown.

When she washed up, she saw shadows under her eyes. She dried her hands on a pair of paper towels.

"What should I do? Go out through the back door and leave that nut Skippy? Though I really can't let him pay for my dinner."

Skippy looked up with a big smile when she settled in across from him. "For a minute I was afraid you'd run out on me."

Carla opened her purse. "I'm paying for my own dinner."

"No no. This is on me."

"I don't want to be beholden to any man just now."

"We'll see."

When the waitress came with the bill, Skippy quick grabbed it and stuffed it in the top pocket of his brown blouse. When Carla reached for the bill anyway, he gently pushed her hand away. "It ain't often a soldier can sit with such a lovely woman."

"Thanks for the compliment, but please let me pay for my share."

He smiled at her winningly. "Someday I'm gonna be a famous playwright and then you'll be glad I bought you a dinner."

"You write plays?" The fellow had a way of getting the jump on one. He was like a bossy rooster. He first made you afraid of him, and then, finding a kernel of corn, a smile, held you in his grip.

He looked down in modesty. "Yeh. That's my dream. I've always loved plays. Novels? You can have them. It's plays that give you the soul of a nation. Like d'great Greeks."

So he too wanted to be an artist. Perhaps someday she could build and paint a stage setting for him.

"That's why I don't regret one sickepit when I ask people for donations. Because I get two things out of panhandling. First, I meet a lot of people and that helps me with characters. And then I get money to help me live while I write my masterpieces."

"That does make it a little different."

"Sure it does. I work mothers with soldier sons for a good cause."

Carla smiled a little even as she shook her head.

"You should come with me some time when I go visit Broadway. It's a ball."

"You go to New York?"

"Yep. When I got my pockets full of money, I take off and go study all the plays. That's my college." He reached for his crutches. "Why don't you wait for me at the door while I pay up."

She shook her head.

"I wanna talk to you some more. You're good for me." And before she could say anything, he was off, hustling over to the cash register, again moving with the speed of a hurrying spider.

Carla sat a moment. "What in the world am I getting into with that man. After what's already happened to me today." She was still sitting when he suddenly showed up at her side.

"I forgot to leave a tip," he said, forgiving himself with a soft smile. He put down a five-dollar bill beside his tea cup. "That should make our waitress happy."

She stared at the size of the tip.

"Yep, easy come, easy go. Now, let's be on our way."

"Wait a minute here, mister. Where to?"

"You got to stay somewhere tonight, don't you?"

"You have a home in the Twin Cities?"

He waggled his head sideways at her. "My home is wherever I set my crutches. Right now it's the Saint Peter Hotel in St. Paul." He held up a hand while holding onto the crutch in his armpit. "Oh, don't worry, I won't bother you. You'll leave for home tomorrow as pure in heart as when you left it."

Carla reluctantly gathered up her purse and got out of the booth. "I never said I'd go along with you."

"Oh, come on. The night's still young. Who knows what great truth we may yet uncover before morning."

"I should tell you to get lost."

"No, no." He ushered her outside. He spotted a yellow taxi waiting in the drive. "Hey, what luck. We can ride in style."

"Wait a minute. I didn't say I was going to go with you."

Holding his right crutch in place in his armpit, he slipped his arm around her. The top of his blond head just barely came to her shoulder.

His voice turned soft and boyish. "At least let me give you a ride downtown."

"I'm going to pay for it then."

"But, sweetheart, I can't be giving you a lift if I don't pay."

She stood very still, not knowing what to do. She looked at the street lamps, then all the way to the Fort Snelling bridge. That darn Oren.

"Sweetheart?"

She thought: "Well, like Tracy would say, you only live once." Aloud she said, "All right."

"Wonderful." Instantly Skippy was a blur of movement. He hopped down to the yellow taxi and opened the back door for her, helped her in despite his handicap, and, throwing his crutches in, slid up on the seat beside her. "You won't regret it," he said. "I just love talking to you. You're one of those wonderful women who know how to listen and be sympathetic and build a man up. Really bright and yet a good listener." To the taxi driver he said, "Saint Peter Hotel."

He talked sweet all the way into downtown St. Paul.

She listened with a wondering half-smile. It came to her that, now that she was not going to marry Oren after all, she was free to do anything she liked. Like Tracy might do. And of course her mother would be glad she hadn't got married. Yes, suddenly she was free, free to go to college and become the artist she'd often dreamed of being. Hey. Maybe things weren't so bad after all.

The taxi pulled up in front of a dark stone hotel with a brightly lit front door. Skippy slipped forward to the edge of the seat, paid the driver, then quickly opened the door on his side and got out with his crutches. Nimbly he helped Carla out and onto the curb.

Just as they were about to enter the revolving door, he snapped his fingers. "I forgot to ask. Where's your bags?"

"I uh . . ."

"It's okay. I don't mean to pry. It's just that if you left them somewhere we should have stopped to pick them up."

"But I didn't say I was going to stay with you."

"But you've got to stay somewhere tonight."

"I think I'll get a room of my own."

"Okay. But come up to my room first a while and let's talk. The night's still young." He gave her his best smile.

What a charmer. And beneath the charm there burned a power of a man. Had he not been maimed by the war, he'd have been a big gun somewhere. "Well, all right. I guess a little while won't hurt. But I want to get a room in another hotel for the night."

"Oh, sure, sure. That's fine with me. Come."

Swinging like a pendulum, he led her with smooth self-confidence across the lobby to the elevator. He punched the button and when the elevator gates opened he helped her inside. The hotel was old and the elevator had open black iron grillwork. The handle to the elevator door was shiny brass. The cage creaked upward, one floor, two floors, all the way up to the tenth floor.

"Here we are." Skippy opened the steel gates and held them back for her, got off himself, then let them slide to with a clang. "This way."

Carla allowed him to nudge her along. She was very tired. Her soul was still numb. Too bad she wasn't Tracy. Tracy would know how to enjoy this.

Skippy opened the door to Room 1017, reached in to snap on the light, and ushered her in. "There you are, my lady."

There was a smell of sweaty clothes in the room. An easy chair faced four large windows. Two hardback chairs stood against the wall. There was a door to a bathroom.

"Sit down, make yourself to home." Skippy bustled about pulling down the blinds, closing an open suitcase and pushing it under the bed, and pulling the tan knitted bedcover straight.

Carla didn't like the mousy look of the beige easy chair. Instead she settled down gingerly on the edge of the bed. She set her purse down beside her and brushed back her hair.

He set his crutches against the radiator under the window and pulled up the easy chair and sat down. "Wow, you're beautiful. Such rich skin. Gold."

"I always freckle a little at first in the summer."

"It's lovely. That soldier friend of yours must've been out of his head to go for the other woman." He shook his head. "Like I said, I just love big blond women." He laughed to himself. "Maybe it's the Napoleon in me to go for big tall women." His eyes began to bend toward her. "I suppose you made the mistake of being good to him before you got married, hah? While the other gal played the professional virgin until she landed him? Know whad I mean?"

"I probably should've been good to him like he wanted."

Skippy paged his nose with his thumb. "You mean to tell me you're still untouched?"

She nodded.

"Well, I'll be . . . I didn't think there was any left."

Carla began to notice other things in the room. Stacked neatly along the far wall were three piles of newspapers: the *New York Times*, the Minneapolis *Chronicle*, the St. Paul *Tribune*. On the bedtable near her lay a pile of books: Shaw, Ibsen, O'Neill, *The Complete Greek Drama*, all of them with varnished backs and white lettering from some library.

He saw where she was looking. "Yeh, I kinda like to keep up on things. I read the *Times* for the news of Broadway. And I read the local papers wherever I am to get the feel of the place. And the books, well, like I told you, I'm going to be a famous playwright someday." His glance fell inward. "You remind me a lot of my sister. She and I was once great pals. We schemed together to get what we wanted in that goddam religious dictatorship we had at home. Ma was like a black widow spider trying to masticate me to make up for her unsatisfied sexual urges. Sis and I even used to kiss each other. And then . . ." His voice trailed off and tears ran down his clear blond cheeks.

The poor fellow.

"And then I lost my leg. From that day on Sis would have nothing to do with me. I just wasn't nice to have around. A messy cripple." His eyes glowed in white hate. "D'bitch. Now she's no better than my mother." He looked down at his hands. They were small and delicate, clean, with the nails pared and filed to perfection.

"I'm sorry to hear that."

He let fly with a raucous laugh. "Yeh. But the roughest was losing that leg. Goddam!" As he spoke the folded trouser leg where his right leg should have been flopped up and down. There was a tinkling sound in it. A surprised look came over his face. "That's right. I forgot." He removed a large safety pin and unrolled the trouser leg a ways, and out popped a thick roll of bills and the tin cup she'd seen him use begging in front of Gambino's. The cup was a collapsible type. He tossed it on top of the pile of the *Times* and folded the money into a clip and slipped it into his back pocket. Then he rolled up the empty pantleg again. As he worked, the stub of what was left of his leg wiggled several times.

"What you must have suffered."

He studied her a moment and then with an easy fluid motion rose from his chair and without his crutches hopped on one leg over to the bed and turned on the bedlamp and then hopped over to the door and turned off the overhead light. The room was abruptly more homelike. "That's better," he said. "I've never liked overhead lighting." He hopped over and sat beside her. He gave her his best boy smile. "It's so good to have you here."

She wondered what Tracy would do with this fellow.

"Hah?" He slipped an arm around her waist and drew her up close for a moment; then let her go. "Such a warm armful. Lord, how I like 'em fulsome. Like you."

"I do feel sorry for you."

"Tell me that someday when the leg that ain't there acts up."

"Does it really ache then like it's still there?"

He rolled his blue eyes. "Hoo. Terrible." He drew her up close again and leaned his head on her shoulder. When she didn't resist he slipped his hand up over her breast.

It was so like Oren. Men.

He pushed his nose into her long hair. "You smell wonderful." He kissed her neck.

A part of her watched herself being touched.

He pushed her back on the bed and with startling strength, using only his arms, lifted her over a little so he could lie beside her.

She thought "Tracy would give this war hero what was once Oren's. Because he deserves something nice for what he's done for our country. I was ready to have a man today and I'm still ready to have a man."

Skippy sensed her surrender. It wasn't long before he'd helped her slip off her shoes and dress and silk stockings and her brassiere.

She resisted him when he tried to remove her half-slip. "Not that," she said.

He undressed himself and again with the surprising power of his arms helped her slide in between the sheets. "Sweetheart. Honey girl." He kissed her chin, finally her lips. "That first kiss is like the first drop of juice from a ripe plum. Sweet."

"Wait," she said, and sat up.

"What's the matter?"

"I've got to go to the bathroom."

"Well, if you gotta go you gotta go."

"Sorry." She slipped out of bed and toed into the bathroom. She closed the door behind her. She decided not to turn on the light. She didn't really need to go to the bathroom. It was more that she'd felt the need to talk to somebody.

She felt around for the seat. She found the cover up and carefully let it down so Skippy wouldn't hear, and then got down on her knees before the toilet, and, resting her elbows on the seat cover and folding her hands, began to pray.

"Dear God, I don't know what to do. My boyfriend has deserted me and married someone else. I am too ashamed to go home. I was ready to switch from living with my parents to living with Oren. But now I'm suddenly on my own and alone. I don't know what to do. I have found this war hero, Skippy, and he wants me. And I was ready to give myself to a soldier. Oren."

There was a sound of water slowly trickling in the tank in front of her.

"I am angry at Oren. And maybe that's wrong. But I can't help it. Help me. What should I do?"

Skippy called from the other room. "Hey? You didn't fall in, did you?"

She shifted on her bare knees. The floor was cold.

"Dear Jesus, is it really wrong for me to hate Oren so? I just have to get back at Oren. We can't just let him get away with what he did to me. I so need to get even."

The water continued to trickle in the tank in front of her.

"Thank you for listening. Thank you. Amen."

She got to her feet and opened the door quietly and settled down on the bed beside Skippy. She sat with her back to him.

"I didn't hear you go tinkle or flush the toilet."

"I was praying to my friend Jesus."

"Jesus. Jesus? Holy smokes." He let out a huge sigh. "Lord. Now I don't know what to do. You're so young. And pure. One minute I want to hug and kiss you, the next minute I want to sit back and just enjoy looking at you."

She let herself sag, and turning lay down beside him again.

Resting on an elbow, he hovered over her. He was a cat that had caught a phoebe and didn't quite know what to do with it.

She straightened her slip down over her thighs, nuzzled her head in the pillow.

"Yet I can't resist you." He leaned over and kissed her.

It was sweet to be touched by a man.

He murmured soft words. "Honey. Honey."

She asked gently, "May I look at your . . . ?"

"Business? Help yourself."

"I mean your stump."

"I'll be goddamned. One minute you act like the Virgin Mary, and the next minute you ask a question that not even a whore would ask. Okay. There it is."

She raised herself on an elbow. The stump resembled the way mother turned in dough over ground meat when she made pig-in-the-blanket. The bunch of flesh bobbed a little on each heartbeat. Beside it his erect penis bobbed to the same heartbeat. Suddenly she yearned to hold this poor man to her breasts. "I just had to see it."

He reached up and pulled the chain to the bedlamp. Only the reflection from the lamps in the street below lit up the gray ceiling.

Soon his slender soft hand was sliding up under her slip and cupping her breast.

She could feel her belly warming toward him.

"I won't hurt you," he whispered. "The good Lord short-armed me."

She let him touch her. She imagined Tracy in her place.

He whispered, "My God, you are a virgin at that. It's going to be awfully tight."

Then it was happening. For a moment she could feel her eyes go cockeyed. She helped him a little.

"Oh, my sister," he whispered in her ear. "How fair is thy love, my sister, my spouse."

Then it was done. He lay spent upon her.

Her eyes steadied in the dark.

Presently he slid off her and lay back in his pillow. His fleshy stump of a leg jerked and bobbed; once it whacked down hard on the bed.

She thought: "Tracy said, 'You just melt, and then pretty soon you just swoon away.' I melted all right but I didn't swoon away." Carla stretched. With a sigh she turned on her side and drew up her knees and curled up into a ball. She felt a draft coming from somewhere and reaching blindly tried to find the quilts.

He felt her reaching and helped her and shared the quilts with her.

She remembered a sermon by Reverend Holly. "Thou shalt not commit adultery." A number of high school girls had become pregnant one spring and he thought it time to preach on the subject of early sex. Now he could preach a sermon about her, Carla Simmons.

Skippy spoke in a low voice. "I can't get over it. You really were a virgin. I shall be forever grateful for this privilege. Because I don't deserve it."

"Don't run yourself down. There's already enough people around willing to do that for you."

"You come from good people. I don't. My family is a mess. And they made a mess out of me."

"Don't say that."

"But I am a mess. You think me a great war hero, don't you? That I lost my leg in a battle? Well, that's a lie. I'm a big fake. I once had osteomyelitis in that leg."

"What!"

"Yeh. It all goes back to the time my ma got mad at me and threw me down an outside stairwell. I was just a snotnose of a kid then. I landed on a steel shoe-scraper cemented into the sidewalk. The scraper caught me across my right thighbone. For weeks that thighbone hurt something awful. It wouldn't heal. Just wouldn't heal. Finally, they had to remove the whole leg."

"Ohh."

"Yeh, it was a roughty." He stiffened beside her; of a sudden climbed over her and on his one leg hopped into the bathroom. He didn't bother to close the door. He hit the seat. "Christ, somebody left the lid down." He groaned and there followed the disgusting sound of loose evacuation.

Skippy wasn't a war hero? She'd given herself to a fake? A gray ache spread through her belly.

After some more groaning, and cussing, he flushed the toilet. Then he was back and climbed over her and lay down on his pillow again. "I'm sorry, but I can't help it. A couple of years after they took away my leg, I had to have my piles removed. My mother took me to a butcher. Because he made a mess of my ass. Sometimes if I'm not careful, I go blah all over the bed. If I can't get to a can quick enough, I go blah in my underwear. When I'm on the road I don't even bother to wash my underwear. I just throw 'em in a wastepaper basket and buy a new pair."

Carla curled herself into a tighter ball.

"So you can see why I don't have any scruples about asking people for a handout." Slipping his hands behind his head, he began to talk up at the ceiling. "Yeh, I'm missing a leg, I've got a bad rectum, I lie like a thief. And I stole that uniform you saw me in tonight. And in my bags I got a Navy outfit and a Marine uniform, which I also stole. Depending on where I am, I wear one of them. If it's near a Marine base, I wear my Marine suit. If it's near a Navy base, I wear that. A couple of times the military police have challenged me to name my unit. I always quick make up a unit on the theory that by the time they can't find it in the records I'm long gone."

Dear Lord. She had to get out of there.

"One of these days, though, the war will be over and then I'll have to go back to being a con man in Calumet City. I got some frien's there in a clip joint and they'll take care of me. I made them a lot of money once, handling suckers coming down from Chicawgo. You might think a hick from the country makes the best sucker. Hnk-uh. It's the big city slicker, the gimbo who thinks he already knows all the angles."

It burst out of her. "That's awful, what you're saying."

"In one joint I had the job of training bar girls. I'd take a new girl and show her the tricks. Get a customer to buy drinks and promise 'm she'll pretty soon take him upstairs to a private room." Skippy laughed. "One girl I taught became a master at it. She'd put on a kittenish act, playfully take her customer's wallet from him when he was about to pay for the drinks, and proceed to help him pay for it. Then she'd put the wallet on the table between them and pretend they owned the wallet together."

"Didn't anybody ever make a fuss?"

"We had cops to handle that."

"What! Policemen on your side?"

"Sure. Cal City hired them and the clip joints paid their salary."

"That's corruption."

"Sure it is, honey. But that's the way it is on the strip. Cal City is the wickedest little town in the USA. That's where life is really lived. Some of the best frien's I ever had live there. They protected me. We were all great buddies together against the world. We schemed and plotted to bring in the bucks. We were good at it."

"Why didn't you stay there?"

"I discovered I could make money faster pretending I was a wounded soldier. And the hours were easier. Then too, like you, lotta women are curious to know what my stump looks like and how it would feel against them while we're doing it. Yep, there's many a cherry I picked that way."

"Ohh!"

"I just might have stayed there in Cal City if a United States Senator hadn't got all hot and bothered about crime. He brought his investigative team down there one week, and things got too hot. It was sort of our own fault. We took to jackrolling some of our richer customers. Say one of my gals spots a fellow with a couple hundred bucks in his wallet. Well, we make damned sure he don't leave the joint with it. We get it all."

"Ohh!"

"Yeh, and if he complains, it's up to me to cool him off. I'd put on my best boy face, and act like I was kind of ashamed of the place myself, and tell 'im, 'Come on, leave quietly. You got what you came for. No need to make trouble now.'"

Carla heard enough. She sat up and swung out of bed.

Skippy laughed to himself. "I used to call my gal friends long distance around the country. New York. L. A. Boston. That cost a lot of money. So I worked out a scheme to make a nickel serve for a quarter. I'd take a desk bell and every time I dropped a nickel in the quarter slot I'd bing the bell. That worked fine until one time I got caught. The phone had just been emptied by a couple of telephone dicks."

In the dark Carla pawed around for her clothes.

"Yeh, I knew how to get by cheap. I used to get ink for my fountain pen from those inkwells in the post office."

It took a while for Carla to straighten out her hose. She found her dress and slipped it on.

"In a fight I always sized up a joint to see how many would be on my side. You know, who'd have sympathy for me because I was a cripple. Before I'd start an argument."

Feeling around, Carla found her shoes and purse.

"Hey, where you going?"

Carla said nothing. She went to the bathroom, snapped on the light, and closed the door behind her.

"Don't take too long in there. I think I got to go again. Damned butcher. Don't know if I gotta go pot or pee. Mixed up the wiring in my ass."

Carla washed up. She combed her hair. She stared at her face in the mirror to see if she had changed any. Except for the shadows under her eyes, she couldn't see she was any different.

"Hey you in there, better make way. I gotta go again." There was a sound of his foot hitting the floor, and then he was clawing at the bathroom door.

Carla, finished, opened up for him.

He skipped by her and aimed his bottom for the seat. "What the hell . . . ? You all dressed up?" He sat down with a plumping sound. "Where do you think you're going?"

"I thought you were a nice man who'd had tough luck in the war. But instead I find out you're a racketeer from Chicago."

"What ain't a racket? All business is a racket." His purplish stump flopped up and down on the rim of the seat.

"Business produces worthwhile things. What does your racket produce?"

A vast fart thundered in the narrow bathroom. "It fills my belly, that's what. And it lets me go see plays on Broadway, that's what." Skippy paged his nose with a finger. "Anything wrong with that?"

She hated him. And she felt sorry for him. "Get your play written and then maybe I'll agree it's been all right for you to have been a flopper." She closed the bathroom door. She crossed the dark room and went out through the door into the hallway. She closed the door behind her softly.

She took the elevator down. She started to cry as she crossed the dim empty lobby. Through tears she saw it was eleven on the wall clock. She pushed through the revolving door. Outside cars and taxis and trucks bruised by. The smell of fired gasoline and burnt oil hung in the air.

"Oh Lord, the shame of it. Now I *can't* go home. That I should land in bed on the rebound with a crook. A one-legged one at that. Och!"

She turned a corner. Tall dark buildings leaned over her. High up at the far end of the street, glowing like an egg illuminated from within, towered the round dome of a cathedral.

Then, numbing over even more inside, she blanked out.

She came to standing in front of a bar. She wasn't sure how long it'd been: a minute, an hour, a day. Her sense of who she was came and went and came again.

She looked at the sign over the door of the bar. Ox-Cart. She pushed through a pair of black leather-padded doors. A jukebox was blasting away; a dozen or so couples were dancing in a small alcove to one side, and everybody at the bar and tables was busy talking and drinking. She stood a moment, looking, wondering. Finally she approached the near end of the shining bar and climbed on a black leather stool.

The barkeep was an old man with a dragging side and a hanging belly. "What'll it be?" He crooked his head, waiting.

"Can I have a glass of milk?"

"Coming up."

A young woman climbed onto the stool next to her. She was a strawberry blond with wide merry lips and mischievous eyes. She ordered a whiskey sour. She took a stiff belt and sighed in satisfaction. She got out a cigarette from her purse and lighted up. Finally she turned and smiled at Carla. "How you doin', honey?"

"I don't know."

"Well, me, I'm dancing like hell and having a whee of a time." She waved the smoke away from her face. "Might as well. Can't be perfect forever, waiting for your man to come back from the wars."

"Your husband in the Army?"

"Yeh, worse luck." The young woman took a deep drag and let it float out of her mouth, slowly. "And you?"

"I got stood up."

"Tough titty. But then maybe you're lucky. At least you won't have the awful feeling your man might not come home. All I can do is touch wood for him and hope for the best. Meanwhile, I'm going to play the field and make sure I don't get pee-gee. Do my bit to help the war effort. And I'm not being dippy about it either."

A sad-dog soldier came up behind them and pushed in between them. He asked Carla, "Can I buy you a drink?"

Carla looked at her milk. "No thanks."

"How about a dance?"

"No."

The young strawberry blond laughed. "Get lost, general, you can't snow her."

The soldier stiffened and the sad-dog expression changed to a bulldog grimace. "Well then, how about you?"

The strawberry blond laughed again. "Don't mind if I do."

The soldier gave his head a shake, dark hair sliding down over his black brows. "Bingo." He led her out on the dance floor.

Carla sipped her milk. "Lips are the front end of the stomach."

The jukebox kept flipping over new records. Sometimes there were cheers when someone recognized a tune. Dancers jostled and swung around. One couple, eyes closed, stood in one spot pressing against each other in a slow undulating rhythm.

Three soldiers sat down on the stools next to Carla. They dropped their blue duffel bags against the brass foot railing. They were different. They'd just arrived from a long ways off. They each ordered a shot of bourbon and a beer chaser. They were still wearing torn battle fatigues and dirty peaked caps and scabby boots. They drank up in two swift moves, first the whiskey and then the beer, and ordered another round.

Carla went in and out of herself. She forced herself to smile, hoping she could steady herself, settle down on some point in herself.

The three drank their next drinks a bit more slowly. They savored each sip, rolling it over their tongues, before swallowing it. They were still suffering from battle exhaustion, eyes staring and fixed on nothing, hands limp, gray haggard cast of sadness drawing at their cheekbones. The one nearest Carla was only a boy, hardly eighteen. He held his beer in both hands, wrists slightly dipped as if he had trouble lifting it. Several times he rinsed his teeth thoroughly with a long sip before swallowing it. The next fellow was older, about twenty-five, with a long nose, lips lifted in a snarl, black eyes sunk deep behind puffy gray eyelids, head tossed back a little as if ready for more shooting. The third fellow stared down at the bar unseeing, brown head tilted forward, lips open in a lost smile.

Here were the true heroes. Neither clerks nor fakes. "You set the date and I'll get the dress."

The three combat soldiers ordered yet another set of boilermakers. Again they savored every drop, roiling their tongues around inside their mouths. The two older men each got out a pack of cigarettes, shook out a single tube and lighted up.

The boy next to her continued to hold his mug of beer as though it were coffee almost too hot to handle.

A moment of clarity came to Carla. "I wonder if the folks have found out yet. If Oren has any conscience at all, by now he should be trying to find out what happened to me." Tears fell into her milk.

The soldier boy next to her slowly turned and looked at her. "You can cry."

Carla nodded.

Two-handed, he sipped some more at his beer.

The second soldier with the long nose leaned around the boy soldier. "We can't talk, lady. The Army."

The third soldier with the lost smile said, "Except for us three, a whole platoon of men blasted to hell. Buddies. Everybody but us."

The second soldier lit up another cigarette. "It's kind of a miracle they fished us out of there and hustled us home."

Carla spotted blood on their fatigues.

"Yeh," the boy soldier said, "we didn't get a chance to change. They run us aboard a military cargo plane and here we are. Good thing there ain't no military police around." He shuddered. "If he wins, it's your life. If you win, well, why not his?"

Carla's neck chilled over.

The boy soldier said, "I'll never forget that poor German kid's face. He was a couple years younger than me. He'd just had a haircut. You could still see where he'd run a comb through his hair—"

"Shut up, Thomas," the third soldier said.

"—tooth marks of the comb were still in it. I knocked the rifle out of his hands and had him by the throat. Up went his hands. I yelled at him in American—'Camerad?'—but he didn't understand me. And that look. Like a little boy worried that his dad's gonna whip him because he's left the cattle gate open, when I'm only a little—"

"Forget it, Thomas."

"—boy myself. It wasn't the look of a cornered rat so much as the look of a poor cornered baby."

"Thomas, shut up, will you?" the second soldier said.

Thomas said, "Richard, I had to kill him. If he wins, it's my life. If I win, well, why not his?"

The third soldier said, "Thomas, we all have our nightmares."

Thomas asked, "Miss, what are you drinking?"

"Milk."

Thomas downed his whiskey and then nursed his beer in two hands again. "I know what I want."

"What do you want?"

"I need to get my cane polished."

Carla slowly finished her milk.

Richard the second soldier said, "You and me and Harold both."

Harold the third soldier brightened. "That would help."

Carla said, "Excuse me, I have to go the bathroom." She took her blue purse and slid off her black leather stool.

"I'll save your seat for you," Thomas called after her.

In the bathroom Carla stopped in front of the mirror. In the reflection she spotted what looked like an envelope on the floor under the door to the far seat. She went over and picked it up. She looked inside. Sure enough, a letter. It was handwritten with a pencil on rough lined paper:

> Darling please be good   I will do all I can to put him in jail I got $200 and I will stay with Mom and I will be home to morraw Hony my head hurts so bad I am going to the farm with you and so please get it
>
> By By Darling

Slowly Carla slipped the letter back into its envelope. Then she carefully placed it back on the floor where she'd found it.

Carla got out her comb and began to smooth down her long gold hair. She stared at her mirrored silver-edged blue eyes. "Tracy?"

The cheery strawberry blond came hurrying in. She greeted Carla with a smile. "Boy, drinking beer, when you gotta go you gotta go."

Carla put her comb away. "Dear Jesus, help me. I don't know who I am anymore."

From her stall the strawberry blond asked, "Otherwise how you doin', honey?"

"All right."

"I saw you talking to those vets at the end of the bar."

"Poor fellows."

"They look like the wrath of God. I'd be careful around them."

"They're heroes. True heroes."

"Yeh, maybe. But when they come back to earth, the first thing they're gonna want is some poontang. So I'd be careful, honey." She flushed the toilet and came out and washed her hands. "And if it was me, I'd skip out the back door right now and try the next bar up the street."

"They lost everybody in their platoon."

"Hey! Careful with that sympathy or you're gonna wind up on the heavy end of a gangshag. Write them off."

"At least they ain't tin soldiers. They've suffered for their country and we back-homers can't be nice enough to them."

The strawberry blond finished drying her hands with a piece of rough tan paper. She shook her head and left.

Carla made up her mind. It was what Tracy would do. Carla threaded her way through the melee of drinkers and dancers and came around the side of the bar. Thomas had saved the stool for her. She climbed up beside him.

Thomas was working on yet another boilermaker. His limp hands had become strong and he held his mug of beer tightly. "What'll you have this time?"

"Another milk."

"Gonna be stubborn about it, huh?"

"My family doesn't believe in liquor."

"Good for you. I admire you. Shall we go?"

"What about my milk?"

"Oh, yeh. First that."

The milk came and young Thomas fished around in the pockets of his fatigue jacket and found a dollar bill. He pushed it toward the barkeep.

Carla took a sip. She looked at young Thomas' lips and liked them. They were soft and full, though the skin around the perfect edges was drawn and tight. She also liked his eyes. They were high blue with dark shadows under them. Had the German boy got the jump on him, young Thomas and his soft lips and sad hungry eyes would be in a grave somewhere, while some German girl back home on the Rhine would be feeling sorry for the German boy.

"Drink up," young Thomas said.

Carla worked at it.

Richard the man with the long nose drank in numbed thought. Harold the man with the lost wary smile nodded at his beer. Both were sucking on yet another cigarette.

"Finished?" Thomas said.

"I guess so," Carla said.

Thomas slid off his stool and picked up his duffel bag. "Let's go then."

"Wait a sec," Richard said. "Where you two going?"

"Find us a dark alley and do a wall job."

Carla thought: "I think I'm gonna blank out again."

Richard slid off his stool too and picked up his duffel bag. "I got a gal friend who paints in a loft over a store. I got a key for it. Can't be having the cops pick you up for fornication in an alley."

Carla said, "A girl painter?"

Harold in turn slid off his stool and picked up his duffel bag. "Wait." He turned to Richard. "Why don't we all go up to your gal friend's loft and lay the hip?"

"Okay, let's go."

Carla said, "This is what Tracy would do."

They walked up the street four abreast, Carla, Thomas next to her, then Richard and Harold. They went east three blocks, then two north. Around the corner at the end of a storefront Richard paused in front of a sidedoor. He fumbled through his pockets, finally found his billfold, and from a small button-down pocket extracted an old rusty key. He tried it in the lock. It worked. He reached inside and turned on a stairwell light. He went up first, carrying his duffel bag, then Harold, then Carla, then Thomas.

Richard opened a door at the top of the stairs and reached in and put on another light and then ushered them inside the loft.

Except for a tiny bathroom in a corner, it was all open. No rooms. The walls were rough plaster, the tie beams and rafters raw wood, the floor oiled fir. Paintings were stacked in rows along one wall, and at the far end was an easel and a model's platform.

Thomas said, "How do you like it?"

Carla said, "There's no beds up here."

"The floor is good enough." Thomas switched his duffel bag from one hand to the other. "I've got a blanket in here we can use." He led Carla to the near corner under a window overlooking the street. "This'll be our corner." He dropped his bag to the floor.

Carla looked over at the paintings and then started toward them.

"Where you going? Come on." Thomas grabbed her by the arm. "You can look at them afters. For now you come here." He got out a khaki Army blanket and spread it on the floor. "There. Plenty of room for the two of us."

Richard and Harold went over to the model's platform and spread their blankets on it. Then Richard came back and turned out the light.

Carla set her purse against the wall. Tracy? She made out Thomas' silhouette against a window. He settled down on the blanket and kicked off his shoes and then slipped out of his trousers and underwear.

Richard started to sing at his end of the loft. His voice was coarse, like a rough saw, but he sang the notes true:

> She was a child of the valley,
> An innocent maiden was she,
> He was a desperate Desmond
> Who owned some property.
> He pursued her over the hills,
> But she was wise to his game.
> He cried, "You'll wed me or else!"
> But this was what she'd exclaim:
>> "No! No! a thousand times no,
>> You cannot buy my caress.
>> No! No! a thousand times no,
>> I'd rather die than say yes."

Harold joined in on the chorus in a curiously high off-tenor voice. He followed Richard a half-note behind and a half-note below.

They sang the second verse:

> That night he crept into her window.
> Oh! how that villain did creep.
> He stole her out of her boudoir,
> Kidnapped her while asleep.
> He tied her down on a railroad track.
> The train came rushing over the hill.
> She cried out, "Oh, my future looks black.
> But, you buzzard, my answer is still:
>   No! No! a thousand times no,
>   You cannot buy my caress.
>   No! No! a thousand times no,
>   I'd rather die than say yes."

Thomas reached for Carla. "Hey, you're as bad as those Belgian girls. Had to undress them too." He pulled her down and gave her a rough shake.

"I think I'm gonna blank out."

Thomas fumbled around, finally managed to pull off her panties. He thrust his knee up between her legs.

Tracy.

Thomas found her right away. It hurt, but thank God it was over in an instant. Not even a kiss.

Thomas rolled over on his side.

Carla stared up at the raw tie beams. She remembered a talk she'd had with Mother just before she left for Fort Snelling. "About men," Mother had said, "Carla, you want to remember that sex is a man's game. When it comes time to go to bed, a woman is just a man's plaything. So you're going to have to put up with it and pretend you're enjoying it if you wanna make him feel like a man." At the time Carla had laughed. "But Mother, suppose I like it?" Mother had cried, aghast, "Why, you're just like your father!"

Thomas was soon snoring beside her, slowly, with long pulls at air. He was like a noisy engine.

Carla remembered Dad talking about the battle he'd been in during the Great War near Argonne. He'd been the only survivor. These three men were the only survivors of the same kind of battle in this war. She wondered if Dad had been this way with Mother when he'd first come home. Maybe that was why Mother never had any fun with Dad. Had Dad done it to some Belgian girl too? Such things were never talked about, of course. Such things were just allowed to die away.

Carla, reaching for her panties, was startled to feel a man's bare ankle beside her. She sucked in a breath. "What?"

"Shh," a voice whispered down at her. "It's me, Richard."

She hugged her breasts. "What do you want?"

"It's my turn now, honey."

"No, no."

Richard settled beside her. "Come now, you're not gonna play hard to get, are you?" Richard's breath stank of cigarettes.

"But Thomas . . . ?"

"He won't wake up. We always give him first dibs."

"Oh, no."

He drew her up close. He was naked, and risen. "Come, my honey con, I sure love punchin' gash."

She fought him. Against the light of the far window she could make out his long nose and odd sneer.

But Richard was too strong for her. He made her take off her dress and then he too found her. They both got sweaty and it wasn't quite as painful. No kisses. He left without saying another word.

"I'm beginning to feel like a pincushion."

Thomas continued his snoring. He lay heavy, all out.

She sat up again. She had barely got her dress up over her head with one arm in a sleeve, when another pair of hands had hold of her. It was Harold. His breath stank like burnt rotted rope. She struggled a moment, first to get further into the dress to free her arm so she could fight him, then to get back out of it. Finally she sagged and gave in.

Harold was kinder. He tried to find her face in the dress to kiss her. He played with her breasts a little. He whispered to her, though what he whispered revolted her. "The lads sure juiced you up for me." And he took longer; and lingered after.

Carla whispered up into the dark. "Tracy."

"What?"

"I don't know who I am."

"Jesus." Then on soft feet Harold too was gone.

A truck shifted gears outside on the street below as it climbed the hill toward the state capitol. Thomas snored. Across the loft one of the other two men began to snore too.

Carla thought of that strange inhuman look in the eyes of all three men: hollow, grey-edged, with the whites of the eyes large and glazed, mouth drawn down in a curve like a fish up on shore gasping for water.

At last, aching, she managed to get to her feet and put on her clothes. She felt around in the dark against the wall and found her purse. She brushed off her dress behind and then quietly, on tiptoe, found the door and went out into the hall and closed the door behind her. Again she brushed her dress down behind and then descended the stairs.

Outside, under the streetlight on the corner, she looked at her wristwatch. It was twelve-thirty.

She wandered past darkened store fronts, across a parking lot, finally arrived at a large square. Because of the war most city lights had been dimmed. She glanced up at the street sign under a weak street lamp. Wabasha and Eighth.

She stood looking at the buildings around her. There were dresses on display behind tall windows. Manikins stood in various poses: legs apart with one arm stretched straight out pointing, legs together and one hand high to touch up the hair, legs astride and arms flung out as though walking. All the hollow manikins were smiling. They'd never had a trouble in the world. They didn't eat. They didn't breathe. They didn't have heartbeat. They had no blood or womb or gall bladder. They had no parents or minister to lay down the law.

What were clothes anyway? Living inside them, even in a nightgown, one was living inside a false front. People took each other for what their clothes made them look like, not for what their bodies really were like. "Under my clothes beats a heart pumping blood all over, works a stomach with food slowly digesting, worms a long set of bowels slowly turning potatoes and meat and beans and lettuce and apple pie and coffee into blah. All you have to do is butcher a chicken for dinner to know that."

A yellow streetcar headed toward her.

Carla watched it until she made out the lighted nameplate in front. *Minneapolis*.

Why not. Stepping off the curb she held up a hand.

The conductor saw her, held his young head to one side a moment, then pointed ahead to a car stop sign at the end of the block. He slowed the streetcar down and kept slowing it until at the end of the block he stopped it.

Carla ran after it. As she approached the yellow back door, it parted for her. She climbed aboard. Before she could decide on a seat the streetcar began to move. She finally picked a seat up front so she could ask the conductor where would be a good place to stay for the night. She brushed down her dress before she settled on the cane-backed seat.

After she'd caught her breath, she looked around and was surprised to see a sailor sitting across from her. When he caught her eye, he smiled and crooked his head as if to say, well, here we are, rattling along alone all by ourselves. He was good-looking: smooth high brow, straight black hair combed pompadour, roguish light-grey eyes, good nose and full lips, and a fine set-out chin. He wore his white sailor's cap at a rakish angle.

The streetcar crossed an intersection, wheels underneath them bungling on uneven steel tracks, sparks flying overhead. Soon they began climbing a long sloping hill.

The sailor leaned over and looked past her out the window. "They even turned off the lights on top of the state capitol, I see."

Carla looked. So they had.

"You're out kinda late, riding the owl car alone."

"What's an owl car?"

The conductor said over his shoulder, "It's the last run of the night. Won't be another streetcar along until five now." The conductor liked Carla but was wondering about her.

The young sailor got to his feet. "Slide over one and I'll sit with you."

Carla slid over one seat. She noticed the young sailor had a strange insignia on his blouse.

He saw her look. "Submarines."

"Ever worry your submarine might spring a leak?"

"You bet. Especially when you almost get rammed."

Tracy would like this fellow.

"Yeh, it happened last week. We were submerged at fifty-five feet, when all of a sudden our sound gear picked up another sub headed straight for us. Bells started ringing. Our commander ordered us to dive to seventy-five feet. And guess what. That other sub ran right over our conning tower. We could hear the swishing of the other sub's screw. Man, it was close. I was right under the conning tower in the control room."

Another hero.

"Yep, next week when I report back for duty in Connecticut, we're going hunting again."

"And the Germans will hunt for you."

"Naturally." He reset his white cap at an even more rakish angle. "After a while you get used to it. And you've got your buddies down there with you. You all work as a team. Everybody is an expert at what he does and you trust each other. I know I'd rather be down there in a sub with torpedoes than upstairs in a destroyer with depth charges. Because we got some secret gear I can't talk about." He smiled at her. "I'm Dewain Hansen. What's your name?"

Really, Tracy would like this fellow. "Tracy."

"Just Tracy? No last name?"

"Tracy's enough for now."

Dim street lamps flashed by. They passed an enormous long building on the left with a high sign: *Montgomery Ward*.

The conductor looked up into an overhead mirror. "Where you getting off, ma'am?"

Dewain spoke for her. "She's coming with me."

The conductor frowned. "Is that what you want, ma'am?"

Dewain smiled at the conductor. There was in his smile the gleam of iron. "Hey, what's it to you?"

The conductor lowered his head, thinking to himself. He rolled his right hand on the controls. Then he looked in the mirror at Carla. "Is this fellow buggin' you?"

Dewain turned to her. "Where you staying?"

"I don't know."

"Then come with me and save yourself some money. I'm going to the Radisson. They're bound to have twin beds there."

The young conductor coughed loudly, then cleared his throat. The streetcar came to the crest of a hill. He called out, "Entering Minneapolis."

The streetcar gathered speed downhill. They passed homes on the left, factories on the right. They rattled past the campus of the University of Minnesota, then trundled across the Mississippi River into downtown Minneapolis.

On Hennepin Avenue, Dewain pulled the bell for Seventh Street, got up and helped Carla to the back of the streetcar and down the steps.

Hennepin Avenue was almost dark. Ahead up the street on Seventh the lights under the entrance to the Radisson glowed muted but inviting.

Carla slowed as they approached the revolving door. She could feel something run down the inside of her thigh. "I better get a room for myself."

"But you're welcome to the other bed in my room. I won't pop your cork. C'mon."

The doorman, standing inside, watched them talk. On the doorman's face was a little boy's expression that had wrinkled intact into an old man's expression.

Dewain said, "I'll register us as man and wife. Then they won't ask questions."

Dewain went up to the front desk while Carla stood to one side. A bellboy standing near the elevator eyed Carla wonderingly. Neither Dewain nor Carla had a suitcase.

Jingling a key, Dewain came over and took Carla by the arm and led her into the open elevator. The bellboy got in with them and, pulling a lever, closed the door. Nose up, the bellboy stared at the numbers of the floors going by. He had white-nibbed pimples.

They got out on the seventh floor. Dewain looked at the tab on the key. "Room 717. This way."

The hallway, carpeted brown, smelled like the musty basement of a church. Their heels made muffled sounds.

Dewain opened up and ushered Carla inside. "Here we are." He snapped on an overhead light. "Well. Not bad." He looked around. "But there ain't twin beds."

Carla held back. The room was a good one though, the big double bed, two brown stuffed easy chairs, an oak writing desk, a dresser with a mirror, a door to the bathroom.

Dewain tossed his white cap on the dresser. "Well, time to pound the ear." He kicked off his shoes. "Sit down."

"I didn't like the way that bellboy looked at me."

"That's just his way. They're all smart alecks. Relax." Dewain smiled up at her. "Look, if it'll make you feel any better, I'll agree beforehand to stay on my side of the bed. We'll declare the middle of the bed no-man's land."

Tracy would probably go along with the suggestion.

"Really. We'll make it a rule that you gotta ask for permission to cross no-man's land. First man to break it gets thrown in the brig."

"I sure don't want this to get back home."

Dewain stood up. "Well, it's up to you. Meanwhile, I gotta go pump ship. Excuse me." Dewain went to the bathroom.

Carla sat down on the edge of the big bed. "I'll always be ashamed to go back home." She got up a second and brushed down her dress behind.

Dewain emerged from the bathroom. "She's all yours."

Wetness kept running down her leg. "I'm not an easy woman."

"Tracy, I'd never say 'she sails' about you."

Carla got to her feet. "Well, I need a bath."

The bathroom, neat and white, smelled good. She undressed and hung up her blue dress. She rinsed out her panties in the wash basin and then let them soak. She kicked off her shoes and rolled off her stockings. She stepped into the shower, pulled the curtain shut, turned on the nozzle, adjusting the hot and cold until she had the temperature just right, then with a gasp took the full spretting steaming blast of water. She scrubbed herself harshly to get rid of the touches of all those men. She toweled herself off briskly and put her slip back on. She wrung out her panties and hung them over a towel rack.

She examined herself in the mirror over the sink. She combed her hair, so many strokes on one side, so many on the other. "Well, I couldn't very well walk the streets all night. And I certainly couldn't lay down on a street somewhere and sleep."

She picked up her dress and stockings and shoes.

She found Dewain already in bed on one side, hands behind his head, elbows akimbo.

Dewain said, "Fresh as a daisy, I see."

She tried to smile.

"Good. Tag the light there, will you? I'm all set for a little kip."

"Sometimes you say things I don't know what they mean."

"Just Navy lingo." He yawned, showing white teeth. "I meant to say, get some shut-eye."

Carla stood uncertainly. "You sure a detective won't come looking in here?"

"Naw. The house dick knows there's a war on and he'll let a lot of things slip by."

"I don't know."

"Speaking of detectives reminds me of a story. There was this rich Chinaman, see. He got kinda suspicious of the way his wife was acting. She wasn't all that hot to have him come to bed with her. So finally he hired a detective to follow her when she said she was going shopping. Couple of days later, the detective made his report. 'I follow her downtown. She go through store and get a taxi on the other side. She go to hotel room. From desk clerk I find out she go to second floor. I go outside and climb up into a tree. I look into room. Pretty soon, he play with she, she play with he, me play with me, me fall out of tree'." Dewain laughed heartily.

Carla didn't laugh.

"Oh. Didn't like that, eh. Anyway, come to bed."

She turned and hung up her clothes, set her shoes neatly under a chair, placed her blue purse on the floor on her side of the bed, and shut off the light. She slipped under the covers.

Dewain yawned loudly again and then turning away from her said, "'Night."

Carla turned her head to the window. She could make out a vague light in the air-shaft outside. "Good-night."

She was grateful that Dewain lying beside her wasn't going to bother her. She decided she liked him. When he went back to his submarine she'd become his pen pal.

If Dad and Mother could see her now . . . ohh.

Noticing that Dewain had fallen into a deep sleep, she quietly got out of bed and went over and pulled the two plush chairs around to face each other. She remembered seeing an extra blanket folded over the foot of the bed. She felt around for it until she found it and then, wrapping herself in it, stretched herself out on the two chairs. There was just enough room for her to lie down comfortably. "Now if the police come bursting in they'll find that nothing's passed between us."

Sleep came over her with a rush. She slept deep and dreamless.

A voice awakened her. At first she didn't know where she was. The prickly plush against her cheek wasn't a pillow.

The voice, Dewain's, spoke again. "Sir, that destroyer is headed straight for us . . . We gotta do a porpoise, sir! Dive! . . . I'm doing the best I can, sir, but that trimming system is on the blink . . . Oh, God we're gonna get rammed! . . . Eeeehh! Aaaahh!" Dewain's voice rose to a terrorized cry.

Carla sat up. Those poor war boys. Really.

"We're going down!" Dewain cried in anguish.

Carla shivered. Then she climbed out of the easy chairs and crept into bed beside Dewain, and with a little moan of a comforting sound slid over and slipped her arms around him and held him close. "Dewain? Everything's going to be all right now."

"Huh? Ohh! What?"

"Shh. It's only a dream."

"Oh."

Carla smiled in his ear. "What a racket you made."

"Did I talk outloud?"

"Enough to raise the dead."

He breathed heavy in her arms. "It was awful. So real. I can still hear that destroyer coming. Straight for us." He gradually woke out of his stiffened state, and rolled and shrugged his shoulders and bicycled his legs. "Thank God it was only a dream."

Carla held him warmly. "You all right now?"

"Yeh. Thanks." Then he said, "Gee, you're a good kid." He turned over in her arms and slipped his arms around her and gave her a good hard hug. "You're a real spuzzy of a sweetheart, girl. The kind of gal a man should have to come home to." He nosed around with his face until his lips found her lips. He kissed her gently.

Carla surprised herself. She kissed him back. Gently.

Dewain rolled his shoulders once again in lazy grace. Then he laughed softly in her ear. "Hey, what about that agreement we had about staying on our own side of the bed?"

"That's right."

"Well, it was my fault really, because I had that dream."

Carla liked that. This fellow was willing to take the blame. She kissed him again.

They lay kissing and pressing against each other and soon they warmed up and the kisses became ardent. He reached for her. He did it in a way that made it seem he didn't really intend to reach for her but that his hand had done it on its own. Her knees weakened and opened. He touched her again and she could feel her insides turn warm and mushy. Burning thoughts flickered like darting fireflies. Oh, this Dewain, oh, did he know how to touch. Yes, it really was like that slide at the playground at home. The more you used it the slicker it got and the faster you slid down it. "My heart now wants what it wants." Since she couldn't have Oren she'd take Dewain. Then Dewain climbed Hebron. "Oh, this Dewain, he makes me feel so full. I've never felt this way before." Then soon she cried out, "Oh, Dewain, I'm beginning to fall. Will you catch me? I'm going to fall out of the tree! Catch me! Ohh."

Presently, as they got their breaths back, Dewain whispered, "I'm sorry. I really hadn't intended . . ."

She whispered, "Now I know what Tra . . . what a friend of mine was always talking about. I could never understand why she let boys use her. But now I know."

"Then you never felt it before?"

"Never."

He stirred on her. "At least we have that together."

"Yes. That's ours."

He slid down beside her, still holding her tenderly. "Wow, now I hope I have another nightmare."

"You." She gave him a playful push.

"You know how it is in a dream . . . you're absolutely helpless. Your brain is okay because you're thinking the right thoughts. Even your hands are okay. But that damned tin fish just won't respond. You never in real life ever get as scairt as you do in a dream. In a dream even your hair is scairt."

"I know. I used to dream Dink was gonna push a baseball bat in through my belly button."

"Who's Dink?"

"A clown back home."

They rested a while. They were wonderfully cozy together.

Dewain asked, "Did you ever have a steady?"

"Yes."

"Where is he?"

Carla took a deep sighing breath.

"You don't have to tell me if you don't wanna."

"I'm trying to forget him."

Dewain gave her a gentle squeeze. "I'm just wondering outloud how come a beautiful girl like you ain't already taken up."

A single hair drifted down her face and tickled her lips. She brushed it aside. It tickled her on the nose next. Carefully she ran a fingernail across her skin and threw it to one side. In a moment it was back tickling her lips again. Or was it another long hair? She tried to push it away with her tongue but then found it in her mouth. With her finger she carefully wiped it away. Then it was gone.

Slowly they fell asleep. Unconsciously they comforted each other's little quivers.

Carla heard it first. Some whispering outside their door. She gave Dewain a little push and whispered in his ear. "Somebody's at the door."

Dewain started up. "Wha—"

"Shh. Not so loud. Somebody's at the door."

Dewain sat up.

A hand touched the doorknob. A man said in a loud whisper, "You sure they're in here, kid?"

"Yes, I brought him upstairs with the girl."

Carla whispered, "It's that bellboy!"

Dewain whispered, "I'll fix that." He hopped out of bed and picked up a chair and propped it up under the doorknob at an angle. He did it so deftly there were no sounds. Then he got back in bed.

"Maybe we better dress," Carla said.

"Good idea. If they manage to come busting in here and find us in bed they'll give us the deep six."

They got out of bed and in the dark hurriedly slipped into their clothes.

Carla remembered her panties in the bathroom and quick got them and slipped into them. They were still damp. She was the first to finish and lay down inside the two plush chairs. She whispered, "I'll lie down here and you lay down on the bed."

"Okay."

There was a solid rap on the door. "Open up. This is the house detective."

Silence.

"Open up, Dewain Hansen. We know you're in there. With a young girl."

Carla's heart thumped, shaking her breasts.

Another voice, heavier than the house detective's, spoke up. "This is the police. Open up."

Carla thought she'd faint. Dad. Mother.

"This is the police. Open up!" A key tickled in the lock. Then someone tried the door. The doorknob made a squinching noise where the chair was squeezed against it. "The bastard's hooked a chair under the knob." Fists beat on the door. "Open up. It's the police. We know you're in there."

Carla shook. "What are we going to do?"

Dim light from the air-shaft gave Dewain's face a spectral look. "They won't do much to me. I'm a sailor on leave. Bawl me out, and then send me home. But you . . ."

Carla realized she hadn't picked up her purse. She felt around for it; tried to make it out in the dim light somewhere; couldn't find it. Terror in a dream could hardly be worse.

Shoulders hit the outside of the door, trying to break in. "Listen, you better open up or it'll just go worse for you. You know you can't have a woman in your room." Again several shoulders heaved against the door. The chair began to slide away from it.

Dewain quick hopped out of bed and tried to shove the chair hard up under the doorknob again. But he was too late. One more surge of shoulders and the door popped in. Someone snapped on the light.

Dewain opened his arms and tried to push them all back into the hall. When that didn't work, he balled up his fists and started punching. He hit the front man in the chest, but then the second man, a tall burly policeman in a blue uniform, threw his arms around Dewain and subdued him.

"Now now, none of that. Cool down, buster. Let's keep our heads and talk this over."

Dewain said, "But I registered us as married."

"I know you did. But the streetcar conductor told us you picked her up on his run."

"So that was the bastard who broke out the flag on us."

"Ha!" the house detective said. "Then this woman isn't your wife." He had a balding head, a wide face with brown eyes, and the beginning of a potbelly. "Is she?"

Dewain lowered his head.

The house detective gave Carla the look of a kindly but nosey old uncle. "Are you of age?"

Dewain spoke up. "What does she look like? Eleven?"

The house detective looked casually around the room. He spotted something. "Ah." He stepped around the two chairs Carla sat in and picked up her purse from the floor. He set it on top of the bureau and began to look through it. "Seems to have the usual kind of things a young lady has in her purse." He paused; flicked a look at Dewain. "What's your name?"

"Dewain Hansen."

"And your wife's name?"

Dewain said nothing.

"Are you AWOL?"

"No. I'm on liberty. Here, I'll show you." Dewain fumbled in a pocket of his blue trousers, finally came up with a folded piece of paper. He handed it to the officer.

The blue officer studied it a moment. "He's Dewain Hansen all right. His papers are okay."

Dewain muttered, "Thanks a million."

The house detective still held one hand in Carla's purse. "And your wife's name?"

Dewain said, "If you must know, her name is Tracy."

"Tracy, is it?" The house detective began to paw deeper into Carla's purse. "Maybe we can find some names in here."

Good thing that torn-up marriage license was floating in the Mississippi River somewhere.

The house detective finally had to give up. "Nothing in here." He turned to Carla. "Just how old are you?"

Glad the man hadn't been able to find her name anywhere, Carla blurted, "Seventeen."

Dewain stared at her. "Holy kaboly! Jailbait." For the first time he looked scared. "Jesus, kid, I wisht you'd told me. That's serious."

"Aha! So you did have relations with this young girl."

"Goddamn."

Carla said, "I'm sorry."

The burly blue officer stepped around Carla's impromptu bed and reached down and helped her to her feet. "I'm sorry, too, Miss, because I've got to place you under arrest."

Carla cringed. Dad. Mother. "Why?"

"You were caught under age with a man in a hotel room."

Dewain had one more shot to fire. "But she wasn't in bed with me when you guys broke in."

The burly officer snapped around at Dewain. "She's jailbait all right. And that's exactly where she's going. At least for the rest of this night. On Monday the Juvenile Court can decide what to do with her."

Carla's eyes rolled wildly. Going to jail. Now for sure her life was ruined.

The house detective looked wonderingly at Dewain. "I wonder what we should do with the young man."

The cop said, "Oh, let the poor bugger go." He glanced at the insignia on Dewain's uniform. "Those submarine guys got it tough enough as it is."

The house detective nodded. "All right, Hansen, you can stay here the rest of the night. But tomorrow I want you out of town."

"Don't worry. I was headed for home in Bemidji in the first place."

"With your bride, eh?"

The cop reached for Carla's purse. "I'll take that. We'll turn it over to the Juvenile Court. And now, Miss Tracy, where's your luggage?"

"I don't have any."

The cop shook his head. "That makes it all the worse." He took her by the arm. "You come with me."

III. THE STALK

CHAPTER EIGHTEEN

CARLA

In her cell were two neatly made-up bunks. A toilet trickled in a far corner. A mirror gleamed over a rust-streaked sink. Above burned a glaring electric light.

Jailbird. She could just hear Mother say it.

Carla missed her purse. When upset there was nothing so comforting as a purse with all its little secrets: notes, comb, addresses, mirror, letters, compact.

Jailbird. She'd never live it down. Nor would her family. Her face drew up into a deep cry. But no tears came.

She teetered over to the bunks and sat down on the lower one. She rocked back and forth.

"Dear Lord, I've made a terrible mistake. It all happened so quick. I should have gone straight home the minute I learned Oren had betrayed me. Dear Lord, please remove this cup from me."

Of a sudden her belly hurt and she had to use the toilet. She barely made it. It was then she became aware of the smells: her own, nose-searing insecticide, moldy mattress, rusting iron. Her mouth tasted like an old radish.

"I might as well be dead."

Presently it was over and she got up and washed her hands and face. The soap had a fine aroma, tar, the only good smell in the place.

She sat down on the lower bunk again. Slowly she removed her shoes and dropped them on the white terrazzo floor. She stretched out on the mattress. She could smell some other woman's hair in the striped pillow.

An hour later she had to rush over to the toilet again. Misery. It racked her until she even had to vomit. She didn't know which way to turn first. Sit or vomit. It was so undignified.

Toward morning she finally slept a little. She dreamed that Oren had murdered his wife Teresita. Carla was about to put her arms around him and comfort him, only to find herself clapped in jail as a co-conspirator. Reverend Holly appeared and told them they were both going to hang.

Monday morning Big Kate, policewoman, came to get her and brought her to Juvenile Court on a lower floor.

When the clerk called out, "Tracy no-last-name," Big Kate helped Carla to her feet and led her up to the bench. Judge Kenneth Roker presided.

Carla didn't like Big Kate with her swinging cantaloupe breasts. There was something cold about all the honey-gold oak railings and tables in the courtroom. The noise in the place hurt her ears. The place smelled like a teakettle that had boiled out dry.

Judge Roker had milk-light blue eyes. "Your first name is Tracy, I see. What is your last name?"

Carla looked down at her hands.

"Can't you speak up?"

Big Kate said, "She wouldn't talk to me either."

Judge Roker turned to Big Kate. "Did you find anything in the mug records?"

"No. She's clean there."

"Tracy, will you please look up at me now?"

Carla managed to look up at the judge.

"That's better." Judge Roker had blond hair, and his cheeks and chin had the pink look of a young man. "Tracy, I want you to understand something. This court is not here to seek vengeance. We're here to understand. And this is especially true of juvenile delinquents." He looked at some papers in front of him. He had long slim almost transparent fingers that trembled involuntarily. "I see you admitted to the arresting officer that you were seventeen."

Carla nodded.

"Tracy, we need to know your last name so we can get in touch with your parents, and then this court can release you to them. This is your first offense, isn't it?"

Carla nodded.

"Tracy, I wish you would speak up. A nod is not enough." Judge Roker stared down at Carla, trying to reach into her, fathom what was going on in her head. "Look, we all make mistakes. It's good that you're ashamed of what you've done, so that you don't want to give your last name." He next picked up her purse and looked through it. He pulled out the fifty-dollar bills. "Where did you get these?"

"Dad."

"You didn't get it hooking?"

"I came to the Twin Cities for a certain reason."

"You're from out of town then?"

Carla fell silent.

Big Kate said, "I might tell you, Judge, the jail matron said this young lady had the quickstep the last two days, so maybe she don't feel so good."

Judge Roker reared up a little. "You mean, this girl was put in jail over the weekend?"

"Yes."

Judge Roker hit his desk with his fist. "How many times haven't I told you people not to put juvenile delinquents in our jail. We have in this county a Home School for Girls where we can put them up for the night. We don't want young first-offenders in jail where they can be corrupted."

"Well, the arresting officer thought it was too late to bring her out there. You know how Veta likes her sleep."

"Yes, I know all about that. Where's the arresting officer?"

"He's home sleeping. He had night duty this weekend."

"And where is the probation officer?"

"He's in the hospital with pneumonia."

"Good Lord, our whole judicial system is in shambles this morning." Judge Roker studied the paper in front of him some more. "I really can't make out here . . . The arresting officer doesn't state specifically that he found her in bed with the sailor."

"He didn't," Carla said. "I was sleeping in two chairs pulled together."

Judge Roker seemed pleased to hear that. "You can talk, can't you?" He smiled down at Carla. "Why can't you give us your last name?"

The fingers of Carla's left hand twitched. "I don't want my folks to hear about this. Please, just let me go, and I'll go right home and face the music there."

"What music, young lady?"

"I can't tell you. Just let me go."

"I'm afraid we can't do that, Miss Tracy. We must make sure that you are safely returned to your family. So they can be there to help you through whatever trouble you're in."

"Please trust me, your honor."

Judge Roker shook his head. "If you won't trust us, why should we trust you?" He leaned down and his eyes turned a soft kindly blue. "You look like a very nice young lady. Tell us where you're from."

Carla thought: "My folks are already going to drive me crazy asking what happened that Oren and I didn't get married."

Judge Roker let his wide shoulders sag. His blue eyes almost closed. "Well, I guess the cat has got her tongue. And the court can't spend any more time on her. We've got a heavy caseload this morning." He mused to himself. "I think this is what we'll do. She is such a nice-looking kid, we'll send her over to the Home School for Girls. When she's ready to tell us where her folks live, we'll call her folks and we'll release her to them. And it'll be all over with." Judge Roker sighed. "Kate, I want you personally to take this young lady over to the Home. Instruct Veta Gulickson to leave this young lady alone until she is ready to talk. And here, I'm making you responsible for her purse and the contents there-of. Sign a release with the clerk there."

"Yes sir, your honor." Big Kate took Carla by the arm. "This way, Tracy. Come." Big Kate stepped over to the clerk's desk, signed a paper, and picked up Carla's purse. Then she led Carla out into the hall.

Big Kate helped Carla into an unmarked police car and they were off. A rainstorm had just passed over the Twin Cities, and the emboweled after-sky was lighted up by an opening blue west. The smell of wet trees coming through the open car window had the sweetness of a flower garden.

They pulled up in front of a dark brick building with a high arched doorway. The grass around the building was fresh with the luminous green of late summer. The place looked like it might once have been the home of a rich family.

Big Kate pulled up on the brake and shut off the motor. "Okay, dearie, here we are. And don't try to run away on me while I'm getting out on my side. Because I can outrun you." She picked up Carla's purse and got out.

Carla waited until Big Kate came around and opened her door.

Inside the building, Big Kate ushered her into the first room on the left. They approached a counter. Behind it sat a black-haired secretary.

Big Kate said, "Tell Veta I have another valentine for her."

"Well, so you have," a voice said. A tall woman wearing rubber-soled sandals had come in quietly behind them. She had greying blond hair done up in a bun in back. Her eyes were a light blue, like Judge Roker's, but they were cold, pitiless.

Big Kate turned heavily on her low heels. "Veta, you sure like to sneak up on a person, don't you?"

"All the better to do my job." Veta inspected Carla from head to foot. "This young lady looks out of sorts."

"Oh, she'll be all right. Judge Roker said to leave her—"

"I know all about that. He just called."

"Oh. In that case I'll be on my way." Big Kate handed Carla's purse to Veta. She tried to fashion a smile for Carla. "Listen, kiddo, you may think it's terrible for your folks to find out what you did. But you'll soon learn that your folks can be very understanding. And forgiving. And that you'll love each other all the more for it."

Carla thought: "But it's happening to me, not you."

Veta took Carla by the arm. "Come with me." Veta led her through a wooden gate next to the counter, then into an office beyond, then into some living quarters. The quarters were nicely done up in light pastels, gray and pink. Two gold-and-black-speckled cats lay sleeping on a light-gold davenport. Veta pointed to an easy chair by the window. "Sit down." Veta herself settled on the edge of a single bed in the far corner. She removed her sandals and slipped on a pair of heavy-heeled black leather shoes. Each heel had a wide steel tip. She began to lace up the heavy shoes. "I'm just back from a long walk, and I've learned that if you're going to walk on cement walks you better wear something rubber-soled." With a flourish of deft long fingers, Veta tied the shoestrings into paired bowknots. "There. That's better." She rose to her feet and stepped over to the davenport, steel-tipped heels clicking where throwrugs didn't quite cover the gold quarter-oak flooring, and settled beside the two cats. "Now, tell me."

"Just let me go. I'm the last person on earth to hurt anybody."

Veta stroked the back of the nearest cat. Its gold tail rose straight up, with the tip vibrating. The other cat, jealous, got up and sneaked under Veta's stroking hand for its share of the petting. Veta laughed. It was an off-key laugh. She gathered the cats up in her bosom. With them peering over her arms Veta for a second resembled heavy-breasted Big Kate. "Tracy is a phony name, isn't it?"

Carla sensed a buzzing about Veta, as if she once might have been insane.

"Come now, tell me a little more about yourself. The public can be merciless with superintendents who let criminals go too soon."

Carla shook her head.

Veta set the cats down on the davenport and got to her feet. "Come, I think I better show you to your room." She took Carla by the arm and helped her to her feet. "This way." Veta slipped an arm around her, long fingers lightly touching Carla under the breast. As Veta stepped past a walnut writing desk near the door, she picked up a ring of keys.

"You're going to lock me up?"

"Come." Veta guided her through the inner office and then through the outer office. "I do have to lock up the Home School for the night, you know." She guided Carla up a hard cement stairwell. At the head of the stairs Veta opened the first door on the right. "But you're free to leave your room any time you want. To go to the bathroom. Visit your neighbors. Come down for meals. And so on."

Carla entered the room. It was pleasant, done in yellow, walls and bedspread, with a blue rug alongside a single bed. There were two large windows. Outside a birch tree nodded in the wind, with occasional gusts reversing the leaves, revealing their gleaming silver undersides. Sun on them sometimes gave the undersides a glittering white cast.

Veta saw Carla looking at the windows. "You better not get any ideas. If you try to open one of them, a light goes on in my office, as well as down in my quarters. The only way out of here is through the front door, and I've got the keys for that." She rattled her ring of keys. "Under-stood?"

"Yes."

"At least you're polite." Veta stroked back her grey-blond hair. "You look like a nice kid just in from the country. When you come to your senses, come down and tell me who your folks are. Then you can be on your way home on the next bus." Veta gave her a final look and left.

Carla sat down on the hard narrow bed. She watched the dancing white-silver undersides of the birch leaves. She longed for home, for crabby Mother and hard-of-hearing Dad and spunky Ivoria. She wished she might be the real Tracy with all her boyfriend problems.

"Somehow," Carla whispered to herself, "somehow I've got to get out of this place and go home. Because this is awful."

Then Carla got down on her knees, folded her hands, and closed her eyes. She raised her face. "O Father, look down at me. I'm in real trouble. I can't let my folks know what I did. That's why I can't tell either the judge or Veta what my real name is. I'm sorry I had to be so foolish that I had to get back at Oren. That was wrong. Reverend Holly once said that the Lord helps those who help themselves. Well, tonight I'm going to try to escape. And forgive me all my sins. In Jesus' name. Amen."

She got back on the bed and stretched out. She looked at the hard yellow-painted cement walls. Vaguely she heard two girls talking in the room behind her. They were arguing about having been caught stealing some silk goods at Dayton's.

When the bell rang for dinner at noon, Carla went down with the other girls to the dining room in the basement. The smell of boiled potatoes and sausage and cabbage was strong. The whole place banged with echoing noises: metal trays, heavy tableware, forks and knives, hard heels, angry hurt voices.

Carla ate with three girls, two brunettes and a black-haired one with kinky marcelled hair. All the girls could talk about was that it wasn't their fault they'd got caught running off with their neighbor's car. A new Buick sedan. It was really the fault of the boyfriend of one of them. He'd stolen the car. When he saw trouble coming, he'd made a break for it and got away and they'd got caught holding the bag. There was a petulant edge to their voices. They kept looking at Carla for her to tell her story.

Carla ate her food. She was going to be gone tomorrow and there was no use making friends with them.

Upstairs in her room again, Carla napped off and on.

She agonized over what she'd done. "I'm never gonna do that with someone I don't love again. Never. Never. Maybe never again with anybody ever." She clenched her fists until her knuckles cracked.

Suppertime she sat with a different trio at a square table. They were more like her: soft, contrite, terribly hurt. They were blonds, two sisters and a cousin, with long straight gold hair down to their shoulders and shadowed blue eyes. Their parents had decided it might be good for them to be punished, to stay in a home of detention, where for once they had to behave or get sent to a real jail. Carla didn't ask what they'd done. They hardly looked at each other, or at Carla. They ate with their heads bowed over their plates. One of them was having her period.

Carla waited until the middle of the night. Then tying her shoes together and hooking them in her belt, she softly opened her door and looked up and down the hall. Everybody seemed to be asleep in their rooms. She could even hear one of the girls snoring. The snoring sounded a little like a gurgling drain in a sink. Carla closed the door, then listened to see if it had set off an alarm somewhere. It hadn't.

On stocking feet she crept down the cold cement stairs. Every few steps she stopped to listen. It was so silent the huge bulky brick building had a sound of its own, as though a big dynamo were humming softly to itself.

She paused at the landing. She glanced ahead toward the front door and saw that it had been bolted on the inside. She'd have to be very careful while sliding the bolt back to make sure it didn't squeak.

But first the keys. She tiptoed to the door of the front office. It was open. She peered inside. Nobody around. With her toes she felt her way across the front office. Slowly her eyes adjusted to the dark, helped a little by the hall light behind her. With a hand ahead of her she finally felt out the counter. She found the little wooden gate and opened it inch by inch. It didn't squeak. Again with her toes and with a hand out ahead of her she found the door to Veta's office. It was closed. She tried the doorknob. Ah. Not locked. She pushed in. Light from a street lamp on the corner helped her make out the door to Veta's private quarters. Stealthily she advanced on the second door.

Before turning the knob, Carla went over what she had to do. Move as quietly as a cat. That ring of keys would probably be on the chair beside Veta's bed. Thank God the superintendent had cats not dogs. Dogs would have barked. Carla had one ankle that cracked now and then, the right one. Perhaps if she kept that leg stiff as she stole along it wouldn't crack. Also she had to watch out for chairs and other furniture not to bump into them. Or trip over a loose rug on the floor.

She tried the knob. It turned without squeaking. Thank God. She entered the quarters. Again the light from the street corner lamp was just strong enough for her to make out the main objects: davenport, easy chair by the window, some other chairs, Veta sleeping in the bed in the far corner.

Veta was snoring. And what snores they were. Veta was like a bladder, a huge one, slowly being filled with air with a rough sucking sound; and then was allowed to deflate through a wabbly aperture with a wet collapsing sound. Perhaps that was why Veta Gulickson had never married.

Carla next saw where the cats were sleeping on the davenport. One of them touched itself over the nose with a sleepy paw. Carla made out the clock on top of a tall radio. She made out both Veta's rubber-soled sandals and her heavy-heeled shoes standing beside the bed. Nearby a pale dressing gown hung from a peg on a coatrack. Next to that stood a chair.

Careful with her right ankle, and stepping in rhythm with the rising and falling of Veta's snoring, Carla advanced across the room. Her eyes were so wide open the margins of her vision sparked. To make sure she didn't bump into anything, she decided not to look at the chair beside Veta's bed until she got there.

Something snapped on with a loud click.

Carla jumped. Her heart pounded loud in her throat. Then she figured out what it was. Refrigerator.

Carla waited until her heart quieted down; then finally looked down at the chair. Ah. The ring of keys.

Carla reached down, making sure her ankle didn't crack. She slipped a finger into the key ring, lifted it off the chair, slowly so the keys wouldn't clink. She had just barely lifted them free of the chair when Veta heaved a huge sigh, took several deep breaths, and then rolled over on her side, facing Carla. Then Veta went back to breathing. But not snoring.

Taking a very slow breath, inside the sigh she longed to sigh, Carla slowly closed her fist over all the keys plus the ring to keep them from tinkling.

One of the cats jumped off the davenport, landing on the floor with a light thump. Then the other cat followed, also landing with a light thump.

"What?" Veta sat up. "What?"

Carla stiffened. She hoped the blue of her dress would blend in with the other shadows in the room.

Veta shook her head and then looked in the direction of the sounds the cats had made.

The cats went arching toward Veta and both leaped up on the bed beside her.

Veta sleepily stroked the cats and they began to purr. "So it was just you. Now you two know I don't like you sleeping up here. Get out of here. G'wan." Veta pushed them off the bed and lay down again.

The cats quit purring for a moment. Then they found Carla's legs handy and started purring all over again. They purred loudly, passing in and out between Carla's ankles.

Carla was petrified. What to do.

Veta looked over at where the cats were purring; then bolted upright in bed. "Who's that! Tracy? Tracy! What are you—"

Carla quick reached down and picked up one of Veta's heavy black shoes, and with a swift chopping motion hit Veta exactly on top of her head with the steel-tipped heel. She put all her strength into the strike. Whunk!

"Tra—" Veta started to say, and then slumped into her pillow.

Carla stared. Knocked out.

Carla whirled, hurried through Veta's office, through the front office, out to the front door. She slid back the bolt. She selected what looked like the right key and tried to insert it into the lock. Didn't fit. In the dim light she tried several more, fingers hurrying but still sure in their movements. The seventh key slipped in. She turned it and the door opened inward. She left the key with the ring in the lock, stepped outside, shut the door carefully behind her. Then still carrying her blue shoes she ran on stocking feet.

She ran hard for a half-dozen blocks. The sidewalk was cold. She could feel her stockings begin to give as though runs were starting in them. Looking up she saw a half-moon hanging in the sky up on the right. It meant she was going south. She had to get to the south end of Minneapolis to reach the road that led home. 169 first. Then 60.

Her chest began to hurt. She slowed down. Her feet stung on the hard cement. She stopped to slip on her shoes. That was better. But it was harder to run in them.

She spotted a blaze of lights ahead. Filling station. The sight of it instantly triggered something in her belly. She had to go to the bathroom. Bad. It had come on her so suddenly she could hardly hold it. She approached the station from the dark side. The bathroom for women was usually around the backside of a station. Sure enough, there it was. *Women*. She didn't bother to turn on the light, not wanting to alert the station attendant that someone was using one of their bathrooms. With vast relief she found the seat in the dark.

Breath back, and with a feeling that things were under control, she stepped outside into the light. She walked around the back of the station, careful to stay out of sight of the attendant. Through the glass front she could make out that he was servicing a car, an old Mercury.

She'd gone about a half block, well into the shadows of the trees, when a car slowed down alongside her, engine idled down. The car kept pace with her. She dared a look. It was the old Mercury she'd just seen. There were three men in it, two up front, one in back. The top was down and folded up neatly behind the rear seat. Moonlight glinted on the men's hair. All three had black glossy slicked-back hair.

"In trouble, miss?" the man in the passenger seat said. He was black, had a pleasant smile. The driver had redbrown skin and an impassive face. The man in back had yellow skin and a quaint wise smile on his thin lips.

Carla didn't quite know what to do. Accept a ride from these strangers and so get that much farther out of the area? Or keep hurrying afoot and hope to get far enough away on her own? By now Veta surely would have recovered from the blow on her head and be on the phone telling the police one of her wards had escaped.

Even as Carla thought "police," there they were. She'd been trying to ignore the men in the open Mercury, looking south, when her eye picked out, some half-dozen blocks ahead, a car with a spotlight coming toward her. If the cops picked her up she was right back where she started from, only worse after having bopped poor Veta. With these three men she had a chance.

"Need a lift, miss?" the black man said.

Carla stopped, and the Mercury stopped with her. "Yes. I missed the last bus to Sioux Falls. And I've got to be home by tomorrow noon. So I'd thought I'd start hitchhiking."

"Hop in. We're headed for Shakopee. That's on 169."

Carla glanced at the approaching police car. It was coming at a steady even pace. She looked at the three dark-skinned men again. They seemed decent. "All right."

The handsome black opened the door, sprang out, and with a gallant gesture waved her into the middle of the front seat.

Carla got in, careful not to crowd the driver.

The black slid in beside her and they were off.

A block farther down the police passed them going north. With a flick of her eyes Carla saw that they weren't looking at her or the other occupants in the Mercury.

The black with a little smile sat against the door. "So you're going home, eh?"

"Yes."

"Where's your purse?"

Carla looked straight ahead. Oh boy.

The yellow man in back said, "Yeh, and your suitcase?"

The redbrown man at the wheel drove along darkly silent.

Carla thought of something. "How come you fellows aren't in the war fighting Hitler?"

The black man laughed. "We're the All-Nations Bunch and we don't believe in war."

The color of the men's skin finally made her realize something. "Why, I'm riding with a Negro, an Indian, and a Chinaman." The men were dressed alike: tan leather jacket, white shirt with red tie, blue pants, white socks with tan shoes. "Are you fellows some sort of . . . ?"

"City gangsters? No. No, we like to score with white women. We first aim to please them and then get what we want."

Oil salesmen. Like those two boyfriends of Tracy back home.

The black man sat very polite and gallant beside her. "You like punch parties?"

"Sometimes."

The yellow man in back thrust a brown bottle in Carla's face. "Maybe you'd like to give your tonsils a bath."

In the moonlight Carla could see, because of the motion of the car, the line of liquor sloshing back and forth inside the bottle. She thought, here we go again. How do I get out of *this* mess?

The black man had an elaborate smile for her. He took the bottle and uncorked it. He held it under Carla's nose. "How do you like that for bouquet, eh?"

The redbrown man was a good driver. They curved around a small lake. There were lights all around the lake, reflecting off the tiny waves. Tall poplars tossed in the night wind.

The black man took a delicate sip. "You sure you don't want a wee nip of the creature?"

Carla stared straight ahead.

They cruised out into the country. Carla several times saw the sign 169 go by. At least they were going in the right direction.

The yellow man in back said, "Where shall we go and have us our All-Nations punch party? Down by the river below Chaska?"

The black man said, "I vote for that abandoned farm house on the other side of Gotha."

"Hey, all right," the redbrown man said. "Remember the last time we were there? And we had that society dame from Kenwood?"

"First she didn't want to. But when we got her turned around, she damned near killed us she wanted so much of it."

The yellow man said, "We actually had to argue our way out of it."

The car crossed a wide bog, then a bridge over a black river, then entered a town. *Shakopee.*

The black man held the bottle under Carla's nose again. "Sure you don't want something against the night chill?"

Carla glanced down at the speedometer. Twenty-five miles an hour. Escape. First catching the heel of one shoe on the toe of the other, and the second heel on a stockinged toe, she quietly slipped off her shoes. She wanted to be able to fly when she jumped out.

"Just a little sip?" the black man urged with a winning voice.

"No."

The yellow man said, "Maybe we better muss up her hair a little."

"No," the black man said, "we'll have more fun if we win her over. Remember, I get first crack tonight."

"Yeh, and I get second," the redbrown man said.

Carla decided to pretend she'd go along with them. Then they wouldn't watch her so close. Lull them into being lax. "Isn't it awful strong that way? Burn your throat?"

The redbrown man said, "Maybe we better get some mix for the lady."

"This time of night?" the black man wondered.

The redbrown man said, "There's an all-night filling station just ahead where we can get some."

The black man asked, "What do you like, miss? Coke? Cream soda?"

"Coke," Carla said.

They drove past a huge brewery and then down under a viaduct. The lights of Shakopee faded behind them. Slowly the highway curved up to a low plateau.

Carla glanced up at the half-moon. Somewhere under it Dad and Mother and Ivoria were sound asleep. Before Carla could stop herself a sob escaped her.

"What?" the politely smiling black man said.

"When do I get my Coke?"

"In a minute, whitey. We're just about there."

Carla asked, "Do you guys do this often?"

"We have a jazz session every two weeks." The black man gave her a knowing look. "You like a punch party now and then too, don't you?"

Carla had never thought of the word "punch" that way.

The black man took another sip and began to sing:

> You can keep a-knockin',
> but you can't come in.
> Yeh, I hear you knockin',
> but you can't come in.
> This trick's busy punchin',
> so you can't come in.

Ahead a half-dozen lights illuminated a small grove of very tall cottonwoods. A red sign winked off and on. In a moment they took a left into a drive-in of a large all-night truck stop.

"Pull up to one side," the black man said. "No need to make this public."

The redbrown man pulled up well away from the pumps.

Several bulking semi-trailers, engines idling, stood waiting off to one side. Two were being gassed up. Through a window Carla could see a trucker near the cash register digging into his pocket for his wallet, the cashier smiling at him.

The black man set the bottle on the floor of the car. He placed a hand on Carla's thigh. "I'll go get you your Coke, pussy. Be back in a jiff." He stepped out of the car.

The yellow man said, "Don't trust her up front there."

The redbrown man slipped an arm around Carla's shoulder. "She won't run." He pushed his nose against her cheek. "Will you?" He

laughed whitely. "She's one of those good clean country girls who secretly likes it."

The yellow man said, "You know, I thought it was my turn first."

"Hey, actually, it's my turn first," the redbrown man said.

Carla felt like a poor rabbit with three dogs tearing at her from
different angles.

Just then the truck driver who'd paid for his meal stepped outside.
He stopped a moment to look up at the half-moon, pried at his teeth
with a toothpick, then sauntered leisurely toward the first truck.

Carla waited until the trucker had kicked rubber all around, and then,
as he climbed in on the driver's side of the cab, she burst free of the hand
on her shoulder, flicked the doorlatch down and the door open, jumped
onto the tar paving, and started running on stocking feet toward the
front truck.

"Hey!" the redbrown man yelled, startled. "Where the hell you think
you're going?"

The yellow man jumped over the side of the Mercury and set out
after Carla. "Stop, you."

Carla leaned down, flying. She'd never run as fast in her life. She
leaped up on the passenger side of the truck cab, tugged at the door,
opened it, and hopped in.

"Hey, what the hell," the trucker said. He was a lean fellow with
powerful arms. His cap was decorated with a half-dozen chauffer license
badges.

Carla pulled the door shut. "Hurry! Drive off!"

"Why, for chrissakes?"

"Just drive off. Now! Please start. Hurry."

The driver's hand lay cupped over the knob of the gearshift. The
turning motor shook lightly into his hand. The trucker leaned forward
and looked past her. "What do they want?"

Carla flicked a look outside too. The redbrown man and the yellow
man had stopped a good dozen feet away, staring at her. "I caught a
ride," she gasped, "with those fellows. At first they looked all right. But
then when they started talking about having a punch party in a
farmhouse with me, I got scared."

The trucker's blue eyes became hard grey. "That why you left your
shoes behind?"

"Yes. Secretly I slipped them off. And then when I saw my chance, I
skipped out. There's a black man with those two and he went in to get
some Coke for a mix. They got a bottle of whiskey."

"The sonsabitches!" The trucker stuck out his clean-shaven chin. He
reached down and picked up a jackhandle. "I'll fix them in a hurry."

"Don't. Just drive out of here. I don't want any fuss."

"What about your shoes? And your suitcase and purse?"

"Never mind about them. Just get out of here. Those men are dangerous. They're part of a gang."

"Well, hell, I don't give a shivagit about that."

"Please. They're dangerous. If you'll look"—just then the black man emerged from the cafe with a couple of bottles of Coke—"they all wear the same kind of clothes. Like a uniform sort of. They're dangerous."

The trucker held his head to one side, considering. "Well, if you say so. And it's true I am in a hurry. Really." He gave it all another turn through his head. "Well, what the hell, I wasn't put on earth to straighten out every mess I run into." He dropped the jackhandle on the floor, shifted into low. The motor swelled and trembled under their feet. Slowly the road monster began to move. The trucker meshed the gears as smoothly as though he were stirring up a pail of slow syrup. In a moment the motor began to blat out the roar of moving power.

Carla sat stiff in her seat, pushing down on the floorboard with her stocking feet to hurry the truck along. She flicked a glance at the side-view mirror. She saw the black man raise his hand and smash the bottles of Coke on the tar surface of the driveway.

Once the trucker had his rig rolling in overdrive, he settled himself comfortably on his special cushion, drew a cigarette from a pack in his shirt pocket, lit up, and let go with a smoky sigh. He flicked a blue look at her. "You haven't got the syph, have you? Full house maybe? Syph, claps, crabs?"

"No!"

"Don't get excited. I was just checkin'."

The powerful headlights of the semi-trailer speared down the highway, picking out advertising signs, single trees, lanes into farmyards, glowing eyes of cattle.

"Where you headed, gal?"

"How far you going?" Carla countered.

"Mankato."

"That's almost halfway home."

"How you going to get from Mankato to home if you don't have any money, leaving your purse and things behind like that?"

"Hitchhike."

"You're takin' an awful chance, girl. Maybe when we get to Mankato you better tell the police what happened to you."

"I'll be all right."

"The cops will call home for you." The trucker ground out his cigarette in an ashtray on the dashboard.

"No, I'll be all right."

They rolled through a sleeping Jordan. They climbed a long slope, the muffler roaring under them like an airplane motor. The trees in the brilliant headlights came at them like great shaggy green monsters, vanishing behind them soundlessly.

The trucker said, "You know, of course, you're lucky you landed with a married man who still likes his wife."

Carla gave him a fleeting appreciative smile.

"How old are you?"

"Old enough."

"Funny you tried to catch a ride home with three strangers instead of catching a train home."

"I can't tell you why."

"Well, I still think you better tell the cops in Mankato what happened to you."

Carla decided to fall silent. The more she talked the more she was in danger of letting slip what had really happened.

The trucker lit himself another cigarette.

The great heavy truck roared up a steep hill on the other side of Belle Plaine. The trucker had to shift down twice to make it.

Carla thought: "People back home are going to gossip like fiends."

The trucker said, "Sleepy? Go ahead, take a short one. There's a pillow up behind you there."

Carla thought it over. She was very tired. "I think I will, if you don't mind."

"Go ahead. I'm used to driving alone at night."

Carla reached back for the pillow. It was a round brown thing, the kind a housewife liked to throw on a davenport. It smelled of old sleep. She placed it against the door and nuzzled her cheek in it. Slowly she relaxed. Warmth rising from the engine under the floorboard helped, and presently, trusting the driver, she fell asleep.

The motor under her snorted several times, and the sensation she was about to slide off the seat awoke her. She sat up, looked around. Ahead and below stretched the lights of a city. "Mankato?"

"Yep, that's her."

Carla rubbed her eyes clear. Her right leg had fallen asleep and it began to sting.

The trucker wheeled the big rig easily down the main street until they came to the Hotel Saulpaugh. He then took a right, and in a moment they were pulling up to a warehouse and then backing toward a big open door where several roustabouts were waiting.

Carla opened the door and started to get out. "Thanks a lot for the ride. I appreciate it."

"Wait a minute. I just can't let you run off like that. I'm a little worried about you."

"I'm all right." Carla's right leg still stung and she wasn't sure she should step down just yet. The leg might cave in under her.

"Listen, I'll grubstake you home, if you'll promise to pay me back." The trucker reached for his billfold in his back pocket. "I just can't let you run off like this. I've got a daughter your age."

"I've got to go. Sorry."

"What's the big rush? Tell me, have you done something wrong? If you have, you know, there's a way of straightening it out."

"No."

"I don't like this, you know."

"I'm sorry. Thanks again." Quickly Carla leaped down, closing the door behind her. Her leg didn't cave in. She hurried back toward the highway from which they'd come. The cobblestones were cold to her feet. She headed for the lighted lobby windows of the Hotel Saulpaugh. She'd wash up in the ladies' room.

CHAPTER NINETEEN
CARLA

When Carla stepped out of the ladies' room she ran into a young policeman in blue. He looked directly at her, at her clothes and then her hair; looked down at a sheet of paper; and made up his mind. He put the paper away in a pocket.

"You're Tracy, aren't you? Come with me."

Carla was crushed. Veta and her cops had caught up with her.

"Come." The young cop took Carla by the arm. "Outside with you." He led her through the leather lobby and out the door and then toward his squad car. "Get in."

The cop drove her to the Mankato city jail. He said little. He ushered her into an office and told her to wait in a chair. He picked up a telephone and dialed a number. "This is Officer Courtney speaking. Mankato. I think we got your gal. Your description seems to fit her . . . Okay. We'll hold her until your man can get her." He hung up.

The officer had troubled eyes. He sat in thought a while. Finally, sighing, he turned to Carla. "Come. There's a cot in the chief's office where you might as well lay down. I'm not going to lock you up in a cell."

Carla meekly got to her feet.

The young officer took her by the arm and led her into a side room. It was mostly bare, desk, chair, a shelf fat with legal books, a hard leather-covered cot. "Sleep while you can." He gave her a little smile, and left.

Carla lay down.

Someone shook the cot and she awoke. Looking up she saw Big Kate.

The woman reached down and helped Carla to her feet. "Sorry kiddo. Where's your shoes?"

When Carla didn't answer, the young officer spoke up. "The trucker said she'd come running up to him on stocking feet."

Big Kate said, "What happened, Tracy?"

Carla said nothing.

"Well, you better come along."

At eleven o'clock Tuesday morning, Carla found herself in Juvenile Court again. Judge Roker was looking down at her, young face hard. To one side stood tall Veta, lightblue eyes glittering. She was wearing a bandage around her head.

"Tracy," Judge Roker said sternly, "I get awfully angry when I learn that the trust I've placed in someone has turned sour on me." He leaned down at her. "Now. I want you to tell me your full name. Where you're from. Exactly how old you are."

"I can't."

"Just why did you run away from our Home School for Girls? We intended to return you to your family, not send you off to jail, like we may have to do now."

"I was afraid."

"I still don't understand how a nice-looking girl like you could let yourself get all mixed up with a sailor in a hotel room."

"But we weren't in bed together when they found us."

"I know you weren't. And that's why I was inclined to go easy on you." Judge Roker shook his head. His manner was hard. "But now, now you're in real trouble. Because Superintendent Gulickson wants you brought into the district court and charged with assault with intent to kill."

Carla cringed.

Judge Roker looked down at her feet. "Where's your shoes?"

Big Kate spoke up. She held a package. "I have them here. The trucker who gave her a ride to Mankato told us about the three fellows she'd escaped from. She'd slipped off her shoes and then run. So on the way back with her from Mankato, on a hunch, I took a look around at that all-night filling station. And sure enough, there they were, in the grass near the entrance."

"Why didn't you let her put them on?"

"I kept them in this bag because I thought you might consider them evidence, your honor."

Judge Roker rolled his big blond head. "For godsakes, Kate, that particular I'm not." He looked down at Carla's feet again. "Give them back to her. Her stockings are in shreds."

Kate handed the bag to Carla.

Judge Roker peered down at Carla some more. "And of course you don't have any friends here in the Twin Cities, do you, who might help you find counsel. Because that's what you're going to have to have, young lady, a lawyer. You're in a bad way, a bad way." He looked down at her feet again. "Put on your shoes at least."

Carla removed the shoes from the bag and put them on.

Judge Roker pondered. He shook his head. "I wish you would cooperate a little more, young lady. It would go a whole lot easier for all of us if you would."

Finally it burst out of Carla. "Oh, your honor, if you'll give me back my purse, I'll go right straight over to the railroad station and buy a ticket home. None of this awful stuff would have happened if my fiance hadn't two-timed me. I was deceived in love, and then I got mad, I guess, and then I did a dumb thing. I'm truly sorry, sir, truly sorry. So just let me go home and everything will be all right. I promise you."

Judge Roker held his head sideways. He wanted to believe her.

Veta saw the judge softening. She stepped forward. "Your honor, I definitely want this case brought into District Court so she can be charged with assault with intent to kill. She may look like an innocent girl from the country, but if you could have seen her face just before she cracked me over the head"—Veta let her eyes close for a second as though in horrible memory—"you'd want the book thrown at her. Her face was vicious. She's dangerous."

Judge Roker said, "Well, Superintendent Gulickson, I know you got hurt, and I know you're angry, but—"

"Why isn't she handcuffed?" Veta demanded. She drew herself up to her full height. Even in her low heavy-heeled black shoes she stood a good half-foot taller than Carla or Big Kate. "I tell you, she's dangerous."

Judge Roker thought to himself a while. "Young lady, you surely are a puzzle to this court. I don't know what to do. In this court, Juvenile Court, we don't have the luxury of being able to appoint a public defender. Whereas in District Court they do." He pondered some more. Then he heaved a great sigh. "In view of Superintendent Gulickson's determination that you must be prosecuted for what you've done to her, you're better off with a public defender. So, with some reluctance, I hereby bind you over to the District Court of Hennessey County."

Veta nodded grimly. "Good!" She glared at Carla. "I'm going to see to it that you're sent to the women's penitentiary! Where you belong."

CHAPTER TWENTY

SKIPPY

Sitting in his room in the Saint Peter Hotel, Skippy studied the advertisements of current plays on Broadway in the *New York Times*. He'd just managed to save up enough money from his panhandling to make another trek to New York.

Finishing the *Times*, he next picked up the Tuesday evening Minneapolis *Chronicle* and began browsing through it. He sat relaxed in an easy chair. It was dark outside and he had a floor lamp turned on beside him. Rain pelted the windows in varying sprays. Every now and then he brushed back his stiff blond hair.

When Skippy turned to the local news section, an item caught his eye:

GIRL HELD IN JAIL WON'T TALK

The tall gaunt blond girl stood in her stocking feet before Judge Roker of Juvenile Court and for the second time refused to give her last name.

Earlier, she had been picked up with a sailor in the Radisson Hotel. It was discovered she was under eighteen, and when she would not tell the court who her parents were, she was sent to the Home School for Girls. The sailor knew her as Tracy but didn't know her last name.

At the Home School for Girls she had hit Veta Gulickson, superintendent, over the head with a shoe and escaped. She got all the way to Mankato when authorities there caught up with her.

Superintendent Gulickson claimed Tracy was vicious, criminally inclined, and wanted her sent up to the women's penitentiary. Gulickson wanted her charged with intent to kill.

Tracy was wearing a blue dress, had blue eyes and straggly light-gold hair. Her height was given as five-foot eight.

Skippy's stub of a leg began to flop up and down. "Gees," he exclaimed softly, "her name ain't Tracy. That's gotta be my gal, Carla Simmons." He stared at the print some more, then carefully cut the item from the paper with a penknife.

Then, suddenly feeling very tired, he went to bed.

Sometime during the night, around three, Skippy woke up with a start. He'd just dreamed that Carla Simmons had been sentenced to be executed.

"By God," he whispered in the dark, "now I know for sure that girl's name ain't Tracy. She really is Carla Simmons." Skippy snapped his fingers. "You know, I'm gonna go over and see that Oren Prince fellow she mentioned over at Fort Snelling."

In the morning he dressed in civvies, a neatly pressed gray suit. He wasn't going to get caught wearing a soldier suit on the Fort Snelling grounds. Being a romantic tramp sometimes had its drawbacks. He caught a taxi out to the Fort.

He scrabbled up the wide steps of the three-story brick Army headquarters and entered the front door. Lunging along on his crutches, on a hunch, he tried the door on the right. He pushed inside.

Four women looked up at him and his missing leg. The dark-haired woman on his right asked, "Can we help you?"

Skippy put on a boyish winning smile. "I'm looking for Oren Prince."

"Mr. Prince just stepped out for a second. Would you care to take a seat?" The dark-haired woman pointed to a chair standing beside a large desk near her.

Skippy settled down on the chair and set his crutches to one side. He looked at the four women with interest. No nookie worth thinking about with the three older dames. But the dark gal was a beauty, and her he could go for. He reset his flame-red tie well up into his white collar and shot his shirt cuffs.

Presently a good-looking dark-haired fellow came in and settled in the swivel-chair beside the big desk. He had shadows under his eyes.

The dark-haired girl said, "Oren, this man asked to see you."

Skippy could see why Carla might have fallen for the fellow. D'bastard was handsome. Then Skippy thought: "But I got what he didn't."

Oren offered a hand.

Skippy ignored the hand. "Can I see you in private?"

Oren glanced at the pantleg folded over Skippy's stub. "What's it about?"

"It's a private matter."

"Can't you tell me the nature of it here? I'm very busy."

Coolly Skippy pulled out the clipping he'd cut from the *Chronicle*. "Maybe this will do." He handed it over.

Oren read a few lines; and turned white. He read as if the print was a magnet and his eyes bits of metal.

"Yeh," Skippy said.

Oren handed the clipping back. He swallowed; and swallowed.

"I'd still like to see you in private a minute."

Oren stood up. "Okay, come with me." Oren led the way outside, down the steps, across the road, and a short distance onto the parade grounds.

A lively breeze had come up, making the tops of the trees ride back and forth. It was windy enough that both Skippy and Oren had to keep combing back their hair.

Oren said, "Well, what do you want of me?"

Skippy balanced himself on his crutches against the wind. "If that gal in the paper was Carla Simmons, she's in real trouble. Because of you."

"What do you know about it?"

"I had dinner with her right after she learned you were married."

"Oh."

"You're a son of a bitch, you know."

"You don't understand. And I'll be damned if I explain it to you."

"Meanwhile, poor Carla's going off to the women's pen."

Oren showed his teeth. "Maybe she wasn't so innocent after all if she was caught in bed with a sailor. She probably had a wild streak in her all along."

"But not as far as you know though, eh?"

"No, goddammit, worse luck. If only she'd've let me in, maybe all this wouldn't have happened."

Skippy sneered. "That dark girl in your office there, was she a virgin your first time with her?"

"None of your goddamn business!"

"Yet meanwhile you've made a tramp and a criminal out of Carla."

"What do you want me to do?"

"You might tell the judge what you know."

"I couldn't do that!"

"If the judge knew she came to the Cities to marry you, only to have her find out you'd in the meantime married another girl, he might understand."

Oren kicked at the green grass.

Skippy shook his head. "Poor Carla, what she hasn't gone through. She must be blown out inside."

"I know. And you don't know how awful I feel about it."

"But not awful enough to go tell the judge what you know."

"Oh, God."

Skippy began to feel a bit sorry for the poor duffer. "That dark girl in the office, she okay for you?"

"Oh, yes. She's wonderful too. And after what's happened, I can see now I didn't deserve her either."

Skippy's eyes opened. He thought: "Well! Maybe this Oren fellow has his side of it too. Hmm. Make a fine point in a play sometime. A nice subtle touch." Skippy asked, "You're getting along with her okay then?"

"We're pumping along just fine."

"She pregnant?"

"Yes."

Skippy murmured. "Yes, millions of sperm at a crack. There's always bound to be one to get through."

"Now I got a question to ask you. What's this to you?"

"I got Carla's cherry. In bed she was as green as April grass."

Oren turned white again. His eyes almost bugged out. "Why, you bastard you! It's *you* who've made a tramp out of Carla then."

Skippy held his head sideways. "Yeh. That's why I'm gonna try to help that poor gal."

Oren stood shaking. The wind kept tousling the dark hair on his forehead.

CHAPTER TWENTY-ONE

SKIPPY

Back in his room in the Saint Peter Hotel, Skippy sat in his chair wondering what to do next.

"I've got to be careful how I go about this. If I go to the judge, he might ask too many questions. Like, what do I do for a living. No, I've got to find somebody else who'll go see the judge for Carla." He twirled his thumbs. "And I don't want to spill the beans for Carla either. She wants to get home without anybody finding out what happened."

When he went down to dinner, he bought himself a new *Chronicle* hoping to find a followup story on Carla's case. He read the paper as he ate his T-bone steak: world news, local news, funnies, sports, financial section, want ads. No mention of Carla. He folded up the paper.

He was sipping his tea when his eye fell on an item on the top fold of the paper. Elmer Dillman, county commissioner, was quoted as saying that social services for the elderly and the crippled were in danger of being neglected while the nation concentrated on the war effort. "We must defeat the Axis powers, Hitler and Hirohito and Mussolini, yes. But at the same time we can ill afford to neglect the indigent and still think of ourselves as a humane civilization."

Skippy set down his cup. "He's the one to see. A do-gooder."

Returning to his room, Skippy looked up Elmer Dillman in the Minneapolis telephone directory.

"Hello?" Dillman had a warm voice.

Skippy introduced himself, then said, "Say, I've got something important I wanna talk to you about. Could I come over?"

"It couldn't wait until tomorrow?"

"No. I don't want to talk about it in your office. I don't want nobody, but nobody, to overhear us."

"I'm busy with my family tonight. I promised my boy I'd watch him in his school play."

"Lemme ask you, did you read in the paper about the girl who's in jail because she wouldn't tell the judge who she was?"

"I did happen to read that."

"I know who she is."

There was a pause. Finally Dillman said, "Just a minute."

Skippy could hear Dillman explain gently to his son why he couldn't go to the play, that something important had come up about a poor lost girl.

Dillman came back on the phone. "Okay. I'll be home."

The taxi pulled up in front of a large two-story white house surrounded by a white picket fence with the lot running down to the bank of the Mississippi. The downtown lights of Minneapolis lay reflected on the river as though they were several galaxies of stars, weaving up and down, appearing and disappearing and then reappearing.

Skippy rang the bell.

The door opened and a friendly round-headed man wearing rimless glasses greeted him. The man's brown hair was parted down the middle and slicked back. "Come in." There was an odd awkwardness about the man. He had to drag his right leg along. Also his right arm seemed stiff. Dillman had had a stroke.

The two men, fellow cripples, hobbled into the living room and sat down across from each other, Dillman on a black leather davenport and Skippy on a chair, a coffee table between them.

Dillman had to lift his right hand with his left hand to place it on his knee. "You said you knew who she was."

"Before I give you her real name, I want you to promise me that you won't tell the judge. You see, my guess is she's so ashamed about what she's done she'll never go home if the news gets out. She's a proud gal. What I want is for someone to just go to the judge and tell him to trust you that you'll make sure she does go home to pick up her life where she left off. See whad I mean?"

The honed edges of Dillman's glasses sharpened the gleam in his light-blue eyes. The eyes appeared to have no lashes. There was in his eyes the knowledge that he someday might have another accident upstairs. "I know Judge Roker. Generally he's a good man. And he might listen to me. But for some reason I've never been able to understand, this superintendent of the Home School for Girls, this Veta Gulickson, has a hold on him of some kind."

Skippy leaned forward. "Is the judge screwing Veta?"

Dillman laughed. It was a wonderful releasing laugh, as if he were a mild god sitting on a little hill contemplating the sexual follies of his countrymen, follies he no longer had to worry about himself. "Maybe he is at that."

"We should all be allowed one mistake. Not that we mean to make it, but when we make it, then a little mercy."

"I agree. Tell me what you know."

Skippy told him.

"Carla let you in on all this?"

"Yes. And this morning I went over to Fort Snelling and burned Oren Prince with what I knew."

"Did he agree with her story?"

"Yes. I felt kind'f sorry for him afters. The woman he married is a peach too. She's pregnant."

"So that explains that. Hmm." Dillman thought some more. A little smile, wise and patient, edged his full lips. "When you're young and ready for love, it's hard to see past wet lips."

"Yeh, when the front ends of our alimentary tracts touch each other, a lot of strange things happen."

A door opened to one side and a handsome tall woman with striking yellow hair entered carrying a tray with hot coffee and cups and saucers and chocolate cookies. She set it all on the coffee table.

"Esther, how nice." Dillman looked at Skippy. "This is my wife. Esther, this is Mr. Kempner."

Esther's eyes were sweet green grapes. "I hope you like coffee."

Skippy said, "You found my weak spot."

"Anything else?"

Dillman shook his head. "Perfect. Thanks a lot."

Smiling, Esther left, tall and lovely.

Dillman sipped his coffee and had himself a bite of chocolate cookie. After a moment he lifted his light-blue eyes and fixed them on Skippy. "Tell me, what's your real interest in all this?"

"She got a raw deal and I believe in fair play."

Dillman continued to fix his eyes on Skippy. They were suddenly the eyes of a man who was tough, inscrutable.

"No, really," Skippy continued. Dillman was never going to find out from him that he'd slept with Carla. "You see, I too once got the shitty end of a stick"—Skippy glanced down at his stump—"and so naturally I've always had an eye out for hard-luckers."

Dillman's glance drifted down to his own right hand and leg.

Skippy waited. He'd almost talked too much.

Dillman sighed. "All right. And now I've got to make sure that this Tracy in the newspaper is your Carla Simmons."

CHAPTER TWENTY-TWO

DILLMAN

The next morning Dillman dragged himself out to his car and one-handed and one-footed drove to his space in the parking area under the courthouse. He took the elevator up to his floor.

Seated at his honey-blond desk at last, he picked up his black phone. "Martha, get me Justin Teague, will you?" Teague was the district attorney. In a moment, Teague was on the wire with his world-weary Irish voice. Dillman listened a few seconds, eyes blinking behind his rimless glasses, finally with a laugh broke in. "Justin, I don't know what I'd do without your citified bullshit. What I want to know is, have you put that case of the State versus Tracy Last-Name-Unknown on the court docket yet? You know, the gal that hit Veta Gulickson over the head with her own shoe?"

"No, as a matter of fact, I haven't."

"Don't. You free this morning?"

"I can see you in a half hour or so."

"Good. Can I first go down and visit this Tracy?"

"Sure. I'll have my gal call them to let you in." Teague paused on the other end of the line. "You know, if this Tracy is a friend of yours, she's damn lucky she didn't blunder into Veta's bedroom when it was Judge Roker's night there."

"So that's the way the wind blows."

"Yeh. That's why I wasn't in a rush about it."

"Good."

Dillman shuffled out to the elevator and took it up to the county jail on the top floor. In a few moments he found himself seated on the lower bunk in Carla's cell, he on one end and she on the other.

The young girl had washed her hands and face, had combed her hair. She looked at him shyly.

"I'm Elmer Dillman. County Commissioner. I want to help you, but I have to know something." He looked around carefully to let her know he didn't mean for anyone to overhear them. "Your name is really Carla Simmons, isn't it?"

Her eyes opened in a frightened stare. "How . . . ?"

"You know Skippy Kempner? A cripple?"

Her blue eyes cleared. "He told you!"

"You really are Carla Simmons then?"

"Yes."

"Good. Don't be afraid. I'm not going to tell anybody. Neither Judge Roker nor Veta Gulickson."

"Nobody must know!"

"How come you hit Veta over the head?"

"When it came over me what I'd really done, I wanted to get home as fast as I could. But then just as I got hold of the keys she woke up."

"But did you have to hit her?"

"What else could I do? She would have stopped me."

"Didn't it occur to you that maybe sneaking into her room was wrong?"

"Sure. But I felt the sooner I got away from all this big city stuff, the quicker I could get it all behind me. Get back to my old life. Now I know it was wonderful."

Dillman studied her as he talked. He liked her. "What do you want to be?"

"Painter. An artist."

"Your father is a sort of artist too, isn't he?"

Carla looked at him puzzled.

"He's a stone mason, not? I've seen some of his work."

"You have?"

"I was born and raised in Hazard, and I often drive through Whitebone on my way home to see my folks."

Carla's face opened in a wide rich white smile. She was with a friend at last. Her shoulders relaxed. "Dillman. I think I remember hearing that name somewhere."

"I had a brother who was quite a baseball pitcher."

"That's where."

Dillman liked her more and more. "Who's your pastor?"

"Reverend Holly."

"Oh yes. Presbyterian Church, right?"

"Yes."

Dillman lifted his right hand off his right knee and placed it on the left. Both his right limbs had begun to tingle in their sockets. "Carla, I'm going to make one call to Reverend Holly about you. But I'm not going to tell him that I met you in jail. It's just that I want to make sure for myself. Because then I can really help you. Okay?"

Carla groaned pleasure. "Oh, it will be so wonderful if I can go back home without anybody knowing."

Dillman nodded. "Just be patient until you hear from me."

"Thank you so much."

Dillman pushed himself upright with a powerful left hand on his left knee. He called the jailer to let him out. With a smile at Carla, he shuffled off for his office again.

His secretary got Reverend Holly on the phone long distance. Dillman told the reverend who he was, and was surprised to learn the reverend knew about him, local boy made good in Twin Cities politics. Dillman asked him what he knew about Carla Simmons.

Reverend Holly's voice sharpened. "Her father and mother have been quite worried about her. They haven't heard from her since she left to get married."

"Ah, yes. What I want to know is, what kind of church member was she?"

Reverend Holly's voice crackled in the receiver. "Why, a fine devout girl. Sang in the choir. Was a confessing member of the church. Why do you ask?"

"Carla will tell you all in good time. Thanks very much. Good-bye." Dillman hung up.

The girl was looking better all the time. She was worth fighting for. Veta was going to have to back down. Veta owed him one. She'd been a mean bitch in several county cases.

Dillman next headed for Teague.

Belve, Teague's secretary, waved him on into Teague's office.

"There you are," Teague said, running a hand through his silver hair, tipping back in his swivel chair.

Dillman stood a moment in the doorway and looked across to where Teague sat in the corner farthest from the door. A lightgreen carpet led from the door to the front of Teague's desk. "You know, Justin, every time I come into this office and I look at that mile-long green carpet of yours, I get the funny feeling that if you had just a little more power, you'd enjoy being Hitler."

"Ho. Irishmen are anarchists. Never."

"The Irish are being pretty friendly with Hitler these days."

"That's because the damned English have been oppressing us since time began."

Dillman shuffled toward Teague's desk and drew up a chair. "About this girl Tracy. I want you to set her free."

"You know her then?" The skin around Teague's nostrils had a bluish skimmilk look as though he might have a cold. His lightgreen eyes had a touch of pink in the corners.

"I know her family. This is what happened." Dillman, not giving names, told what he knew.

"You know all this for a fact?"

"My life on it."

"Hmm."

"Look, we can't send that girl to the Women's Penitentiary all because Veta got zonked over the head."

"Yeh, that damned Veta and her hots."

"Justin, I say it again. We cannot let that girl go to the Women's Pen. We've got to let that girl go back home. And we've got to do it in such a way that nobody ever finds out what kind of mess she inadvertently got herself into."

"So her boyfriend betrayed her, the son of a bitch."

"Yes, he did."

Teague got out a white handkerchief and slowly blew his sore nose. "All right. After I've had a look at her myself, and if I like her, I'll dismiss the action that's been brought into District Court. But, of course, that doesn't end her troubles. The girl is then again in the hands of Judge Roker of Juvenile Court."

"I know. I'll take it from there. Thanks."

Dillman went back to his office. He sat and looked out of his windows onto downtown Minneapolis, at black tar roofs of the lower buildings, at the high Bell Telephone Building, at the spearing Foshay Tower.

Finally it came to him what to do. A smile worked along the edges of his lips.

He called Teague again. "Justin, we know Judge Roker is getting into Veta. I don't suppose they actually cohabit in that apartment of hers in the Home School for Girls. And I don't suppose they'd copulate at his home, what with that battleaxe of a wife he's got. Right?"

"Elmer, where is this line of questioning taking us?"

Dillman laughed. "I want to know where they do their screwing."

"What do you have in mind?"

"I want to walk in on them in *flagrante delicto*."

"Ha! While the crime is blazing, eh?"

"Yeh. That way I might catch Veta in a forgiving frame of mind."

"That's a form of blackmail."

"Not really. It's more like checkmate."

"Well, I can't plead privileged information." Teague allowed himself a laugh. "But one of our finest, you know, Officer Truax, used to hobnob with her at her hideout. But then she switched to the judge and our boy was out. He knew where she had her hideout—"

"Goddammit, Justin, here you're giving me a whole lot of blarneyshit again. What I want to know is, where is it?"

"She's got a cabin on Lake Opal in Wisconsin."

Dillman blinked. "My God, the Mann Act. If somebody wanted to be mean they could raise a big stink about it."

"Yeh, I thought of that too."

"Thanks, Justin. I owe you another."

"It's okay. You're so far behind I won't even bother to collect on this one."

Dillman hung up. His right arm hurt in its socket again; it had set too long in one position. He picked it up and manipulated it a few times. That felt better.

What night would Roker and Veta be most apt to go out to Lake Opal? It wouldn't be a weekend because Roker would have to spend that with the family. It'd probably be in the middle of the week sometime. "Betcha it's Thursday. By God, tonight!" Thursday was the usual club night for men. "I'll bet a dollar to a doughnut he uses that as an excuse."

Dillman dialed the judge's chambers. When a male clerk answered, he said, "This is Elmer Dillman. I was wondering . . . would the judge be busy tonight? I'd like to drop around at his home about a private matter."

The clerk had a heavy voice. "I'm afraid the judge can't tonight. Tonight he goes bowling."

"Oh. I'm sorry. Well, thanks." Dillman hung up.

Bowling?

He next called Veta. "Veta? Elmer Dillman. Say, as your county supervisor, could I drop in on your operation there tonight?"

Veta's voice came throaty over the line. "Oh, Elmer, darling, I'm so sorry, but tonight's my night to go bowling."

Dillman smiled, eyes crinkling up at the corners. Bowling? "Okay. I'll catch you some other time. Thanks."

Dillman went down to the Courthouse Cafe across the street and had himself some steaming wiener schnitzel and apple pie and coffee. From a booth he called his wife to let her know he wouldn't be home until late. Then he got his car out of the parking area under the courthouse, filled up with gas at the corner filling station, got himself a map of Wisconsin. He studied the map and saw that if he took Highway 12 out of St. Paul through Hudson, Wisconsin, and then at Hammond took a country road straight north some twenty miles, he'd hit Lake Opal.

He found Veta's cabin with a little luck. In a roadside cafe near Lake Opal, Dillman overheard a local plumber say something to the waiter that caught his ear. The plumber was having a cup of coffee at the counter.

"Damnedest thing I ever ran into. You know this woman from Minneapolis, the one who's got this cabin out here? Well, she's been complaining about how her sewer line is always plugging up? Twice I had to go out there with my snake to see if I could root it out. But I came up with nothing. So this morning I decided to dig down to the septic tank and see what the hell was going on." The plumber took a sip of coffee and started to laugh. "You'll never guess what I found."

"Yeh?"

"It was full of blown-up condoms. Gas rising from fermenting crap blew them up after they'd been flushed down there. When I lifted off the cement lid to that septic tank, they popped up around me. A couple of 'em took off like great big fat geese and floated away."

"Naw!"

A few minutes later Dillman drove carefully around the lake, following the road closest to the water, at last found a lane with fresh service truck tracks going in and coming out. He drove in and got out of the car and dragged himself around the side of the cottage and looked down toward the lake. There it was. Halfway down the slope lay the fresh signs of a septic tank digging. Veta's place.

He stood a while looking through the tall maples. Their leaves had an aged green look about them, and here and there a single leaf, one in millions, had turned a ripe grape red. Beyond the trees the lake was as smooth as a bared eyeball. It had been aptly named Lake Opal. The nearest cabin was a mile away, on the curving far side to the east. The shores of the little jewel of a lake were still mostly untouched.

He trudged around to the front and was pleased to see it had only one step onto an enclosed porch. He found the screen door open. Checking the lock, he saw he could jimmy it easily in case Veta and Judge Roker decided to lock it. He next checked the main door and found it locked. It had the usual Yale lock plus a dead-bolt arrangement. If tonight they also locked that, he was out of luck. He'd have to ram it with his good shoulder and break in. Well, he'd wait and see.

He next checked to see if the porch floorboards creaked. They didn't.

He went back to Hammond and for dinner had himself walleye fish, baked potato, salad, and a cup of dark tea. The butter on the potato and on the dark bread was so delicious he asked the waitress if it was local butter.

"They make it over in Baldwin. Where all those Hollanders live. They know how to produce rich cream. They run Guernsey cows in with their Frisian-Holsteins."

He nodded. It was what the Frisians did back home in Hazard.

He waited until eleven o'clock, then drove back to Lake Opal. He pulled up a good hundred yards from the entrance to Veta's place and closed the door of his car quietly, with a light click. Then he started out, shuffling along very slowly, leading with his left leg and then dragging his right up even with it, and then the left leg first again. It was slow going, all the more so as he had to be careful the dragging foot didn't make too much racket on the crushed rock drive.

He stopped for breath when he finally got to the screen door. He puffed with his mouth open to keep the sound of it down.

Breath caught, he tried the screen door. Locked. She was there then. He looked around in the darkness. Peering intently, eyes wide open as possible, he made out the vague glint of nickel on a car radiator. Two of them. Judge Roker was there too.

Dillman got out his pocket knife, opened the small blade with the bottle-cap opener on the back side of it, and then gently pried it around in the crack over the lock. He kept up the pressure on the doorknob until, click, it opened. The hooked edge of the bottle-cap opener had done the trick. He closed the knife and dropped it back in his pocket.

He stepped lightly up on the porch with his good leg, eased his bad leg up after it, and then slowly moved across the porch. There were no creaks.

As Dillman was about to try the doorknob of the main door, a thought came to him. Already he could be accused of breaking and entering the way he'd sprung the screen door lock. He'd better not compound it bursting in through the main door. He stood very still. He had to make his next move in such a way that they couldn't strike back at him.

A smile spread over his face. It came to him what to do. He'd enter the house like some neighbor might back home.

He tried the doorknob. Ah. It wasn't locked. The two had apparently decided that a locked screen door was enough. He took a very slow breath, deep, smiled some more, and then, quite casually, pushed the door open and called in, "Anybody t'home? This is Elmer Dillman." Then he reached in, found the light switch, and snapped it on. "Veta? You home?"

Desperate whispers in a room off to one side. Rustling noises of bedclothes being rearranged.

"Veta?"

Silence.

The furnishings in the living room were mostly of rustic design, a lot of pine wood with fat cushions, a halved log serving as a coffee table, several rag rugs, a fieldstone fireplace. Ashes still glowed pink in the grate. There was a good smell of burning oak in the place. The walls, age-darkened knotty pine, had taken on a warm golden hue. A long bank of windows looked out upon the lake.

"Veta?"

More desperate whispers.

Dillman closed the door behind him. He said aloud, as though talking to himself, "She must be here somewhere."

A loud whisper, Veta's. "I know I locked that screen door."

Judge Roker whispered back, "But you couldn't've—"

"Shhh!"

Dillman had to work to keep from laughing out loud. "Is that you there too, Judge?"

Judge Roker spoke up. "Yeh, Elmer, it's me all right. Just a minute." Then the judge said to Veta, "Shh yourself. Let's get up and see what he wants."

Dillman settled into an armchair facing the bedroom. "Take your time. I'm in no rush."

Presently they emerged from the bedroom, both wearing blue bathrobes, sandals, and abashed thickened faces.

Veta quickly went around and snapped on some table lamps, then went over and clicked off the overhead light.

Judge Roker threw a couple of small logs on the still-warm ashes. Almost immediately a flame began to lick at the bark of the bottom log.

The two settled across from Dillman, each in an easy chair.

Veta finally looked Dillman in the eye. "Wasn't that outer screen door locked? I'm positive I locked it."

Dillman raised his good shoulder. "Well, I got in here."

"Very strange."

Judge Roker kept combing his blond hair back with shaky fingers. "What do you want?"

Dillman said, "Justin Teague informs me that he has dismissed the action against a girl named Tracy in District Court. Judge, that puts her right back in your Juvenile Court."

Judge Roker's brows pinched together darkly. "Why did he do that?"

"Because I asked him to. That order to dismiss should reach your desk by ten o'clock tomorrow. And I'd like for you to dismiss all action against that girl by eleven o'clock."

"What!" Veta cried. "When that girl tried to kill me?"

Dillman said, "I don't see you wearing any bandages. So she couldn't have whacked you all that hard."

Rage thickened Veta's face. "Roker! If you let that girl go, I'll never speak to you again. I want her in the pen."

Judge Roker's blue eyes moved from Veta to Dillman to Veta. "Yes, what that girl did should not go unpunished."

Dillman said, "Well now, Judge, I know who she is and I'd like to ask you—"

"You do?"

"Yes. And I want her placed in my custody. Once that's done, I'm going to send her home to her parents. She is a good girl. She was valedictorian of her class this past spring."

Judge Roker swore. "I'm going to haul you into court and have you tell us what you know about her."

Dillman shook his head. "That is privileged information. I'm handling her case as a lawyer and friend."

"Oh."

Veta raged. "Roker!"

Dillman leaned forward. He lifted his right hand with his left and placed it across his lap. "Look, Judge. During the many years that I've observed you, in court, in private life . . . I've seen how you always stressed God, the Bible, the American flag, the sanctity of the home. I've observed how concerned, even tender, you have been when dealing with some of the poor creatures who've had to stand before your bench. You've stressed these things so that troubled juveniles could become better citizens."

Veta was wild. "Roker!"

Dillman went on. "So now I'm requesting that in this matter of the girl named Tracy you be a Christian, that you follow the Golden Rule. One should do unto others as he would have others do unto him."

Judge Roker held up a hand. "You don't have to recite the Bible to me."

Dillman had to admire the spunk of the judge. Here he was, caught fornicating with the very woman who wanted the girl Tracy sent to the women's penitentiary, and yet he was acting as though nothing had happened. "Actually, Judge, the only crime that has been committed here in this case was committed by you, when you sent this poor confused and brokenhearted girl to the Home School for Girls."

"But why couldn't she tell me her name?"

"It was bad enough she herself knew she'd done something wrong. But to add on top of that the shame of having everybody at home know what she'd done—"

"I was trying to be nice to her."

Dillman shook his head. "You could have taken her into your chambers and there had a private talk with her. Where she probably would have told you everything. Yes, Judge, some of your juvenile court sessions are too open to the public."

"Well . . ."

Veta said, "Roker, if you let that girl go—"

"Shut up!" Judge Roker threw Veta a revealing look. "Forgiving is the larger part of justice, you know." Then he looked Dillman in the eye. "All right, I'll put her on probation."

"No," Dillman said, looking momentarily down at his dead arm, "no, I want her forgiven totally. No charges of any kind. The slate wiped clean." He lifted his good hand and pointed a finger at the judge. "I want you to have Big Kate bring Tracy around to my office by eleven o'clock tomorrow morning. And I'll take it from there. Okay?"

Veta scratched at Judge Roker's arm.

Judge Roker withdrew his arm. "All right. Done. And now if you don't mind, I'd like to go back to sleep." He got up and headed for the bathroom.

"Thanks, Judge."

Back in his car, heading for the Twin Cities again, and home, Dillman finally allowed himself a soft laugh. "Yessir. Not once, not once, did I mention, or refer to, where and how I found them. Now I'd call that permissible blackmail."

As he rolled out of the dark countryside into the lighted streets of the city, thinking about Carla Simmons and the kind of future she still might dream of having, he thought of the dream he'd once had. As a boy down in Hazard, Siouxland, where his father had been a tenderhearted minister, he'd been sure that someday he was going to become The President of the United States of America. He had aimed his whole life for this . . . until that one certain morning when he'd awakened in bed to find he couldn't move his right arm or leg.

"Yes, and the hell of it is, I'd have made a great President. Better than the one we have now."

The next morning promptly at eleven o'clock, Big Kate ushered Carla Simmons into Dillman's office.

"Thanks, Kate."

Big Kate's face was all smiles. She approved of what had happened. She gave Carla's arm a pinch.

Carla smiled abashed down at her hands.

Big Kate touched her once more and left.

Dillman got to his feet. "Have a seat."

Carla sat down modestly. Her purse had been given back to her and she held it in her lap. She clutched it tightly.

"Well, we did it, Carla," he said, sitting down.

"Yes. And I'm most grateful. Thank you so very much."

"What are you going to do now?"

"Take the train home."

"Good luck."

Outside the windows pigeons fluttered along the sunny side of several chimneys.

"Carla, may I suggest something?"

"Please do, Mr. Dillman."

"When you get home, write Judge Roker a letter of thanks." Dillman picked up a memo sheet and handed it to her. "I've written down his home address."

She glanced at the memo and then carefully, neatly, folded it and slipped it into her purse. "I'll do that."

"And see Reverend Holly."

"All right."

"Shall I call a taxi for you?"

"No. I want to walk it. The depot isn't far from here, Big Kate says. I want to remember something good about the Twin Cities. After all, they are the big city for us."

Dillman was smiling at her. He swung back and forth several times in his swivel chair. "Have you thought what you might tell your parents when you get home?"

A frown darkened her open blond face. "I'm scared about that. It's a long way home when you're headed for trouble there."

"Naturally."

Her face worked up. "I'm always so ready to panic now."

"I'd tell them everything."

"Everything? Even about finding me that way in the hotel room?" She turned red.

"Well, maybe not that. But I would be quite frank about what Oren did to you." He thought to himself: "She has a real sense of shame. Blush away, girl. It becomes you."

She looked down at her blue purse.

"Will you write me now and then? Tell me how you're getting along?"

She nodded, eyes filling with tears.

"Technically, the judge has placed you in my custody, but I'm not going to bother with that in a formal way. Just drop me a note now and then."

"I will."

"Don't worry. And when you decide to go to college here someday, look me up."

"I will."

"But your best friend is your mother."

"Mother! She'll have a fit. Conniptions."

"She might surprise you." He smiled some more. "There's one other thing."

"Yes?"

"When you get home—"

"Go see a doctor?"

"—go see a doctor."

They'd said it at the same time. It made them both smile.

Carla held out the pinky of her right hand.

He looked puzzled at the extended finger.

Laughing she explained, "When two people say the same thing at the same time, they're supposed to hook their pinkies and spit over their left shoulder."

"Okay," he said, extending the pinky of his good hand. Just before they touched, a vivid spark leaped out between their fingers. "But spit over your left shoulder?"

"Well, maybe not in this neat office." A merry look appeared in her lightblue eyes.

"Good idea."

She stood up. "I mussent take any more of your time. Thank you oh so much."

He got up too. "Don't mention it. And good luck."

"Thanks."

After she'd gone, he sat down and stared out over the city again, the city he'd come to love. He wondered how much longer he had yet to live in it. Every now and then he had the funny feeling that another thunderclap was about to burst within his brain.

CHAPTER TWENTY-THREE

CARLA

As Carla started up the walk, Mother already had the door open for her. Mother said, "Just in time for dinner."

Carla couldn't find her tongue. She stepped inside.

Dad was sitting in front of the radio listening to the war news. He didn't hear the door close. But his keen eyes spotted something off to one side. He rose to his feet all in one move. "Carla! I thought I smelled your perfume."

Mother snorted. "That nose of yours."

Ivoria came running out of her room. "Hey, where's Oren?"

Carla had to fight off a cry. "Well, I guess I might as well just come right out with it. Oren stood me up."

Mother crossed her arms. "He did? Well! Good riddance then. I never did like him."

Dad's eyes took on a hollow white look.

The look instantly reminded Carla of the war-shock look she'd seen in the eyes of the three men in the Ox-Cart Bar. For the first time she truly understood what it had meant for her father to have been at the front.

Ivoria stared at Carla. "You're changed."

Carla laughed lamely. "I'm still your same old sister."

Mother asked, "Where's your suitcase?"

Carla said, "In Oren's office."

"You didn't think to take it along with you?"

"I was so mad I left it with him."

"You've been gone a week."

Dad said, "Let's all sit down now and take it easy."

Carla brushed down her dress in back and settled on the davenport facing the fireplace.

Mother caught the gesture and studied to herself a moment. "I'd still like to know what—"

"Uk uk!" Dad said. "If Carla wants to tell us, she'll get around to it in her own good time."

Carla said, "Well, I just hung around to see the sights." To herself Carla thought: "There I go, lying."

"But where did you stay?" Mother persisted.

Ivoria broke in. "Wasn't we supposed to eat?"

Mother popped up from the chair. "That's right. I bet all the water on the potatoes is boiled right out of the pot."

They were into the meal, Dad already having a second helping of meat and potatoes, when Mother pronounced, "Well, me, I'm glad it turned out this way. And if anybody wants to gossip about it with me, I know just what I'm going to say."

Dad looked sideways from the head of the table. "I don't think you have to worry much. It'll blow over in a week. In little towns like this, the first week everybody's in a swivet over it, then the second week they've forgotten it. The first week you pay with a little shame, the second week you get cake."

Carla had trouble eating. No matter how she moved around on her chair, she couldn't get rid of a hollow feeling in her belly.

Mother asked, "Well, Carla, what next?"

"I'm going to college and study art."

"Where will you get the money?"

"I thought I'd first go to work for a while and then go to Blue Wing Junior College."

Ivoria said, "Well, me, I'm not going to forgive Oren. I liked the other Carla better."

Carla thought: "Nothing gets past Ivoria. Women know."

Mother got up and poured tea. When she came to Carla, she put her hand on Carla's shoulder firmly.

Carla leaned her cheek down on Mother's hand. "Thanks, Mom."

Dad caught the gesture. He fixed Carla with a look that seemed to come right out of the center of his head. "Don't worry. When all's said and done, all the bricks will look like they're in place. Especially if you stand off a block."

The next day, Saturday, Carla walked over to the Presbyterian Church. She found Reverend Holly in his office. She sat down in the usual red armchair. The smell of old moldy psalters was still in the basement.

Reverend Holly leaned back in his swivel chair. "What happened?"

"Oren ran into a beautiful girl and just couldn't wait. She's going to have his baby."

"Not really!"

"Yes. That's what I get for waiting."

"But if that's all the regard he had for you, you're better off without him. What he had for you must've not been very deep."

"She was very beautiful."

Reverend Holly fiddled with his fingers, one moment building a church with them, the next moment cracking his knuckles. "Uh, I had an odd call from Elmer Dillman about you. What was that all about?"

"Oh, I made a little fuss. And he smoothed things over."

"Is it anything I should know about?"

"It's over and done. And I'm back home safe."

"I mean, something you need to square with your Lord?"

"I can handle it. But Mr. Dillman told me to call on you, and so now I have. Everything's all right."

"You know of course the whole town's talking."

"I don't care. I'm just happy not to have Mother mad at me."

Reverend Holly mused to himself. "All right. I won't push any further. But if you ever feel you need to talk about it, come to me."

"I will."

"Do you think you can sing in the choir tomorrow?"

"May I?"

"They'll all be looking at you, wondering, and so on."

"I'd love to sing. Then they can get their staring over with the first Sunday."

Carla was walking past the windows of the Whitebone *Press* when Ian McEachern spotted her. He bounced out of his swivel chair and sallied outside after her. "Carla?"

Carla resigned herself to some more commiseration.

"I heard what Oren did to you." A flush mounted up over McEachern's nose. "I never did like him dating you." His lightblue eyes darted from her lips to her eyes then to her lips. "What are you going to do now?"

"Look for a job."

"How about working for me? I could use another part-time society editor. I offered you that job once before. My friend Tom Lovinger over at Great Plains Manufacturing tells me you're good at design. You could help with layouts."

Carla wasn't sure she wanted to work for so explosive a man. "Well . . . I do need the work."

Carla did well at the job. Her simple prose fit the requirements of the newspaper. The weekly took on a classy look because of her eye for interesting typography.

For her eighteenth birthday, Mother baked a cake and Dad bought her a second-hand typewriter and Ivoria knitted her a pair of woolen mittens. They celebrated quietly at home. After a baked ham dinner, they sat around the fireplace sipping tea. It was almost a happy time.

Early in October Carla had a strange dream. There were footsteps in the dream and they were following her. No matter where she went, to church, to work, to the bathroom, there were the footsteps. When she whirled around, there was no one. It wasn't a ghost walking in her dreams either. It was a real person who somehow always managed to dodge out of sight just as Carla whipped around.

The dream left her with an uneasy feeling of guilt. Brooding over that she remembered there was still one thing left to do. She'd promised Elmer Dillman she would go see a doctor. After that spark had jumped between their pinkies, she owed him that.

With some reluctance she dropped in on their family doctor, Sherman Manning. The nurse ushered her into a little white examining room.

Soon Dr. Manning was sitting before her on a rolling nickel stool, holding a thin folder with her name on it. He glanced inside the file briefly, then looked up. The overhead light gave his cheeks a hollow look, made his fuzzy head seem even more bald. "Well, Carla."

She found herself telling him a little about what had happened to her in the Twin Cities. Not all of it, but enough for Dr. Manning to catch the drift.

He took a sample of her blood for a venereal disease test. Then he examined her.

"Am I all right?"

"Everything looks fine so far. Come back in five days for the lab report."

She swung her legs down from the stirrups. It surprised her she hadn't minded too much he'd seen her intimately. Two months before she hadn't wanted to have him fit her with a diaphragm.

He was about to leave the examining room when a thought struck him. "Maybe you'd better have the rabbit test too, huh?"

Carla shivered.

"When was the last time?"

"I haven't had my flowers since the end of August."

"I guess we better have one then."

When he'd finished, she asked, "How soon will we know about that test?"

"Couple of days. Come back Thursday afternoon."

"I thought maybe I'd missed the month before because of all the commotion."

"Sure, it happens."

Thursday afternoon, the paper out, she walked over to see Dr. Manning.

The nurse, smiling, it seemed specially, ushered Carla into the same white examining room as before. "Dr. Manning will be with you in a moment."

Carla settled on the examining table. There was a smell of mild acid about. Her eyes moved from the sink to a row of bottles to a framed certificate.

Had a life already started in her belly? She recalled the dream with those strange footsteps in it. Maybe it was a baby coming.

There was a rustling sound outside the door. That had to be Dr. Manning picking out her file from the slot on the door. She could sense that he was reading it before coming inside. Then the door opened and Dr. Manning stepped inside quietly. "How are you today?"

"Fine."

He settled on the rolling nickel stool. He opened the file an inch and looked inside. "Well, the lab reports on the VD are okay. But, better yet, your rabbit was cooperative."

She waited.

"You should come to full term around the eleventh of May. A spring baby."

Carla's ears heard the words. But her brain didn't want her ears to.

A baby? And she not married? A flock of blackbirds suddenly surged across the sky above her, in her brain, darkening her world. The sharp overhead light made the baby hair on Dr. Manning's bald head glisten. His blue eyes looked at her mildly, with neither commiseration nor approval; pure doctor. As she stared at him, she saw him melt down on the stool into a puddle of baby hair and pink flesh, and then a pair of blackbirds dove into her eyes.

When she came to, she was lying on the examination table. Dr. Manning was leaning over her, one hand holding her wrist, counting her pulse, the other hand lying coolly on her brow.

"I guess I fainted."

"Yes, you did."

A spring baby.

Dr. Manning said, "I suppose you'll tell the father?"

Which one?

"He'll want to know, won't he?"

Carla sat up very slowly. She had to grab hold of the sides of the examining table to steady herself. "I can't tell him."

"I didn't mean Oren Prince. I meant the real one."

Carla shook her head. "I guess I didn't tell you everything. There was more than one."

"Oh."

"Yes. That's why it's so awful." She moaned. "What a terrible thing I did, to go berserk that night." She tolled her head. "This is what I get for it. The Christians are right."

Dr. Manning picked up her hand and gave it a warm squeeze. "Don't let them get you down. There are worse things than being an unwed mother, you know. Who knows, maybe that child you carry will be a great man. Many a great man has been born with a clouded past."

"Or a great woman."

"Atta girl. Maybe you're going to be the mother of a great soprano."

"Or the first woman President."

Dr. Manning's smile widened. "Carla, you've got the goods. You'll do."

"But what am I going to tell my poor mother now?"

"Your mother will understand."

CHAPTER TWENTY-FOUR

CARLA

Carla went for a walk out into the country, taking the Blue Mounds road north out of town. It was a narrow sunny day in late October. The yellow leaves of the ash trees gave the tasseled cornfields a look of hammered gold.

Suppose she decided to get rid of the baby; how would she go about it? Go to an abortion mill south of Sioux Falls? How would she account for her absence from home and work?

Her nose picked up new smells: stuffy mouselike smell of gravel dust, sugarlike fragrance of old mown grass along the road, dried-semen smell of upthrust ripe ears in the cornfields.

She could still taste the grapefruit she'd had for breakfast. A halved grapefruit first thing in the morning made the rest of breakfast taste sweet. But if one had grapefruit after a bowl of sweetened oatmeal, goodness, how sour the grapefruit tasted then. Or if one ate even a ripe plum after a piece of cake, how puckery sour the plum tasted. She found herself making up a scale of tastes, from sour to sweet: grapefruit, apricot, plum, apple, angel food cake.

The dream she'd had that morning, the one about how she was found floating in the town swimming pool, drowned, with little minnows swimming into her open mouth and coming out of her navel, one after the other, until at last a large snarling pickerel shot into her mouth, where it swallowed all the minnows it could catch up with, then, too fat to make it through her, stayed stuck in her stomach where it kept getting fatter and fatter . . . wasn't that the limit? Where in God's name did such visions come from? It had made her feel, when she awakened, as though she'd just come out of a totally different world.

She felt a tug on her left side, and following the tug turned and stepped down into the ditch and then knelt down in the tall bluestem grass. Her hands seemed to fold of themselves and her face lifted up of itself, eyes closed. She began to pray: "Father, I've sinned. I've been filthy. Sometimes I feel so ashamed. I feel so guilty I sometimes have the skitters all day long. Sometimes I have to pee every ten minutes." Carla pinched back an impulse to relieve herself right there in the ditch.

"Oh, Father, when I once had such wonderful dreams of becoming a good artist and of doing good in the world . . . and now this? Oh, my Father, if it be at all possible, let this burden pass from me: nevertheless, not as I will, but as Thou wilt."

A car came whizzing up; slowed when the driver saw her in the ditch; then slowly picked up speed again and went on.

"Yes, I have sinned and I'm sorry. I'm not asking for a miscarriage. The poor baby can't help it that it was conceived. It was not its doing. Father, whatever I do with it, may it never accuse me of having done the wrong thing."

A soft wind rustled through the tall bluestem beside her. One of the taller grasses touched her nose and lips.

"Yet if I must bear this burden, give me strength in the days ahead. My mother turned out to be very understanding when I first came home. But now with this baby coming, I don't know how she's going to take it. She just might go out of her mind. I will need great strength to tell her. Help me. In Jesus' name I ask it. Amen."

When she opened her eyes, she found sunflowers staring at her.

She got to her feet, climbed out of the ditch, and continued home.

When she came to the first house at the north end of Whitebone, she decided, all of a sudden, to go see her father first, while he was at work. As a little girl she'd often watched him set brick and stone. Dad was putting a new fireplace in Meddy's grandmother's magnificent old house on the hill near the town tower.

She took Barth up to Kniss and then walked south on Kniss. Out of the corner of her eye she caught movement in the various curtains in the kitchens along the street. Most housewives would be making noon dinner for their husbands. They'd all be thinking: "There goes that Simmons girl, stood up by that minister's son."

She found Dad's cement mixer standing in the carriage port of the Queen house. She only had to follow the trail of occasional drops of cement spilled from his wheelbarrow to find him in the basement. He was putting in the under support stones in the basement and from there would run the fireplace up through the floor in the music room. Light from the gaping hole in the floor fell on his graying head.

Dad smelled her before her saw her. "What brings you here?"

"It's my day off. How's it going?"

"It's coming, it's coming." Dad knelt down and with his trowel slapped up a potch of wet gray cement and flished it on a row of fieldstones he'd already laid, a dab here, a dab there, and then with the point of his trowel neatly edged it all along three stones. He carefully set three more stones the size of grapefruit on the fresh cement and pushed them down into it, making the final adjustments by tinking the tops of the stones with the side of his trowel. Finished, he took the point of the trowel and deftly scraped off excess cement from the cracks and slapped that on top of the first stone for the next row.

Carla sat down on a folding stool. She marveled at Dad's skill. He did it all with such an easy motion and accuracy. It struck her that she and her father with their work were making the world a better and more beautiful place to live in. Dad's work might never be recognized for what it was, while she, if she hit it just right, might make a name for herself. She recalled his earlier remarks about stone masons, that if it were not for them, there'd be no lofty noble buildings, no arches of triumph.

Slowly the fireplace went up, stone by stone, each stone exactly put in place. Something of the same sort was going on in her belly. Cell by cell a baby was being built up in her womb, each cell taking up its exact right place in what would someday be a beautiful baby.

"Dad?"

He didn't hear her. Lately Dad had been more lost in himself.

"Dad? I'm going to have a baby."

"Pardon?"

"I'm going to have a baby."

The hand holding the trowel slowly lowered and a potch of fresh mud slid off the tip of it and hit the floor. Dad's eyes opened wide.

Carla was as astounded as he was to hear what her lips had just said. Something in her, dark and deep, not necessarily her conscience, seemed to know what was best to do.

"Couldn't you get out from under him?"

What a strange question that was.

Dad got hold of himself. "Sorry. That slipped out. I didn't mean it that way." Stooping, he scooped up the dropped mud and slapped it in place for the next row of fieldstones. He reached around and picked out a speckled granite stone, gray and pink, and set it in place. "Is Oren the father?"

"No." Carla saw something. "Dad! There's a mouse. Under your jacket there on the floor."

"Is that so?" A smile twisted down Dad's lips. "Well, we'll have to do something about that rascal." Dad went over and stomped on his jacket.

There was a light squeal; then silence. No more movement.

"Dad!"

Dad picked up another stone, a black one, and chunked it into place. "Maybe you should talk to your mother about your baby, not me." He didn't look at her. "Woman's business."

"I thought maybe I should tell you first so that together we could tell her."

"You ain't afraid of her now, are you?" Dad had a way of looking at one, first at what the eyes had to say, then the lips. He was an eye-looker as well as a lip-looker. "She might surprise you. Sometimes just when I think she's going to stick it into me, she comes on like a soft sponge."

"When Mother learns what really happened, she'll flip."

He shot her a look. "Who is the father then?"

"I don't know."

"What!" He stood with his mouth open, so far she could see the right lower tooth capped with gold. After a moment his eyes closed and he stood trembling, remembering something. Then he went back to laying stone.

Carla started to cry. "If you only knew how terrible I felt when I found out Oren had got married in the meantime. I guess I lost my head and—"

"Uk! Uk! God knows what I'd a done if some dame had stood me up. Fair is fair."

Carla wanted to hug her father.

"Nuh, you better run along and go take a nap. Now that you're going to be a mother you better get plenty of rest." A smile edged his thin lips. "And tonight after supper, when you tell Mother, don't let her push you around when she wants details."

Carla's head hurt. It was as though someone had caught her whole head in a nose twist, the kind men used on a horse's nose while shoeing it. She forced herself to eat a little mashed potatoes. Her throat made a clicking sound.

Mother sat like an alert brood hen at her end of the table nearest the kitchen. "If you don't like my cooking, you can take over as cook."

Dad wasn't eating heartily either. And Ivoria was building brown rivers with gravy in her mashed potatoes.

Mother humphed to herself. "A person would almost think you were having morning sickness."

Carla finally managed to say something. "Mother, when I first came home you were quite understanding. Uhh, I uh . . ."

Mother set her fork carefully across her plate. The overhead light emphasized her blond brows and rosy face.

The food Carla had just swallowed wanted to come out again. Tears began to stream down her cheeks. "Oh, Ma, I'm going to have a baby and I'm not married."

Ivoria looked up. "Will the baby be my sister then?"

Dad watched Mother.

Mother's eyes had the look of snow flying past a pair of blue windows. Slowly she got up, and taking a tissue from a pocket in her apron, she came over and dried the tears off Carla's face. "It isn't Oren's, is it?"

"No."

"I guessed as much."

"You guessed?"

"Revenge can be very sweet. I know all about it."

"Oh, Mother."

"Have you told the father?"

"No. He doesn't deserve to know."

Ivoria had a question. "Do you really need a father to have a baby?"

For a second Carla almost burst out with strangled laughter.

Mother said, "Ivoria, I don't want you to be talking to anybody in town about this, you hear?"

"All right, Mother."

"Until we figure out what to do. And after we do, we'll do it, and hold our heads high."

Carla almost exploded with relief.

Later, in her room and ready for bed, Carla wrote two letters. One was to Judge Kenneth Roker. She told him she was living with her parents, had a job with the local newspaper, was singing in the church choir again. The other was to Elmer Dillman, county commissioner. She told him the same thing, except that she added in a postscript that she was going to have a baby.

CHAPTER TWENTY-FIVE
CARLA

Carla next began to dream about snakes. At first it was harmless little garter snakes. In dream she'd be walking in a garden and they'd slither out from under the rose bushes and begin smiling comically at her.

Later on she dreamed about bullsnakes. Usually there were only two of them, male and female, and they were very stubborn about defending their right the lie on the warm stones on the Blue Mounds. They were fiends for eating field mice.

Finally she dreamed about a boa constrictor. In dream she met it while taking a walk in the country. The boa constrictor was lying stretched out in the dead fall grass, almost camouflaged, and it had the most wonderful snake smile, a curving slit up each side of its head, its eyes half-closed in glittering smirk. There was a tall stalk of a compass-plant nearby, and as she stood looking the boa constrictor began climbing the stalk and reached out its forked tongue at her. It made a few funny hhhuhing noises, as though some kind of voice were calling out of old water.

Then the snake dreams stopped.

Carla often caught herself making two unconscious gestures: slowly smoothing her hand over her belly and then right after brushing down her dress in back.

She ran into Bon Prince, Oren's brother, one day at the Palace Cafe. She was sitting alone in a corner having lunch when Bon, coming through the door, spotted her. He came over.

"May I join you?"

"Sit."

The waitress came by and he ordered a chef's salad.

They were almost finished, not having much to say, when suddenly she asked, "Do you ever hear from Oren?"

"Not really. Through Mother and Father a little."

"He's still got some of my things."

"That's Oren. Very forgetful."

She finished her glass of milk. "You haven't found yourself a girl yet, have you?"

"No, worse luck. But I've bought myself a house. On the north end of town. In that new development." Bon sipped at the last of his coffee. "Yes, when it's nice weather, I enjoy sitting on the edge of town, listening to the corn growing out in front of me in the country and the interest ticking behind me in the bank."

Oren was right about his brother.

Bon rippled his muscles. A wide white smile opened his swarthy face. "Maybe I should date you."

"No, thanks."

A week later the phone rang on her desk at the *Press*. It was Olaus Northey, station master, calling from the depot.

"There's a suitcase and a big bag here with your name on 'em."

As a form of self-punishment Carla decided to carry the suitcase and the bag home. People would talk, but so what. They'd be talking worse later on. Besides, maybe carrying the two heavy things might cause her to lose the baby. She had already decided, after many nights thinking about it in bed, that she was not going to have an abortion. But if she could lose it doing something natural, carrying heavy things, well, that was life.

Carrying the suitcase and the heavy bag, Carla found herself surprisingly strong. She only had to set them down once on the way home to catch her breath. The tiny baby in her was already demanding that her body be strong for the big day ahead.

Mother held the door open for her. "So, he finally had the goodness to send them back."

All through November and December, past Christmas, she kept waiting for morning sickness to appear. It never did. Instead she found herself becoming ravenously hungry in the mornings. Sometimes she had a double helping of bacon and eggs and toast. Plus sometimes a helping of cracked wheat cereal with honey and milk and white raisins. She noticed too that while the rest of the family might have sniffles and colds, she always felt wonderful.

Also in the mornings, upon awakening, she found herself craving a man. She felt ripe for it at last. She remembered that swoon she'd had with Dewain the sailor in the Radisson Hotel. "I'm going to fall out of the tree! Catch me!" Had she been made pregnant by Oren, what wonderful times they could be having by now.

"Well, that one time with Dewain will have to do me for a long time."

Tracy Cadwell stopped by. Tracy had come home for the holidays. She'd found herself a good job modeling in Sioux Falls. She came well-groomed, orange hair done up new-style, better fitting clothes, new way of sitting in a chair, new way of setting her feet together. Even her lips were reset. She was wearing a shiny yellow dress. It fit her in an easy loose way, hiding her full hips. Her bobby sox days were over. She was now gold glossy outside.

They were in the living room facing the fireplace, Carla on the davenport and Tracy in an easy chair, with Mother hovering in the kitchen making tea and getting ready to bring out the cake.

"Well, Tracy, who are you dating these days? Brent? Rueul?"

"I've long ago forgot about those two. I've got a new boyfriend." Tracy spoke in a controlled manner. Gone were the breathy spurts of words.

"What's he do?"

"Sells lingerie. Goes to Omaha, Rapid City, Des Moines."

"Does he make you turn to butter too?"

Tracy lifted her chin a little. "Did I ever say that?"

"Yeh. And you also said, the more you use that slide down at the playgrounds, the slicker it gets and the faster you slide down."

"I don't remember saying that."

Carla wondered what Tracy would say if she knew she'd used her name in Minneapolis to hide who she was.

Mother came out with the tea and cake, and then the two talked about things they thought an older woman would like to hear.

After Tracy left, Mother spoke her mind. "That primped up phony. We don't need her kind around."

Carla said nothing.

Mother followed Carla into her room. "And what was that about turning to butter?"

"Oh, Mother, I don't like it when you eavesdrop."

"And about sliding down that slide?"

Carla pursed her lips a moment. "Once a girl learns she can enjoy making love like a man does, she can't stop."

"Nonsense!"

"Tracy used to talk about it all the time."

"Was that what she was filling your head with in high school?"

"She talked about it all right."

"She's got to be lying about that. Only tramps talk that way."

"Then girl tramps can have fun and we can't?"

Mother looked out of the window. The sun was about to set on glittering white snow outside. "I don't believe it. Has it ever happened to you?"

"Once."

"I don't believe it. You've got to be lying."

That night Carla was awakened by a foreign stirring in her stomach. She cupped her hands over her belly. She was now two people.

The next week right after the *Press* was put to bed, Ian McEachern touched Carla on the elbow. "Can I see you a moment?"

"Yes, Mr. McEachern?"

He stuttered. He looked up at the ceiling. His face slowly turned red.

"Have I done something wrong?"

"Carla, have you seen a doctor lately?"

"I saw Dr. Manning last week."

McEachern's lightblue eyes finally managed it. They darted a look at her belly. "What did he say?"

"He says the baby is due sometime around the eleventh of May."

McEachern's face went white for a moment. He had to hold onto a stack of bound paper. "He's sure of this?"

"Yes."

McEachern went into a rage. "I knew that Oren was no good for you. That slimy-handed lecher! That foul-souled fiend! Ruining one of Whitebone's loveliest jewels. I should have canned him earlier. Got him out of town. Despoiler of women. Ach! Something lovely has once again been picked too early. I tell you, our nation, our grand republic, is going to the dogs."

"It wasn't Oren."

"What! He had nothing to do with it?"

"No."

McEachern wanted to question her further; with great effort restrained himself.

"I've decided to have the baby without telling the father."

"You know what'll happen then in this burg."

"I'm ready for it."

He swallowed noisily. "Well, it's your life."

"Are you worried about me at your paper here?" She cupped her hand over her belly.

He turned very red again. "Well, not really."

"I had hoped to earn enough money to pay for the hospital bill."

"You've told your family?"

"Yes. They've known all along."

"And they're willing to stand behind you?"

"Yes."

"Good for them." McEachern paced back and forth, two steps one way, two steps the other way. Suddenly, his lean blond-skinned face shot forward, and he spoke with tight passion. "All right. You just keep working here as long as you can. You were always a noble girl in my eyes and you shall always remain a noble girl in my eyes. Just because you made one little slip doesn't mean you still aren't a good girl."

"Thank you, Mr. McEachern."

CHAPTER TWENTY-SIX

CARLA

Carla was dreaming. A lean mother squirrel was scrambling up the side of an oak with six little baby squirrels, their firm little sucking mouths clamped tight to her dugs. Behind her scrambled six more little squirrels trying to keep up with her. She didn't have enough dugs to feed them all at the same time. A big black Dane dog was barking at them, trying to reach them by making huge jumps up at the tree. The mother squirrel's long auburn tail snapped up again and again. The six little ones still stuck to her kept sucking away, but the other six squeaked pitifully.

Carla decided to help. She gave the big black Dane dog a tremendous kick in its behind. The big dog, stunned, started to yowl and then ran off into the woods. Carla then reached up to the last six little baby squirrels and opening her blouse, offered them her breasts. Strangely she had just the right number. Six of them. As they started to suckle her, just as her breasts began to run with milk, she saw the little squirrels, all twelve of them, like separate wisps, become two plumes of smoke, and suddenly they were two human babies each suckling at a breast, except that now the two breasts belonged to a huge mother squirrel. When Carla realized she'd become a huge fat squirrel, she started to protest, "No! No!" and woke up.

Carla lay lost in the after-grip of the dream. Her nipples hurt. She touched them gingerly and discovered they were wet. She tasted the wet. Milk? Already?

The next afternoon, Friday, her day off, she was home alone when the doorbell rang. When she opened the door, she was stunned to see Oren Prince standing on the first step, Teresita beside him.

Oren and Teresita both looked at her stomach. Oren said, "Bon wrote you were going to have a baby."

"Yes, I am." She saw that Teresita didn't look very pregnant.

"Can we come in and talk about that? Please?"

"I don't need your help."

Oren was very nervous. He kept hacking up phlegm to clear his throat. His soulful dog eyes pleaded with her.

Teresita's dark eyes turned milky. "We understand, Carla. But we'd still like to talk to you."

Carla couldn't resist the softened eyes. She moved to one side and let them enter.

She made them some tea and cut some chocolate cake.

Oren was dressed in civvies, a dark blue suit and a black tie. His brown eyes kept straying to Carla's stomach. He combed back his glossy black hair with jerky fingers. He was so nervous he made a fluttering sucking noise sipping his tea. "Carla, we lost our baby. There was something wrong—" He stopped short.

Teresita was wearing a black suit. She spoke softly. "Doctor said there was something wrong with me." She let her small shoulders settle. "I can never have a baby."

Carla asked, "Did you two drive down?"

Oren sipped some more tea. "Yes."

"Where did you get the gas coupons?"

Teresita said, "We used my father's and our own."

"You have a car then?"

Teresita said, "I do."

"You're from a rich family then?"

Teresita said, "Not really."

Carla looked at Oren. "You're on a weekend pass?"

"Yes. We haven't got much time."

Carla picked up the white teapot. "Freshen your tea?"

"Please."

Carla poured them all a fresh cup. She held out the plate of sliced chocolate cake. Both Oren and Teresita declined seconds.

Oren started again. "About your baby, if you're going to give it up for adoption, could we have it? Keep it family? Instead of giving it to strangers?"

Carla wanted to hit him. Throw the pot of hot tea at him. Keep it "family"? Of course she'd always wanted to keep it "family"—with him.

The shadows under Teresita's eyes darkened as she watched Carla. "We'll be good to it. And we'll let you come and see it whenever you want."

"Thanks."

"No, really."

Carla finished her tea and set the cup and saucer on the coffee table. Carla thought: "One look and you can tell they've worked it out together. He loves her more than he ever loved me. There isn't a chance in the world he'll ever divorce her."

"Carla?"

Carla got heavily to her feet. "I haven't made up my mind what I'm going to do."

Teresita stood up. "We would never have come down if we hadn't heard you were going to adopt it out. I hope you understand we are sincere in wanting your baby."

Oren stood up too. "It would be wonderful if we could though, Carla. It would make up for some things."

"I suppose your brother thought you might be the father of my child?"

"Yes, he did. So did my father and mother. They were all set to blame me."

"Too bad."

"Let's not be bitter now, Carla. What's done is done."

"You mean, what wasn't done is done." Carla showed them to the door. As the sunlight caught their black hair and their dark clothes, Carla remembered the dream she'd had that morning. Then she knew where that big black Dane dog had come from. "The answer is no."

Heads lowered, sadly, Oren and Teresita headed for their car in the driveway.

Carla watched them ride away. She felt good. She'd handled it well.

CHAPTER TWENTY-SEVEN
CARLA

It was March, and clouds came in from the south heavy with rain. Windowpanes streamed water.

Carla quit her job at the *Press*. Both the baby and the weather began to drag her down. She found it hard to breathe, hard to roll over at night.

On her checkups Dr. Manning said she was doing fine. The baby looked like it was going to be a big one, but she should come to term without any problems. He told her to get a lot of exercise.

When the sun came out she took walks.

One evening she ran into Dink Sunstrand. He was raking debris from the city baseball diamond by the river. He'd filled out into a powerful heavy man. He limped on his game leg as he piled up the dead grass. His blue denim clothes were covered with dust. He spotted her between raking motions and stopped to lean on his rake.

Carla was a little breathless from the walk, so she stopped too.

His watery blue eyes were kind. "How you getting along?"

"Fine."

"I hear you're not going to marry the guy."

She found herself holding her stomach. The baby had just then begun to kick up a storm. It liked it when she kept walking and hated it when she stopped to catch her breath.

"Carla, now that we've met here, I'll come right out with it. I'm still willing to marry you. No questions asked. I've been made foreman of my section at Great Plains. So I can provide for the both of you."

"Thanks."

"We can let bygones be bygones."

It warmed her to think that here at least was one person who didn't seem to mind she was having a baby out of wedlock.

A sly smile tugged at his thick lips. "Fact is, I'm even willing to let everyone think I'm the real father. That we didn't dare let it out right away."

That was too much. Carla turned away and headed down the river bank.

Dink called after, "You wanna remember, to a starving man even burnt potatoes tastes good."

Just ahead of her two auburn squirrels chased each other up and around a thick cottonwood. They were going so fast, skirring at each other, they left faint trails behind them around the ochre bark, like ghost grapevines. Carla remembered the squirrel mother and its dozen babies she'd dreamed about. For a second she could almost feel the baby squirrels sucking at her breasts again.

The night before she'd had another strange dream. She'd gone swimming in a nearby ford of the Big Rock River. The stones and pebbles and sand were pink. As she was cupping up water over her breasts, all of a sudden someone came splashing water at her from the side. When she turned to look, she saw the cutest little monkey. It was smiling at her. The monkey was almost human. It didn't have much hair, its skin was almost pink, and if it hadn't been for the toothy monkey mouth, she would have thought it human. She smiled at the little monkey boy— quickly she made out it was a boy—and began to splash water back at it. Just as she was about to reach out and gather up the monkey boy in her arms, it leaped off the pink sand, made two somersaults, then dove for her navel and vanished inside her bowels. My God! She was pregnant. Then she woke up.

On the way back Carla ran into Meddy Queen.

Meddy's haughty air had been replaced by a sad, even broken, manner. That surprised Carla.

Meddy glanced at Carla's stomach. "I'm jealous."

Carla said, "I thought you'd be in school."

"I was in school. But then something happened." Meddy's blue eyes, once sly, were now as soulless as tapioca pellets. "My soldier boyfriend gave me the syph."

Carla was shocked. Meddy, granddaughter of the town's aristocratic Rilla Queen—she have a venereal disease? "I didn't even know you went with a soldier."

"Oh, everybody knew that. Don't we all go out with soldier boys these days?"

"Oh, Meddy, I'm so sorry to hear that." As little girls she and Meddy used to comb each other's golden hair.

"I wish I could have a baby instead of what I had."

Carla felt sick to her stomach.

"You are going to keep it, aren't you? Your own flesh and blood?"

"I'm thinking about it."

"Good luck. And remember what they say: I cried when I had no shoes, until I saw a man who had no feet."

The next Sunday when she arrived early at church to practice with the choir, Reverend Holly stopped her in the hallway and asked her to step into his office a moment. It was obvious he had been waiting for her.

"Carla, don't you think it might be better if you gave up choir for a while? Sat with your folks? Because it's getting to be a little sticky. People are talking."

"Most people have been nice to me though."

"They've only been putting on their manners for you."

"Gossips."

"Girl, girl, you're not married, you're going to have a baby, and yet you haven't come to the church board to confess your sin. You attend Lord's Supper, our sacrament, quite boldly as though you haven't done something that precludes your attendance. One can't attend Lord's Supper without first clearing one's conscience. You know that."

"But that's between God and me."

"So long as you're a confessing member of this church, we're all involved with you."

Carla stood stubborn.

"You haven't once indicated to me that you're sorry. That you sinned. Have you indicated to God that you are sorry?"

Carla remembered how she'd knelt in a ditch and prayed to God. She turned to go. "This is a matter between God and me."

"Wait."

Carla stood in the doorway, looking back.

"Perhaps after you've had the baby, when it won't be so . . . "

"Noticeable?"

"Yes. Then you can sing in the choir again. After some time has gone by and you've made your peace with the church, then we can talk again. All right?"

"I'll think about it."

"Carla, I don't like this."

"I won't sing in the choir anymore. Thank you for letting me sing as long as you did. It was a joy. And I'm sorry if I made a spectacle of myself in church. Bye."

"Please don't leave angry."

"I'm not."

But instead of sitting with her family in the back of the church, she walked home. She decided she wouldn't attend church for a while. Jesus wasn't in that church anymore.

At home she turned on the radio. She had to have voices around her. But no matter what station she tuned in, all were broadcasting a church service somewhere, Lutheran, Reformed, Baptist. When she couldn't find something with music only, she snapped the radio off.

She searched through their record collection and finally found the *Messiah* by Handel. That she loved. She'd sung in an abbreviated version of it once in church. She put it on the phonograph and sat back in a black rocker near the fireplace and listened.

"Unto us a child is born," a hundred voices sang, "unto us."

Carla sat crying.

CHAPTER TWENTY-EIGHT
SADIE

Sadie was cleaning carrots. Carla was in her room taking a nap, Ivoria was in school, and Jake was at work. An April sun shone on the purple buds of the maple outside the kitchen window. Robins had arrived and birdsong was once again a free perfume on the air.

Sadie thought again about what Carla and Tracy had discussed. "'Turning to butter.' Never heard of such a disgusting thing. That's all got to be a flat-out lie."

Sadie realized Carla had thoughts she herself had never dreamed of having, even in her youth, rough as that youth was with her hearty fleshy relatives.

Sadie muttered again as she cleaned a specially long and huge carrot, "'Once a girl learns she can enjoy making love like a man, she can't stop' . . . only tramps think such things."

Sadie handled the big carrot as if it were something she'd never seen before, when of course she'd pared the skin off hundreds if not thousands of them.

That others might have something she didn't have had always galled her. She'd always been terribly jealous of her older sister Ada's secrets. Jealousy was a sin she'd often had to confess before she took Lord's Supper.

Finished with the carrots, she put them in a pot. She dried her hands. Looking in the little mirror she kept over the sink, she saw again how gray was creeping into her long gold hair. It wouldn't be long now and she'd be an old woman. Next month she'd be a gramma. It was all flying past and she still couldn't say she'd ever enjoyed life. Fun.

That afternoon she ran into Rilla Queen on Main Street. Rilla was a stately woman in her seventies, rich, well-read, with blue-gray hair. Rilla had lively vivid brown eyes.

Sadie asked her how she liked the new fireplace.

"Wonderful. Jake does such splendid work." Rilla paused. "When is Carla's baby due?"

"Soon now."

"Lucky girl."

Sadie didn't know why she asked the next question. "How do you like living alone?" Rilla's husband had died the year before.

"Oh, I still miss my husband terribly."

"That was too bad about him. We all felt so sorry for you."

"Yes. But since his going I've learned something about myself. I find myself good company."

"Alone? By yourself?"

"Oh, it isn't half as bad as you might think." A smile, faintly erotic, appeared on Rilla's lady lips. "In Sioux Falls I came across a privately printed book about sex for lonely women. It described self-abuse as actually being a good thing for one, a valuable safety valve to get rid of tension. Well, you know, I'm a woman of seventy-three, brought up to think that self-abuse led to idiocy. During my forty years of married life with my husband, I never once experienced a throe, so you can imagine what my thoughts were."

Sadie suddenly became so embarrassed she began to shy away from Rilla, edging toward the front door of Nelson's Department Store. This she didn't want to hear.

"Still and all, that book put some thoughts into my head. With the result, I'm happy to say, that I induced a throe by myself and found it wonderful. Very refreshing, in fact."

Sadie thought: "Old Rilla has gone dotty." Sadie wanted to run away, yet found herself cemented to the sidewalk.

Rilla noticed Sadie's discomfiture but went on serenely. "One might ask, 'Am I on the path to perdition? Is single ecstasy wicked?' Being of a logical turn of mind, I can't see how occasional self-indulgence can be harmful. I'm not harming anyone. No one else is involved. So I've finally decided that such a glorious and exciting and relaxing experience cannot be wrong or harmful or dirty." On the last word, Rilla Queen stuck out her chin, and then with a little smile at Sadie's unease, sailed on up the street, long bluish-gray dress trailing after her.

Let go, Sadie almost ran into Nelson's, like the snapback of a rubber band released.

Home again, tired from shopping, Sadie thought she might take a nap. It would be a good hour before Ivoria came running in with her busy tomboy schemes.

Sadie shut the bedroom door behind her, drew down the blinds, sat down on the bed, and with her toes kicked off her slippers. After a moment, she remembered she'd just ironed her dress, so she got up and removed it. With a sweeping motion she also threw the white spread to one side, over onto Jake's side of the bed. Then she lay down.

It didn't take but a moment and she was sound asleep. She dreamed. Jake was chasing another woman around a henhouse. Sadie was scandalized and yelled at Jake to quit being such an old fool. He'd unbuttoned his trousers but the funny thing was he was blank there. He kept yelling at the fleeing woman, "I don't like it you call a mouse a rascal." That made him all the more fool. The woman had very blond hair, and once when she turned to look over her shoulder, laughing in high glee, Sadie finally got a good look at her. Why, it was Carla. Except Carla had brown eyes.

Then a funny thing happened. Jake slowly changed. His blue workclothes became a long blue toga, and his heavy leather shoes became sandals, and his blue work cap fell off because his wavy gray hair had grown out all the way down to his shoulders. Jake was Jesus. The Jacob Simmons she'd married had become Jesus the Nazarene. Sadie wanted to yell at him, "You crazy nut, Jesus was sweet and pure and never touched woman, for catsake. Except maybe to heal them."

Then the next thing she knew, Jake the Nazarene saw her, Sadie, and he started chasing her instead. It was her turn to run crying in high glee, looking back over her shoulder. Something showed through his toga, and she liked it because it was the first time she'd seen one, and oh she started to scream in her excitement a man was chasing her, and she could hardly get her breath, and her belly began to feel dreamy, and it opened up like a peony, and she smelled something she'd never smelled before, and her belly began to swell up with swarming bumblebees, and Jesus Jake hurried to take her but when he saw all the bumblebees swarming out of her carcass, he smiled at all the honey in her, and he took of it and ate of it and blessed her; and she thought the spilling out the most wonderful thing that had ever happened to her it ached so sweet.

Sadie woke up. Before she could stop herself her hand found where she'd dreamed there'd been a peony and again before she could stop herself she touched the bud in the center of the peony, touched it again, touched it again, wondering if that was a sin, and then a swarming of needle-pricking stings spread out from the bud and then a drum began to beat in her belly in step with her heartbeat.

She lay breathing heavy. My God. Was that it?

Yes, one did turn to butter. Yes, it was like going down a slide at the playground. Except that to her it was more like going up a slide that got ever slicker the higher up she went.

That tramp Tracy had been right.

Four days later Sadie took another nap in the afternoon. She hurried to take it. She laid herself down exactly the same way, kicking off her slippers, removing her ironed dress, throwing the white spread over onto Jake's side, hoping that somehow she could dream the same dream with Jake chasing her again.

But try as she might she couldn't fall asleep.

Well, she had to have that again. Rilla Queen had said, "I can't see how an occasional self-indulgence can be harmful."

Sadie reached for her little purse of gold fur.

At ten-thirty, after the news, everybody went to bed, Carla groaning with her burden, Ivoria complaining she still wasn't sleepy, and Jake saying he was glad to get some shut-eye after a rough day closing the roof at the Queen house.

Jake was almost asleep when Sadie wiggled on her side of the bed. When he didn't say anything, she jerked again as though she were trying to find the right position. She twitched and fidgeted several more times.

She couldn't figure out what she should say to get Jake to touch her. It'd been so long since she'd tried woman tricks on a man. She was out of practice flirting.

Finally Jake said, "For cripesake, woman, what's up? You're shaking there like you got the heebie-jeebies."

Sadie smiled in the dark. "How's your little rascal these days?"

Jake popped upright in bed. "Pardon?"

"Your little rascal. You know. He hasn't been very naughty lately." A little he-he laugh escaped her.

Jake sat very still. She could feel him staring at her, nosing through what she'd just said. "Are you by any chance referring to my business?"

"When's the last time you kissed me, Jake? Like in the old days."

"You are talking about it then."

"Yes."

Jake slowly lowered himself into his pillow. "Woman, it's too late now. Once you let a man's onions dry up, there's no way you can revive them. You put me out to pasture for keeps long ago."

IV. THE FRUIT

CHAPTER TWENTY-NINE

CARLA

She'd been dreaming about twin calves and had just risen up out of the dream and was thinking to herself that she'd never seen twin calves in her life, when the quake in her belly came. Birth pang. She looked at the luminous dial on the little cream-colored clock on the stand beside her bed. Ten after midnight.

The past week she'd had several good talks with Dad and Mother and both had agreed that if she wanted to keep the baby, fine, she could raise it living with them.

There were times, though, when she felt it would be better for everybody, the baby included, if she were to put it out for adoption. It would be hard to do, but it was probably for the best. When Carla was in that frame of mind, her mother remarked, "Don't look at it when it's born then. Or touch it. If you do, you're lost. One look, one touch, and you'll want to keep it."

The little clock beside her bed made a low buzzing sound. It was an old electric clock and its parts were worn. Sometimes, to keep it running, she had to lay it on its side. Dad had reset the works upsidedown for her once so that the wheels ran in new grooves.

She dozed briefly.

Again a fist reached into her belly and gave her innards a squeeze.

She glanced at the clock. Twelve-thirty. Birth pang all right. The baby was on the way.

She snapped on the bedlamp and got up, heavily, and walked over to the window and looked outdoors. A full moon hung low and red in the east sky.

She turned and stepped back to her bed, the moon in her belly following her reluctantly, as if it had a momentum and a direction of its own. She slipped on a housecoat and softly on bare feet went to the telephone in the kitchen. She snapped on the sink light and drew the phone over to it and dialed Dr. Manning's home number.

"Hello." Dr. Manning's voice was full of sleep.

"This is Carla Simmons. I've just had two cramps. They came about a half hour apart."

"Better get yourself over to the hospital. I'll call them to say you're coming."

"All right."

Carla next opened the door of Dad and Mother's bedroom. "Dad? Fireman? Got your pants ready? The siren's rung twice."

Dad reared up out of bed. She could just make out his figure against the window beyond which lay the pink moonlit lawn. "Be right with you."

Mother said, "Don't you want me to drive you?"

"I want a man to do it, Mother."

Carla moved very erect back to her room and got some clothes ready in an overnight bag.

She looked at the row of art books on the little redwood shelf above her bed: Rembrandt, Wood, Titian, El Greco, Winslow Homer. After a moment's reflection, she picked Grant Wood. Every time she looked at his paintings, she began to feel lonesome for the things he had in them. She also picked up a sketch pad and crayons. She put them all in a grocery sack and set it beside her overnight bag.

The baby in her kicked a couple of times. She could feel it roll around, sharply. It made her feel like she was a gunnysack with struggling cats inside.

She looked down at her troubled belly. "Yes, and what am I going to do with you? Keep you, and have you grow up like you might be my younger sister? A sort of happy afterthought of Dad and Mother? Or give you away and let you grow up with both a mother and a father?"

She looked at herself in the mirror above the commode. Her breasts were like two opulent pears. Yes, and when she walked, her seat hung like two fat pumpkins rubbing against each other.

She wondered which of the five men the baby would take after: Skippy, Thomas, Richard, Harold, Dewain? No one knows which tooth in the buzzsaw cuts off the finger. It nauseated her to think of the men again. Yet one of them was the father.

"Ready?" Dad called from the living room.

"Coming."

Mother stopped her just as she was about to step through the door. "Uhh, I ought to tell you one thing, though. It's probably going to hurt something awful. Worse than anything you ever felt in your life. But just remember this, it's the one hurt that'll be the easiest to forget." Mother started to cry, and turned away and went back to her bedroom.

Dad took Carla's overnight bag and grocery sack. "Let's go."

They were almost at the hospital when another cramp caught her. It was very sharp. "Oe."

Dad stepped on the footfeed and the car leaped ahead.

"Don't," she gasped. "It's all right." She looked at her watch. It was one o'clock.

They rushed past houses with the shades drawn and dark. The good folk of Whitebone were sleeping the sleep of the tired and the just.

The light was on in front of the hospital. Dad pulled to an easy stop and then hurried around the car to open the door for Carla. He helped her out. He reached in and got her bags. He wanted to help her up the steps but she smiled and pushed his hand away.

"I want to do this alone as much as I can, Dad."

The night nurse, a quietly handsome woman with dark hair, efficient in manner, greeted them. She took the bags. "This way. And you can wait here, Mr. Simmons."

Carla said, "Why don't you go home, Dad. It'll be a while yet. Get some sleep."

"No, I'm staying put." He took off his blue work cap and ran a hand through his graying tousled hair. He managed a smile. "It ain't every day a man gets to be a grandfather."

The nurse led Carla to a large white room in back with two beds in it. There was a smell of freshly ironed sheets. "Which bed would you like?"

"I'll take the one by the window. Where I can watch the moon."

The nurse helped her out of her clothes and into a hospital gown.

Carla asked, "Don't I know you from somewhere?"

"I worked for your mother when she had Ivoria."

"Oh, sure. Sally Young. You never got married, did you?"

"No."

"Are you sorry?"

"No. Except I always wisht I'd had a baby." Sally Young had merry brown eyes. There was a touch of sadness along the edge of her lips. "I'm jealous of you. You had the gumption to go ahead and have one anyway."

"It's nice of you to put it that way."

"Too bad we have to get married to have babies."

Carla took comfort from the example of Mary, mother of Jesus. What must Mary's thoughts have been if it wasn't Old Joseph who'd impregnated her? So who did it then? If it was God, then it was someone even eons older than Joseph.

The prepping went smoothly: enema, shaving the pudendum, bath.

Carla asked, "Can I have my dad sit with me?"

"I'll ask Dr. Manning." Sally Young left.

Another surge moved through Carla's belly. It reminded her of a vomiting impulse: once started there was no stopping it. This time there was a bite in it. What was it the Bible said? "In pain shalt thou bring forth children."

The relief after the birthing pain felt wonderful. There was a kind of rolling boil in her belly, a bubbling around, followed by a peculiar snap, of water slapping when one made a whirlpool in a pail.

The door opened and an old woman came in pushing a pail on wheels with a mop in it. She was a heavy woman, wearing a gray hospital work gown, thick calves showing. From the name tag on the gown Carla read that it was Gretchen Hamner. Gretchen Hamner had brown hair, done up in a knot on top, was streaked with gray. Several tendrils of hair refused to be tied back and hung over her forehead. She fixed Carla with a sparkling black look. "Oh. You're the Simmons kid that got knocked up, eh?"

Carla tried to find a smile.

"Well, it happens to the best of us, dearie. Listen, could you hop out of bed a minute so I can mop under it? I've got to move the bed to do it."

"I'm not sure Dr. Manning wants me to move around much."

"Pah. What does a man doctor know about having a baby? Only a woman knows. Me, I kept walking around in my house until I almost had my babies between steps."

Carla swung herself and her belly out of bed and went over to stand by the window. "You had your babies at home?"

"You bet. Out on the farm ten miles from town."

"You weren't afraid?"

Gretchen Hamner snorted. "What's that got to do with anything? If you're knocked up you're knocked up and pretty soon it's gonna come out. What goes in has got to come out."

Carla looked at the moon. It had risen high enough to float over the tallest trees. The pink in it had turned to silver. A single street light at the far end of town twinkled like a distant planet.

Gretchen rolled Carla's bed away from the wall and began swabbing the white terrazzo floor.

"How come you took to mopping floors?"

"It was something to do after my old man died. I like being busy. Besides, I've mopped up behind menfolks all my life." Gretchen swished the mop around, gathering up little lakes of dirty water, and somehow swirled them all up into the mop wringer, and then wrung her mop dry. "If you've looked at floors all your life they finally begin to mean something to you. Floors are like maps. They tell you where you're at. When I walk into a house, or a place of business, anywhere, I always look at the floor first, and right away know what kind of people I'm dealing with."

Another contraction seized Carla. It was a good one and it stung like the dickens. She looked at her watch. 1:50. They were beginning to come faster.

Gretchen saw her grimace. "Good girl. You're takin' it like a real woman." She pushed Carla's bed back in place. "Keep walkin' around in the room here where I've just mopped now. You wanna walk it right out of you."

Too bad Gretchen stank so. Old sweat in old clothes. It was a wonder someone on hospital staff hadn't gotten after her about that.

"Take my daughter now. She just needs to get the tiniest tremor and she runs for the gas mask. No, ma'am, me, I want it nature's way. The right way. The hard way."

Carla began to stroll slowly back and forth beside her bed. "If there's two ways to walk to town, one over a mountain and the other across a prairie, what's wrong with taking the prairie road?"

Gretchen snorted. "But what if there ain't but one way, over the mountain, then what? No, I ain't got much time for all this painless stuff." She swabbed up another little muddy lake and wrung out her mop. "You got to earn your motherhood. When I had each of my half-dozen, I yelled my lungs out. I knew when I had 'em."

The baby in Carla, beginning to feel like two lumps, snuggled down low, down at the very bottom of the bowl of her belly.

Gretchen went on. "Oh, we're so smart with all our gases and stir-rups."

The walking moved the baby even more to the bottom of her.

Gretchen finished swabbing up and wrung out the mop a final time. Then, just as she was going out the door, she said, "Remember, dearie, yesterday is gone, so do the best you can today, because tomorrow may never come."

Something small gave way down there. Carla went over to her bed and pushed the button to call the nurse.

In a moment another nurse stepped in. "Yes?" Her name tag read Nellie Fawcett.

"I felt something give."

Fawcett's hips were curiously swung forward as if she were always ready to receive. The smile of an old campaigner in love's wars was on her lips, drawing them down at the corners. Her black eyes glowed with mischief. "Maybe we better have a peek."

Carla lay down awkwardly and spread her legs.

Fawcett had a look. "Oh. It's just the plug. Some mucous to keep the baby from being infected while you carry it." Fawcett rolled up a little nickel table and, picking up several pads of cotton, cleaned up for Carla. "Hmm. You have some dilation. About four centimeters. Won't be long now. How far apart are they now?"

"There's another one. Oe." Carla looked at her wristwatch. "Fifteen minutes."

"It's beginning to come down the chute then. I better call Dr. Man-ning."

"I already called him."

"I know you did. Because he called me. But he always gets in another nap. No use of him being here until it's about ready to pop."

"Isn't he worried?"

"Oh, he worries all right. But he's only human, you know, and needs his sleep just like you and me. And since he's a busy doctor, he's got to grab it when he can."

"I guess that's right."

"I almost didn't make it over myself," Fawcett said. "Old Virgie wasn't sure she wanted to turn over." When Carla looked at her questioningly, Fawcett added, "I call my old car Virgie because she won't go by herself. She always has to be shoved in the rear before she'll go. Ha."

"You're new here."

"Yeh. I'm a Canuck." Fawcett smirked. "The exchange is better here in the USA. That is, in men."

"You sound bitter."

Fawcett moved around in the room, getting things ready. She moved with a rocking motion, on each step her pelvic front thrusting forward. "And, compared to where I lived, things here aren't quite as primitive. The old Indians there always gave the baby a bath in cold water the minute it was born, even in the winter. If the river or the lake was froze over, they'd chop a hole in it and give the baby a bath in that."

"But that's cruel and inhuman."

Fawcett rocked on her heels. "Oh, is it now. The Indians did it to make sure they had healthy kids. If you was born sickly, you had it. That was one way of making sure you weren't passing on any bad-seed babies." Fawcett smirked a wise smile. "Keep the race up."

"You are bitter."

"Yeh. I'm one of them babies they decided to keep."

Carla stared at her. "You're part Indian, then?"

"All us Canucks west of Winnipeg mostly are."

"Oe."

Fawcett glanced at her wristwatch. "Eleven minutes. Time to call Dr. Manning." With a rolling motion she rocked herself out of the room.

Carla lay alone in the white room. She looked at the moon.

Fawcett came back. "He'll be here in a sec." She approached Carla again. "Maybe I better have another peek." She flipped back the covers. "Ah, about seven centimeters. You're going to have this one quick and easy."

Carla didn't like the way Fawcett peered in at her intimate parts with such easy familiarity, and showed it.

Fawcett laughed. "Yeh, it's times like this when you learn life ain't all sweetness and light. You're lucky you're not having an operation. You should see what happens then. I sometimes double as an anesthetist. The minute he's under, off goes the sheet and all is revealed, the works." Fawcett laughed to herself, remembering something. "Sometimes when they're soaping his testicles so they can shave him there, he has an erection. A nice merry red bell, ready to sound off his charms. Ha. It usually means he ain't far enough under and then I catch hell. But I don't mind. It helps me size up possible candidates for future reference."

Carla was aghast at all she was hearing.

"The same thing is true with you girls. You may be a virgin at home, but in the hospital you're a live carcass and nothing about you is holy."

"Oe!"

"Another one, eh?" Fawcett checked her watch. "Eight minutes. Good." She lifted Carla's sheet for another look. "Yes, you're going to have an easy time of it."

"That last one really hurt."

"Breathe with your whole belly, not just your chest."

"I'll try."

"Relax between contractions. Just let yourself hang."

"You've had a baby?"

"That'd be telling."

A woman in paper slippers slipslapped past outside Carla's door. She had on a white hospital gown too and was waiting for her pains to start. She walked like she had a vast hernia.

Fawcett said, "I see you brought your dad along."

"I wanted a man to bring me to the hospital."

"Got a fix on him, eh? Well, it's okay. An old buck will give you a better time of it than a young one. At least that's what I learned from the love of my life."

"From your father!"

"No, just an old doctor in Winnipeg."

"Oee!"

Fawcett turned professional. "Let it come, let it come. Don't fight it by tensing up. You've got to save your strength for when that horse comes around that last lap. Ha."

Carla let down inside. "That was really a bad one." What a relief it always was afterwards.

"Yeh, I guess I was once a hot item in the hospital corridors. Didn't have time to think about getting up a hope chest, the guys were after me so. Instead, all I had to offer for marriage"—she looked down at her own breasts—"was a hopeless chest."

Carla lay puffing, head hard on the pillow. It was like she was breaking apart down there.

Fawcett's black eyes turned tender. She stood beside the bed and stroked Carla's forehead. "What hair you have, spread out on the pillow like that. Like gold tailfeathers on snow."

Carla ran both hands around and around her mound of a belly. "It feels like I got two in there."

"It sometimes feels like that."

"Will I have the baby in this room?"

"No. For that we go to the saddle room. You sticks your feet into the stirrups and away you ride."

"I want my father in there with me."

"If he don't think it indecent."

"If you were in my place, would you keep the baby?"

"I didn't."

"Then you did have a baby!"

Fawcett smiled a smile full of private mystery. "Sure did. But I wasn't good enough to be its mother."

"You're funny."

"I get paid for that, dearie."

"Then you'd say I shouldn't keep the baby?"

"It all depends on what you want to do afters."

"I want to paint pictures. Become a decorator."

Fawcett cricked her head to one side. "Most husbands won't go for that, you know. And with a baby around, it won't work."

"Then I better give it up. Ohh!"

Fawcett checked her watch. "Four minutes." Abruptly Fawcett became the firm nurse. "Time to move you. I'll get the wheelchair."

"Let me walk over. I want to walk that baby right out of me into the world."

"Good girl." Fawcett helped Carla get up off the high bed, then took her arm.

They moved down the hall into the delivery room. The room was full of shining instruments and nickel tables and glittering white walls. It smelled of arnica and alcohol, like the lotion Dad used on his hands to keep them soft. Handsome Sally Young was already dressed for the delivery, green smock, green cap, green mask. A big thing was about to happen.

They helped Carla onto the delivery table. Fawcett lifted Carla's legs into the nickel stirrups.

Dr. Manning spoke up beside Carla. "Ready to go, I see." He'd come in on rubber-soled feet, dressed in a green gown, green cap, and green mask too. His soft blue eyes were full of anticipation. "Before we go any further, maybe I should have a good listen first." He fitted his stethoscope into his ears and, placing the endpiece on Carla's mounded belly, began listening. He moved the endpiece around, listening intently.

Carla lay puffing.

He was about to quit listening, when suddenly he became very alert. Intense. He moved the endpiece around in jerks, up and over and down the mound of her belly. Then he went back to the place where he'd noted something.

"What's the matter, Doctor?"

"I hear two hearts beating."

"Maybe that's only my heart with the baby's."

"If I count yours, I hear three."

Fawcett said, "Oh, goodie, twins."

Dr. Manning pressed the endpiece deep into the soft flesh of Carla's mound.

Just then the sensation of something letting go, of a blister bursting, opened at the bottom of Carla, and wet warmth spilled down out of her. There was a sudden smell of fresh mucilage in the room.

"What was that?" Carla cried.

Fawcett said, "Just the waters, Carla."

Then something truly astounding happened. A baby cried in the room. It cried out of Carla's partially opened womb, a clear wail of distress and wonderment at what was happening to it.

Everybody looked at each other in disbelief.

Carla cried, "Is it born already?"

"God, no," Fawcett said, "it cried there in your belly."

"I can't believe it," Sally Young said.

"At first I thought it was a fart," Fawcett said. "One of those complaining kind."

"I can't believe it," Sally said again.

"Nor can I." Dr. Manning grew pale, eyes squared. "Never before in my whole life have I ever heard a baby cry before birth. In all the years of my practice."

Carla tried to sit up; Fawcett pressed her down. Carla said, "That was one of those twins still in me crying then?"

"It surely was," Dr. Manning said. He turned to Sally. "We better get moving. I'll quick scrub up and then you help me get my rubber gloves on. Fast."

Carla said, "Doctor, earlier I asked if my father couldn't be with me. He don't need to see it. He can sit with his back to it, facing me, can't he? I want his hand so I can pinch it."

"It's not usually done, young lady."

"Please?"

"Well, I know your father. He won't faint." He turned to Sally. "After you get my gloves on, get him."

Another birthing pain came. It was the worst one so far. Even before Carla closed her eyes the room faded away to a dark gray.

"The first twin is crowning," Dr. Manning said. Then he muttered something to Fawcett not meant for Carla to hear. "If it cried in there, it's already breathing. That could be bad."

Carla heard him. "You mean it could choke in me?"

Dr. Manning leaned down grimly; said nothing.

Fawcett stepped to one side and also slipped on a green gown, green cap, and green mask.

Sally Young came in with Dad. She gave him a green mask and a green gown too. Dad drew up a chair beside Carla, facing her on her right side. He was turned away from what was going on between the stirrups.

Carla squeezed his fingers. "Your hand feels so strong, Dad."

Fawcett continued to be irreverent. "Well, Mr. Simmons, in a minute you'll be seeing your future twice over."

Dad looked stunned. "Twins?"

"There's another one," Carla grunted.

"Push harder," Dr. Manning said. "Come on, just a little more. Ah. Good girl. Now relax."

"Oh, I want to hurry it out," Carla said. "I don't want it to drown." She took a deep breath and shoved until she thought she'd pushed herself inside out.

Dad's face wrinkled in sympathy. "Not too hard. You're turning purple."

"Yes, Dad." With an effort, puffing, sucking air, she said, "I think I'm going to adopt it out, Dad."

Sally frowned. "Then you want your father's grandchildren to be someone else's seed girls?"

Dad said, "What makes you think it's gonna be twin girls?"

Sally said, "Only a girl would cry before it's born."

Carla said, "Things sure have changed. A year ago I hardly knew I went to the bathroom." Carla shook her head. "And now twins yet. Well, this will give the local gossips some real cabbage to chew on. Especially if the twins should happen to turn out to be completely different from each other."

Fawcett said, "Which one of them you gonna throw away?"

"Throw away!"

"Indians always drowned one of them. It was bad luck to keep both of 'em. Besides being hard on the mother."

There seemed to be a lot of pauses. There were people talking and instruments clicking. One moment things seemed to go in a rush; the next moment hours seemed to have passed.

Carla moaned, "Don't let that first one drown in there."

Dr. Manning sat like a master before a console. His gestures were sure and swift. He picked up what looked like a long silver butter-paddle and explored carefully inside her with it. He slipped the lip of it around to one side, then the other.

Again the baby whimpered inside Carla.

Dr. Manning exclaimed softly. "But how is it breathing? Atypical, atypical."

Sally Young was crying. "I'd keep them both if I was you."

Fawcett said, "How will she take care of them? There ain't many men around what'll marry a single woman with two kids."

Dad's face hardened over. "Pardon? What's wrong with us as a family raising them?"

Dr. Manning said, "There's another one. Push, girl, push! It must get out!"

Carla shoved until she reached the bottom of her breath. The corners of her mouth drew back into her cheeks.

Fawcett tried to help by pushing down on Carla's high belly with both hands.

Dr. Manning said, "She better have some help." He picked up a hypodermic needle. "This baby's head is a little large for you. This is novocaine, girl. You won't feel it."

Carla said, "I want to have it natural. Don't take that away from me."

Fawcett said, "Where I came from the midwives give the woman a pinch of snuff. Put it up her nostrils with a goose quill. To make her sneeze."

That crazy Fawcett. Carla couldn't help but laugh. Haha.

And out popped the head. Carla could feel it emerge. "Ahh."

"Atta girl," Dr. Manning said between set teeth. "Now one more big push for the shoulders."

"Dad." Carla squeezed his hand. "Dad, you're always around when I need you, aren't you?"

Dad said, "One more push, girl, and then the little rascal will be safe."

"Push!" Dr. Manning ordered.

Carla pushed.

Dr. Manning caught the baby riding into his rubber-gloved hands. He turned it rightside up. He placed it over Carla's belly. "There's the first one."

"It's a girl!" Sally Young cried. "See! I told you!"

Dr. Manning quickly made sure Carla wasn't bleeding, then turned his attention to the baby girl. A gleaming purple-and-silver cord hung twisting between mother and child.

"It isn't crying now," Carla worried.

"Just a little sleepy," Dr. Manning said. He picked up a big black rubber syringe and squeezed the bulb flat. Then bending the baby's head back, he thrust the syringe's slender nozzle down the baby's throat. He let the bulb expand. It sucked up moisture with a loud wet noise. As he withdrew the syringe, a cry, outraged and furious, followed it.

"Ahh," Carla sighed. The baby lay where but moments before Fawcett's hands had been pressing down on her. The baby felt like a big warm wet cat lying on her. Its arms and legs began to waggle irregularly.

"Don't look at it," Fawcett warned, "if you're not going to keep it."

Sally had to say it. "Keep it."

Carla could see again the faces of all five men: Skippy with his on-again off-again boyish smile, Thomas and Richard and Harold with their harrowed hollow eyes, and gentle Dewain. Which one of those did this first one look like?

Dr. Manning placed two clamps on the cord. Then quite precisely, using a long scissors, he snipped the cord, parting mother and child.

Carla looked up at the white ceiling to make sure she didn't look at the baby.

Her right hand had ideas of its own though. Her thumb touched the baby's shoulder. It felt greasy. Then she brushed the baby's shoulder with the palm of her hand.

"What shall I do, Dad?"

"Carla, you do what you feel you'd like to do."

"That darn Oren. I'd sure like to feel my baby suckling me."

"You mussent think about him anymore. You're shed of him and good riddance."

Fawcett said, "Dearie, you're touching it."

Sally Young said, "To, go ahead and look at it."

Dr. Manning growled a little. "Sally, you know what to do. Take the baby and bathe it. Then measure and weigh it."

Again there were a lot of pauses. Carla drifted.

Dr. Manning leaned over her again. "I think it's time you started working on the second one. How about a little push."

Carla tried. To her surprise there was suddenly another bundle trying to emerge out of her bottom. Compared to the first one this one felt easy.

"Atta girl. Give a good push. More. It's crowning already. Push."

There were some more pauses.

"Push! We're almost there."

Carla gripped Dad's hand and pushed with all she had left. There was a wet slooshing sound, and it was over.

"Another girl!" Sally Young cried.

"Really?" Carla breathed.

"This one's different from the first one," Fawcett said. "Much smaller."

Dr. Manning placed it on Carla's belly too. It wiggled and whimpered a little.

With her thumb Carla touched it. This one felt drier.

"Two beautiful girls," Sally Young said. "How wonderful. You're going to have an awful lot of fun with them, Carla. Girls are always fun to have around."

Carla opened her eyes and looked at Dad. Dad was sitting looking past her like he'd just seen the city dump blow up. He? Grandfather of two little girls?

Dr. Manning cut the second cord. "Sally, you know what to do with this one. Fawcett, wash the mother." Dr. Manning smiled down at Carla.

"And you, my lady, from you I want a few more pushes. Those afterbirths must get out too."

Carla had been aware of more contractions and she rode in behind them with more pushes. In a moment two placentas slid out with soft silky sounds.

"There," Dr. Manning said. He stepped back with a satisfied smile. He looked at the clock. "Three a.m. Good time to start life. That's about the time I usually roll over and think about things for a while." He removed his rubber gloves. He pushed back his green cap, revealing his balding head with its strange baby fuzz.

The second baby girl didn't like the way Sally was cleaning off its fingers and toes, and each time she touched it the infant let out a howl. Soon the first baby girl started to howl too.

"What are you doing to my babies?" Carla asked, feeling anger rise.

"Maybe the cleaning solution is too cold."

Fawcett placed an identification bracelet on Carla's left wrist and then went over and placed bracelets on the two babies' left wrists too.

"I'm cold," Carla said.

Fawcett set a small lamp between Carla's spread legs. It felt like the ardent hand of a man. "That'll warm you up. Besides help you heal faster."

The babies continued to yell and fuss.

"What are you doing with my babies?" Carla demanded.

Sally laughed. "I'm weighing and measuring them. The first baby measures twenty inches and weighs seven pounds six ounces. The second baby measures seventeen inches and weighs five pounds six ounces." Laughing some more, Sally said, "Here, you can have the babies, all shining and clean." She placed the babies back on Carla's belly, face down.

Carla just had to have a look. Which of those men did those babies look like? She took the first baby in her hands, holding it up. It still cried hard in protest, little dark red tongue flittering.

As far as she could see it didn't resemble any of the men. If anything it looked like her own baby pictures. It had blond hair and a long head and blond skin. Its chest breathed in and out in her hands, strong, solid, human. She placed it back on her belly.

She picked up the second one. Again so far as she could see it didn't resemble any of the men. If anything it looked like Dad. It had dark hair and dark skin. Like the first one it seemed to have blue eyes.

Her breasts hurt. "Baby want breakfast? To catch up with your older sister?" Without thinking Carla drew the second little one up close and cuddled it and presented her breast to its little crying red mouth and vibrating red tongue. The moment its tongue touched her nipple, its face softened over and its lips began to work, suckling, suckling. There as a little sound from its bottom and a small black curdle of fecal matter dropped out on Carla's belly. It resembled a little ball of rabbit dung.

Fawcett quickly cleaned it up with a piece of tissue paper. "Should she pacify it so soon after birth?"

"Sure," Dr. Manning said. "There's no milk yet. But there is colostrum. Best possible food for the baby's first meal."

"Oh?" Carla said. "When will the milk come then?"

"Now that the baby's touched your nipple it won't be long. A message just now went down to your breasts for them to make milk."

"Help me hold the first baby in place at the other breast, will you?"

Dad sat smiling.

CHAPTER THIRTY
CARLA

They were having a late Sunday morning breakfast, Carla, Dad, Mother, Ivoria, and the babies Evalyn and Lillian. The June morning sun shone gold in the blue breakfast nook, bouncing off the nickel toaster and the nickel coffee pot and the blue Delft dishes on display on the high shelves. There was a smell of perking coffee and hot oatmeal, and of babies having just been burped in the tight room. Carla, Dad, Mother, and Ivoria were laughing and talking a mile a minute, while the twins slept in their little baskets on a chair beside Carla.

In the middle of it all, Dad asked, "Who's going to church with me this morning?"

Ivoria quick asked, "Can I stay home with the babies? Reverend Holly said Carla could sing in the choir again."

Mother backed her chair an inch. "He did, Carla?"

"Yes." Carla had just nursed the babies but already she could feel milk running inside her maternity blouse. She kept being astonished by all the milk she had.

"Are you going then?"

"Why not? If he's willing to overlook what happened, then the rest of the congregation should too."

"Isn't it sort of rubbing people's noses in it though?"

"They can get used to the idea that I'm having babies without a father. And I'll show 'em that I'll do all right too."

Dad sipped at his coffee. "Just what are your plans about all that?"

"Well, later this summer I'm going to work for Mr. McEachern again. He says I can come home and quick nurse the babies betweentimes."

"And then?"

"A year from now I plan to go to junior college in Blue Wing and take up art and design. I'll work my way through, take care of Evalyn and Lillian, do my studies, all at the same time. I'll show 'em."

Mother smiled. "Maybe some student there will take a shine to you."

Carla shook her head. "It's going to be a while before I take up with a man again."

.voria said, "Maybe a bachelor professor will fall in love with you."

"Fat chance." Again Carla shook her head. "No, I'm off men. I'm ,oing to show you that you really don't need a husband to raise babies."

Dad said, "You won't mind if Evalyn and Lillian have a nice old grandpa though, will you?"

"Of course not, Dad." Carla smiled down at the blond Evalyn and dark Lillian. The babies lay sleeping on their stomachs, heads to one side, facing Carla. Every now and then both Evalyn and Lillian continued to mouth a phantom nipple, little wet lips in sweet sucking motion. Both lay with a fisted thumb at the edge of their soft pink lips. "It may take me years to graduate from college, but I'll do it. I want to know about everything. What I can't get in class, I'll get by reading."

Mother asked, "What are you going to tell those kids of yours someday?"

"The truth, Mother, the truth. So they won't be too shocked by what they run into later on."

Mother said, "I hope you're not going around hating men all your life, for catsake." With a look at Dad, Mother added, "They're not all rascals, you know."

"Hate?" Carla mused, "When I have my little duckies to love and cherish? Never." Carla reached out and placed her hand softly on Evalyn's bottom and then Lillian's. "You little darlings, I could just squeeze you."

Dad said, "Mother, may I bother you for some more coffee?"

Carla felt something in Lillian's diaper. "Oho. So you've got your little bottom all messed up again, have you?"

Mother said, "Such is life."

Roundwind
Luverne, Minnesota